Sunken Castles, Evil P

Lurkers at the Threshold

by Jürgen Hubert

Edited by

Samuel Wells

Cover illustration by

Veronika Sudmann

Cover design by

Maren Happel

ISBN: 978-3-9822171-4-7 (pbk.)

www.sunkencastles.com

Contents

Introduction **7**

1 Those Who Haunt the Works of Man **12**

1.1 The Abodes of the Living 12

1 The Ghosts Haunting the New Mill at the Innerste River 12

2 Foreman Calvör 17

3 The Woman in Childbed 18

4 The Haunting Housekeeper . . . 22

5 The Ghosts' Meal 23

6 Mass for the Ghosts 26

7 Mass of the Dead in Wesenberg . 28

8 The Stolen Goose 29

9 The White Cap 31

10 The Maid Fetches the Alpine Sieve 33

11 The Dance of the Dead 34

1.2 Ruins of the Past 35

12 The Brave Girl in Ohmes 35

13 The Golden Bowling Game (Yburg) 38

14 The Ghostly Mill 40

15 The Glowing Man at the Zehntscheune 41

16 The Irrlicht of Ihlow 42

17 The Black Monk 43

18 Princess Swanwithe 48

2 Those Who Haunt the Wilds **53**

2.1 Haunted Meadows, Forlorn Forests 53

19 The White Girl at the Fecht River 53
20 The Bowling Farmers 56
21 The Headless Man near Münsterhof and the Farmer 57
22 The Headless Man and the Gooseherd 59
23 A Farmer's Fight Against the Headless Man 60
24 The Man Without a Head 62
25 Kleines Clausthal 65
2.2 Over the Hill, Under the Mountain 69
26 Ghostly Activities Around the Nöll 69
27 The Bowling Game Beneath the Hohnstein 70
28 The Meuenloch Cave 71
29 The Brautlachenberg Mountain . 72
30 The Heavily Loaded Men 74
31 Räderberg Mountain 76
32 The Goatherd Boy in the Illgraben 78
33 The Ghosts of the Old Noricans . 79
2.3 Pale Riders 81
34 The Rider without a Head on the Ziegenberg hill near Zwönitz . . 81
35 The Rider within the Beeches of Klosterlausnitz 83
36 The Rider without a Head (Mückenloch) 84
37 The Rider without a Head (Lengfeld) 85
38 The Rider on the Pale Horse . . 86

3 Those Who Roam as Beasts **88**
39 Ghostly Poodle 88
40 The "Lordly Dog" 89
41 The Ghostly Dog 90
42 The Welthund near Stötterlingenburg and Lüttgenrode 91
43 The Cursed Officers 94

44 Ghosts in the Shape of a Dog . . 96
45 The Billy Goat of Büntlitten . . . 99
46 The Pale Horse Haunting the Town Hall of Wernigerode 100
47 The Owl Haunting Saßleben Park 102

4 Those Who Are Denied Peace 104
4.1 The Wages of Sin 104
48 The Men in Zottenberg Mountain 104
49 The Herdess Makes Fried Pudding 107
50 The Golden Bowling Game (Schauenforst) 109
51 The Bride on the Lilienstein . . . 110
52 The Man with the Boundary Stone 112
53 The Man Who Moved The Boundary Stones 114
54 The Coast Warden 115
55 Alfhausen and the Alkenkrug Pub 116
4.2 The Wronged 121
56 Don't Steal from the Dead! . . . 122
57 A Dead Man Searches for his Gown 124
58 The Burial Gown 126
59 A Ghost Searches for his Brain . 128
60 The Ring 129
61 The Shower Maidens 130
62 The Man of Dikjendäl Valley . . 134
63 The Ghost Ship (Emden) 135
64 The Uglei 137

5 Those Who Linger On 140
65 Don't Weep for the Dead Too Much! 140
66 Leave the Dead in Peace! 141
67 The White She-Ghost 142
68 Guests from the Gallows 144
69 Visit of the Hanged Man 145
70 The Ghostly Suitor on Hartenstein Castle 149

71 The Monk on Helgoland Island . 152
72 The Best Religion 153
73 The Ghost Ship (Pellworm) . . . 155
74 Love after Death 155
75 The Dead Bride 158

6 Those Who Find Peace 161
76 The God-Fearing Carter 161
77 Faithful Lights or Errant Lights . 162
78 The Ghostly Light 164
79 The Saved Fiery Man 168
80 The Sneezing Maiden 169
81 The Cowherdess' Buttermilk . . . 170
82 The Little Man at the Barns at Stargard 172
83 A Ghost does a Haircut 173
84 The Salvation of a Restless Ghost between Wredenhagen and Hinrichshof near Röbel 174
85 The Ghost and the Groom 177
86 Ghosts Reaching Salvation 179
87 God's Reward 184
88 The Farmer Who Had Moved The Boundary Stones 186
89 The Unrighteous Plowman . . . 186
90 The Ghostly Wedding in the Deserted Village of Scortowe 188

7 Those Who are Bound and Banished 195
91 An Exorcism in Kirchbrak 195
92 The Ghost Äschamd 197
93 The Banished Paper Miller's Wife 199
94 The Haunt on the Harth 202
95 The Woe Mother 203
96 The Old Linden Tree near Gebhardshagen 205
97 A Shepherd Banishes a Hare . . 207

98 The Banished Villain 209
99 The Ghost of Day Laborer Rossow from Klein-Kelle near Röbel . . . 211
100 The Barber of Penzlin 216

Afterword **223**

The Project **225**

Acknowledgements **226**

A Notes on Germany **228**
A.1 German History 228
A.2 Religion in Germany 231
A.3 The Environment 233
A.4 Rural Life 234

B The Travelogue **237**
B.1 Austria 237
B.2 Czech Republic 239
B.3 France 239
B.4 Germany 240
B.5 Poland 250
B.6 Switzerland 251
B.7 Safety Concerns for Travelers 251

Folklore Collections **259**

Other Sources **264**

People **265**

Places **268**

Timeline **276**

Topics **278**

Impressum **304**

Introduction

Consider the spinning chamber.

The nights of the German winters are long and dark — indeed, close to the winter solstice, there might be as few as eight hours of daylight. Yet in the rural villages of old, the work was not done at nightfall. In particular, the women had to spin the flax that had been harvested in the fall into twine. As heating and artificial lighting were expensive, they gathered at the hearth fire in the main chamber of a farm for these labors. Frequently, several households took turns with hosting such events.

And, in order to pass the time, they told stories to each other.

And the spinning women not alone in these chambers — the men[1] gathered there too, as did the children before they went to sleep. And, as there was little other entertainment to be had in those days before the advent of modern mass media, every-one participated as an audience member or by sharing some of their own tales. Such events became semi-formal gatherings called "spinning chambers", "home gardens", and many other names besides.[2]

[1]While the women had to spin the flax, it appears that the traditional task of the men present was to watch the women do the work. Indeed, some of the tales take note that the labors of the younger and more attractive women present were watched with particular interest.

[2]Though it should be noted that these were not the only gatherings where such tales were told — other opportunities were folk festivals or the ever-popular evening at the pub. Wherever people gathered,

The tales themselves had no single, clearly defined "genre". Some were moral tales emphasizing the importance of virtues and the wages of sin.[3] Others were pure, slapstick comedy. And others still — perhaps told later in the evening, once the little ones had nodded off — were pure horror. In these, the protagonists encountered supernatural forces beyond their ability to control (and, frequently, beyond their understanding as well), and could sometimes consider themselves lucky if they escaped with their lives and sanity intact.

Based on the sheer number of tales featuring them, ghosts were among the most popular topics for such tales of horror. And, as usual with such fireside horror tales, they were most effective if they haunted some nearby place. Terrifying specters might be found in swampy meadows by the river, the castle ruins up on the hill, the boundary to your neighbor's field, even the house next door — lurking just beyond the threshold. The storytellers thus took tales they heard elsewhere, and made them their own — putting them into a local setting and adding some regional elements.

As a veteran player of tabletop role-playing games, this spoke to me. For when we gather together in the here and now to tell stories (whether with friends at the dinner table or on online fanfiction forums), are we really doing anything different?[4] Once again, we take the tales we have heard elsewhere and add elements that matter to us, transforming them into something both old and new. Ghosts remain a popular element of these modern tales.

---

they shared stories — the "spinning chambers" were merely the most formal and inclusive of these meetings.

[3] Which did not necessarily map to modern-day understanding of what constitutes "virtue" and what constitutes "sin".

[4] Well, one difference is that while those old storytellers usually did not worry about narrative consistency overly much and did not bother to slot their supernatural events and entities into neat categories, role-playing gamers tend to over-analyze things. I am no exception, as you shall see.

Thus, when I set out to transform ***Sunken Castles, Evil Poodles*** from a single, self-contained volume into an entire book series,[5] ghost stories made a logical starting point. I didn't have to carefully search dozens of 19th century folklore collections to find examples — I could just open *any* of these tomes[6] at random and be certain that it would contain plenty of useful source material for me to translate. As a result, when deciding on the stories for this volume, it became just as important to consider what I should leave out as to which tales I should include.

The first topic I excluded were hauntings of supernatural animals that were not explicitly described as ghosts. While many of these hauntings probably were probably still considered "ghosts" by the storytellers, there is still enough ambivalence that I decided to leave them for a future volume on animal tales. Nevertheless, a small sampling of animal-shaped ghosts can be found in Chapter 3.

A far more difficult choice I made was leaving out tales of "ghostly processions", such as the "Nachtvolk" ("Night People") of the Vorarlberg region in Austria, or the "Gratzüge" ("Ridge Trains") of the Valais in Switzerland. While the concept of entire processions of ghosts racing along lonely roads in the countryside makes for great yarns, further research[7] led me to the conclusion that these are best understood as a precursor of the "Wild Hunt" phenomenon,[8] which is a topic deserving its own book as well.

---

[5]For more on the overall project, see p. 225.

[6]Well, digital scans of these tomes — thanks to the massive digital scanning efforts of the last two decades, most of these public domain texts are widely available once more.

[7]In particular, *"Ghosts in the Middle Ages: The Living and the Dead in Medieval Society"* by Jean-Claude Schmitt.[Sch98, p. 93ff]

[8]Ghostly or possibly demonic huntsman who ride through the night, often accompanied by hounds of a similarly dubious nature. Variants of the Wild Hunt can be found in much of Western and Northern Europe.

Still, while the remaining 100 tales I've settled on for this volume draw from 43 different sources, they should in no way be considered a representative sample. They couldn't be — there were several hundreds of German folklore collections published in the 19th century alone, and my own exploration of these works is just beginning. Nevertheless, I hope you enjoy these tales — just like audiences of those fireside evenings enjoyed them in previous centuries!

Author's Note

Since the narrators of these tales shared them with a 19th century German audience, they assumed a general knowledge of German history and culture that an international audience is unlikely to have. While I have added explanatory notes to the tales as seemed appropriate, readers with little knowledge on this topic might wish to read my "Notes on Germany" section in the appendix (p. 236) first. Furthermore, these legends are usually highly tied to specific locations of Germany and the surrounding nations. Those who are interested in thise locations might wish to refer to the "Travelogue" section in the appendix, or else consult the online map at `https://sunkencastles.com/german-folklore-map/` while reading this book.

All tales in this book were translated from multiple public domain sources freely available on the Internet as digital scans, each with their own folk tale informants and editoral voices. Thus, the tales have many different narrative styles, which often diverge greatly from modern storytelling expectations (such as clear and satisfying endings). I have attempted to translate these stories as faithfully to the originals as possible, with only slight adjustments for greater readability. Each tale lists the specific source at the end of the text, which can be looked up in the bibliography at the end of the book.

Furthermore, since I wish to encourage wider study of German folklore tales, I am hereby designating all texts in this book written in serif fonts as Creative Commons Zero content (this generally includes the translations themselves, but not the added commentary). They thus can be copied and reused for any purpose without restriction (including commercial applications). For the full terms of the Creative Commons Zero license, see `https://creativecommons.org/share-your-work/public-domain/cc0/`.

1. Those Who Haunt the Works of Man

As ghosts represented the remnants of living people, it is not surprising that most of them haunted the places they inhabited when they were still alive. For story purposes, this also emphasized the horror aspects of the tales. If even your home, the place you should feel the most at ease in all the world, is not secure from otherworldly specters, then no place is truly safe.

1.1. The Abodes of the Living

While dragons dwelled in the wilderness, water spirits haunted lakes and rivers, and dwarves lived beneath the mountains, ghosts could show up truly everywhere to disturb the lives of the living — even at one's place of work.

1. The Ghosts Haunting the New Mill at the Innerste River

The new mill[1] at the Innerste river within the Upper Harz region is said to be haunted. It is believed that the cause for this are the old possessions of the papacy which were destroyed when the mill

[1] There is a "Neue Mühle" road in the Innerste river valley on the western outskirts of the Clausthal-Zellerfeld municipality, which sounds like the most likely location.

was built. For there used to be a monastery where the mill stands now. And when the mill was built during Protestant times, the ghosts of the old monks grabbed the workers by their feet and pranked them constantly. Furthermore, at one particular location a small flame was burning, and a fat monk — a ghost — was visible the entire day. This ghost pointed towards the spot where the flame burned throughout the day. Finally, the workers — who did not know where else to turn, and furthermore suspected that treasures were buried here — fetched a Catholic priest[2] and asked what ought to be done here. After the priest had observed the activities of the ghost for a while, he said: "Yes, a lot of things are here, and for this reason the ghosts cannot rest." He now had the workers dig at the spot where the flame burned according to his instructions, and there they found a thrice-locked chest which was surely filled with money. But the priest said that he would have to take the chest home and speak many prayers over it before the money could be taken out. Thus, they transported the chest to his home on a wagon pulled by four horses, and the four horses were barely able to move the chest from the spot. When the priest did not bring the money within the chest back to the new mill at the appointed time, the workers went to the priest's home. There, they found out that the priest had gone away, but the chest had been left behind. When they finally opened it, there was nothing inside except for a single red pfennig coin.[3] The priest had quietly taken out the rest and sent it ahead to a destination where he himself had planned to go.

When the new mill was already in operation, and leased to the Weibgens[4] in the previous century,[5] the monks and students swarmed across the corridors so much that the mill assistants

[2] Called "Pater" in the German text — which implies a *Catholic* priest, even though the region was now Protestant.

[3] I.e. a copper coin.

[4] A local family which seems to have leased the mill for more than a century, as a subsequent legend starting from the same source elaborates.[Prö96, p. 156f]

[5] I.e. the 18th century.

scarcely dared to fill up the grain when the mill was in operation. At times, the spirits also wore miner's jackets[6] and green miner's hats, and in this form the assistants would see them pour the grain out of the sacks. Once, a mill assistant was working there who was studying the Bible intensively and knew how to deal with the spirits. One Sunday afternoon, he was all alone in the mill and the entire house. He had locked all doors and read in the Bible again. Then, the Devil appeared to him in the chamber. The mill assistant immediately realized that it was the Devil, and demanded to know from him how he had been able to enter. Furthermore, he showed him the page in the Bible which he had opened, and there it was written: "Away from me, Satan!"[7] Then the Devil flew out of the roof with a great noise, and took three shingles with him. No one has been able to put these shingles in again afterwards.

The ghosts, a whole bunch of monks and miners, often appeared in the residential house of the new mill. Frequently, twelve students also stepped inside. Of these, the first one always carried a book, and he browsed in this book for the entire hour from eleven until twelve o'clock. For the ghosts always stepped inside when the clock struck eleven at night, and when the clock struck twelve, they went away again. The first one always stepped towards the table with his book. The second one was also very inquisitive, and looked into the book over the first one's shoulder. But the twelfth student always put a bell on the table when they arrived, and at precisely twelve o'clock he picked it up again when they left. This always made a noteworthy ring when he lifted the bell up from the table.

Among the other spirits that were observed, there were three who had distinctive names among the people of the mill. One of them was "Fateye", and a fat eye hung out of his head. He

[6] "Puffjacke" in the German source which were short miner's jackets mainly covering the shoulders and only reaching down to the waists. They would have either had short sleeves or mere openings for the arms.

[7] Presumably, Matthew 4:10.

wore a white sheet which he had tied into a knot in front of his forehead. This Fateye only ever knocked in order to annoy people, and when there was a racket rising up in the mill and people noticed it, it was always this same evil-minded entity. And then people would say: "Oh, it's Fateye!", and they no longer concerned themselves with it.

Another ghost was called the "Sweeplork",[8] who always swept around the mill with a new broom. But the most welcome entity of all was the "Friendliest". Everyone loved it, even though they did not do as it wished. For it always carried a chair into the chamber which it placed into the center of the room. Then it stood next to the chair and waved to everyone that they should sit down on it. Nobody did this, and when, after one hour and at twelve o'clock, nobody had sat down on it, it took its chair and left through the door with it. But then it no longer looked as friendly, but was sad that nobody had wanted to sit down on its chair. The Friendliest usually appeared every six weeks. It seemed to feel the most comfortable when there was a fairly merry gathering with dancing and zither music, which happened occasionally when a lot of people from the nearby settlements had flour grinded during the night. The Friendliest often stepped into such a cheerful company in the new mill with its chair.[Prö96, p. 153ff]

Commentary: The religious divide between Lutheran Protestants and Catholics that shows up here as a background element is a recurring theme in German folklore, as the Protestant Reformation and its resultant wars and conflicts left their mark on Germany like few other events (interested readers might wish to consult my Notes on Germany in the appendix (p. 236) on this topic). It is significant that the people from a Protestant region nevertheless fetched a

[8] "Fegelork" in German. While "fegen" means "sweeping", "-lork" is not a word I recognized.

Catholic priest to consult with him on a supernatural phenomenon — perhaps they assumed that he would be more useful in dealing with the ghosts of Catholic monks, or perhaps they believed that Catholic priests (due to their greater reliance on rites and ceremonies) were more skilled in dealing with ghosts. The twist where the priest absconds with the treasure nevertheless serves as a dig at the Catholic denomination.

While a fuller exploration of treasure tales will have to wait for a future book, both flames designating a buried treasure and restless ghosts bound to that treasure are well in line with other treasure narratives. Another element we will again see later in the chapter on exorcism (see p. 222) is the difficulty the horses had in transporting the chest — in German folklore, spirits of all kinds can "make themselves heavy" and thus make transporting themselves difficult.

The appearance of the Devil seemingly comes out of nowhere. Why did the Devil appear at this precise time and place — if it was indeed "the Devil" and not some lesser infernal entity (German folklore is often rather unclear on this distinction)? Perhaps he was simply attracted to so many dead souls in a state of turmoil.

I feel that there is more to the "twelve students" in this tale than this text reveals. I am reminded of the text "Die zwölf Johanneße" ("The Twelve Johns"), one of the legends collected by the Brothers Grimm.[GG16, p. 437f] In that tale, a Frankish king had twelve young men who were also called the "German students", and they had powers to travel all over the world on a wheel of fortune — but the Devil took one of them each year as payment. Thus, the twelve students in this tale might also be masters of the black arts, with the book as a tome of magic. But this remains speculation.

The three other ghosts detailed in this story show the range of possible shapes and personalities such spirits might take

— from malicious and annoying to friendly and helpful. Such tales might have been spread to explain the odd noises that might emanate from a mill in operation, or perhaps they were kept alive as pranks and tall tales told by the old hands to the new hires at the mill.

It is worth pointing out, however, that while we are primed by modern media portrayals to think of ghosts as "translucent", none of the ghosts in this tale (or, indeed, most others in this book) are described in such a manner. The ghosts are distinguished by their strange behavior and sometimes bizarre appearances. They might even be entirely invisible at times (such as in "The Ghostly Suitor on Hartenstein Castle", p. 149), but if any appeared "half-visible", the stories generally neglected to mention it. The storytellers and their audiences might have *imagined* that they were translucent, but failing conclusive evidence, we should not make this assumption by default.

2. Foreman Calvör

Rose gold[9] is excavated in a mine in Andreasberg.[10] Rose gold is so valuable that the miners emerging from the mine shaft are searched on their whole bodies. During one particular period of time, many miners died who worked in the mine at night. Eventually, two companions among the miners decided to investigate the reason for those deaths. Around the midnight hour, a terrible roaring and din rose up, and under this noise a frightening ox approached. But when they attacked it with the drill hammer and the two-person drill,[11] the roaring stopped, and soon

[9] Rose gold ("Rotgülden" in the original German) is a gold-copper alloy with a reddish sheen that was often used for specialized jewelry.

[10] Now Sankt Andreasberg, part of the town of Braunlage. Andreasberg used to be a major mining town and, over time, had more than 300 mine shaft for the excavation of iron and silver ore.

[11] The drill hammer ("Bohrfäustel") is used to drive the drill into the ground. The two-person drill ("Zweimenschenbohrer", a term that

afterwards a human voice behind the ox skin pleaded for their life. The miners now tore down the ox skin, and the foreman of the mine, who was named Calvör, appeared before them. He offered them a lot of money if they were to remain silent about this, for he had used the ox skin, which he had hidden within the mine shaft, in order to frighten the miners and then kill them in order to attain a lot of rose gold. But the miners didn't want his money and reported him. As he was about to be arrested, he threw himself into the shaft. For a long time, he haunted the mine and stood in the way of the miners, and frequently they said to each other: "There the tall Calvör stands again with his ox skin!"[Prö96, p. 238f]

Commentary: It gladdens my heart to see that people in folklore developed elaborate crime schemes involving cunning disguises — the Scooby Gang would be proud. Though it is interesting to see that the other miners saw Calvör's ghost once the foreman had actually died as more of a nuisance than an actual threat — he seemed to have been more frightening while still alive.

Even one's home might not be safe from ghosts. While some ghosts were a mere annoyance, others represent a real threat to life and limb, as the following tale illustrates:

3. The Woman in Childbed

In one house in Goslar, a banished pastor stalks women in childbed. For this reason, there is a hook within chambers where women

does not seem to have been used outside of this tale) is presumably a hand-powered drill that requires two people to operate.

who had recently given birth reside. This hook can be hung on the inside of the door. But these hooks are crosses, or at least they used to be crosses, which ensures that no ghost and no spirit has power over these women.

Once, a woman who had recently given birth lived in this particular house, and she had hung up the hook within this chamber and thus was safe along with her children. But she heard tumultous noises from outside. When her husband, who was a miner, came back home, she neglected to tell him about this. But, when it was late in the evening, he heard a terrible sound in the oven. He thought that it was a certain old woman who also lived in the same house and was sometimes smoking a pipe — and that she was rummaging through the oven in search of a piece of coal. Thus, he called out to her that she should come in, for he would provide her with fire. But then the noise became worse. However, the miner then folded his hands and spoke:

"You spirits of Hell, begone,
You have no business here;
This house stands in the domain of Jesus,
Let it rest in peace."

After that, it became quiet in the house. However, in the yard there was a hen with her chicks sitting on a pile of wood. While the noise was going on, she was clucking loudly and fluffed her feathers as if she sought to protect her clutch with her wings. But the next morning, the hen and her chicks were lying dead in the yard. Since the ghost had been unable to do anything to the young mother and her child, he had twisted the necks of the hen and her chicks.

The mother was now quite concerned. Once, when she went out to the yard, she took her school-aged son with her. But when she stood in the yard, the boy suddenly cried in fright: "Mother, look, the pastor is approaching!" Then, everyone saw how he came towards them with widespread arms. But the mother fortunately reached the safety of the chamber, and only dared to get back into the yard in the evening while in the company of her husband. The boy had followed them, and soon again cried: "Mother, look, the pastor is approaching!" Then everyone saw him, but the mother once again reached the safety of the chamber. The husband subsequently visited the clergy, and asked how he should act under these circumstances. The cleric told him that the mother should go to the church the next day and have herself blessed. But, after that, she must not go back to the old house under any circumstance. Instead, he should rent a new domicile, and she should immediately go there from the church.

The cleric then explained that a priest had once been banished into the old house. In front of one chamber within the old house, there was a large lock, and the priest had been confined to that chamber. But now, this priest stalked women in childbed.[12]

The miner and his wife then did as he had been told.[Prö96, p. 90f]

Translation note: This tale, and several others, uses the term "Wöchnerin" (roughly, "week woman"), indicating a woman who has given birth in recent weeks and is now recovering from her ordeal. There doesn't seem to be an English-language equivalent, and thus I have settled on "woman in childbed" when clarification is necessary.

Commentary: As so often with German folklore, this tale raises a number of questions that aren't answered satisfactorily.

[12] At least, this is how I interpret this passage — i.e. the priest was banished into the single locked room, and is now free to haunt the rest of the house and stalk women in childbed. But the original text is somewhat unclear on the precise circumstances.

For starters, why was the pastor banished to another house (presumably, he originally dwelled in some ecclesiarchical building) instead of, say, a remote swamp, hill, or other wilderness area as it is traditional?[13] Was he too powerful to be moved further away?

It's not quite clear from the story, but the implication seems to be that the miner and his wife had rented an apartment in that haunted house. If so, it seems really negligent of the landlord not to tell the miner about the threat that the haunt represented. That is, if the landlord actually knew about this — I wouldn't rule it out that the local clergy hushed the situation up, since a ghost of a priest out to harm women in childbed along with their children would obviously be a huge embarrassment to them. And I shudder to think what kinds of sins he committed in life in order to become such a ghost...

(As a side note, I am also deeply jealous about how the miner was apparently able to rent a new apartment on a day's notice — given my own experiences with apartment hunting all over Germany.)

Not all ghosts were this dangerous, however. Indeed, some only wanted to stay where they once lived, and, in time, mutually beneficial arrangements could be developed.

[13] See Chapter 7 (p. 222) for further details on the theory and practice of exorcism.

4. The Haunting Housekeeper

A woman was buried in Amönau.[14] As the mourners returned from the burial, they saw the woman peer out of the attic window. She was then banished into a swamp, but was able to get out of it again when the swamp was excavated and turned into a pond. After that, she was bound to an oak; but as the tree was felled many years later, the woman was freed from it as well. She still continues to haunt her old home, helps the maid with feeding the animals, starting the hearth fires, and assisting with all sorts of other labors, as then the maids will leave her in peace.[vP85, p. 104f]

Commentary: I wonder what made the ghost return to this house three times even after being deported so rudely. Was it a supernatural compulsion that bound her to the home she once lived in, or did she simply have nowhere else to go? Ghosts, as a rule, do not seem to travel much unless compelled to do so by an exorcist, but precisely *why* they remain in specific places is rarely explained in detail. Perhaps this is part of their punishment when they were forbidden from entering the afterlife.

Either way, the tale makes clear that, upon her death, the woman was no longer considered to be part of the household — only grudgingly tolerated once she became useful and it became clear that it was impossible to get rid of her permanently. This is a remarked contrast to earlier, pre-Christian times when the dead were honored or at least respected — by the time of the 19th century, ghosts were regarded as irritant pests or menaces that the living tried to get rid of.[Lec09, p. 225f] We will see more of this attitude in Chapter 7.

[14] Spelt "Amenau" in the source, this is now part of the town of Wetter in Hesse.

Travelers, too, had better beware — for too many inns reported "haunted rooms" which were hazardous to use as a place of rest.

5. The Ghosts' Meal

Bräuner's *Curiositäten*, p. 336 — 340.[15]
Erasm. Francisci *höll. Proteus*, p. 426[16]

When Frederick III of Denmark[17] called for a public gathering in Flensburg, it occurred that a noble who had traveled there for the occasion could no longer find a room in the inn, as he had arrived late in the evening. The innkeeper told him that all the rooms were occupied except for a single large one. But he himself would not recommend staying there overnight, as it was haunted and uncanny spirits were active there. The noble showed his courage with a smile and said that he was afraid of no ghosts and merely needed a lamp, so that he could better see if anything were to show up. The innkeeper brought him the lamp, which the nobleman put on the table and then reassured himself with waking eyes that no spirits could be seen.

[15] This refers to Johan Jacob Bräuner's *"Physicalisch- und Historisch-Erörterte Curiositäten"*, a collection of "diabolical superstitions" published in 1737.[Brä37, p. 336ff]

[16] This is Erasmus Francisci's (real name: Erasmus Finx) *"Der Höllische Proteus, oder Tausendkünstige Versteller"* ("The Infernal Proteus, or the Thousand-skilled Master of Disguise"), which seems to be a massive, 966 page long compendium of supernatural events first published in 1690. It's a fascinating work that I would love to delve into at length... but then I contemplate phrases like "scope creep" and questions like "do you really want to wrestle with 17th century German while there is still so much stuff in 19th century folklore collections?".[Fra95, p. 426ff]

[17] Frederick III reigned from 1648 to 1670, which gives us a timeframe for this tale.

The night was not yet half over when there was noise in the room here and there, and soon there was one rustling sound after the next. In the beginning, his courage allowed him to remain steadfast against the frightful terrors, but soon, as the noises grew louder, fear mastered him so that he began to shiver, no matter how much he tried to resist. After this prelude of uproarious and tumultuous noises, a human's leg fell through the vent of the room's fireplace. Then an arm, abdomen, chest, and all limbs, and finally, when nothing else was missing, the head. Soon, the parts put themselves together in the proper order, and a whole human body, resembling a servant of a court, rose up. Now more and more limbs fell down, which soon united into human forms, until finally the door of the room opened and the bright mob of an entire royal court entered.

The nobleman, who had stood frozen at the table, trembled and hurried into a corner of the room when he saw that the parade came closer, as he was unable to escape out of the door before the incoming group.

He now saw how the ghosts laid out a table with incredible nimbleness, carried in exquisite dishes, and distributed silver and golden cups. After this was done, one of them walked over to him and indicated that, as a guest and stranger, he should sit down at the table with the rest of them and enjoy their hospitality. When he refused, a large silver cup was handed to him, and he was told to drink from it. The nobleman, who was so dismayed that he had difficulties keeping his countenance, took the cup. It appeared as if they would pressure him to drink, but as he was about to raise it to his lips, he was overcome with a deep dread that shook him to the core, and which made him loudly cried out for God to give him protection and succor. As soon as he had uttered his plea, the entire splendor, the noise, and the whole feast with the splendidly-dressed, proud ghosts was gone in an instant.

However, the silver cup was still in his hand, and while all dishes were gone, the silver cutlery nevertheless remained on the table — as did the lamp that the innkeeper had given to him. The nobleman was delighted and assumed that all this was now his new property. But the innkeeper objected, and finally this matter came to the ears of the king. The king declared that the silver would fall to his purse and confiscated it. Nobody has discovered where it came from, as it was not engraved with heraldry and names as it was the usual custom.[GG16, p. 214f]

Commentary: This is one of the tales collected in *"Deutsche Sagen"* (*"German Legends"*) — the *other* two-volume collection of German folklore by the Brothers Grimm that no one seems to remember these days. Unlike their more popular fairy tale collection (*"Kinder- und Hausmärchen"*, usually known as *"Grimms' Fairy Tales"* in the English-speaking world), this collection focused on local and historic legends that required more understanding of the regional context. This link to local geography and history may explain while it never attained the popularity of their fairy tale collection.[18] It was written early in their career, when they still considered themselves as scientific surveyors of folklore, which is evident in that they cite their sources — unlike the later editions of the *"Kinder- und Hausmärchen"*, which they increasingly rewrote to make them more acceptable "family friendly" mass entertainment for the urban middle classes.

"The lone, haunted room in an inn" is a common narrative element in German folklore, although, usually, such rooms are not haunted by an entire royal court. The precise origin

[18] Indeed, it was only translated into English once — in 1979 by Donald Ward. Unfortunately, this translation hasn't been reprinted in the four decades since, and is thus largely unavailable except at specialist libraries. If my own folklore translations become successful enough to be more than just a hobby project, I *might* create a new translation of this collection of my own — but that's still far away in the future, if it ever happens.

of the ghosts remains a mystery — which is indeed called out by the story itself. We also see one of the most accessible way of driving ghosts and other spirits away — an earnest prayer uttered in fear of one's life or soul.

We should also note that the protagonist was explicitly warned about the haunting of this room, as, indeed, it was common for this kind of narrative. While he seems to have been no worse off for his frightful experience, not all who dismiss warnings of ghosts are so lucky.

Finally, legal disputes over discovered treasures were common enough in the real early modern age — and the ruling noble simply confiscating the valuables once word of their existence reached his ears was one of their hazards.

Churches were already believed to be places connected to otherworldly forces. It is thus not surprising that ghosts appeared in them as well, and tales of masses attended by ghosts were widespread all over Germany.

6. Mass for the Ghosts

1. A devout woman, who lived next to the church, was once woken up during the night by singing emanating from there. Believing that it was morning mass, she hurriedly rose up, got dressed, put on her mantle, and went into the church, whose windows were lit. She sat down on her usual place, opened up her hymnbook[19] and joined in the singing. Then, someone

[19] "Gesangsbücher", or church song books, first started to appear during the Reformation. In the second half of the 16th century they became common and cheap enough thanks to movable type that each member of a congregation could have their own (as it was the case here).

touched her shoulder and whispered to her: "Neighbor, it is late now and you should go home." She turned around and saw a neighbor next to her who had died years ago. Then she surveyed the room and spotted many faces of people who had died. Thus, she hurried out of the church, and, as she closed the door behind her, the last verse of the song ended, and the door snapped shut with a bang so that the tip of her mantle was caught in it. She broke free, and, at this moment, the bells on the church tower rang one o'clock and all illumination within the church ceased.

(Told by Sacristan Hadbusch in Röbel; conveyed by upper class student Pechel from Röbel. The St. Nikolai Church[20] in Röbel is mentioned in Rieberb. 3, 137 ff.)

2. In Hagenow, the ghosts hold mass during the midnight hour before the first day of Christmas.[21] It is custom in Hagenow that a mass is held at 5 o'clock in the morning on that day. Once, a woman went to the church (whose windows were lit) at midnight, erroneously believing that it was 5 o'clock in the morning already. She saw both strange figures dressed in clothes of long-ago times and familiar faces of dead acquaintances. One of them told her to whisper the Lord's Prayer and to hurry out of the church without looking back. She did so, but, when she was already out of the door, she still tried to catch a glimpse. At this moment, the door slammed shut and the tip of her dress got stuck. The woman died three days later.

(Told by Ms. M. Krüger. The same story is told about the church in Dänschenburg[22] near Ribnitz by a seminarian in Neukloster.)

3. There are also reports of a night-time mass in the church of Wustrow near Wesenberg, and a farmer's wife who was woken up by the associated ringing of bells. But, it is not clear whether the congregation consisted of dead people.[Bar79, p. 363f]

[20]The *Nicolaikirche* was built in 1280 and still stands today.
[21]I.e. on the night between the 24th and the 25th of December.
[22]Now part of the town of Marlow.

---

7. Mass of the Dead in Wesenberg

Long ago, Wesenberg was Catholic,[23] and, at the time, it was the custom to hold an early morning mass on Sundays and Wednesdays. Once, there was a woman who woke up one morning in the winter when it was still dark. She heard the ringing of bells and, therefore, believed that she had slept past the start of the mass. Thus, she hurriedly dressed and went into the church. When she arrived, the doors were wide open and the whole church was filled to the brim with people. Before the altar, there were two preachers who distributed the bread of the Eucharist rite.[24] One was wholly unfamiliar to her, but she recognized the other, who had been dead for more than twenty years. She was greatly disturbed by this and quietly went to her chair, kneeled down, said her prayer, and then was about to go home immediately. But then, a woman stepped up to her. This woman was familiar to her, but had likewise died a long time ago. That woman told her: "We dead ones leave the day to you, thus leave the night to us. Go home in peace, but don't look back." With these words, a fright overcame the woman so that she was barely able to stand, but she managed to leave the church and hurry home. But when she was at her front door, she could not resist looking back. The next morning, the piece of her mantle that had been outside at the time was severed as if burned off.[25][Bar79, p. 364]

---

[23] Wesenberg apparently became Protestant no later than 1529.

[24] The Eucharist is one of the major rites of Christianity, where bread (and, in some denominations, wine) is distributed among the believers in memory of Jesus' Last Supper.

[25] See the tale "Leave the Dead in Peace!" (p. 141) for further discussion of the "burning" often associated with ghosts.

Commentary: The essentials are the same in the variants — a woman accidentally wanders into church at entirely the wrong time and is told to leave without looking back. And, like Lot's Wife, she disobeys that command at the last moment, paying the tip of her mantle as the symbolic price — although she loses her life in only one story. In no case we actually learn what she saw when she turned back (although she might not have seen anything), but it may be noteworthy that in the first two fragments she looks back at the very moment the mass is ending. Does the entire congregation shift into some other dimension (purgatory, perhaps)? Obviously, being within the area that shifts back would be perilous for a still-living mortal, but, maybe, witnessing the shift itself is also detrimental to life and soul. And, in the final story, the woman seems to have entered the other dimension itself once she stepped out of her front door, and only found safe refuge when she returned home.

Tales of such "masses of the dead" have a long history — one was written down between 1009 and 1018 by bishop Thietmar of Merseburg where a priest witnessed ghosts celebrating mass in a church and a cemetary. They chased him away two nights in a row, but, when he persisted, they burnt him on top of the altar.[Sch98, p. 37] As we shall see later in the tale "Kleines Clausthal" (p. 65), some people are slow at taking a hint.

8. The Stolen Goose

A long time ago, a goose was stolen from a woman in Osterwieck, and she suspected another woman as the thief. She thus sued her and made her give testimony in court. Both women died soon thereafter.

Then, at a later time, a choir boy heard bells ringing in the St.

Nicolai Church during the night. Full of fear,[26] he jumped out of the bed, got dressed, and went to the church, which he found open and brightly lit. The boy went to his seat and saw many members of the congregation, but he did not recognize anyone nor understood what they were singing. After the singing had ceased, a pastor stepped from behind the altar and walked in front of it, but he did not recognize the pastor either. This seemed strange to him, but he would not be left in confusion for long. Now two women rose and stepped in front of the altar. The boy recognized them as the two above-mentioned women. The pastor interrogated these, which confirmed the innocence of the woman who had been believed to be guilty. At the same time, it became obvious that the thief was still alive, but had now fallen very ill. After this, a woman walked towards the boy, whom he recognized as the sister of his mother, who had died a few years ago. She indicated with a wave that he ought to leave the church. The boy did so, and the church closed behind him with great force. As he got outside, the bell struck twelve o'clock.

Arriving at home, his mother asked him where he had been. He replied that he would tell her in the morning. In the morning, he related everything to her. The mother reported this to the authorities, and the woman designated in the church as the thief of the goose confessed her crime after the pastor had appealed to her conscience at length.[Prö96, p. 57f]

Commentary: While gathering post-mortem information on crimes is convenient, I feel there is some missing information here. If one of the dead women had accused the other, and the other denied it, then how would anyone present actually know who the real thief was? And getting a confession from a severely ill person is presumably a lot easier than one

[26] Presumably out of fear that he was missing a mass in which he was supposed to sing in the choir.

from a healthy person, for the same reason that people getting tortured will say anything just to get the torture to stop.

That the boy did not understand what the ghosts were singing is a recurring element in many ghost tales, where the sole living witness only understands those words relevant to them. At times, this might be an indication that the ghosts come from a long-ago age or from a linguistic minority group (such as in the tale "The Ghostly Wedding in the Deserted Village of Scortowe", p. 188). But, at other times, I wonder if this is more deliberate. Perhaps the affairs of the dead in general are not meant for the living — apart from those specific messages the ghosts wish to pass on to the witnesses.

9. The White Cap

In Gittelde,[27] a pastor with a white cap haunts the lower church.[28] Furthermore, the white cap lies on the altar during the night. Once, there was a girl who said that she would fetch the white cap from the church, and that she feared no one. Thus, she went there and took the white cap from the altar. Then the ghost appeared twice and screamed that she should put the cap back. For this reason, the girl went to the pastor,[29] who blessed her. Then she was supposed to go and put the cap back on the altar. She did so, but once the cap was on the altar, the ghost appeared, took the girl into his arms, and squeezed her to death.

[27] Gittelde is a small village now part of Bad Grund. More than a thousand years ago, Gittelde used to have rights to both hold a market and mint its own coins, hinting at a prosperity the village has long since lost.

[28] That the village has two churches despite its small present-day size is another sign of Gittelde's former prosperity. The "St. Johannes-Kirche" is at a lower elevation than the "St. Mauritiuskirche", and thus the story likely refers to the former.

[29] Presumably, a living pastor — not the ghost.

This pastor — the ghost — is allegedly cursed. And if someone goes there, takes the white cap from the altar, and puts a black cap in its place, and furthermore puts a *Pfennig* coin into the donation box for the poor, then they will have released him.[Prö96, p. 31]

Commentary: There are quite a few German folk tales like this and the following one where a brave young woman does something dangerous as part of a dare. Not all of them end this badly, however.[30]

Most of the details in this story to the imagination. Why is the cap so important to the ghost? Why do the blessings of the living pastor do nothing to protect the girl from death by squeezing? And how has anyone figured out that replacing the white cap with a black cap (not to mention donating to the poor) will be the trick that releases the ghost — and why haven't they released the ghost themselves?

While some buildings might be used by the living for part of the year, they were abandoned at other times. This was especially common for the huts in the high alpine meadows, which were occupied during the grazing season of the summer months, but largely avoided during the colder times of the year. Frequently, imaginations ran wild about what happened at such places when no living soul was supposed to be around to witness them...

[30] For a tale where a plucky girl has better luck in confronting ghosts, see "The Brave Girl in Ohmes" (p. 35).

10. The Maid Fetches the Alpine Sieve

There used to be ongoing hauntings in a certain alpine meadow near the valley of Paznaun. One fall evening during the "home garden",[31] the young men started to talk about this alpine ghost.[32] The maid, who was well-known for her bravery, didn't want to believe any of this. And, when the young men promised her a large amount of money if she were to fetch the sieve[33] from the alpine hut during the night, she immediately accepted their proposal. Her employer[34] was greatly worried when the maid embarked on the hours-long journey. The little dog that accompanied her ran back home again when they were in the vicinity of the hut. The maid, on the other hand, went into the hut, fetched the sieve from the cellar, and cooked a milk soup at the hearth fire. Then, suddenly, a gigantic fiery man stepped towards her, and shouted with a terrifying voice "Tremble!" three times in a row. The maid was overcome with dread, left her milk soup where it was, and ran back home with the sieve at a breakneck pace. There, she met her employer, who was kneeling on the floor with widespread arms and prayed for her. The maid

[31] The "Heimgarten" is a custom explained on page 10 of the same source,[Hau94, p. 10] and seems to be a local variant of the "spinning chamber" of other regions — after work and the evening meal, but before it was time to go to bed, people would gather in the chamber next to the oven and chat, gossip, tell stories, and sing for several hours. That text also notes that neighbors tended to congregate in households where "fresh young maidens" were present.

[32] "Alpenbutz" in German. "Butz" is a widespread Austrian term for troublesome spirits.

[33] Called "Seihe" in the main text and "Alpenseihe" in the title, identifying this term initially gave me some trouble. However, a modern collection of legends from the Vorarlberg region explained this as another term for "sieve".[MM10] Judging from the context, this was likely the milk sieve used by the alpine herders to clean the milk from the herded animals before they processed it further.

[34] "Dienstgeberin" in the German text, i.e. a "(female) giver of service" — not in the sense of *doing* services, but handing out the tasks that need to be completed as part of service.

became very ill soon after and died of consumption[35] within the year.[Hau94, p. 44f]

Commentary: "Fiery men" are a recurring element for many ghosts and revenants, dating back to at least the 12th century.[Lec09, p. 120f] They were commonly perceived to be sinners writhing in hellfire, although in this particular tale, the haunt arrives with no explanation and no background story.[36] Just why this spirit wanted the girl to "tremble" is unclear, but presumably it resented the living on general principle.

11. The Dance of the Dead

A young man once climbed up to the alpine meadow during the winter. He knew that he would encounter no one up here during this time of the year. He spent the night in his hut, but woke up and went outside in order to relieve himself. He noticed that there were lights in the hut next door, and shadows were moving past the windows as if people were dancing there. He thus went to the hut, peered through the keyhole, and now saw several couples spinning in dance. He had not seen any of these people before. As he was freezing, he fetched his overcoat. When he returned and peered through the keyhole again, he noticed that the dancers were covered all over with icicles. Now he startled, for he had recognized his lover, who had died recently. She, too, was wearing icicles in her hair, on her sleeves, on her jacket, and on her skirt. He shuddered, and hurried back into his hut, crawled into his bed, and pulled his blanket over his head. Then there was a knock at his door. He didn't dare bid

[35] "Auszehrung" was usually used to refer to tuberculosis, but other "wasting diseases" like cancer also fit this description.

[36] For further tales of fiery men, see "The Glowing Man at the Zehntscheune" (p. 41) and "The Saved Fiery Man" (p. 168).

the knocker to enter, but then the door opened on its own, and his lover Emma stepped towards his bed and pulled the blanket away from his head. What she told him next has remained his secret for all his life.

(From Wiler)[Jeg22, p. 115f][37]

Commentary: As far as afterlife existences go, this is one of the more cryptical portrayals. While associating cold (and icicles) with death makes sense for the high alpine environment, the story does not explain just why these dead people ended up dancing in that particular hut — and why the young man's deceased girlfriend was among them.

1.2. Ruins of the Past

The history of human habitation in Germany stretches back for millenia, and many buildings and even towns or cities were abandoned due to war or other kinds of disasters. Still, the memory of such events might linger on — in one way or another. And, indeed, it was long believed that the spirits of the dead quickly flocked to places that the living had abandoned.[Sch98, p. 37]

12. The Brave Girl in Ohmes

Farmers sat together in the pub in Ohmes[38] in Upper Hesse and were in a good mood. They were loud and merry. Between all the speeches, bets, and toasts, they hit on the idea of drinking

[37] Spelled "Wyler" in the source, this refers to the village in the Lötschental valley of the Valais in Switzerland.
[38] Ohmes is now part of the Antrifttal municipality.

wine for once instead of schnapps and beer, even though no one in the village had the keys to a wine cellar.

When seeing their long faces after all their bold speeches, the publican's daughter — who had listened to all this — said: "Why so disappointed? I will get some wine!"

The remains of a castle are on a forested height next to Ohmes, and this ruin is called the "Wüsburg".[39] Many walls and rooms still existed at the time. Nobody lived in this forlorn place, but, nevertheless, from time to time bright lights shone here at midnight, and old life reawakened within the castle.

Thus, the girl took a basket,[40] and dauntlessly went into the night. She saw bright light shining in the holes of the old windows, and cockily went into the structure. Inside, all doors were unlocked, and a woman dressed in purest white intercepted the undeterred girl as a ghostly gatekeeper. She asked the girl what she wanted. The girl answered urgently and without any hesitation: She needed and must have wine. Then the gatekeeper took the basket presented to her, went away, and returned after a short while with the basket full of wine bottles.

The girl courteously thanked her, went home with the gift, and the farmers enjoyed the offered vintage with great merriment. But, since they quickly began to appreciate the taste of the beverage, the wine bottles were speedily emptied. The girl

[39] According to Mayor Dietmar Krist of Antrifttal, the site of this castle was most likely the hill to the northeast of the village, which is still called the "Wissberg" today. Its owners were probably the Ohmes family, who were first mentioned in records in 1240 (two years after the village itself was first mentioned). The family seems to have been very wealthy, since they bought an entire village (Bieben, near Grebenau) in 1259. One Siegfried von Ohmes is mentioned in 1276 for receiving half the tithe from Hermannshain, an estate near Vockenrod (also now a part of the Antrifttal municipality). After that year, no further traces of the family can be found, and it is unclear just when their Wissberg estate was abandoned.[MS83, p. 62]

[40] The German word used here was "Mane", which is an Upper Hessian term for a wide, woven basket.

decided once again to fetch more wine, once more took the basket with the emptied bottles, and went back to the Wüsburg. The window holes were still shining, and the girl was only ten steps away from the building when, suddenly, all lights went out and deep darkness fell. No door could be opened now, and the girl had to leave empty-handed.[vP85, p. 111f]

Commentary: It's nice to see that ghosts can get along with their living neighbors, and — as far as we know — the girl didn't suffer any harm for her encounter with the undead. Still, trying to get wine twice was probably too greedy for maintaining good, neighborly relations — so it's no wonder that the ghosts turned off the lights and pretended that they weren't home.

It is unclear whether the wine bottles were "real" and fetched from an heretofore hidden wine cellar (in which case they might have been quite old — but their supply was probably limited), or summoned out of ectoplasm or some other otherworldly substance.[41] If the latter, the farmers don't seem to have suffered any negative effect from it. But, if they had kept some of the bottles and had been able to prove their provenance somehow, I suspect that "ghost wine" could have fetched some good prices — with the right buyers.

On a further note, another short fragment about the Wüsburg named "Der grüne Keller" ("The Green Cellar")[Lyn54, p. 127] mentions a cellar entrance that remained intact for a long time, and people who looked inside mentioned that it "looked green, like a sunny meadow". If this ruin had access to other places on Earth, or even some supernatural otherworld, then perhaps the ghost in this story could likewise retrieve wine from elsewhere instead of her own cellar.

[41] The narrator of this tale probably did not care about such matters, but I was cursed with morbid curiosity.

13. The Golden Bowling Game (Yburg)

It is said of the Yburg[42] castle that it was once built by the Knights Templar.[43] But these knights of the order were eventually all killed in one night, and their home destroyed. Since then, spirits haunt this mountain, giants and dwarves are in the castle, war cries emanate from it, and people who approach during these disturbances will be assailed with thrown rocks. People also have heard laughter, moaning, and wailing from within. Many spirits have also been banished there. The exorcists first put them into sacks, and then carry them out of the houses at midnight. These multitudes of spirits in the old castle frequently play bowling.

A boy, who was gathering wood at the time, heard a noise and went to the castle gate out of curiosity. There, an old man was waiting for him and led him to the living quarters. Inside, he found twelve men with black clothing and white beards, and one waved to the boy and indicated to him that he should set up the yellow pins. The boy did so, but he felt that the ball was far too heavy. When the bells of Steinbach[44] rang twelve o'clock, the men stopped playing, and put a yellow pin into his wood basket as a reward. Then, everything vanished in front of his eyes with the last ring of the bells. The pin was too heavy for the boy, and when he saw a nice heap of firewood next to a tree

[42] The Yburg is a castle ruin on the summit of Yberg mountain close to the village of Neuweier, now part of Baden-Baden. It was likely built around the year 1200, and destroyed for the first time in the year 1333 after its inhabitants raided a caravan belonging to the bishop of Straßbourg. It was destroyed for the second time in 1525 by peasants during the German Peasants' War, and for the third time in 1689 during the Nine Years' War (not to be confused with the Nine Years' War of Ireland). Since 1892, the ruins house a restaurant that caters to hikers and tourists.

[43] There are a number of legends all across Germany about the "final redoubts of the Knights Templar", but alas, in-depth exploration of this fascinating topic must wait for a future time.

[44] Steinbach is a village about 3 km to the west of the Yburg, and now also a part of Baden-Baden.

trunk, he threw the pin on the ground and filled his back-carried basket with wood.

He carried it to Varnhalt[45] and told his father what he had experienced. His father, however, scolded his son for not keeping the heavy pin, for it must have been made out of gold. Then, for the sake of his father, the boy ran back into the forest again and reached the tree trunk where he had found the firewood, but the yellow pin was gone, and there was only a scrawny piece of wood lying there.

Whenever people have business in the forest, they prefer to stay together, or wait next to the road for each other so that they can walk home together. For when they travel on their own, they will frequently be led astray and brought to the castle. Then they have to turn around three times within the ring of the castle fortifications. If they know how precisely they have to turn, they will find the right path again.

(Compare with Mone's "Anzeiger etc.", 1834 volume)[46][Sch46, p. 244f]

Commentary: We will examine how exorcists use remote places as a dumping ground for unruly spirits later, but at least a ruined castle provides some proper ambience when compared to a lonely meadow or hill. It isn't clear how many of these spirits were human to begin with — the reference to dwarves and giants indicate that some, at least, were not. The twelve bearded men seemed fairly human, however — or at least the boy did not recognize any of them as distinctly nonhuman.

[45] Varnhalt is a village on the northwestern slopes of the Yberg, now likewise part of Baden-Baden.

[46] This refers to the *"Anzeiger für Kunde des deutschen Mittelalters: eine Monatsschrift"*, 1834 volume.[Monrg, p. 363f] Its contents are largely identical, but lack the last paragraph of Schnezler's text regarding people losing their way in the forest.

14. The Ghostly Mill

During the Thirty Years' War, there used to be a military camp in a depression at the Weißenstein hill near Wehrda.[47] This depression is called the Goldborn.[48] There is speculation that there used to be a mill at this spot[49] which was destroyed at that time. The fields at this location were ruined as well because of all the fortifications constructed there, which is why the area is now covered by forest and other industries.[50]

On some nights, it is possible to hear noises from there which sound like the rattling of a mill. Furthermore, the local forest wardens have frequently seen a gray man there. Their dogs had cornered this man, but he never answered their questions.[vP85, p. 109]

Commentary: It is not just souls of people who can reappear after death, it seems — buildings can also leave a psychic imprint. Unless, of course, the rattling was an extension of the ghost of the miller — if the "gray man" was indeed the miller. His gray appearance might signify that he was "drained of the colors of life".

---

47 The Weißenstein hill near Wehrda (now a part of the town of Marburg an der Lahn) is home to the remains of Weißenstein Castle, a hill castle whose oldest parts were built in the 8th century. The castle seems to have fallen into disuse after the year 1100 or so.

48 According to this map,[Map] there is a well named "Goldborn" about 1.5 km to the southwest of the castle ruins, in a small depression carved into the side of the forested Mosenberg hill to the south.

49 Considering that this location was up on a hill and away from any major stream, the mill would most likely have been a windmill.

50 From what I can determine from the German phrase "andere Ländereien angelegt", this seems to imply that the old fields were abandoned and new ways of utilizing the land were implemented — possibly the parts that didn't become forests were turned into meadows for grazing.

15. The Glowing Man at the Zehntscheune

Near Lützenkirchen[51] there is a lone house at the boundary of a forest which is called the Zehntscheune ("tithe barn"), presumably because the tithe needed to be delivered there. In the meadow behind the house, there is a rather regular hill with traces of old ditches or ponds. At certain times during darkness, a glowing man is reputed to show up on this hill who guards the treasures that can be found within. This man was allegedly a noble during his life who oppressed the people of the area with the establishment of the tithe. Because of his deeds, he must now haunt the hill after his death. The money, which he buried within the hill while he still lived and now guards after his death, can be dug up. But this is a frightening task. Whoever wants to undertake it must work throughout the entire night and may not say a single word. Additionally, gigantic millstones hang over his head suspended by a thread which devils race through as if they want to crush them down on the bold treasure hunter at any moment. If there is even the slightest cry of fear, the treasure, and perhaps the life of the treasure digger, are forfeit.[Sch97, p. 235]

Commentary: Well, the millstones are certainly a motivation to dig faster — or refrain from making the attempt in the first place.

While a full exploration of the madness that is German treasure hunting folklore will have to wait for a future volume,[52] this tale — odd as it might seem at first glance — actually fits their standard narratives very well. The ghost — a "fiery man", like the one we have seen in the tale "The Maid

[51] Lützenkirchen is now part of Leverkusen.

[52] In the meantime, I recommend reading Johannes Dillinger's *"Magical Treasure Hunting in Europe and North America"* for the methods behind this madness.[Dil12]

Fetches the Alpine Sieve" (p. 33) — is bound to a buried treasure, and can only be released from his turmoil once all the treasure has been retrieved by daring treasure hunters. But the Devil (who has no interest in souls getting released from purgatory) sends evil spirits that conjure fantastic illusions in order to deter any would-be treasure hunters from their task.

Translation note: An "Irrlicht" (a term that could be translated as "errant light" or "mad light") is an entity that is roughly analogous to the English "will-o'-wisp" — a strange light that haunts lonely places and frequently leads travelers astray. While they are not always interpreted as ghosts, this is one of the most common explanations for their existence.

Content Warning: The following story mentions sexual abuse of minors.

16. The Irrlicht of Ihlow

On the southwestern side of the Ihlow Forest,[53] there is a large, now overgrown swamp. On stormy nights a large irrlicht can be seen there. However, this is not an ordinary irrlicht but one that had been punished by God. At the site where the light appears there was once a pond, and even earlier there was a hill. And on this hill, there was a chapel before the monastery in the forest was founded. All Christian people in the surrounding areas had to travel there for prayer and confession, including the young girls. However, the chaplain was a corpulent priest who paid more attention to the young maidens than to his vestments and his scapular. And thus, he did contemptible things to them.

[53]The forest surrounding Kloster Ihlow, a ruined Cistercian monastery that gradually fell into disuse after it became secularized in 1529 during the Reformation.

Finally, it came to pass that the measure of his sins was overflowing, and the ground opened and devoured him along with the hill and the chapel in one horrible night. And so that God's judgment would be recognized in this event instead of attributing it to infirm ground, the irrlicht floats above the site since that night.[Sun69, p. 18]

Commentary: One of the more sordid "ghost origin" tales, showing that sexual abuses committed by priests were on the minds of the people long before the current age — although the (now) predominantly Protestant locals might have had some additional motivation to portray Catholic priests in a bad light.

17. The Black Monk

The fortress of Werfenstein rises up from the stream of the Danube close to the eddy, supported by blocks of granite.[54] There used to be an eerie tower on top of the rocks emerging from the waters next to the castle.[55] The Black Monk resided within these walls, and legends claim that he could not find peace as punishment for the godless deeds he committed while still alive. His appearance was seen as an ill omen.

[54] Castle Werfenstein — located near Sankt Nikola an der Donau — was first mentioned in records in the year 1234, and abandoned near the end of the 15th century. "Werfenstein" could be translated as "rock at the swirl", referring to the major eddy in the Danube river at this location.

[55] This refers to Castle Wörth, which was located on Wörth island which splits the Danube in two. The reunification of the two branches causes the aforementioned eddies. The castle, which was perfectly situated to regulate (i.e. tax) the flow of trade on the Danube, was possibly built as early in the 12th century. As the island represented a shipping hazard, parts of the rock the castle stood upon were blown up in the late 18th century. A few remnants of the walls remain.

Once, Emperor Henry II[56] rode past the Werfenstein with several noble lords, Bishop Bruno of Würzburg[57] among them. Then heavy black clouds arose, and lightning writhed above the waters.

"By God, Lord Emperor", the bishop shouted, "do you see the gigantic, black, threatening figure over there on the battlements of the tower?"

"I only see moss and stone."

"And don't you hear the rustling of the folded robe?"

"The storm wind howls, the thunder cracks."

"Now the Terrible One climbs down, but in his eye glitters deadly revenge!"[58]

"The weather seems to have agitated you, your Excellency!"

Finally, they arrived at Persenbeug.[59]

"This was a marvellous journey — nature is also beautiful when she grumbles" the Emperor said smilingly.

The bishop shook like a leaf, and was unable to find a reply.

Countess Richlita von Ebersberg[60] did whatever she could to

---

[56] Emperor Henry II of the Holy Roman Empire ruled from 1014 to 1024. However, it is more likely that the emperor in this tale is Emperor Henry III, who ruled from 1046 to 1056 — see the comments below.

[57] Bruno of Würzburg was a contemporary of Henry II, but seems to have risen to higher offices only after the latter's death. He first became Imperial Chancellor to Italy in 1027, and then attained the position of Bishop of Würzburg in 1034, which he held until his death in 1045.

[58] It is unclear what the Black Monk wanted revenge for, or against whom he wanted revenge. Perhaps he was undecided.

[59] Now Persenbeug-Gottsdorf, about 17 km downriver of Castle Werfenstein — quite a ride in inclement weather.

[60] This is Richlint, the widow of Adalbero II. von Ebersberg. See the

provide a festive reception to her highborn guests.

"There he is again, the horrible one," the ecclesial lord[61] groaned, "he reaches for me —"

"You seem to be succumbing to a severe fever", said Henry, shaking his head.

"Begone! Begone!" cried Bruno, rose up from his chair, rushed towards the bay window, and flung himself from the window down into the Danube.

But then, a black, shadowed, gigantic figure floated past the window and emitted horrifying laughter.

This time, the Emperor thought that he had seen more than clouds, and heard more than the roaring of the wind.

Once, during the times of the crusades, a ship crewed by Thuringians once drove down the river. Then the ghostly monk showed himself, and distorted his chalk-white face into a malicious grin. Soon, the vehicle drifted towards the rock and capsized. Of all the soldiers and sailors, only one was able to save himself with the aid of a plank.

At a later time, the ghost seemed to strike the empty air with a rod. It didn't take long until a horrible hailstorm shattered forests, seeds, and huts.

At another time, after the monk appeared, a flood occurred of a severity as it has never occurred before, and hopefully will never occur again.

The horrible one also summoned fiery conflagrations which destroyed thriving communities and cities.

---

comments below.

[61] I.e. Bishop Bruno, who continues to witness the Black Monk while the Emperor doesn't.

The last time the Black Monk was allegedly seen, he appeared on the doom-laden battlements of this tower when the Turks threatened Vienna.[62]

He flailed around with a sword as if his intent was to fight a grim enemy.

After that, the tower was torn down, and its stones were used as fortifications against the barbarians.

But even if the fiend has been rendered invisible to observers, he lives on in legend, and superstitious people still make the sign of the cross whenever they perceive this uncanny location.[Bow67, p. 57ff]

Commentary: Many German legends exist in multiple variants, and in such situations it may be instructive to compare these different versions.

In this case, the parallels and differences are particularly interesting. A second version can be found in the second volume of the Brothers Grimm's *"Deutsche Sagen"*.[63] That tale is called: "Der Teufels-Thurm am Donaustrudel" ("The Tower of the Devil at the Danube Eddy").[GG18, p. 182ff]

Major differences include:

1. The Emperor in the Grimm version is Henry III, not Henry II. However, since this tale takes place in 1045 (the year when Bruno of Würzburg died), he technically wasn't emperor yet, since he was only elected to that office in 1046. Nevertheless, he and Bruno were close allies — among other

[62] It is unclear if this refers to the Siege of Vienna in 1529, or the Battle of Vienna in 1683.

[63] See my comments below the story "The Ghosts' Meal" (p. 23) for more on this work.

things, Bruno had courted his future wife Agnes of Poitou for him.

2. In the Grimm version, the spirit appears as "a black man, like a Moor" and introduces himself to Bruno as the latter's "evil spirit", promising that he would soon take possession of the bishop. There is no hint that the spirit is a ghost.

3. "Richlita von Ebersberg" is identified as the widow of "Count Adelbar von Ebersberg". This refers to Adalbero II von Ebersberg, who died on March 27th of 1045.

4. Finally, the ending of the Grimm version links up with actual historical events on Persenbeug Castle, the destination of their journey. The reason why Henry's entourage traveled to Persenbeug in the first place was to sort out the estate of the late count. Unfortunately, on May 27th — two months after the count's death — a load-bearing pillar beneath the great hall collapsed. The king survived with minor injuries, but the countess, Bishop Bruno, and the abbot of Ebersberg Monastery were so severely injured that they soon died of their wounds.

Now, it could be argued that the Grimm version was the more "accurate" version of the legend, but I feel that that would be missing the point — these variations simply show how the same original event (the death of Bruno of Würzburg at Persenbeug Castle) gets told, retold, and embellished until there were multiple explanations for it.

18. Princess Swanwithe

There is a lake near the city of Garz on Rügen island. A castle used to be next to this lake.[64] When this castle was taken by the Christians many years ago, an old heathen king had been living there. This king had been very rich and was so miserly that he always slept next to his treasures of gold and gems, which he had piled up in a large hall deep beneath the castle. He burrowed through these treasures day and night, and, during the destruction of the heathen castle by the Christians, he was buried there so that he died miserably of starvation.

As his soul could not part from his terrestrial possessions, he was subsequently transformed into a black dog which now has to guard the heaps of gold forever. At times, people also see him in his human form, wearing helmet and armor. In this manner, he rides over the city and the lake on a pale horse. Sometimes, he wears a golden crown instead of a helmet while seen in this manner. Others have seen him at night within the Garzer Holz woods on the road to Poseritz,[65] where he wandered around with a black bobble hat on his head and a white stick in his hand.

How this old heathen king can be released from this existence might be related by the following tale:

Once, a king lived in the town of Bergen on Rügen island who had a beautiful daughter named Swanwithe. Many foreign princes visited her in order to court her. But she wanted none of them except a prince from Denmark, who was a noble and well-grown man and whom she liked considerably. He thus became her betrothed groom, and the wedding was planned for the near

[64] This most likely refers to "Garz Castle", an old Slavic fort whose remnants are to the north of the Garzer See lake.

[65] I am not sure of the precise location of these woods, but there is a small forest to the northwest of Garz. It wouldn't be the most direct route to Poseritz, which lies to the southwest of Garz, but it's close enough.

future.

But a Polish prince who had been among her suitors was very upset about this, and because he had a spiteful, malicious character, he spread rumors that the princess led an unchaste life and that she had spent quite a few nights in his company. He knew how to make those tales so believable that everyone trusted his words, and one suitor after another rode away. The prince of Denmark, likewise, no longer wanted to hear anything about the engagement. The tale finally reached the king, and he believed it just like everyone else did, and became so enraged that he beat the princess, tore off her hair, and locked her into a dark tower so that she would never pass in front of his eyes again.

In this tower, the princess lived more than three years, and worried and tortured herself in vain while contemplating how to prove her innocence to her father. Finally, she remembered the tale of the old heathen king and how he might be released from his turmoil. For this would occur when a pure maiden would have the courage to climb the old castle ruins at the Garzer See lake during St. John's Night between twelve and one o'clock while being alone and completely nude. Then she would have to walk back and forth backwards until she stepped precisely on the spot where the door and stairs down to the treasure chamber of the old king were buried during the destruction of the castle. Then she would glide down without harm, and then she would be able to take as much gold and gems as she was able to carry, and go back outside at dawn. Whatever she would not be able to carry herself, the old king would carry after her, so that she would have enough money and possessions for the rest of her life. But, during the entire venture, she must not turn around a single time, and she must not speak a single word either, for otherwise she would not succeed and instead die a pitiful death. The same fate would await her if she wasn't a chaste maiden.

The princess Swanwithe remembered this in her lonely prison, and she contemplated embarking on this daring venture in order to prove to her father and the whole world that she was pure and innocent, and that the malicious Pole had lied to them all. She thus had her plans reported to her father and asked him for permission to pursue them. This was granted to her.

When St. John's Night arrived, the princess walked alone from from Bergen to Garz.[66] And when the church tower clock struck midnight, she took off her clothes and stepped into the castle ruins, where she now walked backwards and forwards while touching the ground with a dowsing rod[67] which she had equipped herself with. She didn't have to proceed in this manner for long when the earth opened up, and she glided gently and slowly into the depths. There, she reached a large hall in which more than a thousand lights were burning, and which was completely filled with large heaps of silver, gold, and gems.

In a distant corner the king was sitting and guarding all those treasures. He was a small, gray man, who waved at her in order to encourage her. But she was unafraid and merely greeted the king silently with her hand. Then, suddenly, many splendidly dressed servants and maidservants[68] appeared. They filled their hands with gold and gems, and the princess did likewise. And, when she had gathered enough, she embarked on her way back, and all the servants and maidservants followed her.

[66] A distance of some 16.5 km — not a particularly difficult hike under normal circumstances, but considering that she presumably hadn't had much exercise for the last 3+ years...

[67] Called a "Johannisrute" ("St. John's Rod") in the German original, which seems to be a local name for the more common "Wünschelrute" (roughly, "fortune rod"). German folklore has a long-running belief in such y-shaped dowsing rods which can allegedly be used to find metals or water sources, and some people still practice such methods today.

[68] The German phrase was "Diener und Dienerinnen" — i.e. "(male) servants and (female) servants", a slightly outdated way of emphasizing that both genders were present, as the base noun ("Diener"/"servant") is male-gendered even though it is also a "neutral" term for the profession of servants as a whole.

As she had already walked many steps upstairs, she all of a sudden became worried whether all those carrying the treasures were really following her. She thus turned around to look at them. But this was her great doom, for suddenly the king transformed into a big, black dog, who jumped towards her with a fiery throat and glowing eyes. And as she cried out "Oh, Lord Jesus!" out of fear and dread, the door above her closed shut with a loud bang, and the stairs sunk down, and she fell into the large hall, where the lights instantly winked out.

She has now been sitting inside this hall for many centuries, and must help the old heathen king guard his treasures. She can only be released if a pure bachelor dares to climb the castle ruins of Garz in the St. John's Night in the same manner as she did and then falls down into the treasure chamber. He must bow before her three times, kiss her, and lead her outside by her hand. He may not speak a single word. Whoever brings her outside shall become her groom and attain so many treasures that he can buy an entire kingdom.

Many have allegedly attempted this daring feat, but none of them have returned. It is claimed that the old, black dog is so terrible to behold that everyone who has perceived it has cried out loud out of dread, and then everything is lost. The last man who has allegedly entered the castle ruins was a shoemaker journeyman named Joachim Fritz. He was of a young, handsome type and was always walking around the castle ruins. But suddenly, he vanished, and no one has ever learned where he had gone. His parents and friends had people search for him in the entire world, but did not find him. He might be very well sitting down there now with the others.

After E. M. Arndt, Märchen und Jugenderinnerungen, I. p. 10-29[Jah86, p. 182ff][69]

[69] I only realized late in the translation process that this is a somewhat abbreviated version of Arndt's original (somewhat overwrought) prose,[Arn42, p. 10ff] but since the core elements are the same, I decided to stick with this version. I also felt no need to elabo-

---

Commentary: The first two paragraphs sound like fairly typical ghost tales as they can be found all over Germany — inconsistent ghostly sightings that might or might not have a common cause. The later sections represent a more coherent tale, and much of it is likely an invention by Ernst Moritz Arndt — though Arndt obviously uses common elements from other treasure tales, including the taboo about not speaking and the demonic black dog as a treasure guardian (who is explicitly identified as a ghost in this version). The nudity during the treasure question is a rarer trope, though not wholly unprecedented.

After her own treasure quest has met such an unfortunate end, Swanwithe herself exists in a half-alive state — bound to the treasure like the heathen king, but still with a chance of returning to life after all this time, with a possibility of rescue (whether her other would-be rescuers can also be rescued is an open question, although there is no mention of whether *they* ought to be kissed). Symbolically, after she has failed to retrieve the treasure she becomes part of it — the "prize" for any "pure bachelor" delving into those ruins.

While the ghosts tied to treasures aren't always explicitly pagan like the "old heathen king" in this tale, grave goods *were* a pre-Christian custom which gradually went into decline as Christianity spread, since Christian theology taught that you couldn't take your wealth with you into the afterlife. Perhaps the abundance of tales that revolve around relieving ghosts of their treasures in order to save them can also be interpreted in this light — as cutting the fetters that bind souls to this world due to remnants of ancient pagan practices.

rate further on the character of the "malicious Polish prince", which likely reflected Arndt's prejudices — Arndt was racist even by the standards of his time.

2. Those Who Haunt the Wilds

While many ghosts dwelled in inhabited places, many more were found outside the towns and villages — in lonely places where few people had a reason to tread. But this, too could be an effective setting for a tale of horror — for just like in modern ghost tales, there was always *someone* who felt compelled to visit the haunted place anyway.

2.1. Haunted Meadows, Forlorn Forests

Meadows were often claimed by the living during the day, as they herded their cattle, sheep, and other domestic animals there. In broad daylight, they seem safe — but at nightfall, the dead might make their presence known. In contrast, forests were often forbidding even during the day, as their interiors were shielded from both line of sight and daylight. Anything might lurk there, just beyond one's vision — and, in folklore tales, it often did.

19. The White Girl at the Fecht River

1. At dusk, it is frequently possible to see a white girl playing in the meadow and the banks of the stream in the Allmendrain field boundary between the Fecht river and the mill water canal of

Ingersheim.[1] One evening, a child from the village — who didn't know about this apparition — was supposed to drive ducks back home that had dallied at the stream. Suddenly, the child saw the white girl skipping around in front of them, always a few steps ahead. The child called out to her: "Come, help me search for the ducks!" But the white girl turned away and did not answer.

As the child could not find the ducks, they ran home and fetched their older brother, who was supposed to help in the search. Both of them saw the white girl sitting in the grass. Whenever they came too close to her, she jumped up, skipped over the small bridge next to the lock,[2] and vanished into the reeds. But, after a few moments, she would jolt out again, wearing a white veil over her head, and folded her hands above her chest.

Now, the boy wanted to approach her and called out to her: "Who do you belong to, girl? You should go home, for the evening bells have already rung!" But, as he received no reply, and the girl skipped forwards as if to mock him, he picked up a stone and threw it at her. However, the stone flew above her head in a high arc, and soon after the girl vanished into the ground. Twice, the siblings heard her shout "Quack! Quack!" with a bright voice from the same location. But the stone had hit one of the ducks that had been sleeping near the ditch, and these now hurried home while quacking and beating their wings.

[1] A "-rain" — frequently encountered as a suffix — is a field boundary, usually between villages. I was not able to identify the "Allmendrain" as such. However, OpenStreetMap shows us that Ingersheim (now located within the Haut-Rhin department of France) has a "Square du Moulin" at the intersection of the Rue de la République and the Rue de trois Epis — and "Moulin" is French for "mill". Google Maps shows us that two minor ditches, streams, or canals meet at this location. Thus, my best guess is that the "Allmendrain" used to be between one of these ditches (the former mill canal) and the river Fecht to the southeast.

[2] The German term used here was "Stellbretter", which could be translated as "control boards" — pieces of wood which can be raised or lowered to control the flow of water in the stream.

According to the account of the children, the white girl skipped or hovered in short jolts, moving at a certain distance above the ground.

2. At another time, in the evening, a girl walked across the large bridge over the river Fecht, which is also an uncanny place at other times. Then, the white girl walked past her, hit her in the face, and sighed: "Oh, why didn't you wish me a good night!" After that, the white girl said something to her, but the girl never shared what she had been told with anyone else as long as she lived. Furthermore, the white girl asked her to come back the next evening. Her mother, a stout-hearted woman, accompanied her. As they reached the spot where the apparition had shown up the previous day, they knelt down and prayed the Lord's Prayer and Hail Mary three times, but nothing happened. But, from this moment on, the girl was unable to see anything white without being overcome by dread, and, at times, she was even suffering from heavy seizures.[Prö96, p. 31]

Commentary: This is the second time that we have seen a "white woman" (well, girl), after the tale "The Brave Girl in Ohmes" (p. 35). "White women" are a recurring theme in German folklore — often representing a ghost, but sometimes a faerie woman or (more often) some entity of uncertain provenance. While the woman in the first story is explcitly described as "dressed in purest white", here it is left unclear whether the girl is dressed in white, has a pallid skin color, or is glowing with white light. This is rather typical for stories featuring them, as is a certain ambivalence about their "true nature".

While the "white girl" in this story does seem to be portrayed as a ghost, I would caution against interpreting such apparitions too narrowly — "white women" (like, say, "black dogs") were ultimately one more tool in the narrative toolkits of German folklore storytellers that could be used and interpreted differently depending on the needs of the story.

That the titular ghost complains that she doesn't get what she needed after failing to indicate in advance what it was that she needed is a rather typical behavior for ghosts — we shall see more examples of this in later chapters. It is not quite clear what the second visit to the bridge was supposed to accomplish, especially since the living girl kept her silence — but considering her subsequent psychological problems, we can probably infer that they did not succeed in releasing the ghost.

Beyond these aspects, it may be significant that her preferred haunt was a field boundary — a threshold place between two different territories. As we shall see later, ghosts were often associated with such locations.[3]

20. The Bowling Farmers

At night, farmers regularly play bowling at the crossroads between Mettman and Lüttges.[4] These farmers used to regularly play bowling at a nearby bowling alley while still alive. When they play, they rarely do so without strife and quarrels. The farmers use their skulls as bowling balls, and their arm and leg bones must take the place of the pins.

They have often been seen by night-time wanderers in this manner.[Sch97, p. 93]

---

[3]See the tale "The Rider without a Head (Lengfeld)" (p. 85) for another example.

[4]This seems to refer to "Hof Lüttges", a historical estate at Niederschwarzbach 24 that is now located in the northernmost part of Mettman.

Commentary: We do not know why these farmers were condemned to such an existence. Perhaps it was punishment for their obsession with this game in life, or perhaps they chose to eternally play bowling, just like many incarnations of the leader of the Wild Hunt chose the eternal hunt over the afterlife. It is also noteworthy that the ghosts have a skeletal countenance, rather than appearing how they did before or immediately after death like most other ghosts.

Crossroads — where the farmers make their appearance — are a traditional spot for encountering uncanny forces.[5] In other tales from German folklore, witches could be spotted at the crossroads as they traveled to their gatherings, spirits assaulting or pursuing travelers were unable to cross them, and the Devil himself could be summoned there, and thus it is unlikely to be an accident that the ghosts choose to play here.

21. The Headless Man near Münsterhof and the Farmer

There is a beautiful forest close to Münsterhof in the Lauenburg district.[6] The path leading through it has high hills on both sides, and a black man without a head resides in this depressed road.

One evening, around ten o'clock, a farmer from Reckow had to pass through this road.[7] His cart was heavily loaded with flour, and thus he only progressed slowly. After he had advanced a short distance along the road, a sack of flour suddenly fell off the

[5] See the tale "The Brautlachenberg Mountain" (p. 72) for another ghostly encounter at the crossroads.

[6] Now Wojciechowo in Gmina Wicko, Poland.

[7] Since the farmer travels towards Reckow — now Rekowo Lęborskie — a likely location for this forested depression seems to be the path between Gościęcino and Tawęcino, directly to the north of Rekowo Lęborskie. Though today, forest only remains on the eastern side of the path.

wagon. The farmer suspected what might be to blame for this, and thus calmly drove onwards. Not long after that, another sack fell to the ground. That, too, didn't bother him, and only after each and every one of the sacks suddenly rolled off the wagon did he stop, climb down, and load everything up again.

But his misfortune was not finished yet. For, as soon as he had driven the horses onwards again, not only the sacks but also the planks and ladders fell off the wagon and were thrown into the sand. This was too much for the farmer, and in his anger he started to swear profusely. As he was saying those curse words, everything that had been scattered was suddenly gathered on the wagon again. The ladders, the sacks, the planks — nothing was missing, and the black, headless man stood next to him and looked him piercingly in the face.[8]

But the farmer took care not to say a single word to the headless man, and instead drove onwards in silence. He then reached his farm in Reckow without further disturbance.

(From Reckow in the Lauenburg district.)[Tem40, p. 258]

Commentary: In German folklore, the color black has a really unfortunate association with sin or malevolence — indeed, in some tales "cursed" people show up whose body have been partially turned black (such as a black lower body, or blackened limbs) because of their sins. Thus, the description of the headless man as "black" should not be read as a reference as to the ghost's ethnicity, but as a visual indicator of his vicious nature.

Strangely enough, many spirits from German folklore — ghosts included — can be driven away by *either* swearing *or* praying. What remains unclear is why certain ghosts can

[8]No, I don't know how that was supposed to work, either.

be driven away in this manner. It is also noteworthy that the ghost in this tale felt compelled to clean up the mess he made before vanishing, yet the farmer clearly believed that any further words on his part would be dangerous.

22. The Headless Man and the Gooseherd

Once, the gooseherd of Reckow herded his geese near this forest. When it was around eleven o'clock in the morning, all geese suddenly rose up into the air and flew towards the pond which was adjacent to the forest.[9] But, before they could reach the water, the black, headless man had them in his hands,[10] and played an abominable game with them. The poor animals, which flew down to the ground out of fear of the horrifying figure, were thrown back towards the sky by the black one as if they were balls. As soon as they had reached the ground down again, he repeated his amusement once more, and it didn't take long until the geese were all lying dead on the ground.

But the gooseherd did not let that distract him, for he had listened to many tales of this haunt, and he had also heard that swearing would immediately drive him away. Therefore, his voice rose up and he started to swear terribly. And indeed — as soon as the curses escaped his mouth, all of the geese revived, and the headless man had vanished.

(From Reckow)[Tem40, p. 258f]

[9]The closest lake visible now (on satellite images as well as OpenStreetMaps) is directly to the west of Rekowo Lęborskie (in Nowa Wieś Lęborska). Another, smaller pond is to the south of Obliwice, about 4 km to the southwest of Rekowo Lęborskie. It is unclear if the ghost's depressed road from the previous tale where he allegedly resides was also in that area, or if he roamed around.

[10]It is not specified how many geese there were, or how large the hands of the ghosts must have been so that he was able to capture them all at once.

Commentary: As we can see here, this particular ghost has a rather cruel streak — frightening and hurting animals for his own amusement like a vicious schoolyard bully. While the tale explicitly describes the geese as "dead", it seems more likely that they were merely incapacitated by the ghost's touch.

We once more witness how swearing has the power to compel this ghost to leave, but, again, we receive no explanation for *why* swearing has this power. Given the ghost's cruel nature, one might be inclined to think that a few curses wouldn't bother him — but apparently, they do.

23. A Farmer's Fight Against the Headless Man

Because of his pranks, the headless man had given the depressed road and the forest such a bad reputation that nobody dared to move through this area — either by day or night. This upset a farmer from Schwartow,[11] who was known in the entire area as the strongest brawler. He thus spoke: "I will teach this black fellow good manners. As I am the tallest and strongest man in the entire land, I shall defeat him as well and thus force him to leave our region so that wanderers will have peace in the future. That he doesn't have a head doesn't bother me. In the worst case, I will simply put one on him."

As he was holding such speeches, he picked up a strong stick and set forth to the depressed road. Once he arrived there, the headless man approached him and gave him a friendly "good evening." The farmer replied equally politely, but then was immediately sharply interrogated by the black one. The latter

[11] Now Zwartowo. This seems to confirm my earlier hypothesis that the depressed road of the tale lies between Gościęcino and Tawęcino, as someone traveling from Zwartowo to Rekowo Lęborskie (again, in Nowa Wieś Lęborska) would likely travel through this area.

questioned him how he dared to enter his depressed road, as the entire world knew that the forest and the road were his uncontested property.

The farmer replied: "What are you telling me, screwhead?[12] Have I questioned you about your business? How dare you talk with me like this?" These brazen words angered the headless man mightily, and thus they started to fight with each other. Initially, luck was on the farmer's side. The black one was lying down and moaned terribly under the fists of the strong farmer. But, soon, the headless one gained the upper hand, stood up, and rose up to his full length, grabbed the startled man, and threw him high up into the air.

When the unfortunate farmer returned to the ground, his whole body was shattered from the fall so that scattered pieces of the corpse were lying at various spots on the road, as well as between the trees. His remains were found by the villagers in this condition the following morning.

(From Reckow)[Tem40, p. 259f]

Commentary: German folklore tales rarely have detailed action sequences, and this remains true for this tale. However, I am suspicious whether the farmer *really* got the upper hand during the early part of the fight, or if the ghost merely pretended to be defeated in order to make the later reversal more shocking.

We also don't get an explanation of what the "full length" of the ghost was, but it must have been significantly larger than his opponent in order to startle the farmer. Certainly, his true strength was tremendous, considering the state the farmer's corpse was found in.

[12] The farmer calls him "Drehkopf" — "turning head", no doubt intended as an insult.

24. The Man Without a Head

1. One evening, when he returned home to Sievershausen[13] from Dassel, the local pastor encountered a man without a head and walked beside him for quite some distance. Finally, the pastor spoke: "All good spirits praise God the Lord!" "And I don't", replied the haunt. Then the pastor spoke: "So go to the Devil, as I shall go to God". Immediately, the apparition vanished. The next Sunday, the pastor held a speech about what he had encountered on the road. Subsequently, he fell ill and was dead four weeks later.

2. Near Markoldendorf[14] there is a memorial stone beneath which a man is buried. This man had ploughed off land from his neighbor,[15] and on the same spot his head was ploughed off in turn. Once, when a coach was driving past with several people sitting inside — a woman was also sitting on the back of the coach[16] — the people sitting within saw a black man without a head walk back and forth. However, the woman who had been sitting on the back of the coach had not seen anything.

3. Within the field boundaries of Einbeck, alongside the road towards Markoldendorf, there a tower called the "Klapperturm" as well as a pub built next to it.[17] Nearby, there is the Tackmanns Graben ditch,[18] as well as a lonely linden tree. This ditch

[13]Sievershausen has now become part of the Dassel municipality.

[14]Markoldendorf is now likewise part of Dassel.

[15]The German term was "abpflügen", with the implication that, by plowing over his neighbor's land, he had taken it away from him. Presumably, the visible plowing lines indicated the boundary lines of his field.

[16]The implication seems to be that the woman was sitting on the outside of the coach, while the others were sitting inside.

[17]There is still a "Landgasthaus zum Klapperturm" restaurant at Klapperturm 1 in Einbeck. According to this article, the tower (whose remains still stand) was built around 1450 as one of eight defensive towers for Einbeck, while the pub was probably built in the middle of the 18th century.

[18]According to an article on the home page of the nearby village of

derives its name from a man called Tackmann. This man had once had stolen a harrow from a field, and for this, his head was ploughed off. He was buried beneath the linden tree. Now, he haunts this spot without a visible head.

4. There is a black pole on the Galgenberg hill[19] near Hardegsen. No shepherd can drive their sheep past it, because they will always run away from there. At this location, a man without a head appears who wears an old Frankish soldier's mantle.[20] He approaches everyone who passes by at night between twelve and one o'clock, but he must remain within a certain circle centered on the pole. People who have seen him have subsequently lost the ability to speak for some time.

5. There is a meadow between Wolbrandshausen and Bilshausen that is said to be haunted. Once, a man who wanted to go to Bilshausen walked along the road between 11 and 12 o'clock. As he was nervous about crossing the meadow, he intended to jump across the stream that was flowing down next to the meadow at its upper end,[21] and continue on his path on

Odagsen,[Oda] Tackmanns Graben lies south of the road, approximately where the railroad tracks are located today. Its biggest claim to fame is the Battle of Tackmanns Graben of May 12th 1479, when the militia of Einbeck decided in a spectacular act of recklessness to charge the forces of William IV, Duke of Brunswick-Lüneburg and Henry III, Landgrave of Upper Hesse on the open fields instead of staying behind the fortified walls of the city. 160 citizens of Einbeck died that day, and 800 more were captured. The city lost two-thirds of its adult male population that day, at least until the captives could be ransomed later in the same year for the enormous sum of 30,000 guilder (gold) coins. It is said that the ghosts of the fallen still reappear there on every May 12th.

[19] "Gallow's Hill" in English, this hill lies just to the east of Hardegsen.

[20] Presumably, this is a reference to the Carolingian Empire or earlier periods, since the concept of a "Frankish" realm largely ceased to exist after the death of Louis the Pious (the son of Charlemagne) in 840, as the empire was divided among his heirs and thus split up into different nations. See the history section in the appendix (p. 236) for further context.

[21] There is a "Gelkentalbach" stream flowing down the northern slopes of the hills between Wolbrandshausen and Bilshausen. Since the

the other side. But, before he could jump across the stream, a "black man without a head" stood before him. The farmer was so "befuddled"[22] by this apparition that he lost all conscious thought, and did not know where he was or where he wanted to go. Then he switched his shoes,[23] and through this he regained his senses and continued on his path.[SM54, p. 202f]

Commentary: The first fragment shows us both the standard discernment approach for distinguishing good from evil spirits[24] as well as the sickening effects that the presence of the dead have on the living. The second and third fragments (which are unsurprisingly from the same region) are representative of the utter contempt farmers had for those who would steal their property. It is unclear if "ploughing one's head off" was supposed to be an official punishment by the authorities for these crimes, or a bit of "vigilante farmers' justice".

The fourth and fifth fragments are more open to interpretation. We do not know why these ghosts haunt these regions in those forms, nor why their presence has such an effect on those who encounter them. And why was "switching one's shoes" believed to ward against evil supernatural forces? I have come across tales where arranging shoes "the wrong way" before going to bed is supposed to protect against

footpath comes from the south until it reaches the stream, and then further follows the stream on the southern side, we can conclude that the meadow was on the southern side of the stream as well (these days, there are fields in this area).

[22]The German term was "verblendet". This has the same root as "Blendwerk" ("blinding work"), a common term for illusions and other malicious magic targeting mind and senses.

[23]It is not clear from context if he switched his left shoe with his right shoe, or if he switched them with another pair of shoes he just happened to have on his person.

[24]See also the footnotes of the tale "Visit of the Hanged Man" (p. 145) for further details on this particular invocation.

malevolent spirits at night, but these stories do not require putting them on.

25. Kleines Clausthal

I. There once was a town near the current-day Clausthal[25] which was called the "kleines Clausthal". This town was supposedly very prosperous. But the richer the inhabitants became, the worse and more godless they behaved. For this, God had sunk the city,[26] and a pond formed at the spot where the church used to stand. The valley is still called the "kleines Clausthal".[27] The church can be seen regularly at midnight between Maundy Thursday and Good Friday. At the same time, a doe can be seen which no one is supposed to hunt. Once, the mountain monk[28] seduced a miner into oversleeping, and after he woke up, he walked along a path that led over the Teichdamm.[29] There, he saw the church of kleines Clausthal. As he was quite astonished about this, he went inside. But he recognized no one among the people within the church, including the preacher. Then, the mountain monk appeared before him again and led him outside, and when he proceeded onwards, the church and

[25] Spelled "Klausthal" in the source, this is now part of the town of Clausthal-Zellerfeld, an important former mining town within the Harz mountain rage. Presumably, this "lost town" derived its wealth from mining as well.

[26] The German word used here was "untergehen" ("going under"), which means both literally "sinking" and "coming to an end". Both meanings of the word seem to apply here. It's not quite one of the "sunken castles" from the series title, but it will have to do for the time being.

[27] The "kleines Clausthal" is a small valley ("-thal"/"-tal" means "valley") to the southwest of Clausthal proper that drains into the Innerste river.

[28] The "mountain monk" or "Bergmönch" is a spirit commonly believed to dwell in mines — called thusly because he usually wears a monk's black robe.

[29] The "Teichdamm" (roughly, "dike of the pond") is a road close to the west end of Clausthal-Zellerfeld, which would have been near the mines in that region.

the path leading to it were gone.

II. There was once a cruel poacher in the Harz region. If he knew that there was a game animal somewhere, then it was not safe from him. Then he heard that, in the midnight hour of Good Friday, a doe with her fawn could be seen that no one is supposed to shoot. But he only laughed about such things. Once, a short time before Easter, he was with merry company.[30] At that occasion, people started to talk about the kleines Clausthal. But as he didn't believe any of these warnings, he only laughed about it all and said: "What's the matter? I will shoot the doe for you, and the fawn, too. And then we shall eat it on the first holiday of Easter.[31] The others tried to dissuade him — but he would not listen.

On the eve of Good Friday, he went into the valley of kleines Clausthal. When he arrived at the pond,[32] he saw a high, dense fog hovering above it. This fog reached up to the sky, and it was impossible to see the pond itself. And there was whispering within the fog as if many voices talked to each other, and there were glimpses of strange figures within. Above the path, too, many figures like merry shadows flitted closer, and they all vanished into the fog above the pond. But none of this did the poacher any harm.

He walked past it, and took position behind a shrub at the exit of the valley, where the first stamp mill of the Innerste is located now.[33] And indeed, the doe with her fawn appeared

[30] I.e. a group of people who had gathered in a pub to drink.

[31] Most likely Easter Sunday. Killed game is usually hung up for several days to soften the meat before consumption. Furthermore, Good Friday and Holy Saturday were both important fasting days. While this poacher might not be personally averse to a bit of blasphemy on those days, it is unlikely that many of his friends would have participated.

[32] Presumably, the "Kleiner Clausthaler Teich".

[33] Referred to as the "erste Innerste-Puchwerk" in the text, this is most likely one of the stamp mills servicing the Bleihütte Clausthal, a lead works facility further downriver. Stamp mills would process ore by

before him. He then shot the fawn. As he saw it fall, he leaped towards it, tied its feet together, and hung it over his shoulders. Then he set forth on the way back.

When he arrived at the spot where the pond is located, he beheld a church at the site where the pond had been only a short time ago. This church was brightly lit, singing was clearly audible, and the organ played amidst it all. "This is strange," he thought, "I ought to go inside." Thus, he stepped within. There, he saw that the church was full of people, but all of them looked as if they had been within the grave for hundreds of years. Their clothing was of a fashion that was unfamiliar to him. He greeted, but nobody greeted him in return. But a few nodded, others shook their heads, waved at each other, and pointed with their fingers at him. The lights on the altar, and the lights on the chandelier burned with a blue flame, and a blue flame flickered out of the cup on the altar. One of the people within the church rose up and pointed him towards the door. The poacher, however, remained in place, looked into someone's hymnbook, and wanted to sing along. Then someone else rose up and pointed towards the door, but he still did not leave and still wanted to sing along. But he could not read the writing, and thus had to give up.

Afterwards, the pastor stepped in front of the altar, but he spoke no human tongue. It was as if wind and thunder filled the whole church, and a blue flame came out of the preacher's mouth. Suddenly, a loud crack reverberated through the church as if the world would end. Then, the pastor pointed towards the visitor and shouted: "Accursed defiler of the sabbath!" And the ghosts rose up against him and howled those words in return. Upon hearing this, the poacher rushed out of the church in fear and dread. The door closed behind him with such force that his heels were torn off.[34] Then he was thrown all the way to

pounding on it, and thus reduce its volume.

[34] This *might* be metaphorical, or perhaps the heels of his shoes were damaged. But then again, you never know with these kinds of tales.

the path, and there he remained lying until the next morning. As he regained consciousness, the pond was quiet, and the fawn was gone. But he himself was deathly ill, and was barely able to drag himself home. After he had lingered on for nine more days, he told his tale and died afterwards.[Prö96, p. 141f]

Commentary: A lot of German folklore tales have descriptions that hardly even qualify as "bare bones". Thus, I really appreciate the amount of special effects that were used to set the mood in this tale — the voices and shapes in the strange fog where the church would form, the eerie ambience in the church with the inhuman tongue,[35] the flickering blue flames, and the entire congregation howling in outrage against the protagonist. Whoever came up with this version of the tale knew what was important for telling a story!

And speaking of the ghostly congregation, presumably these were the "godless" inhabitants of former kleines Clausthal. Were they forced to haunt this uncanny church as an ironic punishment? It's a bit rich that they would get so enraged at the poacher for "defiling the sabbath", even though their own sins were presumably hardly of a lesser nature.

Alas, the mystery of the doe and her fawn remain — just what did they represent that hunting them was forbidden? Were they some kind of metaphor for the sanctity of the Easter holidays, or is there something deeper at play here? Either way, the protagonist decided to break local customs and taboos, despite the stern warnings he had received — and paid the price.

[35]This parallels the tale "The Stolen Goose" (p. 29), which also takes place in a church.

2.2. Over the Hill, Under the Mountain

In German folk beliefs, hills and mountains were long considered to be the residences of the dead — a belief that dates back to old Germanic and Norse myths.[Lec09, p. 149f] It is therefore unsurprising that they still loom large in ghost tales.

26. Ghostly Activities Around the Nöll

The Nöll, a high, forested cone-shaped hill near Friedigerode,[36] is also full of ghostly beings.

The Deaf Huntsman frequently appears there. A forester who was walking through these woods in the evening saw him as a man in green clothing who was measuring the size of a windthrow[37] with his measuring stick. When the forester addressed him, the huntsman vanished, and the wind roared terribly in the forest.

Two girls were in the Nöll near the Teufelskanzel[38] and gathered leaves. Then a woman emerged from between the trees who was dressed as if she was about to attend Communion: All black and white. As she approached, one of the maidens greeted her and asked: "Well, where are you coming from?" But when she was walking past, the woman mutely turned her head towards the maidens. The maidens screamed loudly, for, to their horror, they saw no face, but only a gray larva. But, at the same moment, the apparition vanished and melted. The spirit

[36] Friedigerode is now part of the Oberaula municipality. The Nöll lies to the southeast of Friedigerode, and north of Oberaula proper. Its most noteworthy landmark is an abandoned basalt quarry which dates back to at least the first half of the 19th century.

[37] A stretch of forest where trees were uprooted during a storm.

[38] The Teufelskanzel ("Devil's Pulpit") is a hill to the north of the Nöll and the northeast of Friedigerode.

disappeared in angry, stormy winds, and the forest cracked like thunder. The girls subsequently fled.[vP85, p. 103]

Translation note: Based on legends from nearby Asterode, the "Deaf Huntsman" seems to be a local variant of the Wild Huntsman who is primarily known for the winds that accompany him. The "taub" in "tauber Jäger" most commonly means "deaf", but sometimes means "numb" or "someone who refuses to listen" according to Grimm's Dictionary. Lacking any further explanations for the origin of the name, I left it at "deaf".

Commentary: While the larva-headed woman might not be considered to be the exact same entity as the Deaf/Wild Huntsman, the similarities are strong — both vanish in stormy winds when their supernatural nature is revealed. This shows the overall "toolkit" approach in folklore tales — narrative elements are recycled in a different context.

We cannot be exactly sure that the ghostly woman is actually a ghost, either — the depiction of humanoid beings with the heads of a larvae pops up a few times in association with infernal spirits. It is possible that this ultimately derived from the Roman word "larvae" for malignant dead,[Lec09, p. 128] which Christianity reinterpreted as demonic spirits and diabolical masks[Sch98, p. 11] — but, as so often, a precise classification must elude us.

27. The Bowling Game Beneath the Hohnstein

Once, a herder watched over his herd beneath the Hohnstein.[39] Then, around noon, twelve white-clad spirits approached, and

[39] Called "Hohenstein" ("High Rock") in the original text, this seems to refer to the ruins of Castle Hohnstein near Neustadt/Harz, itself part of the Harztor municipality.

immediately there was a bowling alley where there had been none before. The herder, however, received the instruction that he should set up the pins. The spirits bowled for an entire hour, and as they finished, eleven of them disappeared immediately. Before the final one vanished, he gave the "king" pin[40] to the herder as a reward. The herder carried the pin with him, but it became heavier and heavier until he was unable to carry it. But as soon as he let the pin drop, it turned into the purest gold.[Prö96, p. 238]

Commentary: Like in the tale "The Golden Bowling Game (Yburg)" (p. 38), we can't be sure if spirits here are actual ghosts or some other kind of entity. Do they regularly come to this location for bowling, or was this a one-time event? If they show up more frequently, would-be treasure hunters might be tempted to lurk around in the area...

It is also noteworthy that both tales feature exactly *twelve* spirits playing a bowling game — a curious detail, given that the Yburg and the Hohnstein are more than 400 km apart. Perhaps, like in the tale "The Ghosts Haunting the New Mill at the Innerste River" (p. 12), the twelve spirits might represent a symbolic counterpart to the Twelve Apostles of Jesus, but this will have to remain speculation for the time being.

28. The Meuenloch Cave

The Meuenloch is a cave that has now collapsed, but which used to extend below the church in old times. This cave is also called the Brühlloch because the Brühlweibchen ("Brühl woman") used to live here. Allegedly, this woman can sometimes be spotted sitting under the rock during overcast weather. She wears a

[40] In Germany, the center pin of the nine-pin arrangement is called the "König", or "king".

long black dress and a snow-white veil through which her tear-stained eyes and sad face can be clearly seen. Her sighs can be frequently heard from the depths of the hole.

When boys and girls skip church on Sundays and, instead, lie down on the hill, the Brühlweibchen comes out and scares them, running after them until they get back into church. Furthermore, when children haven't said their evening prayers or refuse to obey their parents, she visits them at their beds, looks at them with her tear-stained eyes, and berates them.[Pan48, p. 68]

Commentary: It is hard to classify this entity as a faerie or a ghost, but considering her weeping and preference for wearing black and white I am inclined towards the latter — and her fixation on Christian rites is probably a further hint.

Finding the location of this tale was tricky — the source claims that the tale is from "Burg in Schwaben", but there is no town called "Burg" (literally "castle") in the Swabia District of Bavaria. However, the source claims that this text is an excerpt from the 56th issue of *"Fliegende Blätter"*.[41] Which, indeed, has a story mentioning the Meuenloch and the Brühlweibchen — but it's about two treasure hunters using a divining rod to search for treasure in the Lower Franconian town of Theilheim.[Heu46]

29. The Brautlachenberg Mountain

About half an hour distant from the old, knightly mountain castle Wildenberg,[42] an enormous, gloomy forest stretches to the southwest into the lowlands of the great valley of the river Laber.[43] The people of the region consider several locations in

[41]An 8-page, weekly magazine published from 1845-1944.
[42]Located in the town of the same name in Lower Bavaria.
[43]One of the tributaries of the Danube.

this dense forest to be haunted, and, even today, tired lumberjacks will hasten their steps to get out of this cursed place before night falls. For the Wild Hunt may encounter those who tarry too long, and they will divert them from their destination with horrendous turmoil.

The Brautlachenberg mountain, in particular, has a reputation for being haunted during the midnight hour. Three black figures will approach a tresspassing wanderer as soon as they reach a swampy crossroads. Two of the paths lead into the depths of the forest, but the main road ascends a tall hill covered by a dense fir forest in the direction of the March of Oberlauterbach,[44] which makes escape for the frightened travelers difficult. Horses rear and refuse to pass this haunted place. Sweating heavily and with hairs standing on their ends, they tread downhill as if suffering under a heavy load, while night-time wanderers will see the three dark figures and hear a disturbing, dull ringing of bells at certain times during the midnight hour.

These three figures are said to suffer for their sin of blasphemy. At this location (called the Brautlache), a bridal wagon once went past when the bells at the Wildenberg castle rang for the evening prayers. The people in the wagon — the bride, the groom, and the bride's attendant — indulged in sacrilegious speeches and blasphemed against both God and the prayers. Immediately, both wagon and horses sunk into the mountain along with the three blasphemers, and the location was transformed into a swamp as an eternal warning.[Pan48, p. 98f]

Translation Notes: The original descriptor used for Oberlauterbach was "Hofmark", which is a term that was only used in Bavaria and Austria and implies a march or territory which had its own jurisdiction for crimes short of capital crimes.

[44] Now part of the town of Pfeffenhausen.

"Lache" is a term for a very small pond or puddle, likely a reference to the swamp in the immediate area. Thus, "Brautlache" could be translated as "Bride's Pool", and "Brautlachenberg" as "Mountain near the Bride's Pool".

The bride's attendant, or "Brautführer", was a male assistant to the bride. One of his jobs was protecting the bride and the wedding guests from bandits and robbers, as well as helping with organizing the event.

Commentary: This is a fairly simple, if effective, story of a ghostly apparition, complete with an origin story (the divine punishment for blasphemy), a remote and spooky location, and some nice special effects (frightened horses and ringing bells). That the haunting appears at the crossroads is in line with their general nature as a boundary space between the mundane world and the supernatural — see the tale "The Bowling Farmers" (p. 56) for another example.

30. The Heavily Loaded Men

It is not safe within the shadow of the Stoffelskuppe.[45] A large meadow there is called the Kuh-Eller[46] and the herders of Roßdorf[47] let their herds graze there. One evening, the headman[48] of Roßdorf walked across this barren mountain area when he spotted two shadowed men on the meadow who walked at an even pace in the distance, barely visible in the gloom of dusk.

---

[45] A mountain of volcanic origin near Roßdorf in Thuringia which is part of the Rhön mountain range.

[46] "Kuh" means "cow" or "cattle", but "Eller" is harder to identify. It seems to be an alternate name for "alder" in parts of Germany, so perhaps it could be interpreted as "cow grazing spot near the alders".

[47] The municipality in the district Schmalkalden-Meiningen in Thuringia, not one of the ten other villages of the same name. It can be translated as "horse village".

[48] Called a "Schulze" in the German text, meaning the Schultheiß — an appointed official in charge of the village.

He was glad to have found company, and hurried to approach them. Now his eyes were able to perceive that the two men were carrying a mighty, oversized and tree-like beam on their shoulders which burdened them to near collapse, and it was barely conceivable how these two people were able to shoulder such a terrible load. The headman was greatly astonished that someone would still work so hard at such a late hour and in such a lonely place, and thus he called out to the two men: "Hey there! Who are you? Where to?" The men did not hear him and did not answer him. He called once more: "Who are you, and where are you going?" Deep silence. Now the headman shouted even louder for the third time: "Hey there, you people? Where do you want to go?" The answer came from both at the same time as if speaking with one mouth, and with a terrible voice: "To the Abode of the Damned!" And then the men pressed forward and vanished into the night. The questioner, however, was overcome with an overpowering terror. And, as long as he lived — which was not for much longer — he was unable to forget that cadence and those words that sounded like the voice of the Last Judgment itself. Other people have seen the heavily-loaded men walking over the meadow, but they took care never to address them with questions.[Bec42, p. 58f]

Commentary: A nice, spooky ghost story with some suitable symbolism — not just in the name of their destination (see below), but also in the burden they carry, which likely represents the burden of their sins that condemned them to this existence. We never learn who they or what their sins were — but this story doesn't need those details to be effective.

The short remaining lifespan of the headmen also reflects the usual theme of German folklore [49] that those among the

[49] Most recently seen in "Kleines Clausthal" (p. 65).

living who get too close to the unquiet dead will soon wither away as well.

Translation note: The destination of the heavily loaded men is called "Ungnadshausen" in the German source, which requires some explanation. "-hausen" is a common enough suffix for villages, since it means "home" or "house" and can designate any place where human habitats can be found — but there is no such village by that exact name in Germany or anywhere else in the world.

However, "Gnade" means "grace" or "favor" — both in the sense of finding favor in the eye of God or before people. "Begnadigen", for example, means "pardoning someone". "Ungnade" means the opposite, finding disfavor in the eyes of God or men. Thus, "Ungnadshausen" is "the home of those who have fallen from the grace of God", or "Abode of the Damned" for short.

31. Räderberg Mountain

(Oral tale)

A butcher from Nassau went away from home in order to trade. On the highway, he soon encountered a coach traveling along the road. He walked after it, following its tracks while lost in thoughts. Suddenly, it stopped in front of a beautiful, large country mansion in the middle of the highway. He had never seen this mansion before, no matter how often he had traveled along this route. Three monks climbed out of the wagon, and the astonished butcher followed them unseen into the brightly lit house. First, they went into a room to conduct the rite of Eucharist for another person. Then, they went into a chamber where a large party of people sat around a table and devoured a meal accompanied by loud noise and shouting.

Suddenly, the man sitting at the head of the table noticed the uninvited butcher, and immediately every noise was gone and silenced. Then, this man rose up and brought the butcher a cup of wine with the words: "Another day!" The butcher shuddered and did not want to drink. Soon after, another man rose up, walked towards the butcher with a cup, and again said: "Another day!" The butcher refused again. After that, a third person approached with a cup and the same words: "Another day!" Now, the butcher drank. But soon after, a fourth person came closer to the butcher, and offered wine yet again. The butcher became extremely scared, and, after he made the sign of the cross, the entire scene vanished and he found himself alone in thick darkness. When morning finally broke, the butcher found himself on the Räderberg mountain,[50] far away from the highway. He traveled a stony, exhausting path back to his hometown, related his experiences to the priest, and died exactly three days later.[51]

There has long been a legend that a monastery used to be on that mountain. Its ruins are still visible, but the monastic order dwelling there has long since died out.[GG16, p. 366f][52]

Commentary: This is one of these tales that focuses on mood rather than explanations. Where exactly was this man-

[50] The exact location of this "Räderberg" is unclear. In his second volume of *"Sagenbuch des preussischen Staats"*, Johan Georg Theodor Grässe speculates[Grä68, p. 711] that this might be a reference to the ruins of the Räderburg (now called "Röderburg") near Roßberg, a village now part of the Ebsdorfergrund municipality — more than 100 km to the northeast of Nassau. If anyone can figure out a more likely location, both me, Mrs. Jaeger of the Nassau Tourist Board, and Dr. Sarholz of the Bad Ems City Museum would all like to know.

[51] It is not clear from the German text whether he died three days after the encounter — in which case he would have needed to travel more than 100 km within three days — or three days after he told his tale to the priest.

[52] If the site mentioned by Grässe is correct, the ruins in question would have been a motte-and-bailey castle (not a mansion) which archaeological finds date to the 13th to 15th century. However, no documents have been found which further explain the nature of these ruins.

sion located, and what was its history? Who were these people gathered at this feast? Why did they toast to "another day"? What exactly did the butcher die of — the fright, the wine he was offered, or the general malaise that seems to inflict many people who encounter the dead? All of these are left to the audience's imagination.

32. The Goatherd Boy in the Illgraben

In the Illgraben[53] valley, the evil souls of the dead suffer for their sins. A goatherd boy had once lost a goat. Since the owner was mad at him, the boy went out to search for it during that same night. He called and called for it, but it didn't answer. He reached the Illgraben, and suddenly he was in front of a great gate which he had never seen before. He knocked on it, and the door swung open. He stepped over the threshold and entered a grand, hall-like kitchen where many maids were working and the most marvelous smells rose up from the pans. This made his mouth water, and he said: "Oh, it is so nice here! If only I could stay!"

But he was shown to a second door, where he knocked again and entered another hall. Inside, he saw many men at a long table who were writing, and, lined up along the walls, there were the most beautiful beds he had ever seen. "I'd love to sleep in such a bed as well", the goatherd boy exclaimed with wide-open eyes. Then, one of the men turned towards him, and said with a dull voice: "Sure, just hold your hand beneath one of the blankets, and you will see how nice it is to sleep in these beds!"

But another one shouted: "No, don't do it! You are a poor, innocent goatherd boy searching for a lost goat! Don't attempt it, for then you would burn your hand — only put the iron tip of your stick beneath the blanket!" The boy approached one of the beds and reached beneath the blanket with his stick. When he

[53] The Illgraben is a mountain valley south of Leuk, in Switzerland.

pulled it out, the iron was glowing, and the stick began to burn. Then he was overcome with fear and dread. He turned around, and started to hurry out of these halls as quickly as possible. As he walked past, he saw that the maids carried the food to the table, and the sounds from the table made it seem as if everything was served on gold and silver plates. When he was outside and the doors closed behind him, a roaring and wailing rose up which made him shiver as if he was standing beneath the glacier, and the cold meltwater was pouring over him.[Jeg22, p. 66f]

Commentary: It is not quite clear how the "evil souls" are punished for their sins beyond the burning beds, although it is possible that more parts of these halls were illusions and thus contained hidden punishments (such as the food actually being made out of some horrible substances). I also found it curious that the man who warned the boy knew so much about him — was this entire scene a trap created merely for the boy, and had they observed him for some time?

33. The Ghosts of the Old Noricans

Allegedly, there used to be a "Norican encampment" founded as protection against the assaults of the Romans in the region known as "Königreich", ("Kingdom") which lies in the southern part of the Neumarkt district.[54] Supposedly, it is still possible to see traces of old walls in this area. One somewhat remote, detached building is said to be a courthouse from this age of antiquity, and the old prison cells are still recognizable.[55]

[54] There is a peak called "Königreich" about 10 km to the southwest of Neumarkt in der Steiermark, so this might indicate the general area.

[55] The site of the capital of the Noricans, Noreia, is now lost. In the 18th century, a location near Murau or Neumarkt was a popular hypothesis, but this is considered doubtful by modern scholars.

The Romans were only able to conquer the kingdom after a long siege, but not before the last man of the Norican defenders had fallen after stalwart resistance.

The ghosts of these brave heroes now persist within the underground rock caves and chambers of the Königreich region. When the land is threatened, they rise to the surface world, light ghostly fires, and admonish the people to get ready to defend their land. This supposedly happened during the Turkish and Hungarian invasions.[56] Likewise, when the French penetrated into Styria for the first time,[57] several inhabitants of the mountains claimed to have seen similar hauntings. Ghostly flames flickered to life, fog-gray figures waved their arms in the air, and when the victorious Frenchmen had pushed the Austrian forces back after a bloody skirmish near Einöd,[58] the ghostly apparitions wailed and plunged down the mountainside.

These were the ghosts of the Noricans of old, who now and forevermore fled into their subterranean graves so that they wouldn't have to watch the ignominy of the defeat, and the oppression by the enemies under which the land was suffering so terribly.[Prö96, p. 238f]

Commentary: Noricum was the Latin name for a Celtic kingdom in the area of modern-day Austria and Slovenia. Despite what the story implies, the Noricans seem to have been long-term allies to the Romans and were gradually incorporated peacefully into the Roman Empire without any noteworthy resistance. But such stories were useful for rallying the national or regional spirit of the living, which is

[56] This refers to the Ottoman wars starting in the 14th century, and the Hungarian invasions of the 9th and 10th centuries.

[57] In 1797 under Napoleon Bonaparte.

[58] This most likely refers to the modern "Wildbad Einöd", a spa and former hamlet that is now part of Dürnstein in Steiermark, which in turn has been incorporated into Neumarkt in der Steiermark.

presumably why someone came up with this particular tale — though it is unclear when precisely the story was first invented.

2.3. Pale Riders

Long before *"The Legend of Sleepy Hollow"* was first published in 1820, legends of headless riders on pale horses were widespread in Germany. The following are a few examples, ranging from the hills of the Southwest to the Baltic Sea coast.

34. The Rider without a Head on the Ziegenberg hill near Zwönitz

A rider without a head allegedly can be seen on the Ziegenberg, a cone-shaped hill with a height of almost 300 Ells.[59] People tell the following legend about this apparition.

In the 17th century, there was said to be a miller in Zwönitz who had a very beautiful daughter. This daughter was secretly engaged to the forester of Grünhain.[60] The forester knew almost none of her other relatives. The miller also had a son, but had renounced him because he married the headsman's daughter without his permission and thus (according to the convictions of that time) dishonored his family.[61] Nevertheless, the siblings

[59]The Ziegenberg ("Goat Mountain") reaches an elevation of 653 meters above the sea level and is located to the southeast of the town center of Zwönitz.

[60]Now Grünhein-Baierfeld, to the south of Zwönitz.

[61]Beyond the status hierarchies described in the appendix, there were a few professions which were generally considered "unclean" by German society, and their members shunned. Executioners were among these social groups. Unsurprisingly, they were also often considered to be highly proficient at magic — another "unclean" trade.

continued to meet at various places, and when the beautiful miller's daughter went dancing in the pub where she had intended to meet her beloved, she met her brother and his wife. And, of course, she couldn't deny him a short dance.

But, in the meantime, the forester had arrived and he hurried from his horse into the dancing hall without changing stride. There, he beheld his bride in the arms of a stranger. When he saw her joking with this stranger in a friendly manner, he was gripped by raging jealousy. He thus lured her to the Ziegenberg hill with flattering words. He pretended that he had lost something in the forest during his gallop, and asked her to help him with the search. The girl accompanied him, suspecting no malice, but when they reached an overgrown spot on the hill, he accused her of infidelity and stabbed her without even listening to her defense. Unfortunately, his aim was only too true, and the unfortunate girl expired within a few minutes — in which she had only enough time to tell her murderer that the alleged seducer had been her brother, who had been unknown to him.

In wild despair, the forester threw himself over the dying woman, but he was unable to bring her back to life. He thus hurried to the dancing hall and cried out to her brother that he had murdered his sister, and wanted to turn himself over to the courts. And this indeed happened. As he sought death, the investigation did not take long, and after only three moons, his guilty head fell on the scaffold in Grünhain. On the spot where the bloody deed was done, a white rose bush was planted whose roses look like they are sprinkled with blood at night, and whose leaves seem to bow down to the ground in grief. But when bad times are approaching, a rider with his head beneath his arm rides forth at midnight from the high court[62] of Grünhain towards the rose tree, stays there for a short time, and then rides back again.[Grä74a, p. 510f]

---

[62] I.e. a court that can rule on capital punishment trials.

Commentary: In this tale, the ghostly rider is compelled to return because of the great crime he committed, and his headless form reflects the nature of his death. It is less clear why his horse is compelled to accompany him — after all, *it* didn't murder its beloved in a fit of misplaced jealousy. At least, as far as we know...

The red-sprinkled white roses are a nice gothic touch, too. Are they haunted by the spirit of his fiancée — and if so, what would happen if you plucked them?

35. The Rider within the Beeches of Klosterlausnitz

During the nights of the new moon, nobody likes to go into the beech woods of Klosterlausnitz,[63] or indeed into their general vicinity, and whoever is able to do so takes a different route that leads around this evil place. For in the night of the new moon, a ghostly horseman rides through the beeches with shouts of "hey-ho" and "hooray". Many have seen that he is missing a head, while others saw him with a hunter's hat. But he rides on a pale horse and that much is certain. It is the spirit of an old huntsman who maltreated the farmers and devastated their fields along with his companions while hunting game. He had impudently bragged that neither God nor the Devil could touch him. This appeared to be true during his life, which seemed charmed. He had received high honors and respect from distinguished people until he reached the end of his life. But then his fortunes changed, for God does not tolerate mockers. Now the huntsman rides around in the hunting grounds he favored when he was alive, and his restless soul waits for deliverance.[Grä74b,

[63] Modern-day Bad Klosterlausnitz. The surrounding forests were well-known for being rich in game and had several game preserves, which lead to the construction of a hunting lodge for Frederick II, Duke of Saxe-Gotha-Altenburg on the grounds of a former monastery. Thus, it seems appropriate that a noble huntsman was said to haunt this region.

p. 342f]

Commentary: Here, the "headless" aspect of the ghost seems more of an afterthought. While the reason for his punishment seems clear enough, it doesn't give an explanation for why he sometimes lacks a head. Thus, it is likely that this narrative element was borrowed from similar tales.

36. The Rider without a Head (Mückenloch)

At the entrance of the Mückenloch Forest,[64] the path leads across a bridge. After crossing that bridge, it is sometimes possible to see a man riding on a pale horse who carries his head beneath the arm like a hat. He pursues people he comes across and likes to lead them astray, but he cannot cross the ditch that is located nearby,[65] and thus people are safe from him beyond it. He can also only leave the forest for a short stretch of the road, and vanishes at the large boundary stone where that stretch ends.

During his lifetime, he was a land surveyor who committed such frauds in this region that he now must haunt this area as a punishment.[Sch46, p. 575f]

Commentary: In this tale, the explanation for the existence of this ghost seems almost like an afterthought. While

[64]Mückenloch (which could be translated as "midge hole") is now part of the town of Neckargemünd.

[65]OpenStreetMap shows a "Mückenlocher Weg" ("Mückenloch Path") leading south from the village itself. This eventually crosses a small stream called the "Haselwiesengraben" ("Hazel Meadows Ditch") shown on Google Maps which runs from north to south, which I suspect is the ditch mentioned in the story.

falsifying boundaries between different lots of lands *was* one of the more common causes for ghosts (as we shall see later), usually the appearance of such ghosts reflects their crimes.[66] Here, on the other hand, the alleged misdeeds might have been ascribed afterwards to a pre-existing ghost narrative.

However, the mention of the boundary stone is in itself significant — representing the threshold between a "safe" region and one where uncanny forces were at work, similar to how crossroads serve as a boundary space between the mundane and the supernatural in other tales.[67]

37. The Rider without a Head (Lengfeld)

There once was a moss-covered stone cross about three and a half feet in height that stood within a hazelnut hedge beneath the village of Lengfeld[68] alongside the cart road to Themar, at a farm boundary[69] where fields were encroaching from the higher side. This cross was only removed recently. According to legend, a horseman lies buried beneath this cross along with his horse. Both were decapitated at this spot during the Thirty Years' War, and during the twelfth hour the rider climbs on his horse which lacks a head just like he does. Then, he slowly rides around the cross, but with the last chime of the bell he vanishes as well.[Sch46, p. 575f]

---

[66] See for example the tale "The Man with the Boundary Stone" (p. 112).

[67] See the tales "The Bowling Farmers" (p. 56) and "The Brautlachenberg Mountain" (p. 72) for examples of crossroads in ghost tales.

[68] Lengfeld in Thuringia.

[69] Called "Rain" in the German, which is short for "Feldrain" — a boundary between the fields of different farms which is sometimes covered by grass, but frequently by hedges or trees. See also the "Allmendrain" in the tale "The White Girl at the Fecht River" (p. 53).

Commentary: In this tale, on the other hand, we do not learn of any crime that might have caused the ghost to reappear — only that he was decapitated, which might have been the result of a skirmish at this site rather than an execution (though the narrative does not specify). That the horse was also decapitated is strange, though — why would their killers bother to do so, if they could just take the horse as plunder? And if they were butchering it for its meat, then decapitation isn't necessarily the usual approach for killing it either.

Once more, the ghost haunts a boundary space — a spot between two lots of land that is not fully part of either. I wonder if the field boundary was established before or after the soldier was killed at this spot. If the former, was the soldier deliberately executed here, and why? Or did getting killed at this location allow the soul of the soldier to manifest as a ghost, while other people who were slain at non-boundary spaces would not have lingered on? And if the field boundary was established later, was it established because neither of the owners wanted to claim responsibility for a haunt on their land?

38. The Rider on the Pale Horse

(Oral tale from Swinemünde)[70]

Uncanny forces are at work in the Tannenkamp[71] near Krummin on Usedom, for people frequently see a rider without a head soaring closer. This rider soon takes on all sorts of shapes and then transforms himself into a large, gray stone. In this form, he remains lying next to the road and frequently causes horses

[70]Now Świnoujście. Świnoujście lies on the easternmost part of Usedom island which now is part of Poland.

[71]This place name could be translated "field of firs". The town of Wolgast to the west of Krummin has a district named "Tannenkamp" — but that district lies at the northern end of town on the mainland, opposite to Usedom island.

to become frightened from its presence. Because of this, many people have suffered great damage to their wagons and their harnesses.[KS48, p. 13]

Commentary: Finally, this headless horseman has no origin story at all — he is just one more protean night terror lurking in the German countryside. Since he is seemingly not bound to this shape, he might have chosen it deliberately in order to frighten the living instead of having his appearance echo his past life.

3. Those Who Roam as Beasts

German folklore is rife with tales of encounters with supernatural animals. While the vast majority of these are presented with no explanation for their existence, a fair number are explicitly described as ghosts. Their most common form was that of a dog — though unlike the "Black Shucks" of the British Isles, they were not necessarily black in color, and their apparent "breed" could vary as well.

39. Ghostly Poodle

Disguised as a black poodle, a student in Würzburg once terrorized the shield guard[1] at the Teufelstor[2] gate for several nights between eleven and twelve o'clock. However, he was eventually shot dead by the guard. As punishment, he must haunt that gate as a black poodle during the same hour of the night.[Baa51, p. 391]

---

[1] A "Schildwache", or "shield guard", was originally the guard standing watch before the armory, but gradually came to mean any guard post.

[2] While there was a Teufelstor gate ("Devil's Gate") in the city walls of Würzburg between 1430 and 1668,[Wue] this is more likely to refer to the Pfaffentor gate("Priest's Gate"), which gained the same name after the Teufelsbarracken ("Devil's Barracks") stables were built nearby in 1812. The Pfaffentor was torn down in 1853, two years after this story was published.

Commentary: While folklore loves ironic punishments, being forced to haunt a location for a death-by-stupidity does seem rather harsh. And it's not exactly fair to the guards that, after they were were terrorized by a student *pretending* to be an evil poodle, they now have to deal with an *actual* supernatural poodle.

"Black poodles" in general are a frequently occurring narrative element in German folklore tales. While they are sometimes interpreted as ghosts, they often represented infernal forces or even the Devil himself, and they were almost always considered to be bad news.[3]

40. The "Lordly Dog"

There used to be a chapel close to Breinermoor.[4] The chieftains of Backemoor[5] were the patrons of this chapel and in it they listened to sermons and submitted to the rite of confession. However, at one time, one of those patrons was such an arrogant, brazen man that the priest was not able to do anything that gained his approval and constantly suffered from his abuse. Usually, the noble brought his favorite big, black dog with him to the rite of confession. Finally, he came up with the blasphemous idea to hold up the beast to the ear of the listening priest during the confession. He did so, and whispered the deeds and pranks of the animal as if it were a human being. The priest supposedly

[3] And, of course, they inspired half of the title of this series. Alas, exploration of "sunken castles" will have to wait for later volumes...

[4] Part of Westoverledingen.

[5] The East Frisian chieftains were a class of nobles that arose during the 14th century when the old, egalitarian social order of the so-called "Frisian Freedoms" declined. The highly defensible East Frisian geography with its multitudes of moors and boglands had allowed the East Frisians to retain some semblance of independence from the German nobility at large, but, in the end, they had to bend their knees to their "home-made" nobles, who eventually assimilated into "mainstream" nobility in the 15h century.

shook his head, but nevertheless gave the dog absolution. After this, the noble broke out into maddened laughter, which rose in volume until it finally could no longer be distinguished from the howling of a dog. Insane, the noble was led away and lived like a dog from this moment on, crawled on all fours and ate from the same bowl as the dog. Indeed, even after his death — which occurred soon after — he was not freed from his curse. For the local people claim that Heaven's just punishment transformed him into a gigantic black poodle with eyes of hellfire. This black poodle shows itself to blasphemous people who visit the pub, but never the church, when they return home from their carousing at midnight.[Sun69, p. 49]

Commentary: Like in the previous story, the black poodle is a ghost who was explicitly punished for his misdeeds in life, although here the crime was a more fitting blasphemy. The association of the black poodle with the forces of hell is made more explicit, however.

41. The Ghostly Dog

At the first boundary stone on the road from Waldwimmersbach[6] to Dilsberg,[7] a black poodle frequently approaches travelers and then silently trots along with them. Its fur gradually brightens, and at the second boundary stone it is completely white. But, from there on, its shade darkens once more, until it is completely black again at the limits of the forest as the traveler reaches the third boundary stone. If it is left alone, it doesn't harm the

[6] Now part of Lobbach. Waldwimmersbach refers to the northern part of Lobbach, which would be closer to Dilsberg than Lobenfeld, the southern part of the municipality.

[7] Part of Neckargemünd. The precise route this refers to is unclear, though it might be along the modern-day road from Lobbach to Mückenloch.

traveler, but if it is asked what it wants, it transforms into a dreadful giant, gives the curious person a mighty slap on the face, and vanishes. How this ghost can be released is just as unknown as why it must haunt this road.[Sch46, p. 577f]

Commentary: Well, that was more random than usual. While we don't exactly have a shortage of black poodles in German folklore, a color-changing poodle is certainly novel. If its range is limited to that particular forest road, why does its brightness increase towards the center?

Just like in the tale "The Rider without a Head (Mückenloch)" (p. 84), the range of the ghost is limited by boundary stones. Did the ghost commit sins there or die there — or was it assigned to this remote region later on by an exorcist?[8]

And like in the tale "The Rider on the Pale Horse" (p. 86), the ghost in this tale (and, indeed, many other folklore tales) has a rather protean nature — allowing for its transformation into a "dreadful giant", even if its ability to do so remains unexplained. Likewise, ghosts distributing "slaps" to those they feel offended by is something we will see again and again in other tales.

42. The Welthund near Stötterlingenburg and Lüttgenrode

The village of Lüttgenrode[9] is located about half an hour to the west of Osterwieck. It was built around a hill which is the site

[8] For a full discussion of the practice of exorcism and its implications, see Chapter 7 (p. 222).

[9] Spelled "Lüttchenrode" in the source, Lüttgenrode became part of Osterwieck in 2010.

of the former convent Stötterlingenburg.[10] There used to be a major forestry office[11] next to the convent, in a building on the northern side of the hill. The house where this office was located is still standing, and its appearance shows the great prosperity of its inhabitants.

It is said of one of these forestry officials: He had a huntsman in his employ who once set his dog against a poor man who had been gathering a bundle of wood. And, when the poor man attempted to defend himself, the huntsman stabbed him with his hunting dagger.[12] Soon after, he fell ill. In his fever-wracked state, he could not stop thinking about his monstrous deed. He then died before a priest could arrive and assist him in preparing for his death.

Since that day, the area has been haunted by an enormously large dog. Eyewitnesses (which, according to their earnest assurances, included most of the inhabitants of Lüttgenrode as late as 1850) compared its size to that of a calf or a donkey. This "Welthund" ("World Dog") — called thusly because it has been spotted in many places — is also said to have a great resemblance to a donkey. It is described as being gray on its back, white on its stomach, and having large, fiery, swollen eyes. It is most commonly encountered by people during the winter after darkness has fallen, and most frequently between 10 and 11 o'clock at night. Its point of origin is within the gable of the foresters' house. It rises from the ground beneath a chestnut tree where the huntsman was buried, for the huntsman was not

[10] The convent of Stötterlingenburg was initially founded in 992 and disbanded in 1552 after the region became Protestant. Its nuns followed the Benedictine rules. Parts of the structure, such as the church tower and a few walls, are still preserved today.

[11] A "Försterei" is a forestry office in charge of the woodlands of a particular region. This particular site was an "Oberförsterei", with the prefix "Ober-" indicating that this was a major branch office in charge of supervising lesser offices.

[12] A "Hirschfänger" ("deer catcher"), this 30-40 cm long blade was used to kill deer and boars, and was generally seen as a badge of honor among hunters.

granted a place in the graveyard because of the murder he committed.[13] It always jumps over the fence at a particular spot, but returns via a different path. It never hurts anyone, but all dogs that sense its presence show their fear through whining or hiding, even if they do not see it. The huntsman who was transformed into the Welthund was also often seen in Heiningen Monastery,[14] which might be explained by the fact that the forests there were under the jurisdiction of the same forestry official.[Prö96, p. 59f]

Commentary: While the cause of the haunting is fairly clear — an unconfessed murder — many of the details remain unexplained. Why is the dog's "point of origin" the gable, even though the text then claims that it rises from the ground at the spot where the huntsman was buried? What do its routes signify — are they the paths the huntsman took in life? Maybe the entrance to the garden used to be at a different spot than it is today, thus requiring it to jump the fence. And why does the ghost appear as a dog in the first place? Was it because the huntsman's dog was involved in the murder? If so, then perhaps there was some resemblance between the huntsman's dog and the appearance of the ghost.

The story implies that if he had received his last rites and confessed his crime on his deathbed, he might have avoided returning as a ghost. This was in line with medieval theology, where ghosts were far more likely to appear if the dying could not be properly guided in their journey to the afterlife.[Sch98, p. 6]

[13] A fate reserved for those who committed heinous sins in the eyes of the church — most notoriously, for those who committed suicide.

[14] The monastery, which used to be located in the village of Heiningen in Lower Saxony, was founded around 1000 by the Billung dynasty of Saxon noblemen, and is located about 20 km to the northwest of Lüttgenrode. The monastery was formally dissolved in 1810, although its church and many of the buildings of the estate still remain.

The notion that the dog appears in Heiningen because it was part of the huntsman's former master's territory is intriguing, though perhaps he did patrol the forests of Heiningen during his life. If so, it seems likely that the ghost now feels compelled to patrol the same lands.

43. The Cursed Officers

A captain of the soldiers who were once quartered in Osterode now haunts this town in the form of a dog. Every evening, around eleven o'clock, it appears at the upper mill[15] at the part of the city wall called the "Schildwache",[16] and slowly walks along the Schildwache until it reaches the Johannistor gate,[17] and turns around at the Johannisbrücke bridge and walks down past the depot,[18] finally vanishing at the Kreits Steg.[19] If you encounter it on its patrol, it will pursue you until you reach your

[15] The Obermühle, or "Upper Mill", was likely built in the 14th century, and is first mentioned in documents in 1402. It is located in the northeastern part of the old town of Osterode.

[16] See the notes for the tale "Ghostly Poodle" (p. 88) for an explanation of the term. In Osterode, there is a road of the same name running along the inside of most of the old city walls, excepting only a small portion in the northeast.

[17] The Johannistor gate was located in the northeastern part of the old town, at the bridge (the Johannisbrücke) over the river Söse. From which we can conclude that the ghostly dog walked along most of the old city walls in a clockwise direction.

[18] The text mentions a "Magazin", which in this context means a storehouse. Looking at the city map, this must refer to the Harzkornmagazin ("Grain Depot of the Harz Region"), which was built from 1720-1722 and, since 1989, serves as the city hall of Osterode.

[19] "Steg" implies a small bridge for pedestrians. While there is no further mention of a "Kreits Steg" in the historic record, according to Ekkehard Eder of the Osterode city archives one such bridge is shown on a city map from 1858. It crossed the river Söse below the Harzkornmagazin into the direction of the Rosmariengasse road on the other side. Furthermore, he pointed out that while he was unable to find the family name "Kreit" within the city records, "Kreit" could also mean "strife" or "quarrel" within the local dialect. Thus, the bridge might be named after a specific incident of strife rather than a person.

own destination. However, it normally doesn't harm anyone, and will only bite those who tease or even beat it. When there were still soldiers stationed in Osterode,[20] the dog always woke up the soldiers standing guard when they were asleep, and did not stop with its scratching, knocking, and barking until they were awake again. It was allegedly a very large dog, and had the shape of a bulldog.[21]

The following is also told in Osterode about an officer. Once, there was a man whose house was supposed to be sold against his will, since he had more debts than hairs on his head. Then he said that his creditors might as well get his house, but no one would be safe from the haunting within it. "Well", the authorities said, "we will be sure to put an end to this". They therefore sent a man to stand guard there. They also told the man — who was armed with sabre and pistols — to shoot immediately if the ghost approached. When the clock struck twelve, a jangling noise came down the stairs, something opened the door to the main chamber, and entered the room. It was a wall clock, which made a horrible noise and almost deafened the guard. The guard took aim, but was unable to fire due to some damage his gun had suffered. The second night, another guard was sent there who was promised a nice sum of money if he was able to take down the haunt. The guard remained stout-hearted throughout. When the large clock approached the guard around

[20] This likely refers to the time when Osterode was part of the Kingdom of Hanover. Osterode was one of the centers of student unrest in 1830 (the others being Göttingen), which likely would have motivated the government to move additional troops there. However, after the Austrian-Prussian War of 1866, the Kingdom of Hanover was dissolved and integrated into the Kingdom of Prussia as the Province of Hanover. Since Osterode was no longer close to the borders of the realm, there would have been less need for soldiers stationed there — and, as the text indicates, this seems to have happened by 1896 (when the legend was published).

[21] The text claims that it resembles a "Fleischerhund", or "butcher's dog" — another term for the Bullenbeisser (German bulldog) breed. They apparently gained this name because they were the only breed fast and strong enough to subdue enraged bulls by biting their noses.

midnight, the guard took aim and, by accident, shot off one of the weights powering the clock. The clock fell apart, and an officer was standing in its place. This officer had been cursed to haunt this house for a long time. The guard received his promised reward, and the officer was likewise grateful for his rescue.[Prö96, p. 192f]

Commentary: The first story follows fairly common narrative conventions. And, while we learn nothing about why the officer was compelled to return as a ghost, it makes sense that he would follow his former patrol route and wake up any soldiers who slacken off.

The second tale, on the other hand, turns into a rather unexpected direction. While one might first be inclined to think that the former owner of the house invented the haunting in order to get his creditors to back off, it turns that the haunting is real — but it's not a haunting by a ghost, but by an officer who has been bound into an animated wall clock for some reason that the story never bothers to explain (though thankfully, the clock never starts singing to a Disney princess). Did the former owner know about this curse — or perhaps even had a hand in it? We can only speculate.

44. Ghosts in the Shape of a Dog

1. At night, a large black dog roams the area near the river Ilme at Oldendorf.[22] This dog has glowing eyes that are as large as cymbals.[23] The locals call him the "Fischhund" ("Fishing

[22] This refers to the part of Markoldendorf south of the river Ilme, which, until 1939, was a separate village by the name of "Oldendorf". Markoldendorf itself is now part of the town of Dassel.

[23] The German text used the word "Becken" which can also refer to basins (including baptismal fonts), or the pelvis. "Cymbal" seemed like the most likely meaning based on the context.

Dog"). This used to be a fisherman who, as he was lying on his deathbed, wished to fish forever after his death. Once, a man from Oldendorf wanted to walk to Holtensen[24] at night in order to visit his bride there. He encountered the Fischhund on the church road.[25] He swung his stick at it, and then the dog rose up on its hind legs, stood tall, and gave him such a mighty slap across the ear that he fell down to the ground unconscious. From this frightful experience, the man first fell sick and then succumbed to madness.

2. A senior forestry official named Molf allegedly built the saltworks in Sülbeck.[26] His portrait hangs within the entrance hall of the senior inspector's official residence. If the picture was taken away from there, he would haunt this place. But, as long as it remains there, a large, black dog as large as cattle haunts the area instead. This dog walks up along the Salzgraben channel[27] in the evenings. Once, young men from Sülbeck encountered it. Believing it to be an ordinary dog, they threw stones at it. But then, the dog stuck out its large, glowing tongue, and its fiery eyes became bigger and bigger. Now, fear and dread overcame the young men, and they fled into a nearby house in wild flight and quickly locked its door behind them. As soon as they had done so, the dog was in front of the door and roared like a lion.

[24] The village to the east of Markoldendorf, now part of Einbeck.

[25] Called "Kirchweg" in the German text, this might refer to the modern-day "Kirchstraße" in Markoldendorf, which is in the center of the settlement.

[26] Sülbeck is another village that is now part of Einbeck. It is famous for its brine springs, and there is archaeological evidence for settlements in their vicinity dating back to 5000 BC. In 1686, the Elector-Prince of Hanover, Ernest Augustus, ordered the construction of the saltworks, which produced 300 tons of salt every year by 1700 — a massive source of wealth, considering the price of salt in those times.

[27] This channel was built by 100 Hanoverian soldiers in order to draw water from the river Leine after Ernest Augustus ordered the construction of the saltworks. This water was used to power the pumps of the facility. Since the dog walked *up* the channel, we can conclude that it started in Sülbeck and then progressed towards the river.

A carpenter from Sülbeck once went outside at night with several others in order to steal fruits. He was about to leave with his loot when he saw the dog on his path at the fence, putting its front paws on the small pedestrian bridge.[28] As the man needed to cross that bridge, he spoke to the dog: "Satan, begone!" and tried to hit it.[29] But he didn't connect with his swing, and merely hit empty air. In the same moment, he received such a mighty slap that he ended up on the other side of the Salzgraben and appeared to be almost dead for half an hour. The other people, who counted a barber[30] among their number, finally managed to revive him and led him home.

3. In Bilshausen, a button maker died who had been an evil man while alive. After his death, a large black dog with glowing eyes and a glowing tongue was lying in front of the door of his former house between eleven and twelve o'clock, frightening passers-by through its countenance. This persisted for four weeks. Only after the priest had blessed the whole house did the dog vanish.[SM54, p. 187f]

Commentary: While the dogs in second and the third fragment are associated with dead people, it is not altogether clear whether the dogs are actually the ghosts of the dead people themselves or merely an associated phenomenon — in particular, the second tale makes the distinction between the ghost of the forestry official and the dog that sometimes appears in his place.

Supernatural entities distributing slaps to those who offend

[28] As far as I can visualize this scene, the fruit orchard was probably a fenced-off area, and the only point of access was via a small bridge across the Salzgraben channel.

[29] It is unclear whether the carpenter tried to hit the dog with his bare hands, or (more likely) with a stick.

[30] A barber would have known some rudimentary, self-taught medical skills, although not on the level of a university-trained doctor.

them is far from uncommon, however — as we have seen before in the tale "The Ghostly Dog" (p. 90).

While dog-like ghosts outnumber all other types of animal-like ghosts in the tales by a wide margin, they were not the only option.

45. The Billy Goat of Büntlitten

A fiery billy goat is frequently seen at night in the Büntlitten area near Dornbirn,[31] and this billy goat is thus called the "Büntlittenbock".[32] Illuminated by the bright glow of its flames, it jumps down from the heights,[33] then back and forth again — an eerie sight! In this manner, it must glow and jump until its hour is past, whereupon it vanishes behind the hill. This spirit has been seen for two hundred years, and it is suspected that it was a man who has committed field sacrilege,[34] or moved boundary markers.[Von89, p. 115]

Commentary: While being forced to haunt the world as a ghost is not an unusual punishment for messing with the fields of other people (as we shall see later in Chapter 4), the

[31] There is a "Bündtlittenstraße" road in the eastern parts of Dornbirn, close to the Fischbach stream, so that's presumably the general area.
[32] I.e. "the billy goat of Büntlitten".
[33] Most likely the heights of the Rhomberg hill located right to the east of the Fischbach stream.
[34] A literal translation of the German term "Feldfrevel", which indicates how strongly the farmers felt about this term. Beyond moving boundary markers, this covers all sorts of thefts from other people's fields.

form of the ghost is not exactly fitting for the crime. Though at the very least, the ghost does command attention and thus represents a warning to others.

46. The Pale Horse Haunting the Town Hall of Wernigerode

Once, the mayor of Wernigerode had the horse of a carter confiscated. Soon after, the unlawfulness of the confiscation came to light. But instead of giving the horse back, the mayor had it killed. The carter then made short work[35] of the mayor, and said: "I wish that my horse will haunt you forever."

Some time later, a man stood sentry at the guard post in front of the (old) post office[36] from 12 to 2 o'clock at night. Suddenly, a pale horse without a head emerged from the yard of the town hall, trotted away across the market, ambled down the Heidegasse alley,[37] and went into the Heidemühlengraben ditch at the Klarenloch hole.[38] From there, it passed beneath the

[35] The German phrase here was "kurzer Prozess" — a "short trial", meaning that the "judgment" against the mayor was brief and possibly bypassed the ordinary judicial process. The implication seems to be that the carter either beat the mayor up or even killed him — probably the former, as the curse would seem redundant with the latter approach.

[36] According to Saskia Düsedau of the Wernigerode city archives, this might refer to either an old post office near the site of the *new* old post office which was built in the late 19th century at Marktstraße 14, or another post office at Liebfrauenkirchhof 2. Since the latter address would not be in viewing distance of the town hall, I am inclined towards the former.

[37] Now the "Heidestrasse", to the northwest of the "Markt" square.

[38] The "Heidemühlengraben" is a (formerly largely, now completely) subterranean ditch that was used for runoff water from the city. It passed beneath the city walls at the "Klarenloch"/"Klares Loch" ("clear hole" — according to Saskia Düsedau, this is an ironic name, since it would occasionally overflow with sewage) next to the Hinterstraße road, and drained into the Ochsenteich ("oxen pond") to the northeast. The pond no longer exists, but it was located between the

city walls until it reached the churchyard,[39] and then went back again along the same route. The guard followed all the way there and back again. On the way back, the pale horse encountered two people. It reared up in front of them as if it wanted to trample them down. The two people were so frightened that they collapsed to the ground. Afterwards, they went home. The next morning, both of them had swollen heads, and one of them died soon thereafter. Many people have seen the pale horse meandering at the so-called Wasser- or Mühlenkulke[40] ditch. Thus, it is still said: "The horse without a head haunts the Mühlenkulke."[Prö96, p. 27f]

Commentary: It's not quite clear why this particular horse should appear headless, unless the mayor had it killed by decapitation. Likewise, if there is a deeper pattern about the places it appeared, it eludes me.

That it caused "swollen heads" in two of the people it encountered is interesting, however — another example of this effect shows up later in "The Woe Mother" (p. 203), as well as a few other tales I have encountered. This hints at a more widespread belief that supernatural entities might create this kind of affliction.

Heltauer Platz and the loop of the 244 federal road.

[39]The church nearest to this spot is the St. Georgii Chapel, to the west on the other side of the railroad tracks.

[40]According to Saskia Düsedau, this would be at the stretch of the Hinterstraße between the Heidestraße and the Gustav-Petri-Straße. A "Mühlenkulk" is a depression in front of the water wheel of a mill which was hollowed out by the swirling waters.

47. The Owl Haunting Saßleben Park

During the times when the plums ripen, Saßleben Park[41] was always visited by a large, mighty owl. The gardener, who frequently had troubles with fruit theft, watched over the garden at night. At the twelfth hour, the large owl arrived, and flew into the direction where the gardener was lying. Then it sat down on a plum tree and started to hoot. The gardener then grabbed a beanpole and swung it at the owl. But, to his horror, the owl became larger and larger. In his fear, he swung at it with full force for the second time, but again, the owl became larger and larger. Suddenly, the gardener lost consciousness. Other people found him in this state the next morning. He died a few weeks later.

The owl was no one other than the former owner of the mansion.[42] It is known that he haunts the area after his death, and regularly has to appear at night around the time when the plums ripen until one hundred years have passed.

(From Saßleben.)[Vec80, p. 27f]

Commentary: Harassing supernatural entities is generally unwise. This includes supernatural animals, which tend

[41] Saßleben (Zasłomjeń) is now part of the town of Calau (Kalawa). Its park was part of the noble estate Schloss Saßleben which dated back to the 14th century, but the mansion burned down in 1945 shortly after the end of the war for reasons unknown. The "Alle Burgen" website has a photo of what it used to look like.[All] The stables and barns of the estate still exist, and are protected as a cultural heritage site.

[42] This most likely refers to a member of the House of Lippe, who gained control of the estate in the late 18th century. In 1879 — one year before Veckenstedt published this tale in his collection — it was sold to a liqueur manufacturer from Berlin. Whether or not he was told about any ghostly owls haunting his new abode is unclear.

to take on a more frightening aspect when confronted — as we have seen before in the tale "The Ghostly Dog" (p. 90).

4. Those Who Are Denied Peace

While, in the distant pagan past, it was seen as nothing unusual that the dead had not departed, by the 19th century the mere presence of ghosts was generally considered to be an affront to the "proper order". The souls of the dead were supposed to depart for their appropriate afterlife (either Heaven or Hell). Thus, they needed some powerful reasons to linger on in the realms of the living.

4.1. The Wages of Sin

The most common assumption was that the ghost had committed some major sin in their life that they had to atone for. Existence as a ghost thus served as a form of purgatory — a state of turmoil that was to be their punishment until their term of atonement had ended. Tales such as these also served as a warning for the living not to commit the crimes for which the ghosts were punished so severely.

48. The Men in Zottenberg Mountain

Medulla by Seyfried, p. 478-481.[1]
Silesiographia renovata c. II. §. 13 by Nic. Henelius ab Hen-

[1]This refers to Johann Heinrich Seyfried's *"Medulla Mirabilium Naturae"*, a book on the "wonders of nature" published in 1679. However,

nenfeld[2]
Beschreibung des Fichtelbergs. Leipzig 1716. P. 59-63.[3]
Ehre von Crain I. by Valvassor, p. 247.[4]

In the 16th century, a man named Johannes Beer lived in Schweidnitz.[5] When, during the year 1570, he once went to the Zottenberg mountain[6] as he usually did for pleasure, he suddenly noticed an opening for the first time. A mighty wind blew into his direction from the entrance. Startled, he fell back. Soon after, however, on Divine Mercy Sunday,[7] he decided to explore the cave anew. He walked into a narrow, straight rock tunnel, followed a distant ray of light, and finally arrived at a closed door that had a glass panel integrated into its frame that projected a marvelous light. After knocking three times, the door was opened for him, and he saw three long, emaciated men in old German garb sitting at a round table within the cave. The men seemed sad and were quivering. Before them there was a gold-

in one scan I found online, the relevant text begins on page 485 instead of 478.[Hei79, p. 485ff]

[2]This is the *"Silesiographiae Henelianae Renovatae"* by Nicolaus Henel von Hennenfeld, a scientific compendium of Silesia published in 1704. The relevant passage starts on page 142 and is mercifully in one of the German portions of the book.[vH04, p. 142f]

[3]This seems to refer to *"Ausführliche Beschreibung des Fichtel-Berges, im Norgau liegend"* — a book published in 1716 and which Google Books attributes to one Johann Christoph Pachelbel von Gehag.[vG16, p. 59ff] This seems to be a distinct and considerably longer work than Kaspar Brusch's *"Gründliche Beschreibung des Fichtelbergs"* from 1612.[Bru12], although it is likely that it is based on this earlier publication.

[4]The first volume of *"Die Ehre deß Herzogthums Crain"* by Johann Weikhard von Valvasor, a natural historian and fellow of the Royal Society in London. This work, published in 1689 with 15 volumes and 3552 large-sized pages, is a groundbreaking compendium on the Duchy of Carniola.[vV89, p. 247ff]

[5]Modern-day Świdnica in Poland.

[6]Now called the Ślęża mountain, which was home to a Bronze Age religious cult center. It now lies within the boundaries of the town of Sobótka.

[7]The first Sunday after Easter Sunday, which would have been on April 12th in 1570.

plated book covered with black velvet.

He addressed them with "Pax vobis!" ("Peace be with you!") and received the reply: "Hic nulla pax!" ("Here is no peace!") Stepping further towards them, he called again: "Pax vobis in nomine domini!" ("Peace be with you in the name of God!") Quavering, with small voices, they replied: "Hic non pax." ("Here is no peace.") When he stepped in front of the table, he repeated: "Pax vobis in nomine domini nostri Jesu Christi!" ("Peace be with you in the name of our Lord Jesus Christ!"), whereupon they fell silent and put the book in front of him. When opened, its title became visible: "Liber Obedientiae" ("Book of Obedience").

Beer then asked them who they were, but they replied that they did not know themselves. "What are you doing here?" — "We await Judgment Day in dread, as well as the wages of our deeds." — "What did you do in your lives?" Upon hearing this, they pointed towards a curtain, behind which all sorts of murderous rifles hung, in addition to skeletons of men as well as skulls. "Do you admit to these evil deeds?" — "Yes!" — "Are these good deeds or evil ones?" — "Evil." — "Do you regret them?" After this, they remained silent, but then quavered: "We don't know!"

The Silesian Chronicle commemorates a castle inhabited by bandits on the Zottenberg, whose ruins are still visible.[GG16, p. 214f][8]

Commentary: These sinners seem to be bound to Earth until Judgment Day as a punishment instead of being consigned to Hell — possibly as a warning for the living. It is

[8]Ślęża mountain apparently was home to two bandits' castles, one in the 13th century and one in the 14th and 15th century. Both were eventually razed.

perhaps telling that, while they recognize their deeds as evil, they are unable to express any regret over them, since that might give them a chance at receiving God's mercy instead of judgment.

The odd element in this tale is the "Book of Obedience". I can only speculate that this might refer to "obeying to the laws of God", but we do not learn whether it contains how these particular sinners failed to obey God or if it contains the Commandments and other rule on how God should be obeyed (and which these people failed to heed).

Alternatively, this book could be an "infernal contract" — they had pledged their soul to the Devil and obeyed him, and now they will reap the "rewards".

49. The Herdess Makes Fried Pudding

A huntsman, who had ventured into the mountain wilderness one late fall in order to shoot chamois, sought shelter in a lonely alpine hut nearby when night began to fall on his way back. There, he first warmed himself at the fire of the hearth which he had lit, ate a bite from his rations, and then laid down on the bed to rest. It might have been around midnight when a herdess stepped out of the cellar and tackled her usual work. She carried the milk containers from down below, skimmed the cream off the milk, stirred the cream in the butter keg, prepared cheese and whey cheese in the kettle, cleaned her milk utensils, and finally made fried pudding. When she was finished, she called up to the huntsman who was lying on his bed and told him that he should come for the meal. The huntsman, however, remained quiet as a mouse, stayed up there, and did not follow the invitation. Then the herdess called again in a very stern manner: "If you don't come down for the meal, I shall tear you apart until you are dust!"

Now the huntsman climbed down from the bed and stepped towards the table. He very much enjoyed the taste of the fried pudding, but he saw a lot of ash on the side of the pan from which the herdess ate. When the huntsman was filled up, he put the spoon away and climbed back to the bed without expressing the slightest thanks to the herdess for the meal. Then the herdess wept bitterly and said: "If you had said a single 'May God repay you!'[9] for the meal, then I would have been released from my torment. But now I must suffer anew for a very, very long time until someone else rests here for the night and, additionally, gives their thanks for the offered meal!" Upon this, she went back to the cellar and was not heard from again.[Hau94, p. 53f]

Translation note: The dish the ghostly herdess prepared is called "Rahmmus" in the German text. I've found a variety of recipes online, but the basics seem to be:

1. Cook cream
2. Stir in flour (sometimes semolina) and sugar, optionally adding eggs
3. Stir until the pudding thickens
4. Fry the pudding in a pan with fat, using a cooking spoon to break the pudding apart into smaller chunks

It's also possible to add raisins or other berries at the end. It's a simple, high-calorie dish for people who have ready access to cream and fat.

Commentary: As seen before in "The White Girl at the Fecht River" (p. 53), a common trend in such tales is that ghosts desiring salvation tend to be bad at communicating

[9] In German, "Vergelt's Gott" — a common way of giving thanks in the Alps and surrounding areas, if somewhat archaic these days. Of course, the invocation of God has special significance in this particular circumstance.

their needs — which, in this tale, isn't helped by the ghost threatening the hoped-for savior with grievous bodily harm if he doesn't come down to eat. Thus, his rudeness in not giving thanks may be understandable, if not entirely excusable.

50. The Golden Bowling Game (Schauenforst)

Long years ago, a brazen and godless knight lived in the Schauenforst Castle[10] who oppressed and plagued the farmers, held up and robbed travelers and wanderers, and who was feared widely in the surrounding areas.

At one time, there had been a hard, long winter, and the sheer amount of snow that suddenly melted afterwards caused rivers and streams to burst their banks. In this manner the terrible flooding destroyed the entire harvest of the poor farmers. However, the cruel and hardhearted lord of the castle still demanded the exact same crushing tribute at the appointed time. And even though he beheld the great destitution and suffering of the farmers, he did not soften to any pleas. Instead, he took the last cow and the last keepsakes from those who could not pay in full at the appointed time, and had everything carried up to his castle.

From this blood money, he commissioned a golden bowling set with silver balls in order to entertain himself after his feasts and drinking bouts. After this, the farmers became terribly enraged, and an old man, whose entire possessions had been taken by the hardhearted knight, spoke a terrible curse that the cruel knight should play with the golden pins until Judgment Day as punishment for his arrogance. And God, who hears the cries of the oppressed, fulfilled the old man's curse and avenged the

[10] Schauenforst Castle, now a ruin near Rödelwitz in Uhlstädt-Kirchhasel, was likely built early in the 13th century, but then gradually neglected and abandoned over the centuries. It was damaged further in the 18th and 19th centuries by treasure hunters.

deprivation of the tormented farmers with severe punishment.

In this manner, it is possible to hear a strange, curious rolling and rumbling from the Schauenforst mountain during quiet, muggy nights. This noise comes from the cruel former lord of the castle, who must play until Judgment Day in the ruins of the fortress deep within the mountain, with the pins which he had, in his arrogance, made with the money extorted from his subjects.[Gre70, p. 124f]

Commentary: In contrast to the earlier tales "The Golden Bowling Game (Yburg)" (p. 38) and "The Bowling Game Beneath the Hohnstein" (p. 70), here we get an explicit origin story for the golden bowling set. While the ghosts in those other tales seem to be eager to give their golden pins away — possibly because they are bound to the treasure, and cannot find release until all of it is gone — the curse the knight in this story suffers under presumably has no such escape clause.

51. The Bride on the Lilienstein

(A poetic treatment by Bachmann can be found in the *Dresdener Merkur* 1826, Nr. 126 and 128.)[11]

A long time ago, a young weaver named Conrad Zeilig lived in Schandau[12] who was upstanding, hard-working, and devout. While he zealously attended the rite of confession, he equally zealously visited the Lilienstein[13] mountain after mass. Once, when he was deeply in contemplation, the lovely figure of a

[11] The *"Dresdener Merkur"* seems to have been a newspaper or other periodical, but I have been unable to find any scans available online.

[12] Now Bad Schandau, this spa town lies close to the Czech border, along a very scenic stretch of the Elbe river I visited during a bicycle trip in 2014.

[13] The Lilienstein ("lily stone") is a prominent mountain about 6 km

maiden approached him. She was beautiful in countenance, and wore a golden chain in her hair. Shyly, the young man asked her first to kiss the hem of her dress, and then, finally, her lily-like hand.[14] Reddened by blossoming love, she pressed her hand towards him and let him do as he wished. When he asked the lost maiden[15] if he would be allowed to lead her home, she replied with a voice like silver bells: "I know the surrounding gorges. I seek something larger — and larger shall be your reward. You have undergone the rite of confession, and next intend to receive the Most Holy. When you do, keep the altar bread, and bring it to me. A devout longing swells my breast, and thus I ask you to bring me the all-reconciling meal!"

The startled weaver[16] was told to come back at dusk, spread out a red cloth beneath a tree, kneel there, and, when she arrived and asked for it, offer up the bread. "But don't be frightened if you see something unusual, or else we will both be lost."

He was ready to do anything for her, except defile the Most Holy. But when she wept two large tears, he was moved to hurry away and fulfill her desire. When he came back and kneeled, a horrible creature suddenly appeared which was half animal, half human. Her arms were the claws of a tiger — she was damned because she had murdered her mother. The stunned weaver crushed the holy bread in his stupefaction and tried to flee, but fell down with a cry. Suddenly, the ground opened up, flames burst out, and the horrible visage was devoured.

downriver of Bad Schandau. It close to Poschdorf, which has been incorporated into Bad Schandau.

[14]The German uses the phrase "Lilienhand" here. This should probably be read as a metaphor for the beauty and delicate nature of her hand, instead of implying that she had flowers growing out of her arm.

[15]In the German text, she is referred to as "Verirrte" at this point, with the implication that she has supposedly lost track of her surroundings. But, of course, the fact that she has "strayed from the path" has metaphorical associations in this tale as well.

[16]In the German source, the weaver is called "Meister" from this point on — implying that he was a master of his trade, despite his young age.

The weaver was lying there unconsciously for two hours. When he woke up, madness took hold of his mind, and he later died with a last glance towards the Lilienstein mountain.[Mei94, p. 31]

Commentary: It is rarely quite clear in these stories whether the "cursed maiden" is actually dead, or was cursed for her sins and imprisoned while still alive. That she appears in a different form that frightens the would-be rescuer is a narrative element that most commonly shows up in tales of "cursed maidens" who need to be kissed three times in order to be freed — first in human form, and then in more frightening guises.

In German folklore tales, altar bread most often shows up as a way of empowering black magic[17]. However, literally or metaphorically sharing altar bread with ghosts is also known to help them move on to the afterlife, perhaps as a remnant of earlier pagan practices.[Sch98, p. 32] Yet the tale explicitly calls this out as sacrilege, and thus this was perhaps perceived as an attempt to cheat and get out of her deserved fate in Hell. Though many other ghosts *do* have rather strange conditions for getting out of purgatory, so maybe she was supposed to do this.

52. The Man with the Boundary Stone

A man once set a false boundary stone in the border areas[18] of Schwerte, and he pursued a lengthy lawsuit over it. However,

[17] Such as in the "Freischütz" legends where ritually desecrating altar bread allows a huntsman to shoot bullets that never miss their targets

[18] The German term used here was "Feldmark" ("field mark") — the lands marked by the boundary stones of a community or estate that have not been used for buildings.

he won the lawsuit because he had bribed false witnesses. As punishment for this deed, he now must carry the boundary stone on his shoulders every night, and walk around in the entire border area. Many people have seen him like this. The boundary stone glows, and every few moments he falls down with it, but he cannot throw it away from his person. Since the fire of the stone burns him, he jumps up and hurries onward while groaning and shouting: "Where should I go with this boundary stone?"[Sta31, p. 274]

Commentary: As we have seen in "The Billy Goat of Büntlitten" (p. 99), German folklore sees moving field boundary stones as a major sin, to be punished with turmoil by haunting the site of their crime as a ghost. This has long precedents — Deuteronomy 27:17 states: "Cursed is anyone who moves their neighbor's boundary stone" (next to curses against people who commit other major sins such as murder or incest). In most such narratives, the ghost of the person who moved the boundary stone is now forced to carry it — and, like in the previous tale, the ghost is wreathed in the flames of Hell. Their punishment can only be ended when the stone is put where it belongs (i.e. at its original position) — but the ghost is unable to figure this out on their own. Such tales first appeared in the 16th century, and continued to be popular all the way into the 19th century.[Lec09, p. 212ff]

Beyond the sin itself, boundary spaces were themselves mystically significant — see the tale "The Rider without a Head (Mückenloch)" (p. 84) for a discussion of this. Thus, the reason for the appearance of "field boundary violators" as ghosts might not merely be the theft, but their meddling with threshold locations that represented entry points for the supernatural.

53. The Man Who Moved The Boundary Stones

Many, many years ago, a greedy man lived in Niederehe[19] who moved the boundary stones next to his neighbors' fields. Furthermore, he constantly lived in strife and had lawsuits with anyone who seemed to oppose him in the slightest. At this time, there were plans for surveying and marking the boundaries of the village forest.[20] This man, who sought to gain an advantage for his community, went into this forest and moved the boundary stones marking the forest belonging to the noble's estate. Since people didn't pay as much attention to the boundary markers in those days, a large piece of land was taken from the noble's estate and incorporated into the village forest, which the village still uses to this day.

However, the unjust man did not enjoy the spoils of his fraud for long. For, when he cut down a tree within the stolen forest, a branch fell off as the tree fell, and bludgeoned him to death. After people had searched for this man in vain for a long time, people finally found him at this location, and wild animals had already feasted on his corpse. But, from this time onwards, this man wandered around in this stolen forest while carrying a heavy stone. And, on quiet evenings, it is possible to hear his wail: "Where do I put it?"[Sch56, p. 30]

Commentary: While this man seemed to be rather unpleasant to be around while alive, it is interesting that the deed that finally did him in benefited not just merely himself, but his entire village. The narrator seems to be deeply offended by the theft from the local feudal overlords (which would be House of Arensberg in this case), while I personally

[19] Niederehe is now part of the Üxheim municipality.

[20] A forest belonging to the village as a whole, as opposed to individuals or the higher-level governments. About one-fifth of all forests in Germany are still municipal forests of this type.

would see this as "stealing from one's oppressors" and thus possibly as an act of civic virtue. This makes me wonder who originally came up with this tale.

54. The Coast Warden

Lorenz Jens Grethen had long traveled the sea, and often made the journey to Greenland.[21] Later on, he received a commission that made him responsible for all affairs concerning the coasts of Sylt, and he did much to reduce thievery.[22] Once, however, he ignored a robbery that resulted in murder. He still haunts the beaches to this day for this reason. However, he rescues castaways at night, wakes up the coast wardens, and motivates them when they slack off. Furthermore, he distributes slaps to beachcombers so that they are not eager to return.

(From Mr. Hansen on Sylt. — A similar tale exists in Dithmarschen[23] of a leaseholder of an outer dike.[24] — In Lauenburg: A coast warden rode along the dike of the Elbe river in order to check up on it. He was forced by others to ride into the waves. Since then, he is seen every night on his white horse.)[Mü45, p. 175]

Commentary: The German title used for this story was "Strandvogt", which requires some explanation. A "Vogt" was an official appointed by a noble to look after one of their

[21] My best guess is that he was part of whaling expeditions in the vicinity of Greenland, since Greenland otherwise wasn't a major trade destination.

[22] Presumably, this primarily refers to beachcombing.

[23] A coastal region north of the mouth of the river Elbe.

[24] The outer dikes were adjacent to the ocean and of lower construction, while the inner dikes were taller and protected the settlements from serious floods. The regions protected by the outer dikes were often used for agriculture, but they were rarely inhabited.

territories. Here, "Strand-" ("beach") is used as a prefix, indicating an official whose primary responsibility was looking after the coasts of the territory. Their most important task was indeed to stop the practice of beachcombing — the practice of the locals to take any flotsam they found for themselves. This was not necessarily limited to obvious valuables such as coin and trade goods — even the wood from a destroyed ship was valuable construction material, since the islands of northwestern Germany did not have many accessible forests. The Strandvogts were not only tasked with stopping this practice, but also returning the property to their proper owners and assisting castaways. I settled on "coast warden" as an approximate translation.

As the notes by Müllenhoff indicate, this fragment is fairly representative of other tales of ghostly officials haunting the shores of northwestern Germany. The one sin the coast warden committed is used as justification for his continued presence, but, even in death, he still follows his duties as he did in life.

Sometimes people interact with the departed because they seek to release or at least banish them. But, at other times, people seek them out for less noble reasons.

55. Alfhausen and the Alkenkrug Pub

Once, there were only eleven houses where the village of Alfhausen[25] is located now. The people who inhabited it belonged to the church parish of Merzen. On every Sunday and holiday,

[25] Alfhausen is now part of the Bersenbrück municipality. Despite what the story claims, the village more likely derives its name from "Alf's house" rather than "eleven houses".

they walked across the heath towards the holy house of Merzen. But the way there was long,[26] and the mood of the churchgoers always brightened when they came close to the barrows[27] on this lonely stretch of land. Here, as the locals tell it, people once had started to build a church. But the Devil tore it down and placed a pub in its place. And this pub was what gladdened the churchgoers now. Here they stopped and refreshed themselves with a mug of beer provided by Alke, as the publican was called. He was a master at keeping his patrons rooted there. "I can only rely on you; we twelve stick together and belong together",[28] as he was fond of saying, and this flattered the farmers, and they were convinced to stay. And when one or the other of the guests replied to his badgering for another round of drinks that they needed to go now if they didn't want to be late for church, the clever man always managed to console them that it was still early enough for sure. Thus, the churchgoers always stayed in the Alkenkrug[29] for too long and arrived too late in Merzen on an almost regular basis. The pastor frequently berated the publican for his evil-minded behavior and warned him, but always futilely. He continued to act as he had always done.

Then, one day, God's judgment fell upon him. His house, which stood on a small hill, sank into the Earth's lap along with his barn, and in place of these buildings the two depressions

[26] Approximately 10 km one way — doable, but not something you'd want to do on what are supposed to be your rest days.

[27] I have found some references[Wikd][Wal] to a "Großsteingrab Wallen", which was located close to the Heiligenberg hill. This hill is now close to the western border of modern Alfhausen, south of the Friesenweg road. The barrow, also called the "Heidenaltar" ("Heathen's Altar"), was apparently a sacrificial altar. However, it was destroyed in the 19th century. I wasn't able to find the precise cause for its destruction, but many such barrows were destroyed in the 19th century by would-be treasure hunters (frequently using dynamite for this purpose).

[28] I.e. he implied that his pub was the twelfth house that belonged to the eleven houses of Alfhausen.

[29] "Alke's Mug", the name of the pub. "Zum Kruge" — "At The Mug" — and variants thereof are very common pub names in Germany.

formed which can still be found at this spot today.

Such an event made a great impression on the people of the surrounding areas, but especially on the former patrons of the Alkenkrug. So that they would no longer have to go past the spot where the pub once stood, they intended to build a church of their own. And, in order to show that they did not want to have anything in common with the godless publican any more, they called their settlement "Alfhausen" — "Eleven Houses".

The construction of the Lord's house was very difficult for the small community, in particular because the stones for the construction had to be carted from far away. Then, suddenly, a shiny gray horse appeared which dedicated its services to this holy cause. Day and night it carted stones to the site until the construction was complete,[30] and then it vanished. No one could say where this faithful helper came from, and where it went. For a long time, the people of Alfhausen still showed the stable to visitors into which they had led horse while the stones were unloaded.

It was just as well that the inhabitants of the "eleven houses" established a prayer house of their own. For if they had been forced to wander the old path to Merzen, then perhaps they would also have witnessed the haunting of the sunken Alkenkrug, and then the publican who had ensnared them so often in the past might now have harmed them as well. For he still dwelled at the location of his former trade. The shepherds of the region, who saw him from time to time, also claimed that if someone circled the Alkenkrug in the hour of the ghosts[31] and called "Alke, come, do you want to go with me?", then the latter would appear and pull the foolhardy person into the abyss with him.

[30]This likely refers to the St. Johannis church, which dates back to the 13th century. However, it might have replaced an earlier construction made out of wood instead of being the first church in the town.

[31]I.e. midnight.

One late evening, the farmer Grumfeld, whose house was not far from Alke's Hollow, sat in the pub together with several other farmers. Everyone praised their own horses, and then Grumfeld said that he had a gray horse that he had so much confidence in that he would dare circle the sunken pub and challenge Alke. The others took him at his word and bet against him for the sum of nine pounds of silver,[32] and the audacious man promised to attempt the daring ride in the next night.

The next day, Grumfeld and his horse headed towards the location which he intended to visit again soon after during the midnight hour. Here he indicated to his horse what would be expected of it. The smart animal indeed seemed to understand, for when its master mounted it, it carried him to his home at lightning-speed. Here the farmer also showed it the large entrance gate, which he intended to leave open during the following night. After that, he gave his horse the best food he had as a reward for the brave ride.

The next night arrived, and Grumfeld and his horse set off for their destination. When he reached the boundary of the water-filled depression,[33] the hour of the ghosts had not quite arrived yet. It was a beautiful, star-lit night, and everything was quiet nearby. Then the rider heard the tower clocks strike twelve, first in Ueffeln,[34] then in Merzen, and finally in Alfhausen. As soon as the last chime had ceased, he shouted:

"Alke, come, do you want to go with me?"

---

[32]Historic German currency systems did not generally use "pounds" (German: "Pfund") as measurements for coins,, which makes me inclined to see this as a reference to the actual weight unit. The exception is the "Karlspfund", which was introduced by Charlemagne but was gradually replaced by the "Mark" starting with the 11th century. If this was indeed a reference to the currency units, then each "Pfund" would have been the equivalent of 240 silver pennies (or 2,160 in total).

[33]There is a small lake between the "In der Heide" and "Friesenweg" roads, which seems to be in the right area.

[34]Now Ueffeln-Balkum, part of the Bramsche municipality.

And from the depth, a dreadful voice replied:

"One shoe I will lace up,
The other one I will slip into,
And then I shall get the Devil!"

How the farmer then spurred his horse! Like the lightning rushing through the air, like the arrow flying from the bow, in that manner they raced through the night — but Alke pursued them in the shape of a large, flaming pole. The spirit approached ever closer, but the hellish chase also got ever closer to the Grumfeld's house. And, just as the fiery pole was about to reach the horse, the horse raced through the lower door of the opened entrance gate, and horse and rider were saved. The glowing "pole", however, rammed the pillar at the side of the great door so that the house shook, and it was still possible to see the burnt spot there for a long time.

The farmer had won the bet, but never again was someone able to convince him to undertake such a dangerous ride.[Cro99, p. 16ff]

Translation note: I first came across an alternate version of this tale, which can be found online on the homepage of the Bersenbrück municipality.[Alk] In that version, the ghost took the shape of a "flaming wheel", which is of course *way* more metal than a mere pole. Thus, I am rather upset that I didn't find a public domain version of this variant that I could work with.

The exact German term used in this story for the form of the ghost was a "Bindelbaum", (roughly, "bundle tree"), which is a long pole used to stabilize hay or other loose material on an overgrown wagon — a picture can be found online at Augustendorf.net.[Bin] Thus, it is perhaps not too surprising that the description of the ghost changed when the very concept of a Bindelbaum fell out of use.

Commentary: As we have seen previously,[35] "sinking beneath the ground" is one of the most common forms of divine punishment in German folklore — though it is rare that the sinner in question is still active like that *after* the punishment. I find the wording of the challenge to be curiously specific, and I wonder how exactly the shepherds learned of it — did they challenge each other on dares until finally one of them found a phrase that would aggravate the ghost enough for him to emerge (to the shepherd's detriment, no doubt)?

It is also noteworthy that Grumfeld reached safe refuge when he crosses the threshold of his own house, even though he had not discussed any "rules" of the engagement with Alke. As with other tales (such as the fourth fragment of "The Ghostly Light", p. 164), the threshold provides at least some protection against outside supernatural forces.

The side story about the construction of the church is interesting as well. Where did that mysterious horse get all those stones (and who loaded them on the cart)? Were they taken from a real world quarry — or a quarry in an otherworld or even by divine miracle (in which case the stone the church was made of might have some supernatural properties of its own)?

4.2. The Wronged

Other ghosts appeared before the living because the living had done *them* wrong. Most commonly, something had been stolen from them.

[35] See, for example, the tales "Kleines Clausthal" (p. 65) and "The Brautlachenberg Mountain" (p. 72).

56. Don't Steal from the Dead!

1. At a time when the graveyard of Einbeck was still at the Neustädter Kirche church,[36] a group of boys went there in order to pick flowers from the graves. One of them died soon thereafter. Then his ghost visibly walked over the plundered grave, and it seemed as if he tried to plant the flowers back on the grave.

2. When the remains of the old nunnery in Fredelsloh[37] were still standing, a maid was told by her employer[38] to scrub a certain chamber. However, as she had forgotten to bring her scrubbing cloth, she took a rag from an old box where the belongings of the nuns who had lived there previously were stored. Then she scrubbed the floor with it, and, after she was done, she hung up the rag in order to dry it.

But, when she was lying in bed the following night, a black figure approached her, grabbed her by her hairs, and pulled her

[36]This refers to the "Neustädter Kirche St. Marien" that used to be located at the Neustädter Kirchplatz square in the old town area (though "Neustadt" means "new town", this is only in comparison to the old old town). Unfortunately, that church was built on a patch of silt, which in 1963 made it necessary to tear it down because of its instability. A new "Neustädter Kirche St. Marien" was built to the west, in the Sülbecksweg road.

[37]Fredelsloh is now part of the town of Moringen. Fredelsloh Abbey was founded in 1132 for Augustine canons, and was expanded into a double convent that included nuns in 1145. However, after a fire in 1290, the abbey went into a long economic and cultural decline. After the region became Protestant in 1542, its endowment was turned into a secular convent for unmarried women (a so-called "Frauenstift"). After the Thirty Years' War, the buildings other than the St. Blasii und Marien church were abandoned and used as a source of stones for other buildings. The church building itself was used as grain storage until it was reconsecrated as a Protestant church in the 20th century.

[38]The German term used was "Herrschaft", roughly translating as "master" but without (unusually, for the German language) designating a specific gender. It seems likely that this took place during the time when the secular women's convent had been installed in the abbey.

into the courtyard of the monastery. There, the figure beat the girl savagely. She then loudly cried for help. A man, who had arrived in the village at that moment and had heard her shouts, hurried towards her location in order to assist her. But a white figure was constantly dancing back and forth in front of him and did not want to let him into the courtyard. He made several unsuccessful attempts to jump over the fence. During the final attempt, the white figure jumped on his back and became so heavy that he fell down. He then was lying there for some time, bereft of his senses. But the girl was found the next morning in the chamber she had scrubbed, and her whole body was covered in bruises. The box with the clothes is still supposed to be in there.

According to another telling of the story, the girl had taken the habit of a nun out of the box, put it on, and made a mockery out of it. For this, a nun appeared to her at night and slapped her. The box with the clothes of the nun was sealed in a wall in order to prevent a repeat of such an incident.[SM54, p. 219]

Commentary: In the first fragment, it's not quite clear whether the boy had to return as a ghost due to his sin of "grave robbing", or because the dead inhabitant of the grave refused to let him pass on until the theft was rectified. Either way, this was a grim punishment for such a minor act of theft.

In the second tale, the girl is punished for disrespecting a dead person's possessions. While this cannot exactly be called a "desecration of grave goods" (since they were not put into the nun's grave), this was taken as a sign of disrespect all the same, since they were obviously important to the nun. Presumably, if those possessions had been used respectfully (such as giving them to another nun to wear), this could have been avoided. Or perhaps not — some ghosts get touchy about *anyone* else messing with their stuff.

The appearance of both a "black figure" and a "white figure" is a curious detail. Were they both expressions of the dead nun's soul, or separate entities? That the white figure jumped on the man's back and subsequently became heavy is a very common type of behavior for spirits from German folklore, which is not only observed among ghosts,[39] but also so-called "Aufhocker"-type spirits of unknown origins and, in rare cases, even werewolves![40]

57. A Dead Man Searches for his Gown

There was a graveyard surrounding the church of Alt-Strelitz,[41] in old times, and like today, the school was in front of it. The cantor lived within the school building. Once, when he happened to look out of the window around midnight, he noticed that a corpse stepped out of a grave, removed his burial gown, and walked away. However, soon after the corpse reappeared, pulled the gown back over himself, and vanished into the grave. The cantor, whose attention was arrested by this, was next to the window the following night and indeed saw the same scene replay itself. On the third night, when the dead man had climbed out of the grave and departed, and the gown was lying on the tombstone, the cantor (who was a brazen man) sneaked out of

[39] Further examples of ghosts jumping on people's backs can be found in the tales "A Dead Man Searches for his Gown" (p. 124), "The Ghostly Light" (p. 164), "The Ghost of Day Laborer Rossow from Klein-Kelle near Röbel" (p. 211), and "The Barber of Penzlin" (p. 216).

[40] While there is a second type of "pressure spirit" that torments sleepers — a phenomenon associated with "sleep paralysis" and often referred to as "night hags" in English-language literature — such beings are rarely described as ghosts in German folklore, and are usually considered demons, fairy-type spirits, witches, or the spirits of other sleeping people who roam outside of their bodies.

[41] Officially, "Strelitz-Alt", a part of Neustrelitz. The historic center — including the church — was destroyed by fire in the final days of World War II, and the remains were razed and replaced with residential housing.

his room and retrieved the latter.

When the dead man reappeared and didn't find his gown, he started a fearsome racket. Soon he knew where his clothing had been hidden, and, when he spotted the thief in the window, forced him with threats to bring the gown outside. The cantor initially did not want to give in, but nevertheless soon made his way to the embittered dead man. But when he had reached the graveyard down below, the haunt jumped on his back and drove him into the church to the altar. There, the cantor had to say the words "Forgotten and forgiven" three times. When the cantor had said those words for the first time, a voice from the distance replied: "Forgiven, but not forgotten!" The same occurred the second and third time when the cantor said those words. Afterwards, the dead man hurried out of the church again with the cantor, and, in front of the door, gave him two terrible slaps. Subsequently, the cantor fell ill and died soon thereafter.[Bar79, p. 221f]

Commentary: As usual, there are more questions than answers here. Why did the dead man leave the grave — and why did he leave the gown behind? How did he find it again — was he able to supernaturally sense the gown, or did he just spot the cantor in the window and put two and two together? The "voice in the distance" is another mystery. If it wasn't the dead man (who was close by), then who uttered those words — given that the voice was heard in the vicinity of the altar, perhaps from Heaven itself? And why this particular phrasing? At least the ghost himself obviously had not quite forgiven the cantor, given the subsequent slaps...

The buried man has a rather more physical presence than many of the "protean" ghosts that we usually encounter. This is in line with old Germanic and Norse beliefs about the undead, but stands in contrast to the "images" that ghosts were interpreted as in first Roman and later Christian belief.[Sch98, p. 13] By the 19th century, when most of these tales were written down, Christian thought on ghosts predominated — but, occasionally, older beliefs still stirred to new life (well, sort of).

As in the previous tale, the ghost jumped on the back of the person who had offended him. While there is no explicit mention of the ghost becoming "heavy", he did seem to be able to steer his victim's path by threat or force.

58. The Burial Gown

Two sisters once lived in a village near Leitzkau.[42] They lived in poverty, for they were spinning flax for other people for pay. They had done this for many years, and turned old and gray over time. But they had not been completely honest at their trade, for whenever they had the opportunity to surreptitiously take some of the flax for themselves that had been given to them for spinning, they did so. From the flax they had accumulated in this manner, they spun the finest yarn, and had linen woven out of it that was fine to a degree that no one else in the village had anything comparable.

One day, one of these sisters died. Her burial gown was made out of this linen. She was buried three days after her death. However, the dead woman found no rest in the grave. Every day, around the time when darkness began to fall, the door to the chamber in which her sister was sitting and spinning opened, and then that sister saw her dead sibling stepping into the chamber dressed in her white burial gown and walking restlessly back and forth. After a while, she vanished again. Finally, the living sister was unable to endure this. She went to the pastor and lamented her distress. The pastor said that he would attempt to bring eternal rest to the dead woman.

[42] Leitzkau is now part of Gommern.

Near the hour of dusk, the pastor indeed visited the old spinning woman. He had brought his Bible with him. And it did not take long until the door quietly opened and the dead woman in her white burial gown entered. But the priest stepped towards her with the Bible in his hand, and spoke to her: "Errant ghost, what do you want?"

Then the dead woman answered with a quiet voice: "I want my honest gown."

The pastor asked the same question three times, and three times the dead woman answered with the same words, whereupon she mutely went out of the door again.

But now the sister confessed everything to the pastor about how she had taken some of the flax, and that the burial gown had been made out of the yarn that had been spun from the flax. Thus, there was nothing else to do but to open the grave and dress the dead woman with an honest gown. As soon as this had occurred, the dead woman was finally able to rest in her grave.

By Fr. Adler senior.[AER88, p. 312]

Commentary: Lacking any other source of income, the women were essentially a form of day laborers — the poorest of the rural poor who eked out a precarious income from work that most households did on their own.[43] It was this poverty that tempted these women to steal — and as a result, one of them did not even get to rest peacefully in her grave while richer people would not have had this particular problem.

I am not quite sure what precisely triggered the haunting — was it being given a gown made out of stolen flax, or not being given a "proper gown"? That is to say, was it

[43]See the section on rural life (p. 234) for a discussion of day laborers.

the sin of thievery associated with the gown that caused her restlessness, or is a "honest gown" necessary for being able to rest at all — i.e. would the burial without a gown also have caused restlessness in the grave?

59. A Ghost Searches for his Brain

(Oral tale from Mettmann)

A man was slain a long time ago near the "Schnabel", at the sunken path "zur Weihe".[44] The murderer used a bowling pin to bash in the skull of his victim. During the court-ordered examination, the skullcap of the murder victim was taken off and the brain was set aside. Later, when the examiners wanted to put it back, they discovered that it had vanished, for a dog had eaten it. Thus, the unfortunate man had to be buried without his brain. Since that time, the man has been walking along the sunken path every night. He carries his skull in his hand and searches for his brain.[Sch97, p. 93]

Commentary: While there are some records of such examinations dating back to the 16th century, forensic examinations only became an established practice in 18th century Germany. Thus, at least this particular variant of the tale must have had a fairly modern origin. While a ghost searching for missing body parts is not exactly an uncommon theme, searching for their brain seems to be an unique variant.

[44] There is a bus stop named "Am Schnabel" ("At The Beak") on the "Gruitener Weg" road in Mettmann, which is close to a "Weihe" (which could be translated as either "harrier bird" or "consecration") road, so this is likely where this story takes place.

60. The Ring

The Bärenburg Castle once stood in the valley of Oppenau, but its remains are no longer visible.[45] Soon after its destruction, a legend arose that a great treasure of gold and other valuables was hidden there. A young, brazen squire[46] from Bosenstein[47] got it into his head to unearth this treasure. His heart greatly desired riches, and a traveling scholar had taught him an incantation for this purpose, as well as how to behave in such uncanny matters.

With great effort, he opened up an entrance and proceeded into the crypt. In it, crumbling skeletons could be found within the coffins, but no valuables were to be seen. Finally, in the last coffin, he discovered the corpse of a maiden of Bärenburg which had not yet undergone decomposition. On the coffin, there was an inscription indicating that she had been the last of her line. On her finger, she wore a glittering diamond, and around her neck a golden chain.

The squire was pleased at this find. He took the ring and the chain, and went home with them. The next day, he wanted to explore further, and went back into the ruins. The maiden whom he had seen in the coffin was sitting at the entrance. "You've taken my ring and my chain", she said, "now give me your hand, for you must betroth yourself to me." The squire shivered cold and hot. He hurried away, and died a few days later.[Sch48, p. 133f]

---

[45] Bärenburg Castle was built in the 12th century, and fell into disrepair after 1470. Some walls of this ruin are, in fact, still visible today.

[46] The German used the term "Edelknecht", indicating a squire who was an adult and had the equipment of a knight, but who had not yet formally earned his spurs.

[47] Bosenstein Castle was built in the 11th century, destroyed during the Thirty Years' War, and razed in 1840. Its ruins can be found in Ottenhöfen, about 12 km north of the Bärenburg. Thus, we can determine that this legend probably takes place sometime between the late 15th and the early 17th century.

Commentary: A "traveling scholar" was a common description for an itinerant mage. The assumption that magic was necessary to unearth treasures was common in Early Modern Europe [48], although we don't actually see the squire do anything particularly magical. Perhaps the incantation was necessary to find the entrance in the first place.

Similar to the tale "The Burial Gown" (p. 126), the maiden seems to be a phyiscal revenant rather than an immaterial specter. It is unclear whether she was already "active" before the squire arrived, although it is suspicious that her corpse was so well preserved. Was it merely because something still bound her to this world (a desire to continue her line), or was she perhaps something similar to a vampire that already haunted the living?

Either way, her mere presence was lethal to the squire (as it is so often the case with the undead in German folklore) — and it is doubtful he would have survived even if he had agreed to the betrothal.

Other transgressions against the departed were likewise prone to creating ghosts — from foul murders, to broken vows, to sins of passion.

61. The Shower Maidens

Once, there were seven sisters which are now well-known to farmers as the "Shower Maidens". They lived peacefully together and made a living from herding their goats. One day, seven noble knights were passing by into the direction of the

[48] I once more recommend the book "Magical Treasure Hunting in Europe and North America"[Dil12] for more on this topic.

Harmer.[49] The knights asked them for something to drink, which the sisters were happy to oblige, for they had their milk kegs in their hands.

From this time onwards, the sisters left their herds, became silent, searched for lonely places in the forest, and yearned for their knights. They no longer looked after their goats, and wolves ate one after another. The knights separated as well, and each sought out the maiden who had offered him a drink. Over time, each couple found each other — one at the Kressenbrunnen,[50] another at the Bärenriegel,[51] one more at a moss-covered cave, and so forth at different places. There they lived and loved each other. Soon, apple-cheeked boys smiled from their beds of moss and delighted in the shining armor of their fathers.

In this way they lived for several loveful years. The knights hid the women so that they could lead them to their castles after their fathers' deaths. Their fathers, however, wanted them to marry rich noblewomen, and when their sons refused to bend to their fathers' wills, they strove to discover the cause for this.

There was a diviner in the region who was able to give them instructions on how they could capture the seven maidens. The grim lords mounted their horses and searched the forest. Once captured, they carried the maidens, as well as their boys, into an old ruin and imprisoned them there so that they would starve. Then, they ambushed each of the knights when they were alone and wanted to bring food to their lovers and children. They were then chained to the walls of the ruin where the maidens were jailed with their children.

49 The German phrase used here seems to imply that this might be a local mountain, but I haven't been able to identify it.

50 I was likewise unable to identify this location, but by implication it is either a well or (more likely) a spring of some kind.

51 This is the only location in the story I was able to identify — it's one of the summits of the "Hohe Bogen" mountain ridge in Bavaria. It is part of the municipality of Rimbach in the Upper Palatine.

When drunken farmers accompanied by their wives (who carried cakes and mead in their baskets) returned from the local Kirchweih festival[52] and passed near this terrible place, the knights pleaded for food for the starving women and children imprisoned within. But the farmers made crude jokes: "The mice are singing beautifully today!", toasted to the health of the old lords before their eyes, and then moved on, plotting how to take possession of the home and property of the seven maidens.

Once the maidens and their boys had passed on, the old lords came and released the knights, as they assumed they had broken their wills. But, in this, they were mistaken, for the sons now attacked their fathers with their short swords. The fight went on for a long time until, finally, everyone had perished.

Then, a great storm arose, and the angered heavens released hailstones as large as pigeon eggs so that all grain on the fields of the drunken, hard-hearted farmers was pounded into the ground and their goats and sheep perished. The stones of ice even struck through their roofs and killed their children in their cradles!

Since that time, hail appears and destroys the harvest of the farmers because they are the descendants of the hard-hearted people who denied food to the starving. Furthermore, since that time, the fathers will no longer live in peace with their sons. However, because of the sin of their forefathers, Christian men will surrender themselves into their fate. For the seven maidens and their boys nourish themselves from the destroyed grain, but they are always hungry and will never be satiated. But if a farmer who is cutting his grain leaves a small sheaf of grain behind, he will be spared from the showers. For this reason, the seven maidens are called the Shower Maidens. If a farmer can

[52]Literally, "Church's Sanctification", this is *the* iconic German folk festival — much more than than the (in my opinion overrated) Oktoberfest. Almost every village celebrates this at the (often only reputed) anniversary of the sanctification of the local church — and since each village has its own date for this, this means that most villagers have several such festivals throughout the year within walking distance.

hear the knights fighting with their ringing weapons, he knows it as an ill omen for his harvest.[Pan48, p. 86]

Translation notes: The original German term "Jungfrau" describing these women does not necessarily imply a virginal status — and in this story it is especially clear that this describes their status as "unmarried women". In general, German folklore does not seem to focus on virginity overly much. However, being an unmarried mother *was* considered shameful.

Commentary: This time, haunted souls return as an entire weather pattern — certainly one of the more powerful manifestations of ghosts. The story doesn't say how wide an area the hail covers, but it is certainly enough to devastate a few local fields.

This particular instance of "ancestral sin" is also interesting. Would the shower maidens pursue descendants of the farmers who moved elsewhere? Or conversely, would they leave farmers alone who do not trace their ancestry to those who had denied them food?

Finally, the practice of leaving a sheaf aside during harvest time sounds like it might be a holdover from pre-Christian practice — leaving one part of the field alone was common in old Germanic beliefs, and is still done in some parts of France.[Lec09, p. 214ff] On the other hand, Leviticus 23:22 and Deuteronomy 24:19 in the Bible also exhort farmers to leave parts of their harvest untended so that the poor, strangers, widows and orphans can use these grain stalks to feed themselves, so feeding the ghosts in this manner could be seen as fulfilment of Biblical practice.

62. The Man of Dikjendäl Valley

The dune valley Dikjendäl lies in the area of old Eidum.[53] During a storm night (some say during Christmas Night of 1713), a sailor who lived in Archsum[54] was stranded there. Under great danger and with strenuous efforts he was able to save himself and his money box on the beach of his home island, and he hoped for a friendly countryman who would take care of him, help him recover, and lead him to his kin. But greedy beachcombers had noticed his arrival, as well as that of his money box. And, instead of aiding him, they pitilessly beat him down with their clubs, and buried him in the sand. The dying man tried to rise up one more time, but the fiends forcefully kicked the head of the unfortunate sailor into the soft ground, lopped off the hand of the sailor's right arm when he attempted to lift it, and carried the money box away. Since that time, a ghost walks around this dune valley where the murder occurred every night, lifting the bloody stump of his cut-off arm and demanding justice. The ghost is called the "Dikjendälmann" after this infamous valley.

(From Mr. Hansen in the Volksbuch of 1844, p. 102.)[Mü45, p. 175][55]

Commentary: Despite many efforts of the authorities throughout the centuries,[56] the inhabitants of the coasts saw

[53]Eidum was a former village on the west coast of Sylt that was destroyed during the All Saints Day Flood of 1436. It was located to the west of modern-day Westerland, a part of the Sylt municipality. The Dikjendäl seems to have been in the general vicinity of the modern "Dikjen Deel" Youth Hostel.

[54]Archsum is a village in the eastern part of Sylt, and is now likewise part of the Sylt municipality.

[55]The *"Volksbuch fur das Jahr 1844"* is available at Archive.org.[Bie44, p. 102] The narrative doesn't differ, but this version is embedded into a larger article about the dunes of Sylt, which is why I stuck with the more self-contained version provided by Müllenhoff.

[56]See the tale "The Coast Warden" (p. 115) for an example.

it as their right to take any flotsam that washed at their shores for their own. While "normal" beachcombing was a nonviolent crime, the temptation to kill any survivors who might have had a claim to the flotsam was often rather strong. Since they were almost always strangers to the beachcombing community, there was little fear of repercussion as long as the bodies weren't found.

That these beachcombers didn't recognize him and killed him off so close to his home — a mere 9 km, perhaps — must surely have contributed to the anguish that the ghost felt.

63. The Ghost Ship (Emden)

At a time when the city of Emden was still flowering, the river Ems was flowing beneath the city walls,[57] and ships of all lands and people filled the harbor, it occurred that a terrible storm broke loose. This storm moved the waters of the North Sea in gigantic masses and waves towards the city, which put the inhabitants in dire straits. During this weather, a merchant ship from Emden, which had long sojourned on foreign and distant seas, approached the city with full sails during the night. Its impending arrival had been signaled when it had reached the mouth of the river Ems,[58] and was now eagerly awaited. Already, it was approaching the mouth of the harbor near the long bridge, close to the protective Delft.[59] Already, it was possible to see

[57] I.e. before the bay of the Dollart to the south of Emden was formed. This occurred during a devastating storm surge in the year 1277, which drowned most of the lands south of Emden. Even today, these lands have only been partially recovered, and the river Ems flows into the bay to the east of Emden instead of forming a recognizable river flowing past the city.

[58] Wikimedia has a scan of the "Typus Frisiae Orientalis" map by Ubbo Emmius.[Wikb] Drawn in 1645, it also shows a map of the Dollart region before the great flood, which should help visualize the geography.

[59] The western branch of the old harbor canals within the old city. Today, there is a street called "Am Delft" next to it.

the dark figures of the sailors moving up and down the ship in the light of the lit lanterns that bobbed and weaved in the wind. Already, it was possible to hear the orders of the ship's captain, who forcefully shouted over the noise of the storm. Already it was possible to hear the clattering of the heavy anchor that tumbled into the depths, when:

Suddenly, an infernal whirlwind[60] broke loose, hurling the mountains of water into the air. The wind whistled so shrilly and strangely that the observers in the harbor were overcome with dread. The ship was suddenly grabbed, lifted up, pushed down, and, with a jolt, lifted up again, twisted around, and stomped into the depths once more. A dreadful cry of despair came from the deck. Were forty weathered seamen, almost all of them sons of Emden, really about to come to such a pitiful end — within sight of their hometown, in sight of their parents and siblings who were assembled on the pier?

A shout arose on the bank: "Where is the barge?" But the harbormaster pointed towards the guard boat that was under lock and key within the Delft, and said coldly and without pity: "The barge stays where it is. It would be useless to have it out there. Furthermore, Elsert Giesberts doesn't deserve any better fate than that which is provided for him now out there!" For the thus-named captain of the ship that was currently sinking was the declared enemy of the harbormaster, and the latter did not know the words "Love your enemies" from the Holy Book, but only the words "Eye for eye, tooth for tooth". And even though the harbormaster had been informed that his own son was on board the merchant ship, his hatred against the captain was so overwhelming in his heart that he did not move any limb towards the rescue of the crew. And, by the time others had forced him to hand over the key, it was far too late. The ship

[60]The text doesn't use the modern "Wirbelwind" ("whirling wind"), but the older "Windsbraut" ("wind's bride") — a word that fits in with the notion that whirlwinds were controlled by living beings, such as witches traveling over land and sea.

went down with the last man amidst the swirl of the mountains of water, and the winds whistled over the city walls in mockery.

But, when a storm approaches from the northwest, the waters of the ocean race against the dike, the air groans and moans, and the winds yell and howl, witnesses may perceive a ghost ship, shrouded in a bluish light, approaching fast during the blackest of midnights. Then the rattling of the ropes, the clanging of the chains, the shouts of the captain, and the ear- and bone-piercing cries of the dying can be heard. And whoever hears those cries shrinks away in dread, and hurries away from the site of the disaster.[Sun69, p. 34f]

Commentary: As mentioned earlier, people who died with strong, unresolved emotions are also prime candidates for haunting this world after death. This crew of sailors certainly qualifies — to expire this close to safety, in sight of their kin, and abandoned to their fate by a vengeful harbormaster was a terribly cruel way to die.

64. The Uglei

Not far from Eutin, there is a small lake within a beech grove. This lake is called the Uglei. Its dark waters are always calm and quiet, and everything around it appears sad and gloomy. The lake did not always exist, but it was a long time ago when it formed.

Up on the hill, where the summer residence is located now,[61] there used to be a castle[62] inhabited by a young, handsome, but wild knight. He loved nothing more than hunting, and early

[61] Presumably the Jagdpavillion ("hunting lodge") in Eutin, which was built in 1776.

[62] There are indeed remnants of old Slavic fortifications in the area.

every morning he ventured into the forest. On his way, he frequently encountered the daughter of a poor farmer, who had to drive her father's horses into the woods for pasture. The knight soon fell deeply in love with her due to her beauty, but the girl refused his pleas and gifts and replied to all his courting that she could not possibly become his wife, as she was only a poor man's daughter. And, yet, the girl had come to care for the handsome knight as well. One morning, when he once more pursued her with his pleas and promises, they came to a depression in the forest where a small chapel was located. Then, the knight led the girl inside. As he stepped before the altar, he spoke: "Here, in the sight of God, I will take you as my spouse, and Heaven may strike me down at this place if I do not stay true to you and fail to keep my word." The girl believed his vow and they met in the forest every morning. But, when the girl reminded him of his promise, he first put it off and eventually he stayed away and did not come back. When she realized that she had been abandoned, she put on a black dress, became depressed, fell sick, and died after a short time.

Meanwhile, the knight had become engaged to a rich countess and the wedding day was set. The wedding was to take place in the small chapel in the forest. But, when the preacher had finished his sermon and the bridal couple wanted to come together, the ghost of the unfortunate girl appeared and raised her finger against the groom. When he sank to the ground out of fright, a terrible storm with thunder and rain broke loose as if Heaven itself was about to collapse. Then the chapel sunk into the waters with everyone inside. The lake has stood at this site since that time. Only the preacher, the bride, and a small innocent girl could be saved, since they had stepped on the wooden stairs of the altar. But, at times, in evenings during quiet weather, it is still possible to hear the small bell of the chapel from the waters.[Sch62, p. 165f]

Commentary: "Trust not the honeyed words of those

more powerful than you, for they will abandon you once they got what they wanted" — a moral lesson that is no less relevant today than it was back then. Though, at least, folklore tales provide the opportunity for post-mortem vengeance — even if it also caused the death of a lot of innocent people in this case.

5. Those Who Linger On

From a Christian perspective, the living are expected to "let go" of the departed, and leave them be once they have reached their proper afterlife. When they fail to do so, the souls of the dead might actually return for a while against their wishes.

65. Don't Weep for the Dead Too Much!

Every tear that is shed for a buried person falls on their shroud and makes it wet.

One of my grandmother's children had died. She lamented and wept for the child profusely. Then the child appeared to her one night and said: "Mother, stop weeping for me! In my shroud, there is only one spot that is still dry, as large as a thaler coin. Once that spot is wet as well, I will not find rest in my grave."[SM54, p. 220]

Commentary: While German culture accepts that grieving for the dead will occur, strong displays of "negative" emotions (excepting perhaps anger) are frowned upon. The traditional funeral process is supposed to ensure that the grieving can be done in what is considered to be a "proper" time and place so that people will "move on". This tale serves to reinforce such cultural expectations.

66. Leave the Dead in Peace!

The husband of a woman living in the village had died. She pitied herself much over this, and always pleaded that her husband might return and give her advice in many things. One evening at dusk, she cried a lot once more, and begged the Lord God to let her husband come back. Then her husband did indeed appear and gave her advice in quite a few matters. But he also added that she ought to have left him in peace. In the end, he wanted her to promise him to do what he had told her. He thus approached his wife and offered his hand. She offered him the handle of a whip, which he took and shook. The next morning, the woman noticed that the handle of the whip was burnt all the way through at the spot where the dead man had grasped it.[SM54, p. 220]

Commentary: Once more, we see that the appearance of the dead among the living is considered a deeply unnatural affair. Here, a departed soul is called back because of a living person's obsessions, though thankfully without lasting harm.

We have seen how ghosts in German folklore are associated with fire and burning before, all the way back to "Mass of the Dead in Wesenberg" (p. 28). Now, we see for the first (but not the last) time that the very touch of a ghost can burn. This seems to be an old Germanic belief, and accounts of this phenomenon exist as far away as Iceland around the year 1000.[Lec09, p. 103] This also cannot be reduced to the usual "ghost writhing in the fires of purgatory" narrative,[1] as the ghost in this tale had already departed for the afterlife and only returned because of his grieving wife.

[1] Beyond the examples provided here, Claude Lecouteux examines this association in greater detail in his book *The Return of the Dead.*[Lec09, p. 218]

It is unclear why she handed him a whip handle in particular, but perhaps it was merely the closest elongated object she had at hand. As we shall see in later tales, people used all sorts of objects in order to avoid shaking a ghost's hand directly.

67. The White She-Ghost

There are female monsters, female devils, female spouses, female fiancées, so why shouldn't there be female ghosts?[2] A long time ago, there used to be a castle between Breinermoor[3] and Backemoor,[4] whose owner was a chieftain.[5] He was also a connoisseur of the arts. He had not found a wife that suited his preferences and, thus, lived as a bachelor from one day to the next without a care. One day, he encountered a painting, a portrait of a young and beautiful maiden. To see her and to fall in love with her was the same. The painting did not leave his side, and the more he gazed at the maiden, the more he was comsumed by desire for her. Thus he pledged: "This beautiful girl shall be my wife, no matter the cost!" He also intended to honor the painting in the same way as the original until he found her.

But, as it happened, the noblewoman was already dead and, thus, could not find peace in the grave due to the sinful idolatry of the knight.[6] As a white ghost, she floated around the castle every night and tried to make the admirer of her beauty understand her predicament. But oh, the pain! The besotted man

[2] This whole sentence is basically a bad German pun where the narrator slapped the female form on all nouns — whether appropriate or not, such as in the case of "Verlobtinnen" ("female engaged people").

[3] Now part of the Westoverledingen municipality.

[4] Now part of Rhauderfehn. Backemoor has a "Borgweg" ("Castle Way") road, which might hint of a fortification in the area.

[5] See my notes in "The 'Lordly Dog' " (p. 89) on the chieftains.

[6] "Knight" should be seen as a reference to the chieftain's status as a noble, not his actual noble rank.

couldn't leave her alone and instead decided to unite with her in death. Thus, he took the painting with him and set himself aflame along with his castle without going through the rite of confession before the act. As he had died in sin, the unfortunate maiden cannot be released and must now haunt the site of a castle as a white ghost. She appears to wanderers during the twilight of the morning and evening, clad in a white, woolly dress shining like phosphorus. Whoever is touched by the dress is hit by blindness or receives burn-like wounds at the point of contact.[Sun69, p. 55f]

Commentary: While being condemned to an existence of a ghost due to one's own sins or mistakes is understandable, here an innocent woman has to leave her (presumably peaceful) afterlife because of a creepy stalker's obsessions with her — and when he dies, *she* has to stay on the earthly plane while *his* soul doesn't seem to be condemned to such an existence[7] (on the other hand, it's probably a small mercy for her that his ghost doesn't show up at this site). There doesn't seem to be any justice here.

While mocking the dead is not exactly the same as yearning for their presence, it is just as inadvisable — for they might take notice, and return at least for a little while.

[7] It is entirely possible that the reason for this is that his soul was directly sent to Hell, however — especially since suicide was considered a particularly grave sin during those times, and doing so because of a lustful obsession would not have helped his case.

68. Guests from the Gallows

Bräuner's Curiositäten, p. 296 — 298.[Brä37, p. 296ff][8]

A publican of a respected city once traveled back home with two wine traders from a wine-growing hill region[9] where they had bought a considerable supply of wine. Their path led past the gallows, and even though they were inebriated, they still spotted three hanged men who had been judged some time ago.[10] Then one of the two wine traders shouted: "Hey, publican of the Bear![11] These three fellows hanging there were once your guests, too!" — "Hey", said the cocky publican, "they can come visit me tonight and dine with me!"

Well, what happened next? When the publican arrived home in a drunken stupor, dismounted his horse, went into his sitting room, and sat down, a great dread overcame him so that he was unable to call for anyone. Shortly afterwards, his servant[12] entered with the intention of pulling off his boots and found his master lying half-dead in his chair. He thus called his mistress, and after she revived him somewhat with potent measures,[13] she asked him what had happened to him. Then he told her that he had invited the three hanged men as guests as he had been riding past them. And when he had entered his chamber, the three of

[8]See the notes in the tale "The Ghosts' Meal" (p. 23) for more on this source.

[9]The German term was "Weingebirge" — "wine mountains". It could be the name of a specific region, but since I could find no region with such a name I interpreted it as a descriptor instead.

[10]The German text used the phrase "lange Jahre" — "long years". This was probably intended as a metaphor for the fact that the hanged men had been hanging there for quite some time, instead of implying it had been many years since their execution. Then again, it cannot be ruled out that the travelers saw an apparition of people who had indeed been dead for many years.

[11]"Bären-Wirt" in the original German — which implies that the pub he ran was named "zum Bären" ("at the Bear") or something similar.

[12]"Hausknecht" — "house squire" in German.

[13]Possibly with hard liquor, although the story doesn't elaborate.

them appeared in the same horrible form as he had seen them hanging on the gallows, stepped into the chamber, sat down at his table, and waved to him that he should approach them. Then, finally, the servant had entered the room, whereupon the three ghosts all vanished. This was initially proclaimed to be a product of the publician's imagination, as, in his inebriated state, he had remembered what he had called out to the sinners while riding past them. But he then laid down in bed and died on the third day.[GG16, p. 435f]

Commentary: The publican in this story calls out to the hanged men in drunken exuberance — paying the ultimate price for his folly. And, as we have seen in other stories such as "The Heavily Loaded Men" (p. 74), being merely in close proximity to the dead can be fatal.

69. Visit of the Hanged Man

(reported as occurring in the year 1661)

Two hundred years ago, a carpenter named Hans Meinecke lived in Wandsbek.[14] At one point, he gained a journeyman named August Hermann Weinrich from the Vogtland[15] in Upper Saxony.[16] This journeyman was a gourmet who never considered

[14]Wandsbek is now one of the seven boroughs of Hamburg. In the 17th century (i.e. the time this story was set in), Wandsbek was a manorial estate. In the 18th century, it became a prosperous town in its own right when it was purchased by the slave trader Heinrich Carl von Schimmelmann, one of the richest men of Europe at the time.

[15]The Vogtland is now a border region between Bavaria, Thuringia, Saxony, and Bohemia in the Czech Republic. It is named after the "Vögte" — officials who ruled the territory in the name of the noble who actually owned the land.

[16]"Upper Saxony" ("Obersachsen") is a historic term for the possessions

the food on Master Meinecke's table to be good enough for him. In particular, he despised the nice groat made out of buckwheat or oats, didn't want to eat it, and called the master's children "groat heads" since they were fed with it in the morning, at noon, and in the evening. This was noted with disapproval by the master's wife in particular.

Over time, the meagre fare caused the journeyman Weinrich to dislike both the beautiful village of Wandsbek and his trade, so he left, enlisted with the soldiers, went to war,[17] fought with bravery, became a flag bearer,[18] and finally a lieutenant. But when the potentates made peace, he and many others were sent off and his glory days were over. Thus, the Herr Lieutenant traveled back again to Hamburg where unrooted people often found ways to earn their living, tried out all sorts of jobs, good ones and bad ones, and finally drifted from the straight and narrow to dubious paths.[19] He thus developed a devious plan together with his wife Margaretha Langin. She went to work as a nursemaid for a rich merchant named Tylo Baren who lived at the Kehrwieder.[20] She claimed that her husband had died in the war, and when he visited her, they pretended that he was her brother. As she had had ample opportunity to explore the house, she carefully rose from her bed one beautiful night, let her husband inside, gathered all the gold, silver, money, and other valuable items together, and, after they had completed this task, both of them walked away with their loot.

of the House of Wettin, which are largely similar to modern-day Saxony and Saxony-Anhalt.

[17] Considering the period this tale is set in, most likely the Thirty Years' War.

[18] "Fähnrich" in German — a military rank that is now similar to the English ensign (i.e. an officer candidate), but was a distinct role in earlier times. This role was given to a soldier who was considered especially reliable and who was expected to carry the unit's flag, never let it go out of his hands, and defend it with his life.

[19] The German sentence contrasts the "gerader Weg" ("straight path") with the "krummer Weg" ("twisted path").

[20] The Kehrwieder is one of the former islands of Hamburg that is now part of the HafenCity quarter.

However, even back then there was an excellent group of night watchmen called the "Räthelwacht". The guards captured them right at the Brooksbrücke bridge[21] and imprisoned them. The lower court convicted them to be flogged at the pillory.[22] One might be content with this kind of punishment for that crime. The lieutenant, however, protested loudly against this judgment and said that this kind of humiliation would be inappropriate for an officer like him and thus appealed to the upper court. The upper court examined the case more closely, and was of the opinion that servants should be more severely punished than other people, since it is easier to protect oneself against outsiders. As further misdeeds of the couple had come to light in the meantime, the woman was beheaded and buried beneath the upper court, but the man was hanged at the gallows on November 11th, in the year 1661.

Many days later, the carpenter Meinecke happened to be traveling home late at night from Hamburg to Wandsbek. And as he passed by the gallows and saw lieutenant Weinrich, his former journeyman, hanging there, he was overcome by a sacrilegious and derisive mood and thus spoke to the hanged man: "Oh, you poor devil, now you are hanging there! If you were with me, instead of here — you would surely eat the groat which you didn't want to eat then and now would love to be a 'groat head' like my children! Well, if you can get away from there, then visit me for the night and be a guest for a meal of groat!"

The cheeky Meinecke was somewhat disconcerted when the poor sinner on the gallows opened his eyes and turned towards him once he had started to address him. But he became horrified to the utmost when, after he had finished with his speech, the hanged man raised and lowered his head three times and

[21] At the time, it would have been a wooden predecessor to the current Brooksbrücke. It was the very first bridge off the Kehrwieder island towards the Hamburg city center.

[22] The precise term for their punishment was the "Staupbesen", a flogging with a bundle of birch sticks which might have stones or even sharp metal fragments embedded within it.

thus nodded as a sign that he would accept the invitation to the nightly meal. Meinecke thus arrived home in a state of great distress, hurried to his bed, and recited the evening prayer,[23] the Lord's Prayer and "All Good Spirits"[24] — more fervently than usual. But around midnight, Meinecke heard a frightful pacing, scratching, and shuffling with jangling of chains, as well as sighing and moaning. It came to a stop in front of his house and knocked on the window sills three times. When he opened them, the poor, hanged sinner himself stood there with his chains around the neck, arms, and legs, smiled at him horribly, and spoke to him in a dull and hollow voice:

"Here I am, and I want my groat. Give me the groat to which you invited me!"

And the carpenter hurriedly put a bowl of groat outside, crawled into his bed, and broke out in cold sweat. He fell sick and remained so for many weeks — and so did the other people in the household who had become aware of the haunting. The bowl was lying empty and shattered in front of the window the next morning.

Thus, take note: You should walk past gallows, high courts, and scaffolds[25] in silence, have thoughts pleasing to God while doing so, plead for deliverance from temptation, and ask God to have mercy for the poor sinners. In no case should you mock

---

[23] Possibly Luther's "Evening Prayer". An English-language version can be found online.[Con]

[24] A traditional invocation against evil spirits, which we have seen before in the first fragment of "The Man Without a Head" (p. 62). One version went roughly like this:

"All good spirits praise the Lord God.
If you are of God, then approach!
If you are of the Devil, then begone!
In the name of Jesus I command you:
Relent from me!"[Lan]

[25] The German term used here for "scaffold" was the vernacular "Rabenstein" — "raven's stone", likely referring to the fact that ravens would be attracted to corpses.

the poor sinners and make light of their fate — for otherwise you might suffer an even worse fate than Master Meinecke in Wandsbek![Ben54, p. 320ff]

Commentary: While the details differ, the sacrilege is the same — mocking the dead on the gallows. Still, at least the carpenter seemed to have escaped with his life, likely because the dead man didn't actually spend any time inside his house.

Some ghosts seem to be fairly self-motivated when it comes to lingering on, usually because they had left some unfinished business behind.

70. The Ghostly Suitor on Hartenstein Castle

(Oral tale. A poetic interpretation by Wiese can be found in J. Günther's *Großes poet. Sagenbuch der Deutschen.* Jena 1846. Vol. 1, p. 123)[26]

At one time, a shadow knight appeared every day at Hartenstein Castle, the ancestral castle of the Schönburg lineage.[27] He

[26]The poetic version (titled "König Vollmer") is largely similar, but the ghost is less of a jerk at the conclusion of the tale.[Gün44, p. 123]

[27]The Schönburgs were a lineage of the German high nobility with two major branches, of which the Schönburg-Hartensteins were one branch, and the Schönburg-Waldenburgs the other. The family still exists, though of course they have long since been stripped of their noble titles, like all members of the former German nobility. Hartenstein Castle itself now exists as a ruin within the city of the same name.

was called "Vollmer, the Ghostly King".[28] It was unclear how it had occurred, but he won the love of the beautiful Kunigunde von Schönburg, and she declared her intention to marry him and no other. Thus, he rode through the castle gate every day on an invisible horse, which no one saw but only ever heard its steps. Then he put it into the stables, and afterwards climbed up the castle stairway — invisible himself, and only perceptible by the echoing of his footsteps. There, his bride came to meet him, and he gave her his hand — this was the only part of the body which could be felt, and it was soft and smooth, but cold as ice. After that, the two talked and flirted with each other in the manner of lovers. Then, they stepped into the dining hall, where the brother of the maiden waited, and all three sat down for the table and ate and drank at their leisure. The food put down in front of the shadow knight and the wine poured into his cup vanished, but nobody saw where it ended up. It was only possible to hear the voice of the shadow groom. The count, who used to dread his ghostly brother-in-law, gradually developed more and more affection for him, for in him he had a constant, faithful adviser and warner of approaching misfortunes. Once the meal was over, the count left the bridal couple, and in this manner they sat together until one o'clock, whereupon the ghostly guest hurriedly took his leave.

In this manner, this state of affairs continued for many years. But, one day, the maiden expressed how much she longed for a kiss from his mouth. And behold, her ghostly groom answered: "Farewell forever! Because I believed in your purely spiritual love, I left my heavenly realm to be with you. But now that you think of base passions, I can no longer stay here. You shall never see me again!" Then he vanished, and the maiden never experienced his presence again.[Grä74a, p. 494f]

---

[28] The German title was "König Vollmer der Geisterkönig". It is not quite clear from this if he was called this because he was a ghostly king, or because he was a king of the ghosts, or both. I went with the former interpretation.

Translation note: Vollmer is called a "Schattenritter" and "Schattenbräutigam" in this text — using the word German word for "shadow" as a prefix to create new compound words in order to describe the "shadowed", invisible nature of the ghost. This should not imply that he was a literal shadow, since he is consistently described as invisible.

Commentary: Let me first state that being asexual is valid, and others should respect people who experience no sexual attraction. Still, the ghostly knight could have handled this better. Sure, he discovered after many years that her relationship needs differed from his own. But I feel that he ought to have let her down gently, instead blaming her for everything — what they had for all these years was real, and was not invalidated by her blooming desires.

(Incidentally, the poetic version of this tale has the ghost explicitly saying that he is not angry with her — implying that she is not to be blamed for unwittingly breaking the "terms of release" from his "heavenly realm". It's still a sad ending, but this hopefully allowed her to move on eventually.)

As a side note, the fact that the ghost was able to warn the count of "approaching misfortunes" implies that he had special intelligence from the ghostly planes of existence — perhaps even getting premonitions of events yet to occur. A very useful trait in an adviser, indeed! The notion that ghosts could provide information about future events has long existed in Christian thought — examples appear as early as an exchange of letters between Saint Augustine and one "Evodius" in 414 AD.[29][Sch98, p. 18ff]

[29]To be precise, in Letter 158 from Saint Augustine, translations of which can be readily found in a variety of online sources.

71. The Monk on Helgoland Island

In the year 1530, our king[30] sent a man to Helgoland who used to be a monk in order to preach the new teachings of Luther. But the people of Helgoland held fast to their old beliefs, mocked the devout man, and wanted to force him to become Catholic again. But, after he stubbornly refused to do so, they finally threw him down from the rocks. They did so at the spot where there used to be a cliff rising out of the waters until a few years ago. This cliff clearly looked like a monk and was thus named this way.[31]

But, on the very first night after his sad end, the ghost of the admonisher showed himself on this cliff. There, he preached the new teachings with a thunderous voice in a manner that caused many people to turn away from the papacy. Soon after, all others followed, as the ghost could find no rest until everyone had been converted. His threatening voice was often heard later on as well, especially when an evil person on the island was about to commit a foul deed.

(Oral tale.)[Mü45, p. 125f]

Commentary: There's nothing quite like a ghost driving home that you should *really* mend your ways and live your life according to the "proper" faith. That he returned to

[30] Most likely the King of Denmark. This would have been Frederik I in 1530, although he generally seemed to have tried to play Catholic and Lutheran interests against each other rather than declaring outright support for one side. His successor Christian III, who took the throne in 1534, was much more blatantly pro-Lutheran, and thus would have been more likely to send preachers to Helgoland.

[31] The "Mönch" used to be a rock pillar at the southern tip of the island which was destroyed in 1947 when the British occupation forces demolished the extensive bunker complexes on the island. Wikimedia has an old photograph of the formation.[Wika]

repeat this message after the inhabitants of the island had brutally murdered him presumably made an even stronger impression.

72. The Best Religion

Diesdorf Monastery lies in the Altmark region, fairly close to Salzwedel. This is one of the oldest monasteries and was founded in 1161 during the times of Margrave Albert the Bear.[32] There were many unmarried women who lived in its convent according to the rules of Saint Augustine. During the time of the Reformation, the two sisters Elisabeth and Ursula von Ritzebüttel[33] lived there. They were unable to decide for themselves which one was the best religion — the papacy or the new teachings of Luther. Finally they agreed that, if one of them were to die first, she should report which of the religions was the superior one. Then, the other one would adhere to that religion afterwards.

As it happened, Elisabeth was the first to pass on some time after that. And soon after, a spirit in her shape visited Ursula. After receiving the question if she had entered bliss, the spirit only answered with the words: "Hardly, hardly!"

Upon hearing this, Ursula decided to change her religion. But when she wanted to go to the church to make her statement of faith, and reached the so-called "Crevice", a dark entranceway from the convent into the church, she suddenly received a slap from an ice-cold, invisible hand. But she declared: "I shall not be deterred by this!", and bravely went onwards and put her intentions into practice. The other nuns of the convent now followed her example, and the convent subsequently became

[32] Albert the Bear was Duke of Saxony from 1138 to 1142, and later became the first Margrave of Brandenburg from 1157 to his death in 1170 thanks to his campaigns against the pagan Wendish people.

[33] Most likely this is a reference to the Lappe dynasty of minor nobles whose family home was Schloss Ritzebüttel in Cuxhaven.

entirely Protestant in this manner.

See also:

Beckmann *histor. Beschreibung v. Brandenburg.* Part 5. Book 1. Chapter 10. p. 154-155.[34] *Ueber die Altmark. II.* p. 202.[35][Mü45, p. 125f]

Commentary: There are a number of tales similar to this where two woman are uncertain about how to live proper, god-fearing lives and then agree that the one who dies first should report back on the truth of the matter.[36] The Reformation and its aftermath[37] were especially fertile ground for such stories, as people found their faiths questioned when the ruler of their fiefdom took on a different religion than their own. What this version of the tale leaves out (but the second citation elaborates on) is that such conversions were not exactly a matter of personal choice — people generally had the option of either converting, or leaving the realm and most of their possessions behind.

Still, that they *had* these options was a step forward established by the Peace of Augsburg, since it allowed those who were otherwise bound to the land (such as serfs) to leave if their choice of religion differed with that of their ruler.

[34] This is Johann Christoph Becmann's *"Historische Beschreibung der Chur und Mark Brandenburg"*. It elaborates on the Reformation in the Diesdorf area, but doesn't mention the legend.[Bec53, p. 154f]

[35] This is Heinrich Christoph Steinhart's *"Ueber die Altmark — Ein Beitrag zur Kunde der Mark Brandenburg. Zweiter Theil."* It does mention the interesting detail that the nuns were under pressure to either convert and stay with the convent as "secular" residents, or follow the monks into exile.[Ste00, p. 202]

[36] See [Sch98, p. 50] for an account written down by the monk Guibert of Nogent, who lived around the turn of the 12th century.

[37] See the notes on German history and religion in the appendix for some further historical context.

The invisible slapping hand might, perhaps, have been a ghost of one of the nuns who had previously lived in the convent, as, of course, they would have disapproved of such a choice.

73. The Ghost Ship (Pellworm)

It was at a time of the year when all ships berthed and all sailors traveled home, but the betrothed of one young woman still wouldn't come. And when everyone else was already home, he had not arrived. Her heart did not want to accept this, and, in the nights, she stood at the waters and wailed and cried for her beloved. Then, one night, the ship arrived which had been lost at sea with her groom. It took her on board, and nobody ever saw her again.

(From Pellworm or Föhr, narrated by Herr Storm.)[Mü45, p. 163f]

Commentary: Short, but simple and effective. Whether she now is dead as well, or if they are joined together in some purgatory or Otherworld on the Seven Seas we can only speculate.

74. Love after Death

1. A woman had died in Drüber,[38] and left a small child behind. This child was not taken care of as well as it ought to have been, for eight days later, at eleven o'clock, the deceased mother entered the chamber in which the child was lying. She went to the cradle, picked up the child, and acted as if she was

[38]Drüber is now a suburb of the town of Einbeck.

breastfeeding it. Then, she gathered the diapers,[39] and walked out of the house and towards the well with them. There, she washed them and spread them out in order to dry them. As soon as she had done so, she returned back to the chamber, where she stayed with the child until the clocks struck twelve. Then, she vanished. The next morning, everything in the cradle was just like it had been in the evening. In this manner, the ghost of the mother visited for one hour every night for four weeks. After that, she did not appear again.

2. A coachman from Dassel once drove out to the field with his horse-drawn wagon. On the way, he encountered a funeral procession, and from the mourners he learned that they accompanied the corpse of a woman from a neighboring village who had recently died. When he returned, he encountered the buried woman. Since she had left a small child behind, she went back to her home in order to breastfeed it.

3. A farmer from Wennigsen[40] once drove towards the forest in the evening in order to fetch wood. On the way, he encountered a funeral procession, but he calmly drove past it and gathered his wood. On the way back, the horses shied. The farmer himself sensed the odor of a corpse, and saw the woman who had lain in the coffin. He had been told that she had left seven children behind, and the husband of the woman had also died, the children were altogether alone. Furthermore, the youngest of the children had still been nursed by its mother before she died. Thus, the deceased mother allegedly continued to feed it until it was capable of eating on its own.

4. A young noblewoman secretly had an affair with one of her father's servants, and ultimately got pregnant. When her father noticed this, he drove the servant away in an utterly humiliating

---

[39]The term used here was not the modern "Windel", but the more archaic "Kindestuch" — i.e. "child cloth".

[40]This is most likely Wennigsen (Deister), since it is closer to Drüber and Dassel (mentioned in the preceding tales) than the hamlet of Wennigsen that has been incorporated into the city of Melle.

manner. The girl, on the other hand, was terrorized and tormented so much by him that she died. Several days after her burial, her ghost was seen at night, wearing a white dress. At first, she visited her lover, and appeared next to his bed as she had appeared in life. He would have liked to ask her why she appeared, but he didn't have the heart for it. In this manner, she appeared to him three nights in a row. On the third night, he finally asked her why she disturbed him. She replied that she was unable to rest because her father had done such a great injustice to him. Thus, he ought to relay this to her father. The servant thus told the father everything, but the latter did not want to believe him, and said harsh words to him. On the fourth night, she appeared to her mother and pleaded with her to tell the father that he ought to forgive the servant — for otherwise, she would not be able to rest. The mother did as she was asked, but without success. After this had not helped either, she appeared to the father himself, told him everything, and asked him to forgive the servant. The father pledged this to her, and kept his word. From this moment on, the ghost was not seen again.[SM54, p. 220ff]

Commentary: On the one hand, it's heart-warming that a mother's love transcends death. On the other hand, we have to contemplate that these children were breastfed by revenants — made only more disturbing that this actually worked. Which is no small thing, since the presence of the dead is usually considered harmful (and, at times, outright lethal) to the living. But, if you want to justify the necromantic powers of a folklore-based character, I suppose "I was nursed by my undead mother" works quite well as an origin story...

In the last story, it's striking that the ghost cannot rest because of the injustice done to her lover — but, at least, the lover still lives, while her father's torments resulted in her own death. While it is touching that she values her lover more than herself, I cannot really call the result "justice".

75. The Dead Bride

Lauf Castle, which is usually called Neu-Windeck,[41] is said to have been uninhabited for a long time before its destruction, as its hauntings could be heard day and night. During that period, a young knight who was foreign to this region sought hospitality in this castle. He had difficulties with finding the entrance during the darkness of the night. The courtyard was covered by tall grass, and his shouts echoed eerily between the lonely walls. Finally, he saw a light in one chamber of the castle, and climbed the stairs towards it. In the old great hall, a young woman was sitting at a table and seemed to be so preoccupied with her thoughts that she didn't notice him as he entered. She was beautiful, like an angel, but the redness of her cheeks seemed to have paled as if from sorrow. When the knight greeted her, she looked up and nodded with her head. When he conveyed his request for hospitality, she rose up, fetched wine and venison as well as all sorts of poultry, and indicated to the stranger that he should enjoy the meal. Bread and salt were missing, but he did not have the courage to ask for these, for the whole situation seemed entirely uncanny — especially since the maiden had not uttered a single syllable so far. But soon, the wine lifted the spirits of the knight, and he started a conversation:

"You must be the daughter of this house?"[42]

She nodded with her head.

"And your parents?"

[41] Neu-Windeck castle — located near Lauf (Baden) — was built around the year 1300, and was described as a "ruin" by 1580.

[42] I.e. the female scion of the noble lineage this castle belonged to.

She indicated a few portraits on the wall, and spoke with a quiet voice: "I am the last of my line."

The beautiful maiden appealed to the young knight considerably, and, since he indulged with his tankard eagerly, his heart opened more and more. He was poor, and thought to himself that he might make his fortune here.

After a few speeches, he took her hand and asked her if she was still unbound.[43]

She affirmed this with another nod of the head, and the knight proposed marriage to her. Her face lightened up. She rose up, took two rings and a rosemary wreath from a drawer, and stuck the latter into her black curls of hair. Then, she waved to the knight to follow her. He obeyed, not without dread, and would have liked to go back on this word. But at this moment, two venerable, festively dressed old men entered who took him and the maiden into their midst and led them to the castle chapel. There, several tombs were located, and on one of them there was a cast iron bishop in full priestly regalia. The maiden touched the iron figure, which quickly rose up and stepped in front of the altar, where the candles lit up on their own. The iron countenance of the bishop seemed to come alive, his eyes shone like a star peeking through light fog, and he spoke with a deep, hollow voice:

"Kurd of Stein, speak whether you want to marry the maiden Bertha von Windeck, and make her your wife?"

The knight quavered like the leaves of an aspen in the wind, the word died on his tongue, and his senses started to fail him. Then, the crowing of the cockerel on a nearby farming estate became audible, the whole congregation vanished, and a terrible whirlwind tore through the chapel which seemed to pull the

[43] In the German, he asked her "ob sie noch frey sey" — "if she was still free", i.e. if she had not yet been married or was betrothed to anyone.

castle into the depths. The knight fell unconscious, and when he revived, he was lying in the tall grass of the courtyard, and his loyal horse was next to him.[Sch48, p. 143ff]

Commentary: The big mystery here is why the ghost of the maiden agreed so readily to the marriage proposal — was this a chance to escape her torment, or was she just lonely? It is also unclear who the two old men were — relatives of the bride, perhaps? The "bishop", on the other hand, doesn't seem to be a ghost or specter like the others, but an animated piece of ironmongery — but was this achieved by the ghost of the "real" bishop, or created by an extension of the bride's will?

The crowing of cockerels — as a signifier of daybreak — often sends supernatural entities away. This is most commonly seen in tales about the Devil, but also shows up in ghost tales from time to time — we shall see another example in the tale "The Salvation of a Restless Ghost between Wredenhagen and Hinrichshof near Röbel" (p. 174). While the cockerel in this tale ends the apparitions, I do wonder what would have happened if the ceremony had actually gone through. Would the maiden have been released from her existence as a ghost? Would the knight have joined her in her ghostly state? Or would they have existed as a union of a living and a dead person, with all the complications this might cause?

On a final note, salt was traditionally used to keep ghosts away[Sch98, p. 29] — which may explain why it was missing from the meal.

6. Those Who Find Peace

Not all ghost tales necessarily end in tragedy. Indeed, many ghosts manage to find salvation and pass on to the afterlife. However, this almost always requires the intervention of a living person, a notion that dates back to at least the 3rd century in Christian thought.[Sch98, p. 43] This living person need not even know that they are helping a ghost or what they need to do to help a ghost move on — an "accidental" salvation of a ghost still counts, as the following tales of ghostly encounters out in the countryside demonstrates.

76. The God-Fearing Carter

Many people have seen a wandering lantern on the Lichtenstein hill[1] near Dorste.[2] In this area, a freight carter once had a minor accident and wished: "Oh, if I had a lantern here! Then I could easily repair this!" Then, suddenly, the lantern was next to him and shone as brightly as three lamps. The carter now quickly restored his cart to its proper working order, and, when he was finished, he wished for the one who had shone for him "three times Heaven and eternal bliss". Then a voice sounded out: "God made you say that, for I have waited for these words for many centuries." The voice also recommended that, if he were to receive illumination from an invisible hand again in the future, he should not ask who it was. Then the voice fell silent. But it

[1] See the sixth fragment of "Ghosts Reaching Salvation" (p. 179) for another tale that features this region.

[2] Dorste is now part of Osterode.

remained bright enough that the carter was able to see the road until he reached Osterode.[Prö96, p. 202f]

Commentary: Unlike other irrlichts,[3] this ghost helps people instead of leading them astray, and earns salvation after receiving the carter's blessing. It is not clear why the soul advises the carter not to inquire after other souls that provide illumination, however — would this drive the ghost away?

77. Faithful Lights or Errant Lights

According to legend, these lights are poor souls which are still barred from Heaven. Thus, they float around and wait for their release. While they are not malicious, they nevertheless like to lead nightly wanderers astray by luring those wanderers towards them. If you pray, they come closer and squat down on your shoulder or another part of your body. They are then felt as a heavy load. However, they will flee from people who are swearing.

A worker from the old mill in Lutzerath[4] once drove towards Lutzerath one night and saw a Treulicht ("faithful light"). As he started to pray, the Treulicht approached and squatted down on the back of the cart. He continued his prayer, and the Treulicht sat down on the head of the horse. As he continued to pray, it sat down on his own shoulder, and finally on a button on his chest. Then, the worker swore, and the Treulicht retreated from

[3] See the notes for "The Irrlicht of Ihlow" (p. 42) for an explanation of this term.

[4] While not shown in Google Maps, OpenStreetMaps displays an Altmühle ("old mill") hamlet to the northwest of Lutzerath proper, close to the L16 road leading west at a spot where the Üßbach stream forms a small loop towards the north.

him and spoke: "You murderer of souls! If you had recited the Lord's Prayer three times, I would have been released, but now I must wander for a long, long time until the hour comes again in which I can be released. Now the acorn falls from the tree, and when that acorn has become a tree, a cradle will be made from boards made out of that tree. Only then it will be possible that a human, who has lain within that cradle as a child, will be able to release me!"

At dusk, an irrlicht joined a man who had been unable to finish his urgent work during the day. Thanks to the illumination it provided, he was able to continue and complete his labors. When he was done, the man said with emotional eyes: "May Jesus thank you for this!" Whereupon the irrlicht responded: "I've waited for these words for many years with great longing. Now I am a child of the eternal life, and you shall become so one day as well."[Sch56, p. 39f]

Translation notes: The original title of this tale was "Treulichter oder Irrlichter". We've covered the meaning of irrlicht in the notes for the tale "The Irrlicht of Ihlow" (p. 42). The "Treu" in "Treulicht could be translated as "faithful", but also as "loyal" or "true". Conceivably, they got their name by "faithfully" accompanying wanderers.

"Arme Seelen" — which I translated as "poor souls" here, although "pitiful souls" would also be appropriate — are considered to be souls who are denied entry to Heaven due to past sins, yet who were not depraved enough to be sent to Hell. They continue to linger on Earth as ghosts, until someone helps them and releases them by fulfilling the right conditions.

Commentary: In quite a few tales, the terms of the purgatory for such "poor souls" can be extremely harsh — the first Treulicht apparently can only be released by someone who fulfills some highly specific conditions, and if that person screws it up, it will be many decades or even centuries until the next candidate gets a chance. I do wonder how these ghosts learn of these candidates — does an angel inform them of who is suitable, or do they have to linger around one specific tree until it is finally cut so that they can check if a cradle is made of it (and stalk the child that lies in it until the child get the opportunity to fulfill its destiny)? That would make the punishment even more horrifying.

On the other hand, helping a "poor soul" — beyond being a laudable act on general principles — can yield an extraordinary reward. If the second ghost can be believed, they implied that the man who helped it earned entrance to Paradise on that single act alone — irrespective of any other sins they might have committed in life.

78. The Ghostly Light

1. A carter had the misfortune that a part of his wagon broke in the dark of night. He was unable to fix the damage even with the aid of the assistant who had accompanied him — namely, to restore the broken wheel, especially since his own lantern had also been lost. As it happened, he was currently at a spot of which he knew that it was supposedly haunted by a ghostly light. Thus, he spoke in his desperation: "Oh, I wished that the light that wanders around these parts came here and shone for me!"

As soon as he had said so, the light was next to him. Now he put the broken wagon back into its proper order with the aid of his assistant, tied the wheel together as well as he was able, and repaired everything else that needed fixing. All the while, the light faithfully gave him light. Then, it accompanied him along the most difficult parts of the route. Once he no longer needed it, he spoke to it: "I have pleaded that you might come and shine for me, and you fulfilled my wish. Now, by the grace of God, go to the place of rest where you belong!"

Afterwards, he heard a voice which was jubilant in joy, thanked him profusely, and spoke that he had granted it salvation with these words. It had waited for this in vain for two thousand years, for however often it had sought to approach people in confidence, they had always shyly fled from it. And none had spoken the words that would have saved it until the carter had done so.

2. A baker in Gelliehausen had ground flour in Benniehausen.[5] When he traveled back late in the evening, he saw a light on the path in front of him. He would have liked to walk besides the light, and thus called out to the light that they should wait. At the same time, he walked faster, but couldn't catch up to them. By continuing to follow them in this way, he eventually became so tired that he laid down next to a haystack. He remained lying there until the next morning, and saw that he was right in front of Gelliehausen.

3. A man from Sebexen[6] had gone to a neighboring village, and was going back home in the hours of darkness. When he reached the so-called Küler[7] (a forest belonging to Sebexen), he saw a light moving around in the shrubbery. He thought that his wife had ventured out with a lamp in order to meet him halfway, and called out: "Come here, and light the way for me!" Suddenly, the thing jumped on his back, and, with force, steered him away from the right path to the depression of the Helgenholtgrund.[8] When he finally got close to the village to

[5] Both Gelliehausen and Benniehausen are now part of the Gleichen municipality. Benniehausen used to have three watermills along the "Mühlenstraße" ("Mills' Road") until the early 19th century, one of which dated back to at least the 14th century. Only one mill building, the "Hessenmühle" ("Hessians' Mill") remains.[Mue]

[6] Sebexen is now part of the Kalefeld municipality.

[7] OpenStreetMap shows a forested hill named the "Kühler" to the northeast of Sebexen. My best guess is that he came from the direction of Ellierode, a village now part of Bad Gandersheim.

[8] I was unable to identify this location. However, "-grund" implies the

the so-called "Krüzhôligen Weg" (a depressed road where two paths crossed), it left him. Now he tried to grab it, but his hands only closed on moss. He kept this moss as a keepsake for a long time.

4. A fisher from Wulften had frequently fished in the territories of Lindau and Hattorf.[9] For this reason, he must now haunt the region. He appears at the boundary of the Rotenberg forest,[10] walks towards the village green, and then moves up alongside the river Oder[11] until he reaches the village boundary. He carries a lantern in his hand, and wears a red frock. This frock has only one coattail, as the other one was once ripped off by a fisher from Lindau when he had fished on that man's territory. People thus call the ghost "Einschooß",[12] and he is also given the mocking nickname "Fränzchen".[13]

When he stood in front of his home, the field warden from Wulften once saw the ghost moving downriver along the Oder[14] in the form of a light. He shouted "Fränzchen!" in order to mock him. Soon, the ghost got in front of his door, whereupon

floor of a valley, and the most logical place would be the valley of a small stream labeled "Wiershäuser Bach" on Google Maps, which flows downhill towards Sebexen from the east. Presumably, he followed the flow of this stream towards his home.

[9] The closest villages to the west and east of Wulften. Lindau has now been incorporated into the Katlenburg-Lindau municipality.

[10] According to OpenStreetMaps, the Rotenberg is a forested hill to the south of Hattorf and the southeast of Wulften.

[11] Not the river Oder that flows along the Polish-German border, but a much smaller river of the same name within the Harz mountain region.

[12] Roughly, "One-Tail", with "Schooß" being the German term for "Coattail".

[13] My best guess here is that this derives from "Franzen", a derogatory nickname for Frenchmen — since the Napoleonic Wars were in living memory, this would have been considered a major insult. The nickname might be a reference to the coattails of French uniforms. The "-chen" in "Fränzchen" is a diminutive, likely referring to his single coattail — "half a dressed-up French soldier", perhaps. If this interpretation is correct, it's no wonder the ghost got so mad.

[14] Interestingly, this would be in the opposite direction of his usual route.

the field warden quickly fled inside his chamber. The ghost was unable to follow him there, but he was aware that the apparition moved in front of the window and noticed how his light illuminated the whole room.

Soon after, the field warden accompanied a traveler to Bilshausen, and returned home at night between eleven and twelve o'clock. Then, suddenly, Einschooß approached him and threw him into a swamp in order to avenge himself. The warden only escaped from him with great difficulty.[SM54, p. 213f]

Commentary: The first fragment is a salvation narrative in line with the others, although, unusually, the spirit tells us just how long it has waited for salvation — which implies that it has lingered on since pre-Christian times. Would it even have been *possible* to release this spirit by invoking one of the pagan gods of old?

The second tale presents the Irrlicht as a haunt that leads wanderers astray — or, at least, bringing them to the brink of exhaustion by driving them onwards. While the distance between the two villages is a mere 1.8 km, we should keep in mind that the baker was presumably carrying a heavy sack of flour (or perhaps transporting it in a wheelbarrow, although the story doesn't mention any details).

The third tale presents the spirit as an outright malevolent entity, exhibiting the same behavior as the ghost from "A Dead Man Searches for his Gown" (p. 124), but with less provocation. The fourth is a more conventional ghost tale — of a person who has to remain on Earth due to some past sins (in this case, poaching) and now follows a regular nightly routine. But he can still be roused out of this routine when angered! It is noteworthy that, while he is ultimately not constrained by the village boundary, the door to the field warden's house still represents a threshold the ghost cannot pass.

Thus, these four short tales show how the same phenomenon (the irrlicht) can be interpreted in different ways depending on the intentions of the storyteller — they were part of a narrative toolkit, not a categorizable real world phenomenon.

79. The Saved Fiery Man

1. Once, a farmer drove through a forest at night. At that occasion, a fiery man spoke to him and asked him to let him sit on the cart as well. The farmer permitted this, and thus the glowing ghost rode with him for some time. When he climbed down, the farmer said to him: "May God thank you for illuminating the path for me!", whereupon the ghost replied: "May God thank you for releasing me!", and vanished. For the "May God thank you!" released him.

(From Buchers)[15]

2. Once, a man drove back home late at night, and, to his terror, saw how a fiery man squatted down on the wagon, facing backwards. Then the carter started to fervently pray, but the fiery entity nevertheless moved closer and closer to him. The carter prayed even more fervently, but the spark-spraying ghost still came closer. Finally, full of fear when the apparition was almost touching him, he recited the Lord's Prayer in utmost zeal. After this, the fiery man spoke: "The Lord's Prayer is worth more than all the others combined, for it has released me!" With these words, he vanished.

(From St. Veit an der Gölsen)[Lee92, p. 362f]

---

[15]Modern-day Pohoří na Šumavě, in the Czech Republic just across the border from Austria.

Commentary: The farmer in the first fragment seems rather unconcerned about the fiery apparition climbing on his cart, and is amiable enough to gracefully thank the ghost for providing his services as a light source. In contrast, the frightened carter in the second tale is practically bullied by the ghost until he recites the words that the ghost wants to hear. The end result is the same — the ghost is released regardless of the intention of the living person who helped them, without the latter even receiving a hint in advance of what would help the ghost.

80. The Sneezing Maiden

There used to be three poplar trees on a meadow between Heidingsfeld[16] and Würzburg. Once, two vintners who were returning home during a night of the full moon saw a beautiful maiden with a white veil sitting there. When they walked past her at a close distance, they heard her sneezing three times. And, as it is custom in Franconia, both of them said: "God bless you!"[17] three times. The maiden replied: "You have released me!" From this hour onwards, nobody has seen the maiden with the white veil again.[Ano77, p. 362f]

Commentary: If you can't be useful to the living so that they bestow their blessings upon you, then — as seen in the previous tale — tricking them works just as well. Which has interesting theological implications — it seems that the conditions of a ghost's release are not dependent on the intentions of the one fulfilling them. They are, effectively, "magic

[16] Heidingsfeld is now a district of Würzburg, south of the river Main and the old town of Würzburg itself.

[17] The German phrase was "Helf Gott!", which translates as "May God help you!". This is no longer in common use, having been replaced by "Gesundheit!"

words" that break the ghosts' binding, and any actual good deeds involved only matter insofar they get the living person to utter them.

Frequently, ghosts were quite willing to approach the living in their quest for salvation — although they would rarely state outright what they needed.

81. The Cowherdess' Buttermilk

The herders of the Zamserloch alp[18] once had to leave a cow behind during the fall cattle drive down to the valley because she limped. The owner, a man named Schueler, went up to the grazing grounds on the very same day in order to fetch his cow, but, since it was already late in the evening, he felt compelled to rest in the alpine hut and wait until the early morning. After Schueler had taken a small evening meal, he climbed on the bed[19] and laid down. Around midnight, a woman stepped out from the cellar, and started to process the milk like it was usually done in the alps. She carried the milk containers out of the cellar, skimmed the cream, and put the leftover milk into the cauldron for the cheese production while she poured the cream into the stirring kettle. After she had added some hot water to the cream, she shook the butter keg with great effort until the butter finally separated. Once this this had occurred, she took the butter from the keg, while she let the milk run into a bucket beneath the keg. Then she invited the man up high on his bed to drink some buttermilk. Undaunted, he climbed down from his bedding and drank from the milk. Immediately,

[18] As far as I can tell, this most likely refers to the high meadows in the Lochtal valley stretching towards the northwest of Zams.

[19] From which we conclude that the bed was elevated in some way, similar to the alpine hut in "The Herdess Makes Fried Pudding" (p. 107).

the herdess stood before him in a snow-white form, thanked him profusely, and told him that she had now been released from her suffering thanks to him. Once, when she had been a herdess on this alp, she had denied a beggar who had asked her for a ladle full of buttermilk. For this reason, she had been forced to haunt this place until Schueler had released her by drinking the milk that had been offered to him. Early in the morning, Schueler went back home with his cow, and was very happy that he had released a poor soul.[Hau94, p. 54f]

Translation note: The ghost is called a "Sennerin", the female form of "Senner" — the herders of the high alpine meadows who would stay up in the mountains with their cattle during the warmer seasons. While this was largely a male profession, this could vary a lot by time and region — there were areas where this was considered a women's job. Elsewhere, the presence of a woman was considered unlucky — and the all-male herders' communities led to legends such as those of the "Sennentuntschi", a sex doll made out of straw that becomes alive and avenges herself on the men who abused her.

Commentary: Refusing a beggar something to drink might seem like a minor sin, but any beggar who ended up in this remote location probably could not expect any other hospitality for many kilometers around — and, depending on the weather and season, hospitality could be considered a matter of life and death. Fortunately, the condition for releasing the ghost was fairly simple (when compared to those of other ghostly hauntings) — although I do wonder why none of the herders who had lived in this hut all summer had helped her.

82. The Little Man at the Barns at Stargard

(By F. C. W. Jacoby at Neubrandenburg.)

Once, when a night guard in Stargard[20] made his rounds and came into the vicinity of the barns of Neubrandenburg,[21] he heard fearful crying from the direction of a nearby wall. He considered it to be his duty to investigate, and he thus saw a little man twist back and forth on the wall who constantly cried: "Help me! Help me!"

He asked: "What am I supposed to help you with?" But the little man gave no answer.

The night guard asked "So tell me, in which way can I help you?" repeatedly, but the little man gave no answer other than his cry for help, and the guard finally turned away from him.

But, in subsequent nights, the little man repeated his cry for help more and more fearfully, and thus the night guard finally said: "I can't help you, and thus may God the Father, the Son, and the Holy Spirit help you!"

As soon as the little man heard this, he thanked the guardsman and then jubilantly ascended to Heaven before his eyes.[Nie59, p. 231]

Commentary: Once more, the ghost is bad at communicating the assistance he needs to end his tormented state. But, as usual, an earnest invocation of God helps. One

[20]This refers to the small town in Mecklenburg-Vorpommern which was renamed Burg Stargard in 1929.

[21]Neubrandenburg lies approximately 8 km to the north of Burg Stargard. Presumably, the barns mentioned here were either next to the road or the city gate leading towards Neubrandenburg, or perhaps owned by people from Neubrandenburg.

might wonder how much the "little man" was capable of clear thought about his situation while in his state of turmoil — was this really the best plan he could come up with?

83. A Ghost does a Haircut

In an inn along the country road, there was a chamber in which nobody wanted to stay overnight, as everyone who rested there had been found dead the following morning. One evening, a noble gentleman arrived at the inn and wanted to stay for the night. But every room was occupied other than this particular one. The innkeeper told him that this room was haunted in some manner; but the guest only laughed and told the innkeeper that he should prepare a bed for him.

This was done. The stranger left the light burning and fell asleep. Suddenly, the door opened, he woke up, and saw how a fat, strong man entered the room who was dressed in a short jacket and was wearing a black velvet cap on his head. He had a shaving kit in a bag under his arm and opened it, taking the shaving razor and running it alongside a leather strip. Every time when he reached the end of the strip, he looked at the stranger and waved at him, indicating that he should allow himself to be shaved. The guest regained his countenance and silently sat down on a chair in front of the fat man. The man silently whipped up foam, covered the guest's face with soap, and shaved him in an orderly manner. Once he was done, he thanked him and said that he was now released from his turmoil. He had once been the innkeeper in this house, and, out of greed, cut the throat of a guest in this very room. He had been doomed to eternally wander[22] until someone was willing to let himself be shaved by him. No one had agreed to this, and thus he had killed them all. Now he had found peace. Then the light went out and the ghost had vanished. The stranger,

[22] I read this as a metaphor for his state of existence as a ghost, as he seemed to have haunted the same inn that he had lived in.

however, appeared the next morning hale and hearthy to the astonishment of everyone.

From Pogge in Pölitz[Bar79, p. 220f][23]

Commentary: Like in "The Ghosts' Meal" (p. 23), the protagonist finds himself in an inn filled to capacity, and is warned that the sole remaining room is haunted — but, like the prince in the earlier tale, he dismisses those warnings. The condition for ending the ghost's personal purgatory seems strange — because he once cut someone's throat, he now needs someone to allow him to put a razor to their throats *without* cutting them? Presumably, haircuts were among the services the innkeeper offered to his guests at the time — usually without any fatal incidents.

I also find it interesting that murdering all those other guests as a ghost did not seem to affect the purgatory directly. Did the ghost only receive one judgment — the one that condemned him to existence as a ghost — and thus the later sins did not matter? Or would he be judged anew, once his first term of punishment was over?

84. The Salvation of a Restless Ghost between Wredenhagen and Hinrichshof near Röbel

In earlier times, there were no mills in Wredenhagen,[24] and the people there had to carry their grain to the nearby windmill in Hinrichshof.[25] This mill stood on the small hill which lies next

[23] "Pölitz" most likely refers to a village now part of the Laage municipality.

[24] Wredenhagen is now part of the Eldetal municipality, to the north of the Mönchssee lake.

[25] Hinrichshof is a hamlet within the Eldetal municipality, to the east of the Mönchssee lake. It is about 4 km away from Wredenhagen — not

to Hinrichshof. However, this windmill is long gone, and only minor remains indicate the position where it once stood. On the other hand, there are currently two windmills at Wredenhagen.

But, at a time when the inhabitants of Wredenhagen still had to bring their grain to the mill of Hinrichshof, it occurred that a day laborer's wife from the former village had to carry a sack of rye to that mill during the twilight hours of the evening so that it could be ground there. Since the woman had neither bread nor flour left in her house, she had to bake bread the next morning out of necessity, and thus immediately carry her grain back home after it had been turned into flour. But the miller was already grinding a lot of flour, and thus the woman had to wait for quite a long time until it was her turn to have her grain ground.

Thus, it was very late when the laborer's wife was finally able to wander back home with her sack of flour on her back. She hadn't yet gotten far when, suddenly, a man approached her from behind. The good woman was quite frightened, for the man didn't speak a word. Furthermore, it was around midnight, and the moon illuminated the scene so hauntingly that she was rather creeped out. Once she had reached the paddock (through which the footpath to Wredenhagen she had picked led), the strange man approached, and offered her to take her load and carry it for some time, as he saw that she was struggling under the weight.

The woman initially didn't want this, staying that she could not ask this of someone else and so forth, but the stranger talked to her in such a friendly and welcoming manner that she was finally willing to accept his offer and now let him carry the sack with the flour.

When they had almost reached the village of Wredenhagen,

too far, but still rather inconvenient if you have to transport heavy sacks of grain and flour.

the cockerel suddenly started to crow. At the first crowing of the cockerel, the strange man said: "You have no power over me yet."[26] He uttered the same after the cockerel had crowed for the second time. But when he heard it for a third time, he said: "Now I must leave. But what will you give me in exchange for carrying the flour for such a long distance?"

"Oh", replied the woman, "what could I possibly give you? I am a poor woman, and have nothing."

"But you certainly give me something!" replied the stranger.

"Nothing more," said the woman, "than my best thanks, and a thousandfold God's reward!"

"God be praised and thanked! I have wandered this world for many years in vain, but now I am released and can finally sleep in peace!" the ghost — for the stranger was such — cried out in joy, and vanished.[Nie60, p. 169ff]

Commentary: Now, I am sure that "being followed home late at night by a stranger" is something no woman wants to experience, and it was made worse by the fact that her poverty meant that she was extremely reluctant to drop her flour and flee. The stranger offering to carry the flour might have been a robber as well, which makes it very understandable that she was reluctant to hand it over. And when he suddenly asked for a "reward" at the end, and insisted that there was something she could give him despite her poverty, it must have been even more alarming.

Everything did turn out well in the end — but really, it says something when the stranger revealing himself as a ghost

[26] The exact German phrase (in dialect and high German) was: "Du deist mie noch nickts!"/"Du thust mir noch nichts!", which could also be translated as "You can't do anything to me yet."

was probably the *least* frightening turn of events for the poor woman in this story.

At other times, the living do know how to help the ghosts — usually, by asking them directly.

85. The Ghost and the Groom

(By the teacher Kaese from Gebhardshagen)

On an estate near Boffzen, the horses always became agitated at a certain time of the night. Furthermore, a spirit frequently appeared to the groom when he wanted to cut fodder for the horses. The groom became afraid from this, and finally asked the pastor what he should do. The pastor told him that he shouldn't be timid under any circumstances. If the spirit were to reappear, he should bravely exclaim: "All good spirits praise the Lord God!" If the spirit replied: "Me too!", then he should ask them after their desires. But if the spirit answered: "Not me!", then he should leave them be and no longer pay them any heed.

The groom resolved to do this, and stand up boldly to the ghost. During the next night, in the hour of the ghosts, he suddenly saw a large, white woman rise up. Then he dauntlessly shouted: "All good spirits praise the Lord God!"[27] The figure replied: "Me too!" Then the groom asked her what she wished of him. She said in reply that she once had pledged a certain amount of flour, milk, and salt to poor people. But she had not given that to them, and thus she could not find rest until the promised goods were given to the paupers. And then she asked

[27] See the footnotes of the tale "Visit of the Hanged Man" (p. 145) for more on this invocation.

the groom if he would take pity on her and fulfill her pledge. The groom promised to honor this. But now she requested that he should shake her hand on this. However, the groom had been warned by the preacher not to give his hand to the spirit under any circumstances. Thus, he quickly grabbed the sharpening stick[28] and held it towards her. The ghost thus grabbed the stick at a spot close to his hand, and the stick was gone as far as she had taken hold of it.

The next day, the groom fulfilled his promise. The following night, the ghost slowly rose up in front of him, made a content and grateful nod, and vanished. She has not reappeared since that day.[Vog85, p. 122f]

Commentary: As we shall see in the next chapter, the groom must first *discern* if the spirit is malevolent or not. Once it is established that she is not intentionally seeking to do harm, he is ready to help her — but, nevertheless, her touch represents danger of which she is apparently unaware. It is not quite clear what happened to the sharpening stick in this tale — if it broke off or partially vanished somehow — but as we have seen in previous tales, such objects are often burned away to a crisp.

Once the unfinished business is fulfilled, the ghost reappears once more for the traditional final thanks to her benefactor.

[28]The German term used here was "Streke", which is described in a footnote as "the device for sharpening the scythe and the miter box". Sadly, I was unable to find a more comprehensive description — "sharpening stick" represents my best guess.

86. Ghosts Reaching Salvation

1. A farmer died. This farmer had also been a sleepwalker. After his death, whenever the others were sitting at the table, he appeared, sat behind the oven, and smoked.[29] Since this was rather uncomfortable for the people in the house, they asked him what he wanted one day. In reply, he said that the money, which had vanished in the house during his life, and which everyone had believed to be stolen, had in fact been taken by him while he was sleepwalking. In this state, he had put it into the attic near the chimney. They ought to take it from there and give it to the poor, and then he would have peace. After this was done, the dead man did not reappear again.

2. Once, a sacristan wanted to transport some hay from the fields. Unfortunately, the rope which was needed to tie the beam that affixed the hay to the wagon[30] was torn apart. As he had no other rope available, he fetched a rope from the church tower. However, he forgot to put it back to its proper place afterwards. Soon after, he died. A few days later, his daughter went into the tower in order to ring the bells. Suddenly, her father stood right in front of her as if he was alive. She asked the dead man what he wanted. He replied that she should bring the rope that was still lying in their house back to the tower. Furthermore, she should shake his hand on the promise that she was really going to do this, and if she promised that, he would not come back. The girl quickly wrapped her apron around her hand, and held it towards him in this manner. When he reached for her hand, the ghost grabbed all the way through the apron.[31]

3. A man in Wulften was very lazy. Whenever he had collected

[29] It is unclear if he smoked a pipe or something similar, or if his entire ghostly form emitted smoke.

[30] See the notes of the tale "Alfhausen and the Alkenkrug Pub" (p. 116) for an explanation of this "Bindelbaum".

[31] The tale does not elaborate if the ghost's hands simply moved through the apron as if it wasn't there, or if the apron disintegrated under his touch.

stones from his fields, he walked with them over the fields of his neighbors until he reached the gates of a meadow so that he could scatter them there. And, in order to make the task easier, he always let a few stones drop on the fields of other people. After he had died, he visited his wife one evening during dusk, and asked her to give him ten sacks. The woman asked him what he intended to do with them. He replied that he would tell her once he returned, and received the sacks. He returned at one o'clock in the night and returned the sacks, and told her that he had gathered the stones from the field which he had willfully dropped them on them while he was alive. He also asked her to pay the owners of these fields a certain amount of money as compensation, pressuring her to promise this and shake his hand on that promise. She agreed to this and gave him her hand. The next morning, the hand she had given him was completely burnt and dropped off. Furthermore, the sacks no longer had a bottom, since the dead man had carried so many stones in them.

4. One noon, a school teacher's maid went to ring the prayer bell. On the way, she saw the figure of a girl sit on a grave. After the same apparition showed up twice more, the maid gathered her courage and asked the ghost what her desire was. The apparition then told her that she had had a child out of wedlock and then killed it. But, because she had died without doing penance for her sin and without having partaken in the rite of Eucharist, she was now unable to find rest in the grave until someone had participated in her stead.[32] The maid promised her to take part in the Eucharist in her place. Then, as the ghost demanded a handshake on that promise, she held out her hand, but she had wrapped her apron around it out of caution. As soon as she had done so, the apron became black and burnt. After the maid had fulfilled her promise and told this to the ghost, the ghost thanked her profusely and vanished before her eyes.

[32]Compare with the tale "The Bride on the Lilienstein" (p. 110) for another example of using the Eurarist in order to help a ghost.

5. A noblewoman was so miserly and hard-hearted that she didn't give any alms to the poor. This went so far that, whenever the poor asked for such, she didn't even give them any skimmed milk, but instead immediately poured the milk into the pig trough. Her maid, on the other hand, was very compassionate, and thus frequently poured such milk into the gutter hole,[33] from which the poor secretly fetched it. For this, she received many "God's rewards".[34] The noblewoman died, but she appeared every day after her death in the house by sitting on the pig trough. The maid, whom she seemed to recognize,[35] finally asked her why she had appeared again. The woman answered that she could not attain the peace of the afterlife, but if the maid were to give her a single of her "God's rewards", then she would be able to reach salvation. The maid answered that she would be glad to give her all her "God's rewards", for she hoped to attain new ones. Thereupon the woman parted from the maid with the most heartful thanks, and said that she would now stay away — for now she would find salvation.

6. The knight Hans von Lichtenstein[36] stood out from many other knights due to his great strength and agility. Due to this, he instilled fear in all inhabitants of the region. But he only used his great power for unrighteous deeds, and he did not want to know anything of faith and godliness. After he had died and been buried, he appeared to his loyal steward on a certain large stretch of land one noon between eleven and twelve o'clock. He was riding on a red horse, and was wearing fiery clothes. "Tell

[33] A literal translation of the term "Gossenloch" in the original German text. This is not a particularly common German word, but the German Dictionary of the Brothers Grimm mentions a "Goszstein",[Deu] which represents a hollow stone in the kitchen (frequently containing a pipe) through which the dirty water can be transported outside into the gutter.

[34] Presumably, the recipients of the milk said something on the lines of: "May God reward you!"

[35] It's not grammatically clear from the German text if the maid recognized the ghost, or vice versa.

[36] This name derives from Castle Lichtenstein to the east of Osterode, in the Harz region — not the Franconian von Lichtenstein lineage.

my wife", said the ghost, "that she should give back the lowest piece of this stretch of land to the neighbor. I once gained this land thanks to a false oath, and thus cannot attain eternal peace, but must remain in Hell forever." The steward promised to faithfully convey his wishes, and went away with the words: "Tomorrow noon I shall report back to you."

After he told the Lady of Lichtenstein of the strange apparition and relayed the order of his deceased master, she replied: "If he has done injustice in his life, then he may suffer for it. I shall not part with any land." The next noon, the steward went to the same spot in anticipation. During the eleventh hour, his master appeared to him in the same clothes, and listened to his wife's message with dread. "Well then," he said, "if my wife has no pity for me, then fetch a pick and a trough tomorrow noon, and bring them here to me. However, you can accompany me this one time, and witness how I fare under my current circumstances." Then he led the steward to a cave entrance in the Lichtensteiner Holz forest,[37] and asked the steward to follow him. When the knight of Lichtenstein had reached his abode, he sat down on a red bed. The room was decorated with red chairs and other red furniture. Soon, red servants appeared, brought red slippers, poured red wine into glasses, and brought red dishes to the table.

After the steward had witnessed all this, he left in order to fulfill his appointed task. The following noon, he went to the usual spot with the requested tools in order to hand them to his lord. The latter soon appeared, and said: "Sit down and stay there until I am finished." The steward did so. Now, the lord started to work with great effort in order to bring the soil, which he had once sworn was his own, to the other lot of land. When the bell struck twelve, the noble returned with the tools, handed them back, gave his thanks, and said: "It was good

[37] The forest surrounding the hill Castle Lichtenstein was built on, located to the northeast of Dorste. It features both a castle ruin and an elongated cave that was rediscovered in 1971 and served as a burial ground for 40 people during the Bronze Age.

that the pick had a long iron top, for else I would not have been able to finish, and then would have to suffer eternal torment." Startled, the loyal servant said: "Tell me, lord, why you consider yourself unfortunate, for you have all those comforts and can ride on a red horse." "Oh", replied the nobleman, "it is precisely this, what is tormenting me. Everything I drink is fire. Everything I eat is fire. Everything I ride on is fire. And everything I breathe is fire. It is altogether terrible, life in Hell. Now that I have given back the land, I have received forgiveness and can get into Heaven. Farewell!" — With these words, he vanished.

Even today, the land can still be seen which the nobleman had transported to the other location. But the spot to which he led the steward to demonstrate his torments is still called "Hölle" ("Hell").[SM54, p. 226ff]

Commentary: Several themes weave through these short tales:

The touch of ghosts burns. As in previous tales, the touch of ghosts is dangerous to others

The ghosts need to address their past sins to move on. Sometimes these sins were acts of deliberate greed or malice, while at other times they were due to carelessness or even out of their control (such as the sleepwalker in the first tale).

The ghosts need a living agent. They are incapable of resolving the situation on their own, and it is only with the help of a living person that their final requests can be completed. Even the knight, who moves the soil he had appropriated while alive under his own power, still needs the tools provided by his former steward to actually complete the task.

87. God's Reward

There once was a woman near Osterwieck who was very miserly. She had a maid who was very compassionate. That maid gave the poor local women much of the wealth of her mistress, and handed them money through the gutter hole.[38] For this, she received all those thanks of "May God reward you!" which ought to have been directed at the woman owning the wealth.

Thus, three days after her death, the miserly woman sat on her old chair behind the oven where she always used to sit, went into the pantry, into the cellar, to the animals in the stable, and rattled mightily with the crockery. Her son finally sent for a few Jesuits who had to ask her for her desires. Then she said that she wanted nothing more than the God's rewards that the maid had received for what she had handed through the gutter hole. The girl was questioned and answered: She should receive them all in God's name. The woman then said that she should shake her hand on this. The Jesuits did not permit this, and instead she had to hold a broomstick towards her. And as she did so, the broomstick splintered into a thousand pieces.

The woman then said: She now could reach grace, if her son butchered a pig, baked cakes from three bushels[39] of wheat flour, and then distributed everything to the poor. This was done, and after that she was transported to the Kibitzbruch swamp[40] in a coach with four horses. She was not seen again.[Prö96, p. 62]

---

[38] See the notes in the previous tale about gutter holes.

[39] "Scheffel" in the original German text. Since many market towns had their own standards for this (and other) unit of measurement, I am not sure which Scheffel standard would have been applied to Osterwieck during the time this story takes place

[40] "Kibitzbruch" could be translated as "lapwing swamp", though considering how many swamps were drained in Germany over the centuries, the name might have outlived the actual swamp.

Translation note: The German text uses the phrase "Gotteslohn" ("God's reward") as both the title of the story and as a shorthand for the thanks the poor give to the maid. The implication is that the thanks the poor give to their benefactor translate into favor in the eyes of God.

Commentary: This is a longer version of one of the fragments from the previous tale. One of the differences is that the maid handed out money to the poor through the gutter hole instead of pouring out milk through it, which at least strikes me as a more hygienic approach.

Whether or not handing out stolen money to the poor can translate into grace in the eyes of God, the ghost of the woman certainly seemed to think so — as she believed that "transferring" this grace from the maid to her would help her escape purgatory. This transferral might not have been a mere metaphor, either — in his "Ghosts in the Middle Ages", Jean-Claude Schmitt tells of an otherwise virtuous monk who suffers in purgatory because he agreed to share his friend's sins.[Sch98, p. 67] If sins can be transferred in the accounting of the afterlife, then why not the reward for good deeds as well?

It is hard to know whether she knew that her touch was dangerous when she requested that the maid shake hands with her, but it certainly parallels similar narratives.

Even though everything else was done as per the ghost's requests, someone (presumably the Jesuit exorcists) didn't trust the situation and sent her off to a remote, uninhabited location — standard practice for exorcism in German folklore, as shall see in the next chapter. How long she had to linger there before moving on to the afterlife is unclear.

88. The Farmer Who Had Moved The Boundary Stones

(From the teacher Ernst in Braunschweig)

Once, a farmer in Lichtenberg[41] died who had moved boundary stones and, in this manner, increased the size of his own land. As a punishment, he then had to carry the boundary stones around in his arms while wandering around on the field at night. People who passed by late in the evening heard him moan and call out: "Where am I going to put them?" One person who heard this gathered his courage and shouted at him: "You old scoundrel, put them where you got them from!" Since then, the haunting had ceased.[Vog85, p. 112]

Commentary: As the conditions for releasing a ghost from their turmoil can sometimes be highly specific and only be attempted once every few generations,[42] "boundary marker ghosts" tend to be among the lucky ones, as many tales such as this one resolve the situation by telling the ghost to put the stones back from where they came from — without even having to specify where precisely this spot was.

89. The Unrighteous Plowman

(From the teacher Hanne in Opperhausen)

In the past, a man with a glowing plow was plowing every night between 11 and 12 o'clock on a swampy meadow between Hunzen and Halle.[43] He was condemned to this fate because

[41] This most likely refers to the district of modern-day Salzgitter.

[42] See the tale "Faithful Lights or Errant Lights" (p. 162) for a particularly extreme example.

[43] This refers to Halle (Holzminden), a municipality in Lower Saxony — not the more well-known city in Saxony-Anhalt. Hunzen is a village which is now part of that municipality.

he once cut away a piece of his neighbor's land with his plow. He had to labor until the entire land, which he had attained unjustly, was returned to its proper owner. However, in each hour he was only able to move a single grain of sand. Many years ago, another man talked with him and offered to plow for him. He did as offered, but once he had finished, the plow and the harness[44] vanished, and the ghost has not returned since then. For the last of the stolen land had been returned to the neighbor thanks to this effort, and thus the unrighteous plowman finally found peace in the grave.[Vog85, p. 118f]

Translation note: The ghostly plowman is described as "falsch" in the text and the title. A literal translation of this would be "false", or "wrong", but in this context I settled for "unrighteous", in the sense of "bearing false witness".

Commentary: This ghost might have reached salvation on his own — eventually. But, as with many other salvation stories, the process is greatly accelerated by the assistance of one of the living.

Finally, at times people might not even realize that they have encountered ghosts — and helped them — until after the fact.

[44]It is unknown if the ghost had ghostly draft animals, or if he pulled the plow himself.

90. The Ghostly Wedding in the Deserted Village of Scortowe

Once, there was an ancient village of the Wends[45] in the Schortental valley near Eisenberg,[46] but this was a long, long time ago. This village was named "Scortowe". Many years ago, this village was abandoned and now nothing of it is visible any more. However, in earlier times it was frequently seen during certain blessed nights[47] and during the right hour — in the middle of the Schortental valley, on a green, quiet forest meadow. But now no one can behold it any more, for it was released from the heavy curse which made it visible in holy nights in every tenth leap year.

Quite a few years ago, there was an honest, poor girl in Eisenberg who had arrived with Protestants emigrating from Salzburg[48] and found a place to stay with compassionate locals. One evening, when it was already turning dark, she was sent out

[45] Short for the Wendish people, West Slavic groups that were gradually pushed back or conquered by the invading Germans. The Sorbian people living in the German-Polish border areas are some of their modern-day descendants.

[46] There is a "Schortental" road in the northeast of Eisenberg which leads to a sports facility on a hill, so this is presumably the general area.

[47] It becomes clear later in the story that "blessed nights" meant the times when the village could be released from its curse.

[48] There were strong Protestant sympathies in the city of Salzburg soon after Martin Luther proclaimed his Ninety-five Theses. in 1517. This was rather awkward for its rulers, since the city of Salzburg was the seat of the Prince-Archbishopric of Salzburg, an ecclesiastical principality of the Holy Roman Empire. Thus, all Protestants were ordered to leave the city by the year 1590 — except for minors below the age of 15, which had to be left behind and were assigned to Catholic families. However, as is explained later, this story took place after the Thirty Years' War — which means that she was more likely part of the 20,000 Salzburg Protestants who were banished from Salzburg in 1731. This time, they had to leave children below the age of 12 behind, which gives us a minimum age for our protagonist.

in order to fetch some feed[49] for the livestock from the Schortental valley. As she was unafraid, she fearlessly proceeded through the rustling woods that were quiet in the evening, until she safely arrived in the meadow in the Schortental where she usually gathered the requested feed. But, instead of the meadow, she beheld an old village before her, which was unknown to her and whose name she did not know. Light shimmered out of its small, old-fashioned houses. Initially she was startled and frightened, but soon she gathered her courage and knocked carefully on the windows of the first, brightly lit house. She asked for directions as well as where she was, and, as she was rather hungry and thirsty, pleaded for a piece of bread and a bit of water to drink. An old man with a white beard and strange garb opened the window, and told the girl to enter. Nervously, she followed the invitation and entered the low chamber in which a merry group seemed to be celebrating a wedding. Demurely, she greeted them, and repeated her request. Upon hearing this, the old man who had invited her bade her to sit down and passed food and drink in strangely-formed bowls and cups to her. As far as she could see, everything in the entire chamber seemed to be like it was from an old, long-ago time: Bowls and cutlery, tables and chairs, everything was fantastically strange and unfamiliar. All the guests wore strange garb out of a long-lost time, with old-fashioned and baggy suits and dresses. The bride was costumed like a nun with a long, flowing veil and severe garb right out of a monastery. The groom, on the other hand, was wearing a luxurious tunic embroidered with gold and silver in the manner of a knight, a long, glittering rapier at his side, as well as a heavy, golden honor chain[50] on his chest.

The old man sympathetically questioned the girl about her situation and circumstances, and, as soon as he had been con-

[49]It is unclear what kind of feed she was supposed to fetch, though grass seems most likely.

[50]As far as I can tell, an "Ehrenkette" ("honor chain") was a chain — often with special insignia — that people wore as a status symbol to signify their importance. The best equivalent modern English-language term is probably "bling".

vinced of her poverty and her good, honest heart, he spoke with the groom for a long time in a strange, unknown language. After that, the knight approached her with a visibly delighted countenance, and said: "My thanks, my child, that you have come here. Soon, we will attain eternal joy and peace."

Then the wedding dances started, which were odd dances accompanied by strange, fantastic music which the girl had never danced to before. Only now and then there was a dance she was familiar with, and she always danced those with the handsome groom. Finally, a weird dance started that involved the most fantastic jumps and turns.

Then, suddenly, in the middle of the merry, carefree pirouettes it suddenly became calm and quiet. Twelve blows of the horn reverberated eerily through the night. Then there was silence once more, and everything vanished at once — the cheerful party of the guests, the merry musicians, the old, peculiar tables and cutlery, the whole strange village.

As the poor girl looked around in consternation, she once again stood alone in the dark night on the quiet forest meadow, and did not know what had happened to her. She quickly hurried home. There, she discovered a beret in her basket which she remembered being worn by the handsome groom. Within the beret, there were quite a few old, heavy gold and silver coins, as well as a rolled-up, yellowed sheet of parchment. The following was written on the parchment in gothic letters:[51]

"In the year 1400, the knight Siegbert von Hainsburg[52] abducted the noble maiden Elsbethe von Kunitzburg[53] from the

[51]The text uses the term "Mönchsschrift" ("monk's calligraphy"), indicating so-called "gothic letters" commonly used in the late medieval period for official documents.

[52]This most likely refers to Haynsburg, now part of the Wetterzeube municipality and about 16 km to the northeast of Eisenberg.

[53]The Kunitzburg was a castle (now a ruin since a siege in 1451) in the Kunitz district of modern-day Jena. Around the end of the 14th century, the castle was in the possession of the Margraves of Meis-

convent at Eisenberg.[54] He married her at the home of a sympathetic serf belonging to the convent,[55] and lived a happy and blessed life with her until his demise. However, after their death this was judged to be a major sin to their account, and they had to spend one hundred years of torment in purgatory. But then, after the convent had long been abandoned and the village of Scortowe had been razed in the Thirty Years War, they had to stage mock weddings in the same location. They were to repeat this in every tenth leap year on the day of the full moon while the sun was located in the sign of Cancer, until a poor, but honest and fearless girl would visit them three hours before midnight and ask for something. Many years have passed since then, and thirty-three leap years have gone by, many people have seen the abandoned village, but no honest girl has dared to approach it alone during the blessed hour. Pray an Ave Maria for our restless souls!"

In this manner, the honest, brave girl had released the poor couple and helped them find peace in the grave. The blessing of this deed remained, however, and showed itself throughout her entire fortunate life. It was as if the ghosts from the village of Scortowe who had attained the longed-for peace were always gratefully watching out for her, and faithfully guarded and protected her.[Gre70, p. 35ff]

---

sen, although it would have been called the Gleißberg, Glisberg, or Glizberg at the time — after the noble line who owned it until 1327. It is not quite clear which noble line Elsbethe was supposed to belong to, although her name indicated that she was born or raised in the castle.

[54]The convent was called "Zum Heiligen Kreuz" ("At the Holy Cross"). It existed from 1219 until 1524, and operated under the Benedictine rules. Now, the only sign of its presence is the "Klosterstraße" in Eisenberg.

[55]The German text uses the term "Klosterhöriger". "Hörig" implies serfdom — they couldn't own land but were bound to their lord. With the prefix "Kloster", it is clear that he was bound as a serf to the convent.

Commentary: Considering all my frustration when other folklore tales leave out vital context, I must say I really appreciate that this one doesn't only provide exposition, but does so on an in-story sheet of parchment to boot!

So, when was this parchment written? Well, it claims that the ghostly weddings started after Scortowe was destroyed in the Thirty Years' War. While historical information on Scortowe itself is scarce (though not completely absent), this most likely occurred at the same time that Eisenberg itself was razed — which was on September 15th of 1646. The first leap year after that (i.e. the first appearance of the ghost village) would have been in 1648. 32 leap years later, or 128 years later, would have been the year 1776.

Sadly, this doesn't fit with the description of the protagonist as a Protestant exile from Salzburg, as the final expulsions of Protestants from the Archbishopric occurred in 1731/32. An alternative interpretation could be that the ghostly weddings started to occur after the couple had ended their 100 year stay in purgatory in 1500. Depending on whether the year 1500 counts as the first leap year for this calculation, the letter could have been written either in the period from 1628 to 1632, or from 1632 to 1636. Unfortunately, both of these occurred before the likely destruction of Scortowe in the Thirty Years' War, so that approach doesn't help us either.

However, it is clear that the parchment was written some time before this story occurred. For one thing, the parchment is described as "yellowed" (although perhaps the presence of the undead caused the parchment to age faster). For another, the village only appeared in every tenth leap year, and since only 33 leap years had passed since the first occurrence by the time the letter was written, its next appearance was obviously some time away.

Thus, let's tackle this problem from another side and assume that the story takes place in 1732 — shortly after the final wave of expulsions from Salzburg. The "full moon" when "the sun was located in the sign of Cancer" would have been July 8th that year. Assuming that the parchment was written in the final period before the salvation of the village, the first haunting would have occurred four times forty years (i.e. ten leap years), or 160 years ago. Thus, the first haunting would have been on June 25h of 1572 — long before the destruction of the village. The parchment itself would have been written sometime between 1700 and 1704.

The question remains who wrote the parchment, and why. Since it writes about the couple in the third person, it was probably not written by either of them — but it cannot be ruled out. Presumably, one of the other villagers was the author (since the author seems to include themselves among the "restless souls" — though this makes me wonder just why the villagers had do be dragged out of the afterlife for this, even though the sin was not theirs). So why did they write it so many years before the next appearance of the village? Did they hope to pass it on to the living somehow, so that a suitable candidate would appear some three decades in the future when the village appeared next? If so, they seem to have failed in this endeavor, since they ultimately stuffed into the beret along with the other gifts to the girl (who was ignorant of their circumstances). At this stage, it was certainly nice of them to provide the girl with some explanation for what she had experienced, but it doesn't seem to have actually helped them in any way.

Speaking of the villagers, the serf who allowed the knight and his bride to marry took a huge risk in defying his masters in the convent in this way. Perhaps, as a "Wend" (i.e. one of the Western Slavic people remaining in the German-colonized territories), he resented his German feudal lords, while the knight actually seemed to know their language and thus might have been viewed as more sympathetic. Nevertheless, he must have been quite confident that no one else in the village would report this wedding.

As for the abduction itself, we should probably assume that the bride cooperated in the abduction. Monasteries and convents were a favorite dumping ground for excess sons and daughters of the nobility, and the actual consent of these descendants was a secondary concern. This is likely what happened to Elsbethe, and it is entirely possible that she knew Siegbert before her exile — perhaps their love affair was even the cause for her banishment. Nevertheless, she had violated the monastic vows she had been forced to take, and he aided her in this — and violating oaths, even if forced ones, was seen as a very serious matter.

7. Those Who are Bound and Banished

Not all ghosts go gently into that good afterlife, but remain on Earth to trouble the living. And when no one knows how to speed their passage along, the living resort to the next best option — calling an exorcist. Whether they were priests or practitioners of black arts, the goal of such exorcists was *not* to banish the ghost into the beyond. After all, the presence of the ghosts on Earth represented a form of purgatory and thus (presumably) God's judgment — and no efforts by mere mortals were sufficient to overcome this judgement other than by the precise means which God had stipulated.

Instead, if the exorcists succeeded in banishing the ghost, they would remove them to some remote place where they could trouble the living no more.

91. An Exorcism in Kirchbrak

(From the teacher Hanne in Opperhausen.)

The house in Kirchbrak where the merchant Othmer now lives used to be haunted. Eventually, exorcists arrived in order to carry the uncanny guest away. However, the first exorcist was unable to do so, even though 16 horses were harnessed before the wagon. For this man had once walked across a rye field and an ear of grain had been caught in his shoe buckle. Thus, he now had no power over the ghost. But soon another exorcist arrived who defeated the ghost. The haunt begged and pleaded, but to no avail, and he was banished into the Wollenwebersberg hill.[1] This hill is reputed to be haunted to this day. An old woman from Kirchbrak told the following: "My father watched over the horses grazing there one evening. It was very dark, and when the bells struck twelve, he wanted to go home. Thus, he threw the bridle over the horse that was next to him. However, as he looked closer, he saw that he had caught a wholly unknown creature. My father was overcome by fear and was unable to move from the spot. The apparition only vanished once he had uttered the Lord's Prayer."[Vog85, p. 103f]

Commentary: A common theme in tales of exorcisms involving priests is that the priests must be "without sin" — or else the priest will have no power over the spirit. This does not merely apply to ghosts, but to demons or other types of spirits (such as kobolds) as well. Even such a minor sin as accidentally taking a single ear of grain from a field might be sufficient to disqualify the exorcist! I wonder if this applies to all spirits, or merely the most powerful — or perhaps to those spirits who are the best informed about the sins of priests. If the first, then a lot of would-be exorcists would have to abandon their "careers" after the first attempt. Or perhaps only sins count which the priest has not confessed yet and received absolution for.

We also see for the first, but not the last time how a ghost subject to an exorcism makes themselves heavy in order to be moved to their place of exile. This kind of "passive resistance" to being moved seems to derive from old Germanic beliefs, as similar narratives also show up in Icelandic sagas.[Lec09, p. 98] The apparition of the ghost (if it even was the same

[1] I was unable to identify the precise location of this hill. However, "Wollenweber" seems to be the name of a family that lived in this region,[Nam] and thus this hill might have belonged to that family.

entity) as a "wholly unknown creature" shows the protean nature of ghosts, as in (for example) the tale "The Rider on the Pale Horse" (p. 86) — they are no longer bound by the shape they had in life. It is not clear whether the inability of the herder to move from the spot was from "mere" fright or from some supernatural effect caused by the ghost — if such a distinction is meaningful in either case.

92. The Ghost Äschamd

A ghost named "Äschamd" haunted the old town hall[2] in Weißenhorn in Swabia for a long time. He was bound into a tin pitcher by a Capuchin monk and buried within the Äschachwald forest,[3] which lies about a quarter of an hour distant from Weißenhorn.

"There" (as told by the narrator) "he now drives around at night on a two-wheeled cart harnessed behind a decrepit mare and makes terrible noise. You can hear his frightful howling all the way to the city, but he cannot get closer than the Rothach.[4] If you approach, he drives after you, addresses you by name, lures you, and invites you to get on the cart. If you follow the invitation, the mare rages and snorts, and sprays fire. The journey with these appartions then races onwards above the treetops with the speed of a storm, but as soon as dawn arrives, he will throw you into a pond. If you refuse to climb on the cart, he will

[2]Most likely the "Schranne" at Hauptstraße 11, which was originally built in 1356 and now serves as a cultural center.

[3]The forest — now called "Eschach-Wald" — is located directly to the west of Weißenhorn, and seems to have been partially cut down and replaced by an industrial park. Which makes me wonder if the mandatory environmental evaluation made before its development included checking for toxic ectoplasmic waste.

[4]While I was unable to identify the precise river, based on the name it should be one of the tributaries of the river Roth that flows through Weißenhorn, perhaps the Nebenroth that largely follows the course of the main river. Or perhaps this stream ceased to exist when the industrial park was built, so let's hope that it wasn't necessary for warding the ghost away from the city.

race through the forest with dreadful wailing so that the trees in his path will be torn away. But in the next morning, none of the damage will be visible.

Sixteen years ago, a tailor journeyed with Äschamd, and died after three days. He also wanted to dump a weaver into the pond near Weiler.[5] Dawn broke, and he threw him off at the dike of the pond instead. He lifted the skirts of women and smacked them with a stick until they were barely able to walk.

(From my brother Georg.)[Pan55, p. 110f]

Commentary: Based on the large area the ghost could roam in, and how troublesome he remained even after his banishment, the Capuchin monk didn't do a particularly thorough job. Perhaps he thought that the ghost would remain within the tin pitcher, but, if so, he was obviously mistaken.

It is also noteworthy that the ghost doesn't merely appear on his own, but shows up complete with cart and horse. If these were merely extensions of his own ghostly substance (which shouldn't be ruled out, since many ghosts can transform into all sorts of shapes) or if they were different spirits altogether remains unclear. Either way, he clearly enjoyed terrifying the locals.

[5] "Weiler" is a common term in southwestern Germany for "hamlet" and thus shows up in a lot of place names in the region. The closest candidate would be a group of houses just south of the Holzschwang district of the city of Neu-Ulm, but it lacks any identifiable pond. It is possible it was drained since then.

93. The Banished Paper Miller's Wife

Behind Goslar, there used to be a paper mill.[6] An old couple lived within who had only one son. As he grew up, he found himself a woman whom he loved, but his parents could not stand the relationship. Nevertheless, he could not be deterred and courted her. Soon after the marriage, the paper miller's wife died and the paper miller handed over the premises and everything within them to his son, moved to Goslar, and established his own household there. Time passed, and the young woman gave birth to a son. The two maids had to keep watch with the new mother.[7] When the hour was approaching midnight, the two girls became tired along with the mother, and all fell asleep. When they woke up the next morning, the boy lay dead next to the mother, and nobody knew what caused his death.

More time passed, and the young paper miller's wife gave birth to a little girl. Subsequently, everything happened again as before. Some time after the death of the daughter, the woman gave birth to a boy again. At that time, there was a new maid among the two maids watching over her. She chatted with and told things to the other one, and in this manner both stayed awake. But it was a wonderful night, the moon was shining brightly, and when the hour approached eleven o'clock, the new girl said that she wanted to step outside for a moment. There

[6]This might refer to the Grand Ducal papermill at Oker (which now is the easternmost district of Goslar itself), which was founded in 1580, and was a major supplier for the assorted ducal offices as well as the (now defunct) University of Helmstedt. On the other hand, I've found an online post by a local historian[Gos] referring to a historic paper mill in the valley of the Grane river, south of the Granestausee (barrier lake) and to the northeast of Hahnenklee, the southwesternmost borough of Goslar. Since the paper mill seems fairly affluent (two maids, a guard, and the ability to afford a town retirement home for the father), I am inclined towards the paper mill in Oker.

[7]The German term used here was "Wöchnerin" — see the translation notes for "The Woman in Childbed" (p. 18) for an explanation of the term.

was a large side building opposite of the paper mill, and as she was outside, there was suddenly a noise coming from this building. Then, a window opened and a white figure looked outside. As the bell struck twelve, the white figure closed the window, walked across the floor, and went away.

When the young master woke up the next morning, the maids told him of these events. He initially did not want to believe this, and decided to stay awake with them himself the following night. As soon as the bell struck eleven, the figure appeared again, and the young paper miller recognized his mother. At twelve o'clock, the figure threw the window shut and vanished. The next day, the old paper miller was brought to the mill. He, too, stayed awake during the night and was able to convince himself that the first two children had been killed by none other than his wife.

He thus sent out a call for discalced monks[8] who could banish the ghost. The physician and the midwife were fetched as well, in case something happened to the mother while the ghost was to be banished from the chamber in which she was lying. The monks ordered the miller to leave everything open in the house, and he did so. However, when the guard passed by, he closed the main entrance and the window of the main chamber. First, the two monks drew three circles on the floor of the mother's chamber. There was a young monk and an old one. The young one sat down at the bottom of the bed at a small table, took his large book, put it down before him backwards, and started to read in it. The old one stood next to him.

As the hour struck eleven, the old woman appeared at the window of the side building. When she had looked outside for a while, she closed the window and entered the main house.

[8] Monks of religious orders who either wore only sandals or walked barefooted — most likely Franciscans. The German term, "Barfüßer", implies that they went barefooted, although this might merely be a general reference to these orders instead of actually true in the case of these specific monks.

At the first circle, she stopped. Then the young monk asked: "Spirit, declare if you are a good spirit or an evil spirit! Thus I command you to speak!" She did not reply and he asked for a second time. But she did not answer again, and when he asked for the third time, she confronted him that he had once had stolen a penny from his mother. While he replied that he had bought paper with this money, he still had to stand up, and the old monk sat down in his place.

When he talked to the ghost, she began to shake and confessed that she could not rest, for she had not wanted his son to court his wife, and that she was responsible for the death of the two children. And if the girl hadn't stayed awake this time, the third child would have suffered the same fate. Then the monk commanded her to leave for the Red Sea, but in response she started to beg. She asked them to leave her a corner in the house, even if it was only a hole she could climb into. Then this monk asked her son and her husband whether they would be content if she were stay within the house. These two did not want to abide by this, and said: "No, she should go to the Red Sea." As soon as the bell struck twelve, she turned around and vanished, and left a terrible stench behind. When they went down to the main chamber where the guard had closed everything, they discovered that she had taken a panel of glass from one of the window frames with her. But from this time onward, she never reappeared again.[Prö96, p. 88ff]

<u>Translation note:</u> The German word used for the banishment process in this story was "verweisen" — roughly "telling someone to leave a certain place". This word, in itself, does not usually have supernatural associations, although the approach in this story certainly does. "Banishing" seemed like the best fit for this context.

Commentary: This story provides us with a lot of interesting details on ritual exorcism. Once the spirit shows up, the first step is the discernment we have seen before[9] — determining whether the ritualist is encountering a benevolent or a malevolent spirit. This was of vital importance, since evil spirits could appear in any guise, and thus the ritualist couldn't determine the nature of the spirit by appearance alone (for a full discussion of this topic, I recommend the book Knowing Demons, Knowing Spirits in the Early Modern Period).[BRW18]

Then the younger monk (the apprentice?) fails to control the spirit, as he has committed a minor sin in the past (it is not clear why "buying paper" with the stolen money should be an excuse — perhaps he needed it for his religious studies?).

When the actual exorcism occurs, the goal, as usual, is not about sending the ghost to the actual afterlife — this is beyond the power of the exorcists. The monks cannot do anything about the (self-inflicted) state of purgatory the ghost is in — all they can do is to send her somewhere where she will do no harm. Like Andres in "The Barber of Penzlin" (p. 216), she attempts to plead her way out of this fate — but unlike with Andres, her pleas fall on deaf ears. Which is not surprising, since she just confessed to murdering two children and the intent to kill the third one, too.

94. The Haunt on the Harth

There is a spirit haunting the forest of Malberg, which also called "auf der Harth" ("on the Harth"),[10] and many people

[9]See the tales "The Man Without a Head" (p. 62) and "The Ghost and the Groom" (p. 177) for further examples.

[10]The exact position is unclear to me, although by implication this probably refers to one of the hills to the northwest or northeast of the village of Malberg.

could tell of the pranks he[11] played on them. A Capuchin monk thus led the spirit away from this forest, and to another, where he could no longer bother anyone. A woman, who was part of the procession,[12] told the Capuchin: "Let me see the spirit." The Capuchin replied: "Step on my right foot with your left foot, and look back over my left shoulder." The woman did so immediately, but fainted before the eyes of everyone present, and fell down to the ground unconscious.[Sch56, p. 31]

Commentary: It is not entirely clear whether the spirit transported here was ever human to begin with — it could be a ghost, or something else entirely. Clearly, its default state seems to be invisible, while many other ghosts and spirits can be seen by ordinary people.

"Looking over someone else's shoulder" to see something otherworldly is a narrative element that shows up in other German folklore tales from time to time, but it's not quite clear how this works — is it part of a spell, or just a general ability of people standing on the threshold of the supernatural?

95. The Woe Mother

Near the end of the previous century,[13] the Wehmutter ("Woe Mother") lived in Augsburg. She was a midwife, and during emergency baptisms she baptized the child in the name of the Devil. After her death, she returned as a haunt in various forms, such as a dog, a calf, and similar beings. She was a dreadful

[11] While the spirit is referred to as male, this does actually mean that the spirit was actually gendered — the term used in the German text ("Spukgeist" — "haunting spirit") is gendered male by default.
[12] Presumably, the procession transporting the spirit.
[13] I.e. the 18th century.

menace, and she became a threat to women in childbed[14] and small children in particular. She made her presence known to them through pitiful whining.

During the Twelve Nights of Christmas,[15] she traveled through the streets. People who cheekily looked out of their windows would pay for it with swollen heads. There was no peace until a priest banished her into the Danube near Regensburg. Others claim that a Capuchin monk had banished the Woe Mother into the Wertach river.[Pan55, p. 111]

Translation Note: "Wehmutter" is an archaic term for "midwife", which derives from "Wehen" ("contractions") and "Mutter" ("mother"). However, I suspect that in this case the word is intended as a pun — "Wohl und Wehe" is the German counterpart to "weal and woe", with "woe" representing both physical pain and mental anguish. Thus, I settled on "Woe Mother" as a translation.

Commentary: Infant mortality rates were much higher in previous centuries, and any incident where a newborn child died without baptism was considered a major tragedy, since their souls were potentially lost to Heaven (the fate of these souls is a major element of certain other folklore tales, but this does not need to detain us at the moment). In the absence of a priest, midwives were authorized to conduct emergency baptisms if it seemed that the child would not survive. Thus, a midwife baptizing such children in the name of the Devil must be seen as especially reprehensible (and beliefs in such were probably linked to beliefs in witch cults).

[14] I.e. women who had given birth in recent weeks. See "The Woman in Childbed" (p. 18) for an explanation of the term.

[15] The "Rauhnächte" (roughly, "hairy nights"), the twelve nights between Christmas and Epiphany, are a time when the boundaries to the supernatural are growing thin according to German folklore. In particular, the Wild Hunt is known to be especially active during that time, and sensible people usually stay at home after nightfall.

Banishing the ghost into the Danube near Regensburg — a distance of more than 120 kilometers — seems strange. Why at this spot? It is tempting to assume that the locals didn't want to have the ghost anywhere near them, and did not care if it then bothered people elsewhere. Perhaps dumping your own unruly spirits on your neighbors was a common practice — and possibly a profitable one for exorcists, if they could get hired to banish the same spirits several times in a row. Banishing her into the Wertach, a small river that flows into the Lech river within Augsburg itself, seems more reasonable. Still, while she is unlikely to be able to harm young mothers and infants from within the waters, I can't help but wonder if she subsequently posed a threat to fishermen and other people of the river.

96. The Old Linden Tree near Gebhardshagen

(From the teacher Hanne in Opperhausen)

It wasn't all that long ago that there was an old linden tree in front of the Hagenholz forest[16] near Gebhardshagen.[17] The locals claimed that a bailiff[18] had been banished into it.

A long time ago, a bailiff named Droste lived on the estate at Gebhardshagen. But this bailiff was such a miserable person that he was condemned to return after his death as a ghost. He had no rest in his grave, but haunted the estate every night. No servants thus wanted to remain there, no animal remained healthy, and, to make it short, this situation needed to be resolved and the ghost had to be banished.

[16] The entire forest to the south and west of Salzgitter was called the "Hagen", as it was shaped in the form of a hook ("Haken" in modern German). The "Hagenholz" seems to be the stretch between Gebhardshagen and Calbecht (another borough of Salzgitter).[Was]

[17] Gebhardshagen is now one of the boroughs of the city of Salzgitter.

[18] The German title, "Amtsmann", implied the most senior administrative retainer of a territorial lord.

But who would be able to accomplish this? Assorted exorcists arrived, but he reproached each of them for their long lists of sins,[19] and thus he remained where he was. Once, a priest arrived who believed himself free from all sins. But the ghost nevertheless knew something and spoke: "Some time ago you walked through a field, and an ear of grain got stuck in your shoe buckle. You did not return this ear from where you attained it. Thus, you have stolen and do not have any power over me now!" Therefore this priest likewise had to leave without success.

Finally an old hermit arrived. When the ghost saw him, he started to wail loudly, and pleaded that, if only he'd be assigned to a spot in the garden, he'd be completely peaceful there. The old one did not agree with that proposal, but said that the ghost would have to leave the estate and even the village. Then, 16 horses were harnessed to a wagon, and the ghost was put on it with great labor and effort. But the 16 horses were barely able to pull him from the spot, as he put that much strain on the wheels. Just before the Hagenholz forest, the ghost was unloaded and banished into a hole by the hermit. A linden tree was then planted into the hole.

The old one, however, left for the hills above Gebhardshagen after this event, where he lived until the end of his days in a moss-covered hovel. The remains of this hovel can still be shown today. In memory of this old man, the hill above the site of the hovel is now called "der Einsiedler" ("the Hermit") today.[Vog85, p. 98f]

Commentary: Once more, we witness how exorcists (especially "priestly" ones, it seems) fail if they have committed any sins whatsoever in their past. Presumably, this limits the number of people who can work in this profession, although maybe it is only the more *powerful* ghosts who know this

[19] The German phrase used here was "Sündenregister" — "ledger of sins"

much about their would-be exorcists. Or, possibly, the most evil ones — perhaps they have a "hotline to Hell" where the Devil (who is not interested in having priests succeed) tells them about their sins.

And even after one exorcist finally managed to get the better of him, he was able to slow down a wagon pulled by sixteen horses — which speaks of the ghost's power. This echoes the tale "An Exorcism in Kirchbrak" (p. 195), though we do not know why sixteen horses were chosen in both tales to transport the ghost. Perhaps the people involved started with fewer horses, but then doubled their numbers after each failed attempt.

It is not quite clear to me why the linden tree was planted into the hole he was banished into, except perhaps to "plug the hole". If so, perhaps he is now free once more after the linden tree was cut down.

So far, we have mostly seen priests and monks working as exorcists — which is only proper, since their very profession was supposed about protecting their flock from supernatural evil. But exorcism was not merely done by the ordained — indeed, it could be a lucrative side business for many people.

97. A Shepherd Banishes a Hare

A hard-hearted farmer woman on the Breitenstein[20] near Sulzbach in the Upper Palatinate gave her servants bad bread, overburdened them with work, and was a godless person. After she had died, she had to run around as a hare, and generally plagued

[20]The town of Königsstein in Bavaria has a district named Breitenstein, which lies downhill from the ruins of Castle Breitenstein.

the servants and the animals, which often broke free from the chains and ran around wildly in the stable.

The herder, who knew how to use magic, was subsequently called in order to drive the haunt out of the house. He was promised a large reward. The herder first banished all hares into the yard, and then into the main chamber. Here, he held an open sack before the hares, and summoned the shape-changed hare into it. That one asked to be granted the space beneath the stairs, but the herder denied this request. It would even have been content with the hinges of the door, but to no avail — it had to go into the sack, and the herder went into the forest with it.

There, the hare now sits on a tree stump, covered with cobwebs and wailing. Late-night wanderers see it around midnight, and avoid this uncanny place.

(From my sister Susanna.)[Pan55, p. 103f]

Commentary: As we have established,[21] it is not uncommon for ghosts to reappear in animal form — though hares are much less common forms for ghosts than dogs (three-legged hares in particular were frequently believed to be witches in disguise, however). The attempt at bargaining for even a small space within their former home is also in line with other exorcism tales. But being bound to a single, small tree stump (and covered by cobwebs, no less!) seems like an especially harsh fate — other ghosts tend to have more space to roam in after their banishment.

[21]See, for example, the tales "Ghostly Poodle" (p. 88) and "The 'Lordly Dog' " (p. 89).

98. The Banished Villain

(From the teacher Frau Bleßmann.)

A certain noble once used to live in the Kleines Schloss mansion in Wolfenbüttel.[22] He perpetrated many acts of villainy while he was alive, and, after he died, he could find no rest in the grave for this reason. He roamed around as a haunt and terrified the inhabitants of the mansion. They were in dire straits, but had no idea how they might get rid of this evil guest. Finally, they turned to an old woman who lived in the city who was widely rumored to be a witch, and asked for her help. What the witch told them, they put into action. This occurred in the following manner.

Late one evening, one person arrived with a coach. He commanded the ghost: "In the name of Evil,[23] get inside!" The ghost was not able to resist this, and took a seat. The coachman drove him to the old execution site near the Lechelnholz wood,[24] at the old road to Braunschweig. It was midnight when they arrived. Now, the coachman commanded the ghost: "In the name of Evil, get off!" The ghost obeyed. As soon as he had stepped out of the coach, the servant turned around and drove away rapidly. The ghost shouted and hurled insults, but to no avail. The coachman did not look back,[25] drove his horses

---

[22]The Kleines Schloss, a side building of the larger Schloss Wolfenbüttel palace, which was first built in 1643, initially housed the princely heirs of the Duchy of Brunswick-Lüneburg, then a knight academy, and finally the Duke himself until it was sold off to private owners. Someone more obsessive about these things than I am might be willing to research nobles with a bad reputation who lived and died there in order to identify the titular character of this story, but this tale might not be based on an actual person to begin with.

[23]The German text is grammatically unclear whether this refers to "Evil" as an abstract moral force, or the "Evil One" — i.e. the Devil.

[24]A forest stretching north of Wolfenbüttel, towards Braunschweig. According to OpenStreetMap, it is now called Lechlumer Holz.

[25]In some variants of this basic narrative I have come across, the entire

onwards, and happily arrived back in Wolfenbüttel. In this manner, the people of the châteu got rid of their nasty guest.[Vog85, p. 194f]

Commentary: As we can see, the people of the mansion are not particularly choosy when it comes to the method of ridding themselves from the ghost — it's the results that counts, even if it means seeking aid from a witch and invoking the forces of Evil.

It's not quite clear from the story itself why an old place of execution would be considered an appropriate place to banish a ghost to, apart perhaps from its overall association with death. However, while researching this site, I came across the book *"Ringelstein im Kreise Büren"* which mentions that this site saw heavy use during the witchcraft trials under the reign of Henry Julius, Duke of Brunswick-Lüneburg. Henry ruled from 1589 to 1613,[Voe10, p. 143f] and was particularly fanatical about the persecution of witches, even by the standards of his time. The execution site of the Lechelnholz saw heavy use for this purpose, described as looking "like a small forest" due to the sheer number of poles the witches were tied to as they were prepared for death by the pyre. On some days, as many as a dozen alleged witches were burnt here. This might have contributed to the eerie nature of this place even beyond that of a "normal" place of execution, and could explain why this was seen as a convenient spot to banish a ghost to.

banishment becomes invalid if the coachman does look back.

99. The Ghost of Day Laborer Rossow from Klein-Kelle near Röbel

(By *, Pastor in *)[26]

Some years ago, a day laborer named Rossow lived in Klein-Kelle[27] near Röbel. As long as he had lived, no untoward things were said about him, and as far as people knew, he was an unpretentious, honest man and loyal worker. Nothing further was known that mattered for either his fame or his infamy. But as soon as he had died, strange stories about him started to circulate in the region.

It was claimed that he appeared to his now-widowed wife in his former house almost every night, soon after dusk. A depression had formed in his grave-mound.[28] Out of this hole, which he had made, he emerged every evening and then made his round of visits in Klein-Kelle. He also extended his tour through the ford between Zierzow and Sietow and over the border bridge between the two villages.

It thus seems that ghosts do not like to go on the direct path through meadows and water-filled ditches, but to meander on established paths. Or perhaps it was conversations with spirits

[26] Sic. I am interpreting this as an anonymous source — a pastor who didn't want to admit that he was interested in such tales.

[27] If I am understanding the website of the Röbel-Müritz administration[Amt] correctly, the location of Klein-Kelle of old seems to be identical with the "Gutshof" estate in modern-day Groß Kelle. On the other hand, the Wikipedia entry for Groß Kelle[Wikc] claims that Klein-Kelle was about 2 km distant from Groß Kelle, and that now only ruins remain of the hamlet.

[28] The German phrase "Grabhügel" (literally, "grave hill") used here is more commonly associated with the old burial mounds of pre-Christian times (which were often linked to revenants, or physical undead rather than the more spectral ghosts of later tales), and it would be unusual for a "modern" grave to be an actual mound. I am reading this as a metaphor for his grave rather than an actual physical description, but I cannot say for sure.

dwelling in the territory of Zierzow that interested the wandering ghost Rossow, as spirits have been known to be quite active there since earlier times?

For, as legend has it, a white maiden appears during the night on the border bridge between Sietow and Zierzow. A woman also told me of a time when she had lived in Zierzow with her parents as a girl. Whenever she had been out to cut herbs, a hare — not a natural one — had appeared and sat down on her back. She hadn't just felt it, but also really seen it when it had jumped off her back. Even my staid, calm riding horse once seemed to have been terrified by a spirit. At one time, around 10 o'clock in the evening, I rode into the ford of Zierzow. I had not been able to see an outline of either a human or an animal, yet my horse shuddered in fright and sped up into a hurried gallop. It almost seemed as if this fear came over the terrified animal by an invisible being. Whether it was Rossow or another spirit that had taunted me, it was sufficient confirmation for the commonly-held opinion that spirits congregate on this road.

Our Rossow is also alleged to have wandered on this road, and this particular matter shall no longer concern us here.[29]

But in his former house in Klein-Kelle, Rossow no longer appeared as a friendly guest, but as a rummaging, taunting presence. He indicated his presence through all sorts of noises. He knocked on doors, on windows, rattled on the chain which was used to lock the main door from inside, rummaged beneath the kettles, pushed over standing objects, and even knocked things with the axe. But his favorite activity was to sit on the spinning wheel belonging to his wife as well as the one of his niece, which had remained in the house after his death. The spinning wheels then made the most peculiar sound, and then people said: "Now he sits on the spinning wheel again!"

[29] I am not sure where precisely Rossow was buried, but presumably it was somewhere near his home. That ford is about 4 km to the north-east of Groß Kelle, which is quite the trip considering he supposedly did it every night.

It wasn't just the neighbors who visited in order to witness these strange occurrences, but people from nearby villages came as well to confirm the reality of these apparitions for themselves. And it was not only the people of the lower estates either, for the name "Rossow" became known to people of more distinguished standing. Even the secretary of the estate in Groß Kelle, to which Klein-Kelle belonged, was motivated to visit Rossow's house in the evening hours several times. However, Rossow seemed to respect this man. Perhaps he was afraid to be dragged before the court by him. In the presence of the secretary, Rossow did not show even a single sign of his presence.

I cannot recall just how long the ghost Rossow haunted his former house. But I know that a farmer from Sietow was asked to find a so-called exorcist who would be able to put a certain troublesome spirit (who might have been the ghost Rossow) to rest.

This helpful farmer had fetched the miracle worker by horse, but this courtesy would have nearly brought him great misfortune. In the presence of the spirit, both riders passed over a high bridge. The ghost might have anticipated what was intended to happen to him. As the farmer first reached the bridge, his horse reared up and threw the rider off. He was a lucky dirt-rider,[30] however. The fall from his horse cost him neither arm nor leg, nor caused him any injury. He fortunately was able to recapture his escaped horse, and he swung himself back up on it. He then led his exorcist to the place said to be haunted by the spirit.

The exorcist first walked around the ghost in a circle in a grave and solemn manner. After he had thus bound the ghost into a circle, he took his rod, whipped his ghost with it, and made ever-closer circles around him. When the frightened ghost no longer knew where he should go, his tormentor, the mighty

[30]The German term used here, "Sandreuter" (or, correctly spelled, "Sandreiter"), can be translated as "Rider of Sand", a humorous description of someone who is thrown off his horse while escaping serious injury.

exorcist, put an open bottle in front of him. In his fear, the poor ghost did not know where else to go. He slipped into the bottle, but there he was trapped. The exorcist already had a plug in his hand, and quickly put him on the bottle. Now, the ghost was unable to escape.

The exorcist then carried his bottle to a deep swamp and let it sink there.

There the ghost might rage in the bottle as much as he wants, but the rest of the world now has peace from him until, one day, he might be released from his jail.

But however plain the impression was that day laborer Rossow gave during his mortal existence, later on some people believed to have discovered something extraordinary about him. They claimed that he had a Dühmk in his storage box, a demonic entity, which supposedly helped him diligently in his labors and businesses. After his death, it was said that his nightly travels were to visit this Dühmk. And since Rossow had sold it his soul, he therefore had found not any peace in his grave.[Nie60, p. 98f]

Commentary: It is not in fact clear if the spirit of the house was actually Rossow — unlike in many other ghost tales, he never appeared in a visible form, but made his presence known through telekinetic manipulation of the house he haunted. It might actually be a completely unrelated entity (possibly infernal in origin), and the association with Rossow could have been a posthumous slander.

The "Dühmk", which may or may not be responsible for the appearance of the ghost, is one of many examples of demonic household spirits from northeastern Germany. Such spirits were said to be very useful to those who owned them, but, as they were creations of the Devil, their owners usually tried to get rid of them before they died so that their souls wouldn't be forfeit.[31]

We do not know what caused the alleged wanderings to that bridge, if the bridge was indeed haunted by the same spirit. The "white maiden" and the hare were probably unrelated tales. If, after Rossow's death, the "Dühmk" lived somewhere to the north of that bridge, we could speculate that Rossow's chest was sold off or otherwise taken to that area. Or perhaps the Dühmk returned to Hell to visit its master, and there is a Hellmouth in the general vicinity.[32]

The description of the exorcism itself is also noteworthy. We know that exorcists can bind spirits into particular areas, but this is usually done at the intended destination of the spirit. Here, this magic is used for the initial confrontation with the spirit instead — negating the ability of the spirit to move around. This certainly has advantages over arguing with the ghost directly, since that might lead to embarrassing revelations about your past sins.

Modern ghost tales tent to portray ghosts as "incorporeal" — being able to move through walls, objects, and even people without any problems. That it is possible to seal a ghost within a bottle[33] is, perhaps, more evidence that ghosts in German folklore were not assumed to be incorporeal as such and thus cannot move through solid objects — though they can slip through very small openings. Or, perhaps, the bottle was enchanted in some way in order to hold a ghost — as usual, the story neglects to provide us with any such details.

---

[31] The rich folklore surrounding such "familiars" and household spirits will unfortunately have to wait for a future volume in this series.

[32] Entrances to Hell where witnesses could behold familiar faces writhing the flames of Hell were far from unknown in German folklore. One such example is in the sixth fragment of "Ghosts Reaching Salvation" (p. 181).

[33] This is not the only possible container — consider the tin pitcher from the tale "The Ghost Äschamd" (p. 197).

Leaving the ghost inside the bottle and sinking it into a swamp seems unusually cruel even by the standard of such tales, however — usually, ghosts had at least some space to roam even after their banishment. But that perhaps fits with the general callousness towards ghosts in German folklore — ghosts had done something bad in their lives to deserve existence as a ghost after their deaths. If their freedom to act was further constrained as part of an exorcism, then this might have been seen as just punishment and their own fault, no matter how cruelly they were treated.

For the most part, the exorcists in our stories seemed to know what they are doing. But how do you enter such a profession — and what kinds of challenges might beginning exorcists have to face?

100. The Barber of Penzlin

More than eighty years ago, a field medic named Andres lived in my old house. This man must have committed a very serious sin in his life, for he found no rest in his grave. Soon after he was buried, people started saying "Andres is haunting [this place]". In particular, he caused lots of trouble in his former residence by pranking the inhabitants in the evenings and at night, frightening them with loud thumps, and otherwise becoming a major pest. But he was also spotted in other houses and likewise became a nuisance there.

At this time, a smith named Jost lived in Penzlin. He had a stable on the outskirts of the town, beyond the gate where the Mühlenstraße street is located now. In this stable he kept his supply of black coal,[34] and he fetched them with a sack

[34] That is to say, bituminous coal.

whenever he needed more. One time, when he arrived as usual, he was startled to discover Andres sitting on the coals, appearing just as he did when alive, and sneering at him. Jost attempted to beat him and drive him away, but this was futile as he was unable to hit him. And as soon as the poor smith had lifted his heavy sack on his shoulders, the former medic perched down on top of it and increased the already heavy load to such a degree that the poor man was unable to carry it away and had to throw it back on the ground. This was all the troublesome ghost had wanted, and, as soon as this was accomplished, he stepped down from the sack and stood next to the smith, made faces, and struck out his tongue without bothering to evade the angry but futile strikes of the smith. But as soon as Jost shouldered his coals again, Andres returned to his previous seat, and thus the tortures continued until the poor victim had finally carried his sack home with tremendous efforts. This bullying continued on a regular basis whenever Jost wanted to fetch coals so that the poor man started to shiver and hesitate whenever he thought of going to his coal deposit. Furthermore, Jost was hardly the only one suffering like this; Andres went after almost everyone with his stupid pranks.

Around this time, there was a woodturner journeyman working in the area. He was reputed to be far-traveled and trained in the black arts.[35] He also owned a black wooden hand and was able to capture and exorcise ghosts with it. However, this man received requests for help so frequently that he was hardly able to sleep in his bed but had to spend night after night capturing and banishing ghosts. This became too much for him and thus he packed his backpack and traveled onwards. But, before he left, he had taught the bloodletter Peter some of the intricacies of his arts. He formally instructed Peter in exorcism and left him a black wooden hand for this purpose.

Thus, it was Peter who was called for help when the haunting became such a nuisance that it began to bother more than one

[35] I.e. magic, especially the more dubious sorts.

victim. Peter didn't have to be asked twice but immediately appeared at the right time armed with his black hand and with a sack for imprisoning the ghost. This was a weapon that was dangerous for the ghost. All resistance was futile, and it had to go into the sack. Delighted about his successful capture, Peter closed the sack tightly and walked with him out of the city so that he could assign a new residence to his captive in an area that was as remote as possible. In the beginning, the captive in the sack suffered this in silence, but when the heard the whispering of the water and realized that they were near the small mill,[36] he wanted to be carried no further and made himself so heavy that Peter had to throw him on the ground. But Peter was not amused. He worked the recalcitrant ghost over with his black hand until the latter cried out in pain and begged for mercy. He merely asked that Peter tell him where he wanted to carry him. "To the Burbrook[37] meadow" was the reply. "To the Burbrook?" cried the prisoner full of fear. "There are already three priests there from old times! I won't be able to get along with them, and then I will suffer. Take me wherever you want, just not there!" "Well, if you insist, you can go to the Soltborn[38] hill" the exorcist replied, and, as the field medic was satisfied with this, he loaded him up and walked onward.

When they had reached the Grapenwerder Bridge, Andres made himself heavy once more. This enraged Peter considerably. Immediately, he threw down the sack with its contents and once more worked over the field medic with his black hand. But the latter spotted a small opening in the sack that had appeared during the fight, and immediately he fled into the outside

[36] An online source,[Kro] which also tells the story, identifies this as the name of a small bridge on the footpath to Klein-Lukow, which is to the northeast of the town of Penzlin itself.

[37] The suffix "-brook" signifies a "Bruchwald", a swampy and permanently flooded forest. The same website[Kro] identifies the "Barbrook" (also known as "Warbrook") as a flooded meadow to the right of the footpath to Klein-Lukow.

[38] The Soltborn is part of the Grapenwerder, a low hill chain north of Penzlin.

world and hid under the bridge, leaving the exasperated Peter behind. Peter could have recaptured the escapee, but he was too exhausted. For it was already evening, and he was tired from carrying and fighting the field medic. Thus he limited himself to assign the unruly ghost to the bridge and bind him there. Then he returned to the city, but threatened Andres that he would come back and bind him to an even more lonely place if he dared to play his pranks here as well.

In the city, people now had peace from the field medic, but the hauntings were much worse at the bridge. Andres let nobody pass easily, and soon there were loud complaints about him from every side. He frightened the horses of one person and he got the cart stuck of another. In other incidents, he threw rocks at passersby, tore at their hairs, sat on their backs, and displayed similar outrageous behaviors.

Once, Peter and his son also rode this way because he wanted to take the horses out for grazing. As he rode along the road without a care and stepped into the banishment circle, the embittered ghost jumped him and harried him greatly. Peter jumped off the horse in order to defend himself as well as he was able, but he didn't have his black hand with him and thus the ghost was too strong for him. It wasn't long until the ghost had dragged his enemy into the ditch, and now he made a serious effort to push him into the soft mud and suffocate him. Peter was now in no little danger and thus called to his son: "Leave the horses alone, and hit the bastard[39] in the head!" His son didn't have to be asked twice and immediately started swinging a stick. He did hit with the stick, but unfortunately not the ghost but his father's head. The poor man was close to defeat and he was barely able to shout to his son: "Stop the swinging boy, you are going to kill me otherwise!" In this way Peter and Andres wrestled with each other for a long time. Finally, Peter was able to escape. He ran home and soon returned with the

[39]The German term used here was "Hund" ("dog"), but I feel that "bastard" expresses the sentiment better.

black hand and a sack. Now the barber was forced to surrender, but there was no longer any possibility of mercy. No matter how much he writhed and protested, he had to go into the sack. When Peter had finally exhausted his desire for vengeance, he put the sack on his back and carried his prisoner to the Soltborn hill. There he created a new circle which Andres was not allowed to ever leave, and, as far as anyone knows, never has.

Only once did people hear from Andres again, when the bloodletter Kunz got too close to him while chopping trees and bushes. For Kunz owned a piece of land on the Soltborn hill which he had recently bought, and, in contrast to his predecessor, he intended to make use of every square foot of land. For the latter had never farmed many of the nooks and crannies of the land, including the piece that was adjacent to the Soltborn. As Kunz reached this location, which was partially within the banishment circle, the barber did not want him to continue clearing the land. As no amount of pleading made a difference, Kunz threw his hatchet at his opponent in order to get him out of the way. But this did not help. For once, he never hit, no matter how often he threw his hatchet. For another, he always fell on his back after each throw. Thus, he finally had to give up clearing the land at this spot.[Bar79, p. 169ff]

Translation notes: Andres is called a "Feldscheer" in the original text, which were people who treated wounded soldiers. They did not generally gain their medical knowledge through academic education, but by on-the-job training from barbers, farriers, and sometimes torturers. Needless to say, actual medical knowledge tended to be low in this profession. This should be read as synonymous with "barber" — i.e. Andres is the "Barber of Penzlin" mentioned in the title.

Both Peter and Kunz are called "Adersmann" — literally "Vein Man", which should be understood as "bloodletter". This was also part of the profession of a barber (although neither Peter nor Kunz are referred to in this manner), and thus the central struggles in the story are between different barbers. I can only speculate on whether the narrator did this on purpose.

Commentary: I love this story in so many ways. For starters, it says a lot when a very small town like Penzlin (which had 4,177 inhabitants in 2017, and was likely smaller during the time period the story takes place in) has so much trouble with unruly ghosts that the woodturner-exorcist was kept busy almost every night. And when Peter wants to dump Andres at a random meadow, he is informed that there are already three other ghosts there (of priests, no less!). You get the impression that (a) Heaven, Hell, and Purgatory are largely empty, and the dead just linger on, and (b) exorcists have been dumping hazardous ectoplasmic waste out of town for a long, long time. Presumably, as the towns grow larger the ghosts will have to be relocated again — a job for future exorcists.

The powers of the titular ghost get a lot of details. He doesn't have the killing or sickening touch that many other ghosts of German folklore have, but he does have the abilities of many other "pressure spirits" that allow him to increase his weight when being carried by someone (whether he is carried voluntarily or not).[40] He can be seen by and interact with normal people and animals. He is also apparently either hard to hit by nonmagical weapons, or even entirely unable to be struck by them. He does not seem to be able to pass through objects like modern portrayals of ghosts, since the sack is able to contain him effectively — although even a small rip in the sack is enough to let Andres escape. It is also possible that the sack is magical (although the story never mentions this), since he displays tremendous strength in his battle with Peter and is capable of rooting an entire cart to a particular spot —

[40] See the comments for the tale "Don't Steal from the Dead!" (p. 122) for more on this phenomenon.

why else would he be unable to rip open the sack by himself? Finally, Andres' claim about the three ghostly priests seem to imply that ghosts can affect each other in some way — although he might have been lying.

We also get a good look at the profession of "exorcist", which apparently was a part-time job instead of a full-time profession. The tools of the trade include the magic wooden black hand, which apparently skilled exorcists can create on their own (like the woodturner did for Peter). It is never quite clear how the black hand is used as a weapon — if it emits some anti-ghost magical ray or if the exorcist simply needs to hit the ghost — though personally, I am inclined towards the latter. The second tool is a sack for transporting ghosts in — as mentioned above, it's not clear if the sack is magical in any way, although the story never treats it as more than an ordinary sack that is merely used for an unusual purpose. In this, it fulfills the same role as the tin pitcher in "The Ghost Äschamd" (p. 197).

Finally, the exorcist needs to create a banishment circle in order to bind ghosts to a remote location where they cannot bother anyone. This circle is not mentioned as being visible to normal people, but it is very effective against ghosts, and the circle does not have an "expiration date" since Andres never left his circles under his own power — although Peter was capable of removing him from the first circle he had created around the bridge (perhaps this is another property of the sack). If exorcists were organized in a more professional manner (instead of pursuing it as the part-time job we see here), they probably ought to take notes on where precisely they bound each ghost — in order to prevent nasty surprises for future generations.

Afterword

As we have seen, ghosts take on many forms. They might appear just as they did in life — or with missing body parts or discolored limbs. They might retain human form — or take on the shape of animals or even not-quite-inanimate objects.

But whether they seem harmless, or whether their very presence causes the living to wither and die, ghosts were not a comfortable presence for the living. While accommodation with revenants might have been possible during the age of the old pagan German or Slavic people that once inhabited these lands, once Christian thought spread, the presence of ghosts was increasingly seen as an aberration. Whether they were sinners who were forced to serve out a term of purgatory on the mortal plane, unfortunates who had to remain behind through no real fault of their own, or self-willed souls who still wanted to accomplish some final task before ascending to the afterlife, all of them were eventually expected to move on — and if they refused to do so, the living did not hesitate to call for a specialist who would imprison them in the remote wilderness until the end of time.

For the living, these narratives of ghosts were both consoling and liberating. "Consoling" because the presence of ghosts showed that there was an existence after death, and that rewards of bliss and peace awaited those who worked for them with good deeds and prayers. And even if enough sins weighed on them to deny immediate entrance to Heaven, redemption was still possible for all but the truly damned with the assistance of kindly living people.

And "liberating" because the souls of the dead had no claim on the lives of their descendants. Either they moved on to Heaven or Hell, where they were out of reach in any but the most extreme circumstances, or they remained behind as a punishment for their sins. And in that case, forcibly removing them from one's home with the aid of exorcists was not seen as disrespect or even disloyalty towards an ancestor, but merely a restoration of the proper order. It was considered kind for the living to help them move on, but the living were not expected to rearrange their daily lives according to the whims and desires of their deceased relatives.

Thus, while tales of ghosts could provide thrills aplenty for those late-night storytelling sessions in the spinning chamber, they allowed safe escape even for those who believed in such specters. Just as the gathering in the communal chamber and the tales themselves ended, so would the presence of ghosts end in one way or another, and it was safe to go to bed and have dreams unburdened by the unruly dead.

Still, the sheer popularity of ghost tales ensured that the undead would always return — and I, too, have barely started my exploration of this subject. Nevertheless, for now it is time for me to move on to another topic from German folklore — an entity scarcely less popular and just as variable as ghosts. Tempter and fool, trickster and adversary — we will examine the Devil himself in his many guises. Thus, keep an eye out for the next book in this series:

Volume 2: Old Goatfoot

The Project

This book is part of an ongoing project that strives to make old German folk tales accessible to an international audience by translating them into English. As there are tens and possibly hundreds of thousands of German folk tales that have never been translated into English before, this project is not intended to end any time soon.

Interested readers can subscribe to the project newsletter at `https://sunkencastles.com`. Newsletter subscribers will receive at least one free translation every month, as well as information about further publications and related information.

Those who wish to support the project further can subscribe to the project's Patreon campaign at `https://www.patreon.com/sunkencastles`. Currently, subscribers receive at least 1,000 words of translations and commentary every Monday. Higher-level subscribers can also receive book manuscripts, including a "Master Volume" of all translations released on Patreon so far, or even suggest topics for future translations.

I am also available for reader feedback on my writings (including any errors I made), insights from the perspectives of other folklore enthusiasts, and any questions you may have about German folklore. You can reach me at sunken.castles.evil.poodles@gmail.com.

Acknowledgements

Any book of this size builds on the work of others. This is more literally true for this book than many others, as I indebted to the labors of many scholars from past centuries (see the following bibliography for a list). But many living people have earned my gratitude as well.

Like most books of this size, ***Sunken Castles, Evil Poodles*** required a team effort to get ready for publication. First and foremost among my many helpers is Samuel Wells, whose editing helped me tackle the grammar and style errors in my manuscript. Any remaining errors are purely my own.

While I understand the Franconian and Bavarian dialects well enough, I frequently struggled with the many other permutations of the German language I found in the source material. Thus, I wish to thank Vera Jüterbock and Olaf Wilsing-Jüterbock for their assistance with deciphering Low German fragments, as well as **Tanelorn.net** forum users 1of3, 6, Aedin Madasohn, BBB, Candero, Chiarina, Chronist, Der Tod, Edvard Elch, Faras, Fezzik, Damion, Ham's the R, Haukrinn, Huhn, Megavolt, Roach, Samael, Selganor, Sir Mythos, Shadom, Sphyxis, Tarin, and unicum for help with linguistic challenges, as well as obscure bits of Germany trivia and technical assistance.[41]

Beyond the linguistic challenges, I also had to reach out

[41] The German-language discussion thread will remain active for future translations and can be found here: `https://www.tanelorn.net/index.php/topic,108095.0.html`

to local expertise several times when trying to decipher obscure place names or historical details. I am indebted to Saskia Düsedau of the City Archives of Wernigerode, Ekkehard Eder of the City Archives of Osterode, Patricia Jaeger of the Tourist Information Office of Nassau and Dr. Hans-Jürgen Sarholz of the Bad Ems City Museum, and Dietmar Krist, Mayor of Antrifttal.

I used LaTeX for compiling this work in both PDF and reflowable text formats. In this, the **tex4ht** package currently developed by Michal Hoftich was invaluable, as was his technical advice for getting the reflowable ebook format precisely as I wanted it.

Finally, I wish to thank my Patreon backers, whose support kept me motivated during the writing process and helped pay for the costs of publication.

Explorer: Erin McGann, Mathew Michanie, The Curious Jalebi
Scholar: Amanda Kauer, Arc Dream Publishing, Babbaboosh, c, Captain Button, Cheryl Fuller, Colin Rowe, David Azzageddi, David Dorward, Daylan, Denis J Mc Carthy, Der Schweizer Schrättlig, Ephorea, Eric Horstman, Gotteswaise, k grunge, Kent Crispin, Lynn Hardaker, Mac (The Maniculum Podcast), Quinn Bicer, Robert Anstett, Robin D. Ashe, Sam, Samantha Sage, Scott Harris, Stephanie, Terry Champlin, Trez Laforge, Wayne's Books
Enthusiast: Clara Skrippek, DD, Eleanor Konik, Ellie Soleayst, Fletcher Haug, Granger Huntress, Greis RPG, harley stroh, Jenny Asencio, Kim Wedlock, Lahsbee, Laura Gibbs, Max Rohleder, Nicole Rivette, Pixellance.

A. Notes on Germany

A.1. German History

The notion of Germany as a distinct region dates back to the Roman era, when the regions east of the river Rhine were referred to as **Germania**. While the Romans were able to establish the provinces of Germania Superior and Germania Inferior along the Rhine, and the province of Raetia included parts of southern Germany close to the Alps, further expansion was halted by the **Battle of the Teutoburg Forest**[1] in 9 AD. This was later developed into the "founding myth" of Germany and supposedly symbolizes the fierce independence of the German people — somewhat ironically, as many prominent Germans throughout history were never shy about appropriating Roman heritage when it suited them.

The next major turning point in German history was the reign of **Emperor Charlemagne**, who expanded the Frankish Empire over much of central and western Europe during his reign (from 768 to 814). Naturally, both the French and the Germans claim him for their own, and his deeds[2] and travels feature prominently in many German folk tales.[3]

[1] The Teutoburg Forest is a hill region straddling the border area between modern-day Lower Saxony and North Rhine-Westphalia, close to the city of Osnabrück.

[2] Which included many wars against the pagan Saxons, massacring those who refused to convert to Christianity.

[3] As do his "final resting places". Not unlike King Arthur of British myth, Charlemagne is reputed to sleep under many, many different hills until he is needed once more.

After his death, his possessions were split between his heirs. The eastern lands eventually formed the kernel of the **Holy Roman Empire**,[4] which was established when **Otto I** was crowned emperor by the pope in 962. These emperors were never absolute rulers of the realm — formally, they had to be chosen by the prince-electors, the most powerful lords of the Empire.[5] Their ability to get things done as an emperor was thus limited by their personal power as a ruler of one of the larger German domains — as well as their relationship with the current pope, as there was a constant struggle between the emperor and the papacy for supremacy.

Nor were the prince-electors the only rulers of note — thanks to complicated succession laws, marriages, wars, and political alliances, there were at times more than 200 more-or-less independent fiefdoms in the Holy Roman Empire. This chaotic situation made it imperative for local rulers to be able to defend themselves, resulting in the construction of more than 20,000 castles over the course of German history. The vast majority of these became ruins after their strategic importance declined.[6]

Towns and cities, too, became more and more assertive — parlaying their wealth into greater political independence and becoming an important player in the politics of the Empire in their own right. The greatest expression of this trend was the formation of the **Hanseatic League**, which, at its peak during the 13th to 15th centuries, had more than 200 member towns.

The greatest political and social upheaval in the history

[4] Possibly the most blatant appropriation of Roman culture in the history of Germany.

[5] To make matters more complicated, three of these were usually archbishops of the Roman Catholic Church, and who controlled large lands in their own right.

[6] That hasn't stopped them from being scenic locations for ghost tales, though.

of the Holy Roman Empire was the Protestant Reformation, which started in earnest when **Martin Luther** nailed his Ninety-five Theses criticizing the Catholic Church on the doors of the Wittenberg castle church in 1517. As movable type had recently been introduced to Germany by **Johannes Gutenberg**,[7] these theses were copied and spread like wildfire. The Reformation soon transformed into a larger political conflict, as many rulers and cities (especially in the northern parts of Germany) aligned themselves with the Protestants, while the emperor and many southern domains remained Catholic. The Reformation also triggered a series of peasant uprisings culminating in the **German Peasants' War** (from 1524 to 1525) seeking secular in addition to religious reformation. However, Martin Luther and his supporters sided with the nobility and condemned the peasants, who were ultimately crushed along with the religious reformers supporting them.

The Holy Roman Empire managed to paper over these conflicts for a while with the **Peace of Augsburg** of 1555, which established both the right of the local ruler to choose whether his land should be Protestant or Catholic,[8] and the right of subjects who followed a different faith to move to another domain that was more accommodating. But this agreement gradually broke down until it ended with the **Thirty Years' War** (from 1618 to 1648) — a conflict that was mostly fought in Germany but involved most European powers and devastated the region. The horrors of this war made a deep impact

[7] Johannes Gutenberg did not invent movable type when he built his first printing press using this technology in 1450 — this honor likely belongs to some 11th century Chinese inventors. However, thanks to the comparably simple Latin alphabet the German language uses, movable type was much easier to implement in Germany and thus was embraced enthusiastically by many entrepreneurs. While Gutenberg is mainly remembered for printing the Bible cheaply, most of the pamphlets in circulation should be seen as the predecessors to modern-day tabloids in both content and character.

[8] Anabaptists and other splinter groups needed not apply — they were persecuted as heretics by both confessions.

and remained a fertile subject for folk tales even centuries later.

While the Holy Roman Empire limped along for a few more centuries, it finally came to an end when **Emperor Francis II** abdicated in 1806, after he lost decisively in the **Battle of Austerlitz** against the forces of **Napoleon**. While Napoleon was eventually defeated in 1815, most Germans still felt humiliated by the Napoleonic Wars and yearned for a strong Germany that could assert itself on the European scene.

This was the climate when first the **Brothers Grimm** — and then many others inspired by them — started to collect German folk tales in an increasingly organized manner, and it is from this era that I have gathered most of the tales for this book. It was their hope that by collecting such tales, they could do their part in forming a strong German national identity and thus a stronger German nation — whatever form it might take.

They could not have known that their dreams would culminate in the horrors of two world wars. But that is a story for another day...

A.2. Religion in Germany

By the time most of these folk tales were written down, Germans were mostly split between two Christian denominations. The geographical distribution of these denominations — Lutheran Protestantism and Catholicism — was largely determined by the outcome of the Thirty Years' War and the preferences of the local rulers. Catholic priests were beholden to their bishops, archbishops, and ultimately the pope himself. Lutheran Protestants had their own hierarchies, led by officials appointed by the local secular rulers.

Catholicism had a rich mythology of saints, pilgrimages, as well as the notion of purgatory, a place where the souls of sinners could "purge" their sins through suffering before entering Heaven — all of which were fertile fodder for folk tales. Protestant theology rejected all of these, yet elements persisted in folk tales even in Protestant regions — portraying ghosts as being in a state of purgatory, or even considering Catholic priests as superior in the art of exorcism.

Other Christian groups such as Anabaptists showed up from time to time in smaller communities, but they were widely distrusted by the larger denominations and frequently persecuted by both religious and secular authorities. The major exception was Calvinism, which managed to establish itself in the Swiss Confederacy.

Jews were another religious minority who were at times grudgingly tolerated in German towns, but at many other times violently persecuted. Forbidden from owning land and barred from most professions, they were largely limited to working in trading, finance, and money lending. While these were lucrative, this was used as an excuse for further hatred and envy from other Germans — inflamed by Church propaganda portraying Jews as collectively responsible for the death of Jesus, even more than a millennium after the event. Vile slanders against Jews were common, such as accusations of well poisoning, altar bread desecration, and ritual satanic child sacrifice.[9] These slanders were frequently used as the pretense for pogroms, driving out Jews from cities and fiefdoms or even killing them. This reached its low point during the Holocaust of the 20th century, where the Third Reich and its many willing helpers murdered millions of Jews[10] all across Europe. But even after that, antisemitism was not

[9] I wish I was kidding about this, but I am not. Such slanders were widespread in folk tales, and these tropes endure even to this day — as the "Pizzagate" conspiracy fantasy of recent years shows.

[10] As well as other minority groups, such as homosexuals and Sinti and Romani people.

gone, and anti-semitic conspiracy fantasies continue to circulate in private.

A.3. The Environment

The southern border regions of Germany, as well as most of Austria and Switzerland, are dominated by the European Alps. These are Europe's highest mountain range, with 128 peaks higher than 4,000 meters. Much of the southern and central areas of Germany are covered by smaller mountain and hill regions whose elevations gradually decline as they approach the northern lowlands. The northwest is largely flat, criss-crossed by a vast system of drainage canals and dikes that drain the former marshes into the North Sea (this was still very much an ongoing process during the 19th century, and many "marsh colony" settlements were founded during this period). In contrast, the northeast has numerous small rivers and lakes that drain into the Baltic Sea on their own, as the Baltic Sea has weaker tides and the terrain is not as flat.

A number of large rivers flow through Germany, such as the Rhine, the Danube, the Elbe, the Weser, and many others. Before the spread of the railroad network, these represented the main trade routes of Germany and most large cities can be found on their banks.

During the 19th century, about 26% of Germany was covered by forest. This was something of a historic low, due to the increased demand for timber spurred on by industrialization (today, forest coverage has recovered to 31%). Nevertheless, forests featured prominently in folklore, and the National Romantic movement sparked renewed interest in both forests and the other (more-or-less) "natural" environments of Germany.

Thanks to the warming effects of the Gulf Stream ocean current, Germany has a thoroughly temperate climate despite its fairly northern latitude, with four distinct seasons of spring, summer, fall, and winter. There are no clear "wet" or "dry" seasons — precipitation can occur throughout the year. However, due to the chaotic arrangements of mountains, islands, peninsulas, and oceans, these seasons did not represent stable weather patterns, and it was always possible that days or even weeks with weather that was too hot, too cold, too dry, or too wet for the season could occur. The farmers had to plan accordingly and hope that the harvests would be bountiful enough to feed themselves and their kin during the cold, dark winter season when snow frequently covered the land. It is perhaps not surprising that there were plenty of "weather superstitions" that attempted to predict the weather for the growing season based on various signs and omens.

A.4. Rural Life

Throughout the Middle Ages, society in Germany was largely divided into three social classes — "those who work" (the peasants), "those who fight" (the nobles), and "those who pray" (the clergy). While there were always groups of people who didn't fit neatly into these categories (such as the rich merchants of the cities whose wealth and power surpassed that of many nobles, or the "robber knights" — nobles who preyed on the merchants and were little more than bandits with fancy castles), this division remained largely intact into the 19th century and was not questioned overly much. Even the failed revolutionaries of 1848 merely wanted greater rights and representation for the non-nobles, but (unlike in France) did not want to abolish the aristocracy.

Nevertheless, by the early 19th century, even peasant life

had began to change. Serfdom — the practice of legally binding farmers to both their soil and the feudal landowners — had been abolished within living memory. This was not necessarily out of altruism — noble landowners had begun to recognize that tenant farmers would be more motivated to work hard and pay high rents for the land they leased than serfs, who knew that any excess production would be confiscated by their lords.[11]

Still, the rural peasantry maintained their own social hierarchies. Due to rapid population growth spurred on by agricultural reforms, the number of peasants increased, while the number of farmers inheriting land from their parents remained fairly constant. As a result, farmers and their wives were masters of their own large households just as nobles were masters of their estates. Beneath them were maids ("Magd") and farmhands ("Knecht") — laborers who worked for room, board, and paltry wages, and who could only gracefully quit their jobs once each year (usually in the spring). In larger farms, there was often a distinction between senior and junior maids and farmhands. Even worse off were day laborers ("Tagelöhner"), who usually lived in tiny hovels and had to scrounge odd jobs from day to day.[12] It was these rural poor who flocked to the new industrial heartlands of Germany in search of a better life — and, despite the many horrors of the Age of Industrialization, this often *was* a step up from the deprivations of rural life.

Not all people living in the countryside worked the fields

[11] That the landowners no longer had any obligation to look after the welfare of tenant farmers might have been an added benefit from the perspective of the nobles.

[12] While I am as much for dismantling predatory capitalism as the next guy, I am deeply suspicious of nostalgic visions I have come across which yearn for the past when "everyone lived on their own land, and produced what they needed for themselves" — since this ignores the inconvenient fact that land ownership was never equally distributed, and the rural peasantry of old had just as many inequalities as the modern-day workforce.

directly, however. There was a range of artisans whose work supported the farmers, from the village smith to the millers who transformed the raw grains into flour. The priests, too, were important as shepherds for the souls of the villagers. Any of these could show up as the protagonists of their own folk tales.

B. The Travelogue

For those who are curious about where these stories took place (and maybe even visit these sites), I have created a list of real world locations that correspond to the individual stories. The villages, towns, and cities where the stories take place are listed by country, state, and postal code. An online map showing the locations of all stories from both this book and my Patreon site can be found at `https://sunkencastles.com/german-folklore-map/`.

It should be emphasized that the regional distribution of tales in this book is not in any way representative of the distribution of folklore tales as a whole, merely of the tales I have come across and translated first. *All* regions of Germany have numerous stories, but time and space prevented me from showing more than a non-representative sample.

B.1. Austria

Lower Austria

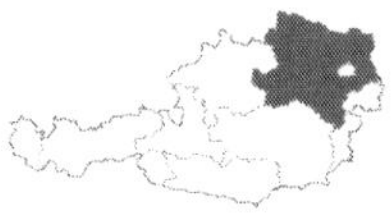

3161 St. Veit an der Gölsen: "The Saved Fiery Man" (p. 168)

3680 Persenbeug-Gottsdorf: "The Black Monk" (p. 43)

Styria

8812, 8820, 8822, 9323, 9360 Neumarkt in der Steiermark: "The Ghosts of the Old Noricans" (p. 79)

Tyrol

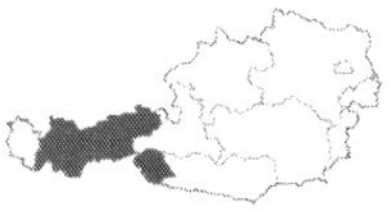

6511 Zams: "The Cowherdess' Buttermilk" (p. 170)

Paznaun Valley: "The Herdess Makes Fried Pudding" (p. 107), "The Maid Fetches the Alpine Sieve" (p. 33)

Upper Austria

4381 Sankt Nikola an der Donau: "The Black Monk" (p. 43)

Vorarlberg

6850 Dornbirn: "The Billy Goat of Büntlitten" (p. 99)

B.2. Czech Republic

Author's note: The territory of the modern-day Czech Republic was home to millions of Germans, and the following tale is from this group. That most of their descendants were expulsed from this region after WWII was a direct consequence of the war of aggression waged and genocide perpetrated by the Third Reich in Eastern Europe, which resulted in the deaths of approximately 345,000 citizens of Czechoslovakia.

Jihočeský kraj (South Bohemian Region)

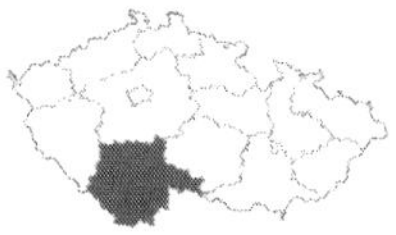

382 83 Pohoří na Šumavě: "The Saved Fiery Man" (p. 168)

B.3. France

Author's note: Befitting its status as a border region that frequently changed hands, the Alsace had a German-speaking minority for a long time. The following tale is from this region.

Grand Est Region

68040 Ingersheim: "The White Girl at the Fecht River" (p. 53)

B.4. Germany

Baden-Württemberg

69151 Neckargemünd: "The Ghostly Dog" (p. 90), "The Rider without a Head (Mückenloch)" (p. 84)

74931 Lobbach: "The Ghostly Dog" (p. 90)

76530, 76532, 76534 Baden-Baden: "The Golden Bowling Game (Yburg)" (p. 38)

77728 Oppenau: "The Ring" (p. 129)

77886 Lauf (Baden): "The Dead Bride" (p. 158)

Bavaria

84076 Pfeffenhausen: "The Brautlachenberg Mountain" (p. 72)

86150–86199 Augsburg: "The Woe Mother" (p. 203)

89264 Weißenhorn: "The Ghost Äschamd" (p. 197)

92281 Königstein (Oberpfalz): "A Shepherd Banishes a Hare" (p. 207)

93359 Wildenberg: "The Brautlachenberg Mountain" (p. 72)

93485 Rimbach: "The Shower Maidens" (p. 130)

97070–97084 Würzburg: "Ghostly Poodle" (p. 88), "The Sneezing Maiden" (p. 169)

97288 Theilheim: "The Meuenloch Cave" (p. 71)

Brandenburg

03205 Calau (Kalawa): "The Owl Haunting Saßleben Park" (p. 102)

Hamburg

"Visit of the Hanged Man" (p. 145)

Hesse

35037, 35039, 35041, 35043 Marburg an der Lahn: "The Ghostly Mill" (p. 40)

35083 Wetter (Hessen): "The Haunting Housekeeper" (p. 22)

35085 Ebsdorfergrund: "Räderberg Mountain" (p. 76)

36280 Oberaula: "Ghostly Activities Around the Nöll" (p. 69)

36326 Antrifttal: "The Brave Girl in Ohmes" (p. 35)

Lower Saxony

05528 Bilshausen: "Ghosts in the Shape of a Dog" (p. 96), "The Man Without a Head" (p. 62)

26632 Ihlow: "The Irrlicht of Ihlow" (p. 42)

26721, 26723, 26725 Emden: "The Ghost Ship (Emden)" (p. 135)

26810 Westoverledingen: "The 'Lordly Dog' " (p. 89), "The White She-Ghost" (p. 142)

30974 Wennigsen (Deister): "Love after Death" (p. 155)

37130 Gleichen: "The Ghostly Light" (p. 164)

37181 Hardegsen: "The Man Without a Head" (p. 62)

37191 Katlenburg-Lindau: “The Ghostly Light” (p. 164)

37199 Wulften am Harz: “Ghosts Reaching Salvation” (p. 179), “The Ghostly Light” (p. 164)

37186 Moringen: “Don’t Steal from the Dead!” (p. 122)

37520 Osterode am Harz: “Ghosts Reaching Salvation” (p. 179), “The Cursed Officers” (p. 94), “The God-Fearing Carter” (p. 161)

37539 Bad Grund (Harz): “The White Cap” (p. 31)

37574 Einbeck: “Don’t Steal from the Dead!” (p. 122), “Ghosts in the Shape of a Dog” (p. 96), “Love after Death” (p. 155), “The Man Without a Head” (p. 62)

37586 Dassel: “Love after Death” (p. 155), “Ghosts in the Shape of a Dog” (p. 96), “The Man Without a Head” (p. 62)

37589 Kalefeld: “The Ghostly Light” (p. 164)

37619 Kirchbrak: “An Exorcism in Kirchbrak” (p. 195)

37620 Halle (Holzminden): “The Unrighteous Plowman” (p. 186)

37691 Boffzen: “The Ghost and the Groom” (p. 177)

38226, 38228, 38229, 38239, 38259 Salzgitter: “The Farmer Who Had Moved The Boundary Stones” (p. 186), “The Old Linden Tree near Gebhardshagen” (p. 205)

38300, 38302, 38304 Wolfenbüttel: “The Banished Villain” (p. 209)

38312 Heiningen (Lower Saxony): “The Welthund near Stötterlingenburg and Lüttgenrode” (p. 91)

38640, 38642, 38644, 38690 Goslar: “The Banished Paper

Miller's Wife" (p. 199), "The Woman in Childbed" (p. 18)

38678 Clausthal-Zellerfeld: "Kleines Clausthal" (p. 65), "The Ghosts Haunting the New Mill at the Innerste River" (p. 12)

38700 Braunlage: "Foreman Calvör" (p. 17)

49594 Alfhausen: "Alfhausen and the Alkenkrug Pub" (p. 116)

Mecklenburg-Vorpommern

17094 Burg Stargard: "The Little Man at the Barns at Stargard" (p. 172)

17207 Groß Kelle: "The Ghost of Day Laborer Rossow from Klein-Kelle near Röbel" (p. 211)

17207 Röbel: "Mass for the Ghosts" (p. 26)

17209 Eldetal: "The Salvation of a Restless Ghost between Wredenhagen and Hinrichshof near Röbel" (p. 174)

17217, 17219 Penzlin: "The Barber of Penzlin" (p. 216)

17235 Neustrelitz: "A Dead Man Searches for his Gown" (p. 124)

17255 Wustrow: "Mass for the Ghosts" (p. 26)

17255 Wesenberg: "Mass of the Dead in Wesenberg" (p. 28)

17440 Krummin: "The Rider on the Pale Horse" (p. 86)

18299 Laage: "A Ghost does a Haircut" (p. 173)

18337 Marlow: "Mass for the Ghosts" (p. 26)

18574 Garz/Rügen: "Princess Swanwithe" (p. 48)

19230 Hagenow: "Mass for the Ghosts" (p. 26)

North Rhine-Westphalia

40822 Mettmann: "The Bowling Farmers" (p. 56), "A Ghost Searches for his Brain" (p. 128)

51371–51381 Leverkusen: "The Glowing Man at the Zehntscheune" (p. 41)

58239 Schwerte: "The Man with the Boundary Stone" (p. 112)

Rhineland-Palatinate

54579 Üxheim: “The Man Who Moved The Boundary Stones” (p. 114)

54655 Malberg: “The Haunt on the Harth” (p. 202)

56826 Lutzerath: “Faithful Lights or Errant Lights” (p. 162)

Saxony

01812–01814 Bad Schandau: “The Bride on the Lilienstein” (p. 110)

08118 Hartenstein (Sachsen): “The Ghostly Suitor on Hartenstein Castle” (p. 149)

08297 Zwönitz: “The Rider without a Head on the Ziegenberg hill near Zwönitz” (p. 81)

Saxony-Anhalt

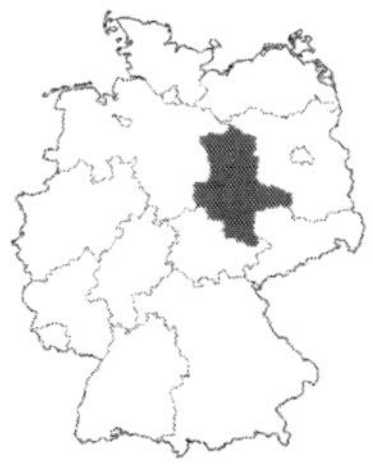

29413 Diesdorf: "The Best Religion" (p. 153)

38835-388356 Osterwieck: "God's Reward" (p. 184), "The Stolen Goose" (p. 29), "The Welthund near Stötterlingenburg and Lüttgenrode" (p. 91)

38855, 38875, 38879 Wernigerode: "The Pale Horse Haunting the Town Hall of Wernigerode" (p. 100)

39175, 39245, 39264, 39279, 39291 Gommern: "The Burial Gown" (p. 126)

Schleswig-Holstein

23701 Eutin: "The Uglei" (p. 137)

24937–24944 Flensburg: "The Ghosts' Meal" (p. 23)

25849, 25845 Pellworm (municipality): "The Ghost Ship (Pellworm)" (p. 155)

25980 Sylt: "The Coast Warden" (p. 115), "The Man of Dikjendäl Valley" (p. 134)

27498 Helgoland: "The Monk on Helgoland Island" (p. 152)

Thuringia

07407 Uhlstädt-Kirchhasel: "The Golden Bowling Game (Schauenforst)" (p. 109)

07607 Eisenberg: "The Ghostly Wedding in the Deserted Village of Scortowe" (p. 188)

07639 Bad Klosterlausnitz: "The Rider within the Beeches of Klosterlausnitz" (p. 83)

98590 Roßdorf: "The Heavily Loaded Men" (p. 74)

98660 Lengfeld: "The Rider without a Head (Lengfeld)" (p. 85)

99768 Harztor: "The Bowling Game Beneath the Hohnstein" (p. 70)

B.5. Poland

Author's note: The territory of modern-day Poland was home to millions of Germans, and the following tales are from this group. That most of their descendants were expulsed from this region after WWII was a direct consequence of the war of aggression waged and genocide perpetrated by the Third Reich in Eastern Europe, which resulted in the deaths of approximately 6 million Polish people.

Województwo Dolnośląskie (Lower Silesian Province)

55-050 Sobótka: "The Men in Zottenberg Mountain" (p. 104)

Województwo Pomorskie (Pomeranian Province)

84-351 Nowa Wieś Lęborska: "A Farmer's Fight Against the Headless Man" (p. 60), "The Headless Man and the Goose-herd" (p. 59)

84-352 Gmina Wicko: "The Headless Man near Münsterhof and the Farmer" (p. 57)

B.6. Switzerland

Canton of Valais

3918 Wiler: "The Dance of the Dead" (p. 34)

3953 Leuk: "The Goatherd Boy in the Illgraben" (p. 78)

B.7. Safety Concerns for Travelers

After reading these tales, you may wish to visit some of these places where they allegedly took place on a future vacation. Which I think is great — my research has certainly made *me* yearn to explore Germany and the surrounding lands in person!

However, you should be aware that racism and other forms of bigotry are still a problem in many parts of Germany. And unfortunately, as a cisgender heterosexual white male German, I am not really qualified to give good safety advice on this matter. Tourist-heavy regions should probably fine, at least during the day and early evening. Beyond that, the best gauge of the expected level of bigotry in any given community are probably the election results of the *"Alternative für Deutschland"* (or "AfD" for short), the most powerful nativist political party in Germany at the moment. The latest election results for any given community can usually be found in their Wikipedia entry (in the German-language version, at least). If they are above 20 percent, then this certainly should be taken as a warning signal!

If you have the time to spare, you might also want to email the local tourist offices in advance about your safety concerns. At the very least, it will help raise awareness that safety *is* a concern for tourists who are people of color, which means that it is in the interest of local businesses and politics to fight bigotry if they want more tourist revenue.

Either way, if you have visited these locations and some experiences to share — good or bad — then I'd love to hear about them! Please send your reports to sunken.castles.evil.poodles@gmail.com.

Folklore Collections

[AER88] Adler, Eberth, and Richter. Sagen aus der Provinz Sachsen (V). Zeitschrift für Volkskunde, 1:310–313, 1888. Available at Archive.org and Google Books.

[Alk] Alkensage @ Bersenbrueck.de. `https://www.bersenbrueck.de/staticsite/staticsite.php?menuid=2592&topmenu=2995`. Accessed: 2022-02-13.

[Ano77] Anonymous. Der Sagenschatz des Bayernlandes. I. Bändchen. Kreis Unterfranken. Verlag der H. Staudinger'schen Buchhandlung, Würzburg, 1877. Written in Fraktur font. Available at Archive.org and Google Books.

[Arn42] Ernst Moritz Arndt. Märchen und Jugenderinnerungen. Erster Theil. Zweite Ausgabe. Verlag von G. Reimer, Berlin, 1842. Written in Fraktur font. Available at Archive.org and Google Books.

[Baa51] Bernhard Baader. Volkssagen aus dem Lande Baden und den angrenzenden Gegenden. Verlag der Herder'schen Buchhandlung, Karlsruhe, 1851. Written in Fraktur font. Available at Archive.org and Google Books.

[Bar79] Karl Bartsch. Sagen, Märchen und Gebräuche aus Meklenburg. Erster Band: Sagen und Märchen, volume 1. Wilhelm Braumüller, k.k. Hof- und

Universitätsbuchhändler, Wien, 1879. Written in Fraktur font. Available at Archive.org and Google Books.

[Bec42] Ludwig Bechstein. Der Sagenschatz des Frankenlandes. Voigt und Mocker, Würzburg, 1842. Written in Fraktur font. Available at Archive.org.

[Ben54] Otto Adalbert Beneke. Hamburgische Geschichten und Sagen. Perthes-Besser & Mauke, Hamburg, 1854. Written in Fraktur font. Available at Archive.org and Google Books.

[Bie44] K.L. Biernatzki. Volksbuch fur das Jahr 1844, mit besonderer Rücksicht auf die Herzogthümer Schleswig, Holstein, und Lauenburg. Schwer'sche Buchhandlung, Kiel, 1844. Written in Fraktur font. Available at Archive.org and Google Books.

[Bow67] Ludwig Bowitsch. Vom Donaustrande. Verlag von A. Pichler's Witwe & Sohn, Wien, 1867. Written in Fraktur font. Available at Archive.org and Google Books.

[Cro99] W. Crone. Aus der Heimat. Sagen und sagenhafte Erzählungen des Kreises Bersenbrück. R. van Acken, Lingen, 1899. Written in Fraktur font. Available at Archive.org.

[GG16] Jacob Grimm and Wilhelm Grimm. Deutsche Sagen. Erster Theil, volume 1. Nicolai'sche Buchhandlung, Berlin, 1816. Written in Fraktur font. Available at Archive.org.

[GG18] Jacob Grimm and Wilhelm Grimm. Deutsche Sagen. Zweiter Theil, volume 2. Nicolai'sche Buchhandlung, Berlin, 1818. Written in Fraktur font.

Available at Archive.org.

[Grä68] Johann Georg Theodor Grässe. Sagenbuch des Preußischen Staats. Zweiter Band, volume 2. Verlag von Carl Flemming, Glogau, 1868. Written in Fraktur font. Available at Archive.org and Google Books.

[Grä74a] Johann Georg Theodor Grässe. Der Sagenschatz des Königsreichs Sachsen. Zweite verbesserte und sehr vermehrte Auflage. Erster Band, volume 1. G. Schönfeld's Verlagsbuchhandlung, Dresden, 1874. Written in Fraktur font. Available at Google Books.

[Grä74b] Johann Georg Theodor Grässe. Der Sagenschatz des Königsreichs Sachsen. Zweite verbesserte und sehr vermehrte Auflage. Zweiter Band, volume 2. G. Schönfeld's Verlagsbuchhandlung, Dresden, 1874. Written in Fraktur font. Available at Google Books.

[Gre70] Kurt Gress. Holzlandsagen: Sagen, Mährchen und Geschichten aus den Vorbergen des Thüringer Waldes. Verlag von Ed. Ma, Leipzig, 1870. Written in Fraktur font. Available at Archive.org and Google Books.

[Hau94] Christian Hauser. Sagen aus dem Paznaun und dessen Nachbarschaft. Verlag der Wagner'schen Universitäts-Buchhandlung, Innsbruck, 1894. Written in Fraktur font. Available at Archive.org and Google Books.

[Heu46] J. Heuchlinger. Die Schatzgräber (Schluß). Fliegende Blätter III. Band, Nro. 56., 3(53):57–60, 1846. Weekly illustrated magazine. A scanned version can be found here: `https://digi.ub.uni-heidelberg.de/diglit/fb3/0061/image`.

Accessed: 2022-02-13.

[Jah86] Ulrich Jahn. Volkssagen aus Pommern und Rügen. Verlag von H. Dannenberg, Stettin, 1886. Written in Fraktur font. Available at Archive.org.

[Jeg22] Johannes Jegerlehner. Walliser Sagen. H. Haessel Verlag, Leipzig, 1922. Written in Fraktur font. Available at Archive.org.

[KS48] Adalbert Kuhn and Wilhelm Schwartz. Norddeutsche Sagen, Märchen und Gebräuche aus Meklenburg, Pommern, der Mark, Sachsen, Thüringen, Braunschweig, Hannover, Oldenburg und Westfalen. F. A. Brockhaus, Leipzig, 1848. Written in Fraktur font. Available at Archive.org and Google Books.

[Lee92] P. Willebald Ludwig Leeb. Sagen Niederösterreichs. Verlag von Heinrich Kirsch, Wien, 1892. Written in Fraktur font. Available at Archive.org and Google Books.

[Lyn54] Karl Lyncker. Deutsche Sagen und Sitten in hessischen Gauen. Verlag von Oswald Bertram, Cassel, 1854. Written in Fraktur font. Available at Archive.org and Google Books.

[Mü45] Karl Müllenhoff. Sagen, Märchen und Lieder der Herzogthümer Schleswig, Holstein und Lauenburg. Schwers'sche Buchhandlung, Kiel, 1845. Written in Fraktur font. Available at Archive.org and Google Books.

[Mei94] Alfred Meiche. Sagenbuch der sächsischen Schweiz. Verlag von Bernhard Franke, Leipzig, 1894. Written in Fraktur font. Available at Archive.org and Google Books.

[MM10] Wolfgang Morscher and Berit Mrugalska. Sagen aus dem Paznaun und dessen Nachbarschaft. Haymon Verlag, Innsbruck-Wien, 2010. The snippet preview available at Google Books did not include any page numbers.

[Nie59] A. Niederhöffer. Mecklenburg's Volkssagen. Zweiter Band, volume 2. Verlag von Heinrich Hübner, Leipzig, 1859. Written in Fraktur font. Available at Archive.org and Google Books.

[Nie60] A. Niederhöffer. Mecklenburg's Volkssagen. Dritter Band, volume 3. Verlag von Heinrich Hübner, Leipzig, 1860. Written in Fraktur font. Available at Archive.org and Google Books.

[Pan48] Friedrich Panzer. Bayerische Sagen und Bräuche. Beitrag zur deutschen Mythologie. Erster Band, volume 1. Christian Kaiser, München, 1848. Written in Antiqua font. Available at Archive.org and Google Books.

[Pan55] Friedrich Panzer. Bayerische Sagen und Bräuche. Beitrag zur deutschen Mythologie. Zweiter Band, volume 2. Christian Kaiser, München, 1855. Written in Antiqua font. Available at Archive.org and Google Books.

[Prö96] Heinrich Pröhle. Harzsagen zum Teil in der Mundart der Gebirgsbewohner. Zweite Auflage in einem Bande. Hermann Mendelsohn, Leipzig, 1896. Written in Fraktur font. Available at Archive.org and Google Books.

[Sch46] August Schnezler. Badisches Sagen-Buch. Zweite Abtheilung: Von der Ortenau bis zum Mainthal, volume 2. Creuzbauer und Kasper, Karlsruhe, 1846. Written in Fraktur font. Available at

Archive.org and Google Books.

[Sch48] Aloys Wilhelm Schreiber. Sagen aus den Rheingegenden, dem Schwarzwalde und den Vogesen. Dritte Auflage. Zwei Theile in einem Bande. Jos. Engelmann'sche Verlagsbuchhandlung, Frankfurt am Main, 1848. Written in Fraktur font. Available at Archive.org.

[Sch56] J. H. Schmidtz. Sitten und Sagen, Lieder, Sprüchwörter und Räthsel des Eifler Volkes, nebst einem Idiotikon. Erster Band: Sitten., volume 1. Fr. Linz'sche Buchhandlung, Trier, 1856. Written in Fraktur font. Available at Archive.org and Google Books.

[Sch62] Ottmar Friedrich Heinrich Schönhuth. Die Burgen, Klöster, Kirchen und Kapellen Badens und der Pfalz mit ihren Geschichten, Sagen und Märchen. Verlag von Ih. Geiger, Lahr, 1862. Written in Fraktur font. Available at Archive.org.

[Sch97] Otto Schell. Bergische Sagen. Gesammelt und mit Anmerkungen herausgegeben. Baedersche Buch- und Kunsthandlung und Buchdruckerei, Eberfeld, 1897. Written in Fraktur font. Available at Archive.org.

[SM54] Georg Schambach and Wilhelm Müller. Niedersächsische Sagen und Märchen. Vandenhoeck und Ruprecht, Göttingen, 1854. Written in Fraktur font. Available at Archive.org and Google Books.

[Sta31] H. Stahl. Westphälische Sagen und Geschichten. Büschter'sche Verlags-Buchhandlung, Elberfeld, 1831. Written in Fraktur font. Available at Archive.org and Google Books.

[Sun69] Franz Sundermann. Sagen und sagenhafte Erzählungen aus Ostfriesland. A. H. F. Dunkmann, Aurich, 1869. Written in Fraktur font. Available at Archive.org and Google Books.

[Tem40] Jodocus Donatus Hubertus Temme. Die Volkssagen von Pommern und Rügen. Nicolaische Buchhandlung, Berlin, 1840. Written in Fraktur font. Available at Archive.org and Google Books.

[Vec80] Edmund Veckenstedt. Wendische Sagen, Märchen und abergläubische Gebräuche. Verlag von Leuschner & Lubensky. K. K. Universitäts-Buchhandlung, Graz, 1880. Written in Antiqua font. Available at Archive.org.

[Vog85] Theodor Voges. Sagen aus dem Lande Braunschweig. Verlag von Benno Goeritz, Braunschweig, 1885. Written in Fraktur font. Available at `https://dlib.rsl.ru/viewer/01004457405`. Accessed: 2022-02-13.

[Von89] Franz Josef Vonbun. Die Sagen Vorarlbergs. Verlag der Wagner'schen Universitaets-Buchhandlung, Innsbruck, 1889. Written in Antiqua font. Available at Archive.org and Google Books.

[vP85] Hermann von Pfister. Sagen und Aberglaube aus Hessen und Nassau. R. G. Elwert'sche Verlagsbuchhandlung, Marburg, 1885. Written in Fraktur font. Available at Archive.org and Google Books.

Other Sources

[All] Saßleben @ Alle Burgen. https://www.alleburgen.de/bd.php?id=30719. Accessed: 2022-02-13.

[Amt] Groß Kelle @ Amt Röbel-Müritz. https://www.amt-roebel-mueritz.de/verzeichnis/visitenkarte.php?mandat=119619. Accessed: 2022-02-13.

[Bec53] Johann Christoph Becmann. Historische Beschreibung der Chur und Mark Brandenburg. Christian Friedrich Voß, Berlin, 1753. Written in Fraktur font. Available at Archive.org and Google Books.

[Bin] Bindelbaum @ Augustendorf.net. http://augustendorf.net/index.php/politik/bild/35-vorgestern/detail/923-kornernte. Accessed: 2022-02-13.

[Brä37] Johann Jacob Bräuner. Physicalisch- und Historisch-Erörterte Curiositäten. Jung, Frankfurt, 1737. Written in Fraktur font. Available at haab-digital.klassik-stiftung.de.

[Bru12] Kaspar Brusch. Gründtliche Beschreibung des Fichtelbergs. Samuel Seefisch, Wittemberg, 1612. Written in Fraktur font. Available at Google Books.

[BRW18] Michelle D. Brock, Richard Raiswell, and David R.

Winter, editors. Knowing Demons, Knowing Spirits in the Early Modern Period. palgrave macmillan, Switzerland, 2018.

[Con] Daily Prayers @ Concordia Publishing House. https://catechism.cph.org/en/daily-prayers.html. Accessed: 2022-02-13.

[Deu] Goszstein @ Deutsches Wörterbuch. https://woerterbuchnetz.de/?sigle=DWB&lemma=goszstein#0. Accessed: 2022-02-13.

[Dil12] Johannes Dillinger. Magical Treasure Hunting in Europe and North America. A History. Palgrave Macmillan, 2012.

[Fra95] Erasmus Francisci. Der höllische Proteus oder tausendkünstige Versteller. Wolfgang Moritz Endter, Nürnberg, 1695. Written in Fraktur font. Available at Archive.org and Google Books.

[Gos] Papiermühle im Granetal @ Goslarer Geschichten. http://www.goslarer-geschichten.de/showthread.php?2651-Papierm%FChle-im-Granetal. Accessed: 2022-02-13.

[Gün44] J. Günther. Großes poetisches Sagenbuch des deutschen Volks. Erster Band, volume 1. Verlag von Friedrich Mauke, Jena, 1844. Written in Fraktur font. Available at Google Books.

[Hei79] Johann Heinrich. Medulla Mirabilium Naturae. Hofmann, Nürnberg, 1679. Written in Fraktur font. Available at DeutschesTextarchiv.de.

[Kro] A. C. F. Krohn. Der spukende Barbier zu Penzlin. http://www.lexikus.de/bibliothek/Der-spukende-Barbier-zu-Penzlin. Accessed: 2022-

02-13.

[Lan] Alle guten Geister loben Gott den Herrn @ Landschaftsverband Westfalen-Lippe. `https://www.lwl.org/medienarchiv_web/detailansicht?id=166614`. Accessed: 2022-02-13.

[Lec09] Claude Leconteux. The Return of the Dead. Ghosts, Ancestors, and the Transparent Veil of the Pagan Mind. Inner Traditions, Rochester, Vermont, 2009.

[Map] Goldborn @ Mapcarta. `https://www.lwl.org/medienarchiv_web/detailansicht?id=166614`. Accessed: 2022-02-13.

[Monrg] Mone. Literatur und Sprache. Anzeiger für Kunde des deutschen Mittelalters. Dritter Jahrgang, 3:363–376, Nürnberg. Available at Archive.org and Google Books.

[MS83] Josef Martin and Alfred Schneider. Antrifttal im Wandel der Zeiten. Beiträge zur Geschichte des ehemals mainzischen Gerichts Katzenberg und des Dorfes Bernsburg im Antrifttal bis zur Bildung der Großgemeinde. Selbstverlag der Gemeinde Antrifttal/Vogelsbergkreis, Antrifttal, 1983.

[Mue] Mühlen @ Heimatverein Benniehausen e.V. `http://benniehausen.de/Gewerbe-damals-u-heute/Muehlen/`. Accessed: 2022-02-13.

[Nam] Namenliste Ortssippenbuch Kirchbrak @ Kreibaum.de. `https://www.kreibaum.de/projects/namen-kirchbrak`. Accessed: 2022-02-13.

[Oda] Eine der größten Katastrophen für Einbeck @ Odagsen.de. `https://www.odagsen.de/index.php/chronik/54-odagsen/chronik/geschichtliche-entwicklung/41-1479-schlacht-an-tackmanns-graben`. Accessed: 2022-02-13.

[Sch98] Jean-Claude Schmitt. Ghosts in the Middle Ages: The Living and the Dead in Medieval Society. University of Chicago Press, Chicago and London, 1998.

[Ste00] Heinrich Christoph Steinhart. Ueber die Altmark. Ein Beitrag zur Kunde der Mark Brandenburg. Zweiter Theil., volume 2. Heinrich Christoph Steinhart, Stendal, 1800. Written in Fraktur font. Available at Google Books.

[vG16] Johann Christoph Pachelbel von Gehag. Ausführliche Beschreibung Des Fichtel-Berges. Johann Christian Martini, Buchhändler in der Nicolai-Strasse, Leipzig, 1716. Written in Fraktur font. Available at Google Books.

[vH04] Nicolaus Henel von Hennenfeld. Silesiographiae henelianae renovatae. first volume, 1704. Written in Fraktur font. Available at Digitale-Sammlungen.de.

[Voe10] Johannes Voermane. Ringelstein im Kreise Büren. Universitätsbibliothek Paderborn, Büren, 1910. Available at `https://digital.ub.uni-paderborn.de/retro/urn/urn:nbn:de:hbz:466:1-15298`. Accessed: 2022-02-13.

[vV89] Johann Weikhard von Valvasor. Die Ehre deß Herzogthums Crain, volume 1. Wolfgang Moritz Endter, Leybach, 1689. Written in Antiqua font.

Available at Archive.org and Google Books.

[Wal] Wallen 2 @ Steinzeitforschung.de. https://www.steinzeitforschung.de/2020/01/07/nr-210-wallen/. Accessed: 2022-02-13.

[Was] Burg Gebhardshagen — Am Anfang War Ein Adelsgeschlecht @ Wasserburg Gebhardshagen. https://sites.google.com/view/wasserburg-gebhardshagen/die-burg/chronik-der-burg. Accessed: 2022-02-13.

[Wika] File:Wd b163.JPG ("Der Mönch auf Helgoland") @ Wikimedia Commons. https://commons.wikimedia.org/wiki/File:Wd_b163.JPG. Accessed: 2022-02-13.

[Wikb] File:Blaeu 1645 — Typus Frisiæ orientalis.jpg @ Wikimedia Commons. https://commons.wikimedia.org/wiki/File:Blaeu_1645_-_Typus_Frisi%C3%A6_orientalis.jpg. Accessed: 2022-02-13.

[Wikc] Groß Kelle @ Wikipedia. https://de.wikipedia.org/wiki/Gro%C3%9F_Kelle. Accessed: 2022-02-13.

[Wikd] Großsteingrab Wallen @ Wikipedia. https://de.wikipedia.org/wiki/Gro%C3%9Fsteingrab_Wallen. Accessed: 2022-02-13.

[Wue] Teufelstor @ Würzburg Wiki. https://wuerzburgwiki.de/wiki/Teufelstor. Accessed: 2022-02-13.

People

Adalbero II. von Ebersberg, 44, 47
Adler, Fr. senior, 127
Agnes of Poitou, 47
Albert the Bear, 153
Alke, 117–120
Andres, 216–220
Arensberg
House of, 114
Arndt, Ernst Moritz, 52
Augustine of Hippo, 153

Baren, Tylo, 146
Beer, Johannes, 105, 106
Bergmönch, 65
Bertha von Windeck, 159
Billung dynasty, 93
Bishop of Würzburg, 44
Black Monk, 43, 46
Brothers Grimm, 231
Bruno of Würzburg, 44–47
Brusch, Kaspar, 105
Bräuner, Johan Jacob, 23
Brühlweibchen, 71, 72
Bärenburg family line, 129

Calvör, 18
Charlemagne, 63, 119, 228
Christian III of Denmark, 152

Deaf Huntsman, 69
Dikjendälmann, 134
Donald Ward, 25
Droste, 205
Duke of Brunswick-Lüneburg, 209
Duke of Saxony, 153

Elisabeth von Ritzebüttel, 153
Elsbethe von Kunitzburg, 190
Emma, 35
Ernest Augustus, Elector of Hanover, 97
Ernst, 186

Fateye, 14
Fegelork, 15
Francis II, Holy Roman Emperor, 231
Francisci, Erasmus, 23
Frederick I of Denmark, 152
Frederick II, Duke of Saxe-Gotha-Altenburg, 83

Frederick III of Denmark, 23
Friendliest, 15

Giesberts, Elsert, 136
Grethen, Lorenz Jens, 115
Grumfeld, 119, 120
Grässe, Johan Georg Theodor, 77
Gutenberg, Johannes, 230

Hadbusch, 27
Hanne, 186, 195
Hans von Lichtenstein, 181
Hansen, 115, 134
Heinrich Carl von Schimmelmann, 145
Henry II, Holy Roman Emperor, 44–46
Henry III, Holy Roman Emperor, 44, 46
Henry III, Landgrave of Upper Hesse, 63
Henry Julius, Duke of Brunswick-Lüneburg, 210

Imperial Chancellor to Italy, 44

Jesus Christ, 19, 28, 51, 71, 163, 172, 232
Johann Christoph Pachelbel von Gehag, 105
Johann Weikhard von Valvasor, 105
Jost, 216

King Arthur, 228
Krüger, M., 27
Kunigunde von Schönburg, 150
Kurd of Stein, 159

Langin, Margaretha, 146
Lappe family line, 153
Lot's Wife, 29
Louis the Pious, 63
Luther, Martin, 152, 153, 188

Margrave of Brandenburg, 153
Margrave of Meissen, 191
Martin Luther, 230
Meinecke, Hans, 145
Molf, 97
Müllenhoff, Karl, 116

Napoleon, 231
Nicolaus Henel von Hennenfeld, 105

Ohmes family, 36
Othmar, 195
Otto I, Holy Roman Emperor, 229

Pechel, 27
Peter, 217–219

Richlint von Ebersberg, 44, 47
Rossow, 211–214

Satan, 98
Schueler, 170

Schönburg family line, 149
Schönburg-Hartenstein family line, 149
Schönburg-Waldenburg family line, 149
Seyfried, Johann Heinrich, 104
Shower Maidens, 130, 132
Siegbert von Hainsberg, 190
Siegfried von Ohmes, 36
Storm, 155
Swanwithe, Princess, 48, 49, 52
Sweeplork, 15

Tackmann, 63
Twelve Apostles, 71

Ursula von Ritzebüttel, 153

Vollmer, the Ghostly King, 150

Wehmutter, 203
Weibgen family, 13
Weinrich, August Hermann, 145
Wettin, House of, 146
Wild Huntsman, 70
William IV, Duke of Brunswick-Lüneburg, 63
Wollenweber, 196

Zeilig, Conrad, 110

Äschamd, 197, 198

Places

Alfhausen, 116–119
Alke's Hollow, 119
Alkenkrug, 117, 118
Allmendrain, 53, 54
Alps, 228
Alt-Strelitz, 124
Altmark, 153
Altmühle, 162
Am Delft, 135
Amenau, 22
Amönau, 22
Antrifttal, 35, 36
Archsum, 134
auf der Harth, 202
Augsburg, 203
Austria, 73, 80

Backemoor, 89, 142
Bad Ems City Museum, 77
Bad Grund, 31
Bad Klosterlausnitz, 83
Bad Schandau, 110, 111
Baden-Baden, 38, 39
Bavaria, 73, 145
Benniehausen, 165
Bergen
  on Rügen, 48, 50
Bieben, 36
Bilshausen, 63, 167
Bleihütte Clausthal, 66
Bohemia, 145
Bosenstein Castle, 129
Bramsche, 119
Braunlage, 17
Braunschweig, 209
Brautlache, 73
Brautlachenberg, 73
Breinermoor, 89, 142
Breitenstein, 207
Brooksbrücke, 147
Brühlloch, 71
Burbrook, 218
Burg Stargard, 172
Bärenburg Castle, 129
Bärenriegel, 131
Bündtlittenstraße, 99
Büntlitten, 99

Calau, 102
Calbrecht, 205
Carniola
  Duchy of, 105
Carolingian Empire, 63
Castle Breitenstein, 207
Castle Hohnstein, 70
Castle Lichtenstein, 181, 182

Castle Persenbeug, 47
Castle Werfenstein, 43, 44
Castle Wörth, 43
China, 230
Clausthal-Zellerfeld, 12, 65
Cuxhaven, 153
Czech Republic, 145

Danube, 43, 45, 72, 204
Dassel, 62, 96, 156
Delft, 135, 136
der Einsiedler, 206
Diesdorf, 153, 154
Diesdorf Monastery, 153
Dikendäl, 134
Dikjen Deel Youth Hostel, 134
Dilsberg, 90
Dithmarschen, 115
Dollart, 135
Dornbirn, 99
Dorste, 161, 182
Drüber, 155, 156
Duchy of Brunswick-Lüneburg, 209
Dänschenburg, 27
Dürnstein in Steiermark, 80

East Frisia, 89, 142
Ebersberg Monastery, 47
Ebsdorfergrund, 77
Eidum, 134
Einbeck, 62, 63, 97, 122, 155
Einöd, 80
Eisenberg, 188, 190–192
Elbe, 110, 115
Eldetal, 174
Emden, 135, 136
Ems, 135
erste Innerste-Puchwerk, 66
Eschach-Wald, 197
Eutin, 137

Fecht, 53–55
Fischbach, 99
Flensburg, 23
Franconia, 169
Frankish Empire, 228
Fredelsloh, 122
Fredelsloh Abbey, 122
Friedigerode, 69
Föhr, 155

Galgenberg, 63
Garz (Rügen), 48, 50, 51
Garz Castle, 48
Garzer Holz, 48
Garzer See, 48, 49
Gebhardshagen, 177, 205, 206
Gelkentalbach, 63
Gelliehausen, 165
Germania, 228
Germania Inferior, 228
Germania Superior, 228
Germany, 228
Gittelde, 31
Gleichen, 165
Gleißberg, 191
Glisberg, 191
Glizberg, 191
Gmina Wicko, 57

Goldborn, 40
Gommern, 126
Goslar, 18, 199
Gościęcino, 57, 60
Grand Ducal papermill, 199
Grane, 199
Granestausee, 199
Grapenwerder, 218
Grapenwerder Bridge, 218
Grebenau, 36
Greenland, 115
Groß Kelle, 211–213
Großsteingrab Wallen, 117
Gruitener Weg, 128
Grünhein, 81, 82
Grünhein-Baierfeld, 81
Gustav-Petri-Straße, 101
Gutshof (Groß Kelle), 211
Göttingen, 95

HafenCity, 146
Hagen, 205
Hagenholz, 205, 206
Hagenow, 27
Hahnenklee, 199
Halle (Holzminden), 186
Hamburg, 145–147
Hardegsen, 63
Harmer, 131
Hartenstein (Sachsen), 149
Hartenstein Castle, 149
Harz, 65, 166
Harz, Upper, 12
Harzkornmagazin, 94
Harztor, 70
Haselwiesengraben, 84
Hattorf, 166
Haynsburg, 190
Heidegasse, 100
Heidemühlengraben, 100
Heidenaltar, 117
Heidestrasse, 100
Heidestraße, 101
Heidingsfeld, 169
Heiligenberg, 117
Heiningen, 93
Heiningen Monastery, 93
Helgenholtgrund, 165
Helgoland, 152
Heltauer Platz, 101
Hermannshain, 36
Hinrichshof, 174, 175
Hinterstraße, 100, 101
Hof Lüttges, 56
Hohe Bogen, 131
Holtensen, 97
Holy Roman Empire, 188, 229–231
Holzschwang, 198
Hunzen, 186
Hölle, 183

Ihlow Forest, 42
Illgraben, 78
Ilme, 96
Ingersheim, 54
Innerste, 12, 66

Jagdpavillion (Eutin), 137
Jena, 190
Johannisbrücke, 94
Johannistor, 94

Kalawa, 102
Kalefeld, 165
Katlenburg-Lindau, 166
Kehrwieder, 146, 147
Kibitzbruch, 184
Kingdom of Hanover, 95
Kingdom of Prussia, 95
Kirchbrak, 195
Kirchstraße, 97
Klapperturm, 62
Klarenloch, 100
Klares Loch, 100
Klein-Kelle, 211–213
Klein-Lukow, 218
Kleiner Clausthaler Teich, 66
kleines Clausthal, 65, 66
Kleines Schloss (Wolfenbüttel), 209
Kloster Ihlow, 42
Klosterlausnitz, 83
Klosterstraße, 191
Kreits Steg, 94
Kressenbrunnen, 131
Krummin, 86
Krüzhôligen Weg, 166
Kuh-Eller, 74
Kunitz, 190
Kunitzburg, 190
Königreich, 79, 80
Königsstein in Bavaria, 207

Laber, 72
Landhasthaus zum Klapperturm, 62
Lauenburg, 57, 115
Lauf (Baden), 158
Lechelnhoz, 209
Lechlumer Holz, 209
Leine, 97
Leitzkau, 126
Lengfeld, 85
Leuk, 78
Leverkusen, 41
Lichtenstein, 161
Lichtensteiner Holz, 182
Liebfrauenkirchhof, 100
Lilienstein, 110, 112
Lindau, 166
Lobbach, 90
Lobenfeld, 90
Lochtal, 170
Lower Saxony, 228
Luzerath, 162
Lötschental, 35
Lüttgenrode, 91–93
Lüttges, 56
Lützenkirchen, 41

Main, 169
Malberg, 202
Marburg an der Lahn, 40
Markoldendorf, 62, 96, 97
Markt (Wernigerode), 100
Marktstraße, 100
Marlow, 27
Melle, 156
Merzen, 116, 118, 119
Mettmann, 56, 128
Meuenloch, 71, 72
Moringen, 122
Mosenberg, 40

Murau, 79
Mönch, 152
Mönchssee, 174
Mückenloch, 84, 90
Mückenloch Forest, 84
Mückenlocher Weg, 84
Mühlenkulke, 101
Mühlenstraße, 165, 216
Münsterhof, 57

Nassau, 76, 77
Neckargemünd, 84, 90
Neu-Ulm, 198
Neu-Windeck, 158
Neubrandenburg, 172
Neue Mühle, 12
Neukloster, 27
Neumarkt district, 79
Neumarkt in der Steiermark, 79, 80
Neustadt/Harz, 70
Neustrelitz, 124
Neustädter Kirche St. Marien, 122
Neustädter Kirchplatz, 122
Neuweier, 38
Nicolaikirche, 27
Niederehe, 114
Noreia, 79
Noricum, 80
North Rhine-Westphalia, 228
North Sea, 135
Nowa Wieś Lęborska, 59
Nöll, 69

Oberaula, 69
Oberlauterbach, 73
Obermühle, 94
Obliwice, 59
Ochsenteich, 100
Odagsen, 63
Oder (Harz), 166
Ohmes, 35, 36
Oker, 199
Oldendorf, 96
Opperhausen, 195
Osnabrück, 228
Osterode, 94, 95, 161
Osterwieck, 29, 91, 184
Ottenhöfen, 129

Pellworm, 155
Penzlin, 216, 218, 221
Persenbeug, 44, 47
Persenbeug-Gottsdorf, 44
Pfaffentor, 88
Pfeffenhausen, 73
Pohoří na Šumavě, 168
Poland, 86
Poseritz, 48
Prince-Archbishopric of Salzburg, 188
Province of Hanover, 95

Raetia, 228
Reckow, 57–59
Red Sea, 201
Regensburg, 204
Rekowo Lęborskie, 57, 59, 60
Rhauderfehn, 142
Rhine, 228
Rhomberg, 99
Rhön Mountains, 74

Ribnitz, 27
Rimbach, 131
Roman Empire, 80
Rosmariengasse, 94
Rotenberg, 166
Roth, 197
Rothach, 197
Roßberg, 77
Roßdorf, 74
Räderberg, 77
Räderburg, 77
Röbel, 27
Rödelwitz, 109
Röderburg, 77
Rügen, 48

Salzburg, 188, 192, 193
Salzgitter, 186, 205
Salzgraben, 97, 98
Salzwedel, 153
Sankt Andreasberg, 17
Sankt Nikola an der Donau, 43
Saxony, 145, 146
Saxony-Anhalt, 146
Saßleben, 102
Saßleben Park, 102
Schauenforst Castle, 109
Schauenforst mountain, 110
Schildwache, 94
Schloss Ritzebüttel, 153
Schloss Saßleben, 102
Schloss Wolfenbüttel, 209
Schnabel, 128
Schortental, 188, 189
Schranne, 197
Schwartow, 60
Schweidnitz, 105
Schwerte, 112
Scortowe, 188, 191, 192
Sebexen, 165, 166
Sietow, 211–213
Sievershausen, 62
Silesia, 105
Slovenia, 80
Sobótka, 105
Soltborn, 218, 220
St. Blasii und Marien, 122
St. Georgii Chapel, 101
St. Johannes-Kirche, 31
St. Johannis church, 118
St. Mauritiuskirche, 31
St. Nicolai Church (Osterwieck), 30
Stargard, 172
Steinbach, 38
Stoffelskuppe, 74
Straßbourg, 38
Strelitz-Alt, 124
Styria, 80
Stötterlingenburg, 92
Sulzbach, 207
Swinemünde, 86
Swiss Confederacy, 232
Sylt, 115, 134
Söse, 94
Sülbeck, 97, 98

Tackmanns Graben, 63
Tannenkamp, 86
Tawęcino, 57, 60
Teichdamm, 65
Teufelsbarracken, 88

Teufelskanzlei, 69
Teufelstor, 88
Teutoburg Forest, 228
Theilheim, 72
Themar, 85
Thuringia, 145

Ueffeln, 119
Ueffeln-Balkum, 119
Uglei, 137
Uhlstädt-Kirchhasel, 109
Ungnadshausen, 76
University of Helmstedt, 199
Upper Hesse, 35
Upper Palatinate, 207
Upper Saxony, 145
Usedom, 86

Valais, 35
Varnhalt, 39
Vienna, 46
Vockenrod, 36
Vogtland, 145

Waldwimmersbach, 90
Wandsbek, 145–147, 149
Wasserkulke, 101
Wehrda, 40
Weihe, 128
Weiler, 198
Weißenhorn, 197
Weißenstein, 40
Weißenstein Castle, 40
Wennigsen (Deister), 156
Wernigerode, 100
Wertach, 204
Wesenberg, 27, 28
Westerland, 134
Westoverledingen, 89, 142
Wetter (Hesse), 22
Wetterzeube, 190
Wiershäuser Bach, 166
Wildbad Einöd, 80
Wildenberg, 72
Wiler, 35
Wissberg, 36
Wittenberg, 230
Wittenberg castle church, 230
Wojciechowo, 57
Wolbrandshausen, 63
Wolfenbüttel, 209
Wolgast, 86
Wollenwebersberg, 196
Wredenhagen, 174, 175
Wulften, 166, 179
Wustrow, 27
Wörth, 43
Würzburg, 88, 169
Wüsburg, 36, 37

Yberg, 38, 39
Yburg, 38

Zams, 170
Zamserloch, 170
Zasłomjeń, 102
Zehntscheune, 41
Ziegenberg, 81, 82
Zierzow, 211, 212
Zottenberg, 105, 106
Zum Heiligen Kreuz, 191
zur Weihe, 128
Zwartowo, 60
Zwönitz, 81

PLACES

Äschachwald, 197
Üxheim, 114
Üßbach, 162
Ślęża, 105, 106
Świdnica, 105
Świnoujście, 86

Timeline

01st century
9, 228
03rd century, 161
08th century, 40
768, 228
09th century, 80
814, 228
840, 63
10th century, 80
962, 229
992, 92
1000, 93
11th century, 119, 129, 230
1009, 29
1014, 44
1024, 44
1027, 44
1034, 44
1045, 44, 46, 47
1046, 44, 46
1056, 44
1100, 40
12th century, 43, 129, 154
1132, 122
1138, 153
1142, 153
1157, 153
1161, 153
1170, 153
1200, 38
13th century, 77, 106, 109, 118, 229
1219, 191
1234, 43
1259, 36
1276, 36
1277, 135
1280, 27
1290, 122
1300, 158
14th century, 80, 89, 94, 106, 165, 190
1327, 191
1333, 38
1356, 197
1400, 190
15th century, 43, 77, 94, 106, 129, 229
1430, 88
1436, 134
1450, 230
1451, 190
1470, 129
1479, 63
1500, 192

TIMELINE

16th century, 26, 105, 113, 128
- 1517, 188, 230
- 1524, 191, 230
- 1525, 38, 230
- 1529, 28, 42, 46
- 1530, 152
- 1534, 152
- 1542, 122
- 1552, 92
- 1555, 230
- 1570, 105
- 1572, 193
- 1580, 158, 199
- 1589, 210
- 1590, 188

17th century, 81, 129, 145
- 1612, 105
- 1613, 210
- 1618, 230
- 1628, 192
- 1632, 192
- 1636, 192
- 1643, 209
- 1646, 192
- 1648, 23, 192, 230
- 1661, 145, 147
- 1670, 23
- 1679, 104
- 1683, 46
- 1686, 97
- 1688, 88
- 1689, 38, 105
- 1690, 23
- 1700, 97, 193

18th century, 13, 43, 79, 109, 128, 145, 203
- 1704, 105, 193
- 1713, 134
- 1716, 105
- 1720, 94
- 1722, 94
- 1731, 188, 192
- 1732, 192, 193
- 1737, 23
- 1776, 137, 192
- 1797, 80

19th century, 22, 69, 100, 104, 109, 117, 234
- 1806, 231
- 1810, 93
- 1812, 88
- 1815, 231
- 1820, 81
- 1830, 95
- 1840, 129
- 1848, 234
- 1850, 92
- 1853, 88
- 1858, 94
- 1866, 95
- 1892, 38
- 1896, 95

20th century, 122, 232
- 1929, 172
- 1939, 96
- 1945, 102
- 1947, 152
- 1971, 182
- 1989, 94

21st century
- 2010, 91

Topics

abbot, 47
abdomen, 24
absolution, 90, 196
academy
    knight, 209
acorn, 163
affair, 156
agriculture, 115
alder, 74
All Good Spirits, 148
All Saints Day Flood, 134
alphabet, 230
alpine
    ghost, 33
    hut, 33, 107, 170
    meadow, 33, 34
altar, 28, 30–32, 67, 125, 138
    bread, 28, 111, 112
    sacrificial, 117
altar bread desecration, 232
Amtmann, 205
Anabaptism, 230, 232
anchor, 136
animal, 22, 205
    draft, 187
    game, 66
    wild, 114
April
    12th, 105
apron, 179, 180
archbishop, 229, 231
arm, 24
armor, 48, 131
armory, 88
arrest, 18
artisan, 236
arts
    black, 16, 195, 217
ash, 108
assistant
    mill, 13
attic, 179
    window, 22
Aufhocker, 124
Austrian-Prussian War, 95
Ave Maria, 191
axe, 212

bachelor, 142
back-squatting, 212
bailiff, 205
baker, 165
ball
    bowling, 38, 56
    silver bowling, 109

bandit, 74, 106
  bandits' castle, 106
banishment, 38, 204, 217
  circle, 219, 220, 222
baptism
  emergency, 203
  in the name of the Devil, 203
barber, 98, 220
barefooted, 200
barge, 136
barking, 95
barn, 102, 172
barrow, 117
basalt
  quarry, 69
basket, 36, 190
  wood, 38
  woven, 36
battle
  open field, 63
Battle of Austerlitz, 231
Battle of Tackmanns Graben, 63
Battle of the Teutoburg Forest, 228
Battle of Vienna, 46
battlement, 44, 46
bay, 135
bay window, 45
beach, 115
beachcomber, 115, 134
beachcombing, 115
beam, 75
beanpole, 102
beautiful
  maiden, 169
bed, 78, 148, 157, 170
  red, 182
beech, 137
  forest, 83
beer, 36
beggar, 171
bell, 14, 27, 28, 73, 85, 138, 182, 196, 200, 201
  church, 29, 38
  evening, 54
  prayer, 180
Benedictine rules, 92, 191
beret, 190, 193
berry, 108
bet, 33, 119, 120
betrothal, 129
betrothed, 155
Bible, 14, 127, 136, 230
Bindelbaum, 120, 179
binding, 219
birch
  stick, 147
birth, 199
  out of wedlock, 180
bishop, 44, 47, 231
  cast iron, 159
  of Straßbourg, 38
bituminous coal, 216
black
  arts, 16, 195, 217
  bobble hat, 48
  cap, 32
  coal, 216
  dog, 48, 51, 52, 89, 96–98
  dress, 138

man, 47, 57, 59–62, 64
pole, 63
poodle, 88, 90
robe, 65
velvet, 106
velvet cap, 173
wooden hand, 217–219, 222
Black Shuck, 88
blanket, 34, 78
blasphemy, 73, 74, 89, 90
blessing, 20, 98, 191
blindness, 143
bloodletter, 217, 220
blue
flame, 67
light, 137
boar, 92
bogland, 89
bone, 56
book, 14, 200
gold-plated, 106
Book of Obedience, 106, 107
border bridge, 211
bottle, 37, 214, 215
wine, 36
boundary
farm, 85
marker, 99, 114
stone, 84, 90, 112, 114, 186
bowl, 148, 189
bowling, 38, 56
alley, 56, 71
ball, 38, 56
golden bowling set, 109
pin, 38, 71, 128
box
donation, 32
money, 134
brain, 128
branch, 114
bravery, 189, 191
brawler, 60
bread, 158, 175
altar, 28, 111, 112
bad, 207
breastfeeding, 156
bride, 73, 74, 97, 138, 150, 189
bride's attendant, 73, 74
bridge, 54, 55, 84, 94, 98, 135, 147, 213, 218, 219
border, 211, 212
bridle, 196
brine
spring, 97
British occupation forces, 152
Bronze Age, 105, 182
broom, 15
broomstick, 184
brother, 54
brother-in-law, 150
buckle
shoe, 195, 206
buckwheat, 146
bull, 95
Bullenbeisser, 95
bunker, 152

burial, 22, 92, 157, 216
  gown, 124–127
  mound, 211
buried person, 140
burning touch, 143
burns, 180
bush, 220
butcher, 76, 77
butter, 170
  keg, 107, 170
buttermilk, 170
button maker, 98
Butz, 33

cake, 132, 184
calf, 92
  ghost, 203
Calvinism, 232
camp
  military, 40
canal
  harbor, 135
  lock, 54
  mill water, 53
Cancer, 191, 193
candle, 159
cantor, 124, 125
cap
  black, 32
  black velvet, 173
  white, 31, 32
capital
  crime, 73
  punishment, 62, 63, 82
captain, 94, 136, 137
captivity, 63
Capuchin, 203
  monk, 197, 204
caravan, 38
carousing, 90
carpenter, 98, 145, 147–149
  journeyman, 145
cart, 57, 162, 168, 219
  two-wheeled, 197
carter, 100, 161, 164
castaway, 115
castle, 36, 38, 39, 43, 48, 49, 72, 106, 109, 131, 142, 143, 149, 158, 160, 190, 229, 234
  bandits', 106
  chapel, 159
  hill, 40
  motte-and-bailey, 77
  ruin, 38, 40, 49–51, 106, 182, 190
Catholic, 28
  priest, 13
Catholicism, 15, 152, 188, 230–232
cattle, 74, 171
  drive, 170
cave, 80, 105, 131, 182
cellar, 33, 107, 108, 170, 184
  wine, 36
chain, 137, 148, 212
  golden, 111, 129
  honor, 189
chair, 15
  red, 182

chamber
main, 208
spinning, 7, 33
treasure, 49
underground, 80
chamois, 107
chandelier, 67
channel, 97, 98
chapel, 42, 89, 138, 159
castle, 159
chaste
maiden, 49
cheese, 107
production, 170
whey, 107
chest
thrice-locked, 13
chest (body part), 24
chestnut
tree, 92
chick, 19
chieftain, 89, 142
East Frisian, 142
of Backemoor, 89
child, 155, 156, 204
child sacrifice, 232
chimney, 179
choir, 30
boy, 29
chopping wood, 220
Christian, 42
Christianity, 228, 231
Christians, 48
Christmas, 204
Day, 27
Night, 134
church, 20, 26–31, 65, 67, 71, 72, 90, 117, 118, 122, 124, 125, 153
bell, 29, 38
tower, 92
tower clock, 50
churchgoer, 117
circle
magic, 213
warding, 200, 201
Cistercian
monastery, 42
city
archive, 100
hall, 94
wall, 63, 88, 94
clergy, 20, 234
clock
church tower, 50
tower, 119
wall, 95
weight, 96
cloth, 111
clothes
fiery, 181
club, 134
coach, 62, 76, 184, 209
coachman, 156, 209
coal, 19
bituminous, 216
black, 216
coast, 115
warden, 115
coattail, 166
cobwebs, 208
cockerel, 176
crowing of the, 159

coffin, 129
coin, 119
  copper, 13
  gold, 63, 190
  silver, 190
  thaler, 140
commission, 115
confession, 30, 42, 93, 127, 196
  rite of, 89, 110, 143
confiscation, 100
confusion
  supernatural, 64
consecration, 122
construction, 118
consumption, 34
container
  milk, 107, 170
convent, 92, 153, 191, 194
  secular, 122
conversion, 152, 154
copper, 17
  coin, 13
corpse, 114, 124, 129, 156
  shattered, 61
count, 47, 150
countess, 47, 138
country road, 173
court, 82, 213
  high, 148
  lower, 147
  royal, 24
  servant, 24
  upper, 147
courthouse, 79
courtship, 138, 199
courtyard, 123, 158, 160
cow, 109, 170
cradle, 132, 155, 163
cream, 107, 108, 170
creditor, 95
crime, 73
  capital, 73
cross, 19
  sign of the, 77
  stone, 85
crossroads, 56, 85
crowing of the cockerel, 159
crown
  golden, 48
crusades, 45
crying, 172
crypt, 129
cult
  center, 105
cup, 67, 189
  gold, 24
  silver, 24
  wine, 77
currency, 119
curse, 109, 188
cutlery, 189

dagger
  hunting, 92
dance, 82, 190
dancing, 15, 34
  hall, 82
Danish
  prince, 48, 49
daughter, 48
dawn, 49, 197, 198
day, 28

day laborer, 175, 211, 214, 235
dead
  mother, 155, 156, 200
death, 92, 155
deathbed, 97
debt, 95
decapitation, 62, 63, 147
December
  24th, 27
  25th, 27
deer, 92
defeat, 80
demolition, 43
demon, 214
depressed road, 57, 59, 60
depression, 40
desecration
  of altar bread, 232
Devil, 14, 16, 57, 62, 83, 89, 107, 117, 120, 160, 207, 209, 214
devil, 41, 142
diamond, 129
diaper, 156
Dienstgeber, 33
dike, 115, 137, 198
  inner, 115
  outer, 115
dining hall, 150
discalced
  monk, 200
discernment, 202
disguise
  as black poodle, 88
dish
  red, 182
ditch, 62, 84, 211, 219
divine
  punishment, 42, 65, 74, 117
Divine Mercy Sunday, 105
diviner, 131
divining rod, 72
doe, 65, 66
dog, 40, 88, 92, 94, 128
  black, 48, 51, 52, 89, 96–98
  black poodle, 88, 90
  Bullenbeisser, 95
  Fischhund, 96
  Fleischerhund, 95
  German bulldog, 95
  ghost, 203
  little, 33
  poodle with changing fur color, 90
  white poodle, 90
doll
  sex, 171
donkey, 92
door, 212
dowsing rod, 50
draft animal, 187
Dresdener Merkur, 110
dress
  black, 138
  white, 143, 157
drill
  hammer, 17
  hand-powered, 18
  two-person, 17
drinking bout, 109
duck, 54

dune, 134
valley, 134
dusk, 53, 74, 111, 180, 211
dwarf, 38
dynamite, 117
Dühmk, 214

ear of grain, 195, 206
Easter, 66
Sunday, 66,. 105
ecclesiastical principality, 188
eddy, 43
egg, 108
embroidery, 189
emperor, 44–46, 229, 230
employer, 33
encampment, 79
engagement, 138
engraving, 25
enlistment, 146
entrance
gate, 119, 120
hall, 97
Epiphany, 204
estate, 114
eternal life, 163
Eucharist, 28, 69, 76, 180
evening, 23, 54, 143, 216
evening prayer, 148
Evil, 209
evil
soul, 78
examination
forensic, 128
execution site, 209
exorcism, 20, 22, 200, 205, 215, 217, 232
exorcist, 38, 195, 206, 213, 218, 221, 222
eye
fat, 14
fiery, 90, 92, 97

faerie, 72
false
oath, 182
witness, 113
farm boundary, 85
farmer, 35, 36, 56, 60, 83, 109, 119, 120, 132, 138, 156, 168, 179, 186, 207, 235, 236
farmhand, 235
farrier, 220
fasting, 66
father, 49, 50, 156
fawn, 66, 68
fear, 41
feast, 109
feather, 19
feed, 189
Feldrain, 85
fence, 93, 123
field, 40, 62–64, 114, 235
boundary, 62
rye, 195
sacrilege, 99
warden, 166, 167
field medic, 216, 218, 219
fiery
billy goat, 99
clothes, 181

eye, 90, 92, 97
man, 33, 168
finance, 232
fir
tree, 86
fire, 19, 45, 113, 183
ghostly, 80, 99
hearth, 22, 33
spitting, 197
town, 124
fireplace, 24
firewood, 38
Fischhund, 96
fisher, 97, 166
fishing, 97
flag, 146
bearer, 146
flame, 13
blue, 67
flaming
pole, 120
wheel, 120
flax, 126, 127
Fleischerhund, 95
Fliegende Blätter, 72
flirting, 150
flogging, 147
flood, 45, 115
flooded
forest, 218
flooding, 109
flour, 57, 108, 175–177, 236
flower, 122
foam, 173
fog, 66
folded
robe, 44
footpath, 64
ford, 211, 212
foreman, 18
forensic examination, 128
forest, 36, 40–42, 45, 48, 57, 59–61, 69, 70, 72, 82, 84, 90, 93, 114, 138, 156, 165, 166, 168, 182, 188, 189, 197, 202, 205, 206, 208
beech, 83
flooded, 218
village, 114
warden, 40
forester, 69, 81, 82
forestry
office, 92
official, 92, 93, 97
forgiveness, 157
fort
Slavic, 48
fortification, 40, 46, 137
fortress, 110
fortune, 191
France, 234
Franciscans, 200
Franks, 16, 63
Frankish king, 16
Frauenstift, 122
Freischütz, 112
French, 80
Friday
Good, 65, 66
fried

pudding, 107, 108
Frisian Freedoms, 89
frock
red, 166
fruit, 98
theft, 102
full moon, 169, 191, 193
funeral procession, 156
furniture
red, 182
Fähnrich, 146

gable, 92
gallop, 212
gallows, 144, 147, 148
game (animal), 66
garden, 206
gardener, 102
gate, 78, 94
entrance, 119, 120
gatekeeper, 36
gem, 48–50
German bulldog, 95
German Peasants' War, 38, 230
ghost, 13–15, 19, 23, 24, 27, 31, 32, 36, 45, 52, 59, 63, 67, 72, 74, 75, 80, 90, 91, 93, 95, 108, 109, 113, 120–122, 127, 128, 138, 142, 149, 150, 152, 156, 157, 166, 171, 173, 177–182, 186, 187, 191, 192, 195, 197, 200, 201, 205, 206, 208, 209, 211, 213, 214, 217–219, 221, 222, 232
alpine, 33
calf, 203
dog, 203
glowing, 168
headless, 57–60, 62–64
of a pastor, 18, 19
ship, 137
snow-white, 171
spark-spraying, 168
village, 192
white, 142
ghostly
horseman, 83
giant, 38, 91
girl
innocent, 138
white, 53–55
glacier, 79
glass, 201
glass panel, 105
glowing
ghost, 168
man, 41
plow, 186
tongue, 97, 98
goat, 78, 130, 132
fiery billy, 99
goatherd
boy, 78
God, 62, 65, 83, 107, 109, 148, 172, 177, 195
invocation of, 108

God's reward, 176, 181, 184
gold, 17, 39, 48–50, 71, 129, 146
  coin, 63, 190
  crown, 48
  golden bowling pin, 109
  golden bowling set, 109
  golden chain, 111
  golden plate, 79
  rose, 17
gold-plated book, 106
Good Friday, 65, 66
goose, 29, 30, 59
gooseherd, 59
Gospel of Matthew, 14
gothic letters, 190
gown
  burial, 124–127
  honest, 127
grain, 14, 132, 174, 175, 236
  ear of, 195, 206
  of sand, 187
  storage, 122
grass, 189
grave, 67, 80, 122, 124, 126, 180, 205, 209, 216
  mound, 211
graveyard, 93, 122, 124, 125
gray
  horse, 118, 119
  man, 40
grazing, 40
great hall, 47, 158
greed, 114
green
  man in green clothing, 69
groat, 146–148
groom, 48, 73, 138, 155, 177, 178, 189, 190
grove
  beech, 137
guard, 147, 199–201
  night, 172
  post, 88, 100
  shield, 88
guardian
  treasure, 52
guilder, 63
gutter hole, 181, 184

habit
  nun's, 123
hail, 132, 133
Hail Mary, 55
hailstorm, 45
hair, 49, 219
hall, 78
  dancing, 82
  dining, 150
  entrance, 97
  great, 47, 158
hamlet, 211
hand
  black wooden, 217–219, 222
hanged man, 144
hanging, 147

Hanseatic League, 229
harbor, 135, 136
    canal, 135
harbormaster, 136
hare, 207, 208
    supernatural, 212
harness, 87, 206
harrow, 63
harvest, 109, 132
hat
    black bobble, 48
    miner's, 14
hatchet, 220
haunt, 208
haunting, 12, 23, 33, 91, 95, 100, 115, 158, 193, 195, 216, 217, 219
hay, 120
haystack, 165
hazelnut
    hedge, 85
head, 24
    swollen, 101, 204
headless
    ghost, 57–60, 62–64
    horse, 100
headman, 74
headsman, 81
hearth, 107
    fire, 22, 33
heath, 117
heathen
    king, 48, 49, 51, 52
Heaven, 90, 138, 161, 162, 183, 204, 221, 232
    may strike me down, 138
hedge
    hazelnut, 85
Hell, 19, 106, 113, 182, 183, 207, 215, 221
helmet, 48
hen, 19
herb, 212
herd, 70
herder, 74, 170, 171, 208
herdess, 107, 108, 171
hermit, 206
hero, 80
high court, 148
highway, 76, 77
hill, 36, 40–42, 57, 63, 69, 72, 91, 99, 117, 137, 144, 196, 202, 218, 220, 228
    castle, 40
hinge, 208
Hirschfänger, 92
Hofmark, 73
holiday, 116
Holocaust, 232
Holy Saturday, 66
Holy Spirit, 172
home garden, 33
honest
    gown, 127
honesty, 188, 190, 191
honor chain, 189
hook, 18, 19
horn, 190
horse, 13, 58, 73, 82, 85, 86, 100, 119, 120, 138, 156, 162,

177, 184, 195, 206, 213, 219
gray, 118, 119
headless, 100
invisible, 150
pale, 48, 83, 84, 100
red, 181, 183
riding, 212
white, 115
horseman, 85
ghostly, 83
hospitality, 158, 171
hovel, 206, 235
howling, 197
Hungarian invasions, 80
hunter
treasure, 41, 72, 109, 117
hunting, 65, 137
dagger, 92
lodge, 137
huntsman, 83, 92, 107, 108
husband, 146
hut, 34, 45
alpine, 33, 107, 170
hymnbook, 26, 67

icicle, 34
idolatry, 142
illness, 68
illusion, 64
imprisonment, 49, 147
incantation, 129
incineration, 143
industrial park, 197
inebriation, 144, 145
infant mortality, 204
inn, 23, 173
inner dike, 115
innkeeper, 23, 173
innocence, 49
innocent
girl, 138
insanity, 90
invisibility, 150, 212
invisible
horse, 150
iron
ore, 17
irrlicht, 42, 163
island, 43, 134, 152

jacket, 34
miner's, 14
Jesuit, 184
jewelry, 17
Jews, 232
Johannisrute, 50
journeyman
carpenter, 145
shoemaker, 51
woodturner, 217
Judgment Day, 106, 109, 110
July
8th, 193
jumping, 99, 190
June
25th, 193

Karlspfund, 119
keg
butter, 107, 170
kettle, 212
stirring, 170

keyhole, 34
king, 25, 47–51
  Frankish, 16
  heathen, 48, 49, 51, 52
  pin, 71
Kirchweih, 132
kiss, 51, 111, 150
kit
  shaving, 173
kitchen, 78
knight, 38, 109, 130–133, 137, 158, 159, 181, 182, 189, 190
  academy, 209
  robber, 234
  shadow, 149
knightly
  order, 38
Knights Templar, 38
knocking, 212

Lache, 74
ladder, 58
lake, 48, 59, 137
lamp, 23, 165
land
  stolen, 187
landlord, 21
lantern, 164, 166
  wandering, 161
larva, 69
larvae (lemures), 70
Last Judgment, 75
last rites, 92, 93
Last Supper, 28
laughter, 45
  maddened, 90
lawsuit, 112, 114
leaf, 69
leap year, 188, 191–193
leaseholder, 115
leather
  strip, 173
leg, 24
letters
  gothic, 190
Liber Obedientiae, 106
lieutenant, 146, 147
light
  blue, 137
lightning, 44
linden
  tree, 62, 205, 206
linen, 126
little
  dog, 33
  man, 172
lock, 20
  canal, 54
locked, 136
looking back, 27
Lord's Prayer, 27, 55, 148, 163, 168, 196
love, 111, 150
lover, 34, 157
lower court, 147
lumberjack, 73
Lutheranism, 152, 231
Lutherans, 15

madness, 97, 112
magic, 64, 81, 208, 217
maid, 22, 33, 78, 122, 180, 181, 184, 199, 235

maiden, 111, 142
  beautiful, 169
  chaste, 49
  pure, 49
  white, 212
maidservant, 50
man
  black, 47, 57, 59–62, 64
  fiery, 33, 168
  glowing, 41
  gray, 40
  in green clothing, 69
  little, 172
  poor, 92
mane, 36
manor, 145
mansion, 76, 77, 102, 209
mantle, 26, 28
  soldier's, 63
March
  27th, 47
march (territory), 73
mare
  decrepit, 197
Mark, 119
market, 100
marriage, 199
  proposal, 159
mass, 27, 30, 110
  morning, 26, 28
Maundy Thursday, 65
May
  12th, 63
mayor, 100
mead, 132
meadow, 40, 41, 53, 63, 74, 169–171, 186, 188–190, 211, 218
  alpine, 32–34
meltwater, 79, 109
memorial
  stone, 62
merchant, 146, 234
  ship, 135, 136
Middle Ages, 234
midwife, 200, 203
militia, 63
milk, 107, 131, 177
  container, 107, 170
  processing, 170
  sieve, 33
  skimmed, 181
  soup, 33
mill, 12–15, 40, 101, 162, 174, 175
  assistant, 13
  paper mill, 199, 200
mill water canal, 53
miller, 81, 175, 236
  paper miller, 199, 200
millstone
  suspended, 41
mine, 17, 65
  shaft, 17
miner, 14, 17, 19, 20
  miner's
    hat, 14
    jacket, 14
mining, 17
  town, 65
monastery, 13, 77, 93, 123, 153, 189, 194
  Cistercian, 42

monastic
  order, 77
  vow, 194
money, 13, 33, 41, 49, 110, 146, 179, 180
money lending, 232
monk, 13, 14, 45, 76, 152, 154, 201, 202
  Capuchin, 197, 204
  discalced, 200
  monk's robe, 65
moon, 175, 199
  full, 169, 191, 193
  new, 83
moor, 89
morning, 27, 28, 143, 156
  mass, 26, 28
moss, 44, 166
mother, 157, 199, 200
  dead, 155, 156, 200
mound
  burial, 211
  grave, 211
mountain, 69, 72, 73, 77, 80, 105, 110, 171
  monk, 65
  range, 74
  volcanic, 74
mourner, 22, 156
moveable type, 26, 230
mud, 219
murder, 82, 92, 93, 115, 128, 134, 180
  by throat-cutting, 173
  matricide, 111
murderer, 82
music, 190
musician, 190
mute, 63
Mönchsschrift, 190
Mühlenkulk, 101

Napoleonic Wars, 166, 231
Nassau Tourist Board, 77
neighbor, 27
new moon, 83
niece, 212
night, 28, 42, 56, 88, 92, 135, 216
  guard, 172
  watchman, 147
night hag, 124
Nine Years' War, 38
Ninety-five Theses, 188, 230
nobility, 89, 234, 235
  high, 149
noble, 23, 41, 89, 114, 145, 209
nobleman, 173
noblewoman, 156, 181
noon, 180, 182
Noricans, 79, 80
November
  11th, 147
nudity, 49
nun, 92, 122, 123, 153, 154, 189
  nun's habit, 123
nunnery, 122
nursemaid, 146

o'clock
  01 (afternoon), 150

01 (morning), 27, 63, 180
05 (morning), 27
09 (evening), 191
10 (evening), 57, 92, 212
11 (evening), 14, 63, 88, 92, 94, 98, 155, 167, 186, 199, 200
11 (morning), 59, 181, 182
12 (midnight), 14, 15, 17, 27, 30, 36, 50, 63, 66, 73, 85, 88, 90, 95, 98, 118, 119, 124, 137, 148, 156, 167, 170, 175, 186, 196, 199–201, 208, 209
12 (noon), 38, 181
oak
tree, 22
oat, 146
oath
false, 182
violated, 194
Oberförsterei, 92
ocean, 115, 137
officer, 95, 147
Oktoberfest, 132
omen
ill, 43
oppression, 80
order
knightly, 38
monastic, 77
religious, 200
ore, 66
iron, 17
silver, 17
Ottoman wars, 80
out of wedlock birth, 180
outer dike, 115
oven, 19, 179, 184
overcoat, 34
oversleeping, 65
owl, 102
ox, 17
skin, 18

paddock, 175
pagans, 228
painting, 142
palace, 209
pale
horse, 48, 83, 84, 100
pantry, 184
papacy, 12, 153, 229
paper, 201
mill, 199, 200
miller, 199, 200
Paradise, 150
paralysis
sleep, 124
parchment, 190, 192, 193
parish, 116
passion, 150
pastor, 30–32, 62, 117, 126, 127, 177, 211
ghost of a, 18, 19
pasture, 138
patrol, 94

Peace of Augsburg, 154, 230
peasant, 234, 235
peasantry, 235
penny, 119
pfennig
  red, 13
Pfund, 119
phosphorus, 143
physician, 200
pick, 182, 183
pig, 184
  trough, 181
pile
  wood, 19
pilgrimage, 232
pillar
  load-bearing, 47
pin, 56
  bowling, 38, 71, 110, 128
  golden bowling, 109
  king, 71
pipe, 19
pistol, 95
pitcher
  tin, 197
Pizzagate, 232
plank, 58
plate
  golden, 79
  silver, 79
plow, 187
  glowing, 186
plowing, 62
plowman, 187
plum, 102
  tree, 102
poacher, 66, 67
pole, 120
  black, 63
  flaming, 120
Polish
  person, 50
  prince, 49
pond, 22, 42, 59, 65–68, 74, 100, 197, 198
poodle
  black, 88, 90, 91
  changing fur color, 90
  white, 90
poor
  man, 92
poor soul, 162
pope, 229, 231
poplar
  tree, 169
portrait, 97, 159
post office, 100
poultry, 158
poverty, 126, 188, 190, 191
prank, 216
prayer, 13, 42, 72, 73, 162
  All Good Spirits, 148
  evening, 73
  Hail Mary, 55
  Lord's Prayer, 27, 55, 148, 163, 168, 196
praying, 33, 191
preacher, 28, 138, 152, 178
preaching, 152
pregnant, 156
pressure spirit, 217–219, 221

priest, 20, 42, 77, 89, 92, 98, 195, 204, 206, 218, 222, 231, 232
  Catholic, 13
priestly
  regalia, 159
priests, 236
prince, 48, 209
  Danish, 48, 49
  Polish, 49
prince-elector, 229
princess, 49, 50
principality
  ecclesiastical, 188
printing press, 230
prison, 49
  cell, 79
processing
  milk, 170
procession, 203
  funeral, 156
production
  cheese, 170
Protestant, 13, 28, 188, 192
  Reformation, 230
Protestantism, 13, 92, 122, 154, 188, 230, 232
pub, 35, 62, 66, 82, 90, 117–119
  sunken, 119
publican, 36, 117, 118, 144, 145
pudding, 108
  fried, 107, 108
puddle, 74
Puffjacke, 14
pump, 97
punishment
  capital, 62, 63, 82
  divine, 42, 65, 74, 117
pure
  maiden, 49
purgatory, 29, 191, 192, 221, 232

quarry
  basalt, 69

rag, 122
Rahmmus, 108
railroad
  track, 63
rain, 138
raisin, 108
ransom, 63
rape, 42
rapier, 189
razing, 191
razor
  shaving, 173
reading backwards, 200
recipe, 108
red
  bed, 182
  chair, 182
  dish, 182
  furniture, 182
  horse, 181, 183
  pfennig, 13
  servant, 182
  slipper, 182
  wine, 182
reed, 54

Reformation, 26, 42, 153, 154
regalia
  priestly, 159
religious
  order, 200
residence, 137
restaurant, 62
reward
  God's, 176, 181, 184
rider
  headless, 81–86
riding
  horse, 212
rifle, 106
ring, 159
  diamond, 129
river, 12, 43, 45, 53, 72, 94, 96, 97, 109, 115, 135, 197
  mouth, 115, 135
road, 76, 90
  country, 173
  depressed, 57, 59, 60
robber
  knight, 234
robbery, 115
robe
  black, 65
  folded, 44
  monk's, 65
rock, 219
  formation, 43
rod, 45
Roman Catholic Church, 229, 230
Romans, 79, 80, 228, 229
rope, 137, 179
rose
  blood-sprinkled, 82
  white rose bush, 82
rose gold, 17
rosemary wreath, 159
royal court, 24
Royal Society in London, 105
ruin, 36, 77, 110, 129, 131, 211, 229
  castle, 38, 40, 49–51, 106, 182, 190
Rule
  of Saint Augustine, 153
  of Saint Benedict, 92, 191
rumor, 49
rye, 175, 195
  field, 195
Räthelwacht, 147

sabbath, 67
sabre, 95
sack, 14, 57, 180, 208, 216, 218, 220–222
sacrilege
  field, 99
sacristan, 179
sail
  full sails, 135
sailor, 45, 134, 136, 155
saint, 232
salt, 97, 158, 177
saltworks, 97
salvation, 165, 171, 187

sand, 58
    grain of, 187
sandal, 200
Saturday
    Holy, 66
Saxons, 228
scaffold, 82, 148
scapular, 42
Scheffel, 184
Schildwache, 88
schnapps, 36
scholar
    traveling, 129
school, 124
Schultheiß, 74
scrubbing, 122
seaman, 136
secretary, 213
seed, 45
seizure, 55
seminarian, 27
semolina, 108
Sennentuntschi, 171
Senner, 171
Sennerin, 171
sentry, 100
September
    15th, 192
serf, 191
sermon, 89, 138
servant, 50, 144, 147, 156, 205, 207, 209
    of the court, 24
    red, 182
sewage, 100
sex
    doll, 171
sexual harassment, 198
shadow
    knight, 149
shaft
    mine, 17
shaking hands, 178–180, 184
shapechanging, 86
sharpening stick, 178
shaving, 173
    kit, 173
    razor, 173
sheep, 63, 132
sheet
    white, 15
shepherd, 63, 118
shield guard, 88
shingle, 14
ship, 45, 136, 155
    ghost, 137
    merchant, 135, 136
shoe, 120
    buckle, 195, 206
shoemaker
    journeyman, 51
shroud, 140
shrub, 66
Siege of Vienna, 46
sieve, 33
    milk, 33
sign of the cross, 46
silence, 41, 49, 58
silt, 122
silver, 50, 119, 146
    bowling ball, 109
    coin, 190
    nine pounds of, 119

ore, 17
plate, 79
sin, 43, 143, 191, 206, 216
singing, 26
sinking
beneath the ground, 43, 117
sisters, 126
skeleton, 106, 129
skimmed milk, 181
skin
ox, 18
skirmish, 80
skirt, 34, 198
skull, 56, 106, 128
skullcap, 128
slap, 97, 98, 153
by a ghost, 91
slave
trader, 145
Slavic, 137
fort, 48
sleep, 228
paralysis, 124
sleepwalker, 179
slipper
red, 182
smith, 216, 236
sneezing, 169
snow, 109
snow-white
ghost, 171
soap, 173
soil, 182
soldier, 45, 94, 146, 220
Hanoverian, 97
soldier's mantle, 63
son, 199
soul, 204
evil, 78
poor, 171
selling one's, 214
soup
milk, 33
spa town, 110
spark-spraying ghost, 168
spinning, 126
chamber, 7, 33
flax, 126
wheel, 212
spirit, 19, 23, 38, 65, 177, 201, 202, 211–213
white-clad, 70
spitting
fire, 197
spouse, 138
spring, 131
brine, 97
squire, 129
St. John's Night, 49–51
stable, 88, 102, 118, 150, 184, 208, 216
stairs, 150, 208
stamp mill, 66
starvation, 48, 131
Staupbesen, 147
stench, 201
steward, 181, 182
stick, 78
birch, 147
white, 48
stirring kettle, 170
stolen
land, 187

stone
  construction material, 118
  memorial, 62
  shapeshifted form, 86
storage
  grain, 122
storage box, 214
storehouse, 94
storm, 42, 69, 132, 135, 137, 138
  night, 134
  surge, 135
  wind, 44
Strandvogt, 115
stream, 53, 54, 63, 109, 166
student, 13, 14, 88
suffocation, 219
sugar, 108
suicide, 18, 143
suitor, 49
sun, 191, 193
Sunday, 14, 28, 72, 116
  Divine Mercy, 105
  Easter, 66, 105
sunken
  pub, 119
surge
  storm, 135
surveyor, 84
swamp, 22, 42, 73, 74, 167, 184, 214
swearing, 58, 59, 162
sweeping, 15
swollen head, 101, 204
sword, 46, 132
table, 76
  head of the, 76
tailor, 198
taxation, 43
teacher
  school, 180
thaler, 140
theft, 98, 201
  of fruit, 102
thief, 29, 30, 125
Third Reich, 232
Thirty Years' War, 40, 85, 122, 129, 146, 188, 191, 192, 230, 231
thunder, 44, 138
Thuringians, 45
Thursday
  Maundy, 65
tin
  pitcher, 197
tithe, 36, 41
toast, 77
tomb, 159
tome of magic, 16
tongue
  glowing, 97, 98
torment, 191
torturer, 220
tower, 43, 44, 46, 49
  church, 92
tower clock, 119
town
  fire, 124
town hall, 100
tracks
  coach, 76

trader
  slave, 145
  wine, 144
trading, 232
treasure, 13, 26, 41, 48, 50–52, 129
  chamber, 49
  guardian, 52
  hunter, 41, 72, 109, 117
tree, 69, 114, 163, 198, 220
  chestnut, 92
  fir, 86
  linden, 62, 205, 206
  oak, 22
  plum, 102
  poplar, 169
  stump, 208
treetop, 197
Treulicht, 162
tribute, 109
Trinity, 172
trough, 182
  pig, 181
tuberculosis, 34
tunic, 189
tunnel
  rock, 105
Turks, 46
Twelve Nights of Christmas, 204
twilight, 143

unchaste, 49
upper court, 147

valley, 65, 66, 78, 170
  dune, 134
vanishing, 91
veil, 189
  white, 54, 169
velvet
  black, 106
vension, 158
vestment, 42
village, 116
  forest, 114
  ghost, 192
vinter, 169
violated oath, 194
virginity, 133
Vogt, 115, 145
vow, 138
  monastic, 194

wagon, 13, 73, 87, 156, 164, 168, 195, 206
wailing, 155
wall, 79, 172
  city, 63, 88, 94
  clock, 95
wandering
  lantern, 161
war, 146
  cry, 38
warden
  coast, 115
  field, 166, 167
  forest, 40
watchman
  night, 147
water
  hot, 170
  wheel, 101
wave, 135

weapon, 218, 221
weaver, 110–112, 198
wedding, 48, 74, 138, 189, 191, 194
    day, 138
Wednesday, 28
well, 40, 131, 156
    poisoning, 232
Welthund, 92
Wendish people, 153, 188
werewolf, 124
whaling, 115
wheel, 164, 206
    flaming, 120
    of fortune, 16
    spinning, 212
    water, 101
whining, 204
whirlwind, 136, 159
whispering, 66
white
    cap, 31, 32
    dress, 143, 157
    ghost, 142
    girl, 53–55
    maiden, 212
    poodle, 90
    sheet, 15
    stick, 48
    veil, 54, 169
    white-clad spirit, 70
    woman, 36
widow, 211
wife, 142
Wild Hunt, 9, 57, 73, 204
wind, 69, 136, 137
    blowing from an entrance, 105
    storm, 44
windmill, 40, 174
window, 200, 212
    attic, 22
    bay, 45
    frame, 201
windthrow, 69
wine, 28, 36, 37, 77, 144, 150, 158
    bottle, 36
    cellar, 36
    cup, 77
    red, 182
    trader, 144
winter, 28, 34, 92, 109
witch, 136, 208–210
witchcraft trial, 210
witness
    false, 113
wolf, 131
woman, 28, 29
    in childbed, 18–20, 204
    white, 36
wood, 38, 92, 156
    basket, 38
    chopping, 220
    pile, 19
woodturner, 217, 222
    journeyman, 217
World War II, 102, 124
World Wars, 231
wound
    burn, 143
wreath
    rosemary, 159

Wünschelrute, 50

yarn, 126, 127
year
leap, 188, 191–193

zither, 15

Impressum

Jürgen Hubert
c/o AutorenServices.de
Birkenallee 24
36037 Fulda

Printed by Amazon (see following page)

Printed in Poland
by Amazon Fulfillment
Poland Sp. z o.o., Wrocław

10448953R00172